PRIVATE LIFE O

Praise for *Private Life of an Indian Prince*

'In my opinion, Mulk Raj Anand's best work ... There is a special poignancy about this book, because it is the off-shoot of a personal experience ... One of Somerset Maugham's finest novels, *Of Human Bondage*, had a similar origin. ' – K.P .S. Menon, *The Times of India*

'[Dr] Anand's novel ... carries a preface by Prof. Saros Cowasjee who writes concisely and illuminatingly on the personal and impersonal background of the story. The information that the novel is an outcome of Dr Anand's personal experience accounts for the spontaneity and fluidity of the narrative.' – *The Statesman*

'[Anand] in the widest sense is a political novelist; he sees his characters and their actions in relation to India and also in relation to the world outside India. This is one of the chief sources of his strength, as is very plainly shown in his new novel ... filled with characters excellently rendered in a sharp, sardonic manner.' – Walter Allen, *The New Statesman and Nation*

'Absolutely contemporary in its theme and presentation, this new book by the foremost Indian novelist of today is likely to take us deep into the obscure corners of India where he has always led us in his well-known previous works, *Untouchable, Coolie, The Big Heart,* etc.' – Steve Smith, *Spectator*

'*Private Life of an Indian Prince* is a much better book than most. My anxiety to avoid exaggeration has made me open with a cool sentence, but I do not really want to disguise the warmth of my response to such spirited writing. Here is India in her colour, squalor, variety and valour in an age of transition.' – Paul Bloomfield

I have referred to its [*Private Life of an Indian Prince*] vivid sense of history, its richness of incident and character, its considerable narrative power, and, above all, its fearless compassion. *Private Life* will surely take its place as an integral part of Anand's "work in progress", the *comedie humaine* for twentieth century India.' – K.R. Srinivasa Iyengar, *Indian Writing in English*

PRIVATE LIFE OF
AN INDIAN PRINCE

MULK RAJ ANAND

With an introduction by
SAROS COWASJEE

HARPER PERENNIAL
Modern Classics

HARPER PERENNIAL

Published in 2008 by Harper Perennial,
an imprint of HarperCollins *Publishers* India

First published by Hutchinson (London), 1953
Published by Bodley Head (London), 1970

Copyright ©Lokayata: Mulk Raj Anand Centre, 2008
Introduction Copyright © Saros Cowasjee, 2008
P.S. Copyright © Saros Cowasjee, 2008

2nd impression 2015

ISBN: 978-81-7223-760-8

HarperCollins *Publishers*
A-75, Sector 57, Noida, Uttar Pradesh 201301, India
1 London Bridge Street, London, SE1 9GF, United Kingdom
Hazelton Lanes, 55 Avenue Road, Suite 2900, Toronto, Ontario M5R 3L2
and 1995 Markham Road, Scarborough, Ontario M1B 5M8, Canada
25 Ryde Road, Pymble, Sydney, NSW 2073, Australia
195 Broadway, New York, NY 10007, USA

Typeset in Perpetua Std 12.5/14
Jojy Philip New Delhi - 15

Printed and bound at
Thomson Press (India) Ltd

AUTHOR'S NOTE

The neutral 'I' of the first person singular has tended, in this book, to become a character in his own right. Most writers know how a character in a novel sometimes takes control and runs away with the story. The author has been content to allow Dr Shankar to take possession of the narrative, as well as become Sancho Panza to the Prince's Don Quixote. Therefore the 'I' in this novel is not to be mistaken for the author, who has reverted to the Indian tradition of anonymity and looks on, like Siva's searing third eye, at the unfolding of this tragi-comedy.

INTRODUCTION

After calling *Private Life of an Indian Prince* (1953) Dostoevskian in 'scope', the Australian novelist and critic, Jack Lindsay, went on to say, 'If Anand had written nothing else, his place in the history of the novel would be secure — his place as a profound interpreter of Indian life in a phase of pervasive crisis.' This was a daring statement to make at a time when *Untouchable* (1935) and *Coolie* (1936) — the two novels that catapulted Anand to fame — were still being used as yardsticks by which his successive novels were judged.

The British critics were unanimously enthusiastic. Walter Allen called *Private Life of an Indian Prince* 'a most impressive work and [Anand's] finest for many years'; John D. Stewart thought it was 'a most rewarding and memorable novel', and Paul Bloomfield hailed it for its 'spirited writing' and summed up the book as 'brilliant'. In odd contrast to all this was the Indian response. Many of the Indian critics argued that Mulk's genius lay in portraying the disfranchised of society, the untouchable and the outcast, and that in portraying the Prince he was out of his depth. Their own notion of morality prevented them from sympathizing with the plight of a decadent prince. They refused to see the human tragedy, and with Shavian pragmatism concluded that the protagonist, broken down by debauchery and greed, had met the fate he justly deserved. M.K. Naik, regarded as an eminent critic of Indo-Anglian fiction, had this to say as late as 2005:

> The two major aspects of *Private Life of an Indian Prince* are: one, it is a political chronicle and, secondly, it is a study in abnormal psychology, and the author is successful in dealing satisfactorily with neither.... Anand is mainly the novelist of the underprivileged – untouchables, coolies, peasants. It is almost ironic to find him now shedding tears over an abnormal Maharaja rushing from one sexual escapade to another.

Naik has missed the point altogether. The novel is not about a Maharaja's sexual escapades but, to use Anand's own words, 'is a study in pity, absolute pity for those who love absolutely – in this case the prince.' Whether Anand is successful or not is a different question. To my mind he is – absolutely.

Fifty years have passed since the novel was first published. The critics have had their say and it is now time for the Indian reader to pass judgement. And whatever that judgement may be, no attentive reader can miss noticing Anand's expert craftsmanship, the almost perfect fusion of history and fiction, the depth and sharpness of his characterization, and the episodes, not one but many, that retain their vivacity long after we have laid the book aside.

After a stay of twenty-five years in England, Anand returned to India in 1945 to witness the country win independence and the 562 princely states merge into the

Indian Union.[1] In 1948 he wrote *Private Life of an Indian Prince* (published 1953), not so much to show the demise of the princely order as to provide therapy for his own illness. (Anand had suffered a nervous breakdown over an affair with a hill-woman and had been advised to write the anguish out of his system.) His knowledge of the princes and their administration was there to give his fictional episodes the detail and immediacy of a painfully reconstructed past. He had been a tutor to the Rana of Bhaji, a tiny principality in the Simla Hills, for two summers, and he had known the Patiala court through Lalla Man Mohan — an ex-secretary to the late maharaja. Above all, as Anand puts it:

> My knowledge of Indian life at various levels had always convinced me that I should do a *comédie humaine*. In this the poor, the lowly and the untouchables were only one kind of outcasts. The middle sections and the nabobs and rajas were also to be included as a species of untouchables. Unfortunately, there has not been time to show the poor-rich of our country, who deserve pity more than contempt.

The material he required was all there. But it was the conjoining of a personal crisis and clear political vision which helped to make *Private Life of an Indian Prince* into a great historical novel and a work of art at the same time.

[1] 'The diversity in size, population and revenue earning of these princely states was mind-boggling', writes Mohammad Ali Shafiq in *Princely India Revisited* (2003). 'On the one hand were the dominions of the parsimonious Nizam of Hyderabad and Berar spread over a whopping 82,700 square miles, with a population of 14.5 million.... On the other hand was the statelet of Vejanoness in Kathiawar, reigned over by a Thakur, whose 184 subjects lived on a 22-acre estate, yielding a princely sum of Rs 450 per annum.'

The title, *Private Life of an Indian Prince*, is a misnomer. There is nothing 'private' about Victor's life – the word is used to cater to the average British reader's nostalgia for the mystery and romance surrounding the Indian princes, and thereby promote the book's sale. As an intimate revelation of the princes, the book is tame compared to scores of others – especially William Knighton's *Private Life of an Eastern King* (1855). Anand's title apparently owes itself to Knighton's, and there are other similarities between the two works (similarities not uncommon among books on Indian princes). But the aims of the two writers are very different. Knighton's objective is to expose the opulence, waste and cruelty at the Oude court in Lucknow, while Anand's objective, as he has already informed us, is to do a *comédie humaine* with the avowed aim of regaining his equilibrium after an unfortunate love affair.

Maharaja Ashok Kumar (known as Vicky to his close friends) chooses to assert complete independence for his small kingdom of Sham Pur rather than join the Indian Union. A febrile romantic who has inherited more of the vices than the virtues of his ancestors, he is encouraged in his histrionics by his nymphomaniac mistress, Ganga Dasi, a powerful and illiterate hill-woman, whose spell holds him in a grip beyond all counsel. His prospects of success for an independent Sham Pur are slim to begin with, and they vanish quickly when he starts exacting huge taxes from his starving peasantry to feed his mistress's greed. This brings him into a dangerous confrontation with his subjects at a most inopportune time. If he meets Ganga's challenge with hysterical tears, he meets the political challenge from his people and the Government of India with self-deluding lies. Needless to say he loses both contests: his mistress elopes with his Political Secretary, and the Indian States Department forces him to sign the Instrument of Accession. Exiled in London, he seduces a shop girl with princely finesse. But he cannot forget his mistress and has her paramour murdered only to end up in a madhouse from the shock of what he has done.

Though a knowledge of the political background is not essential to the appreciation of this work, it does help to explain certain gestures and actions of the Prince. On the surface of it, Maharaja Ashok Kumar's bid for independence might seem absurd, but not if one bears in mind what the British Government had led the princes to believe for nearly a century. Her Majesty Queen Victoria, in 1858, gave her celebrated pledge to 'respect the rights, dignity, and honour of the native Princes as our own'. His Majesty King George V reaffirmed this promise in words noticeably intractable: 'Ever to maintain the privileges, rights, and dignities of the Indian Princes, who may rest assured that this pledge is inviolate and inviolable'. Representatives of the Crown in subsequent years repeated these promises, but when Independence came to India and Pakistan in 1947, all that the princes got were advice and admonitions. The princes, whose dynasties had faithfully stood behind the Crown through two world wars and fought the nationalists at home to defend the Raj, regarded this as an arrant breach of trust. The British Government, for its part, argued that its pledges to the princes rested on Paramountcy (on the fact of their supremacy throughout India), and not merely on treaties and assurances. With their withdrawal from the rest of India, Paramountcy automatically lapsed and the British were thus no longer in a position to offer protection. However, there was an alternative for the princes: they could unilaterally declare independence if they so wished. Paramountcy would not be transferred to any successor government, they were assured. But this was small comfort to most of them. Lord Mountbatten, then Viceroy and Governor-General of India, urged the princes to forget about independence and to accede to either India or Pakistan. The majority of them reluctantly took his advice. By the date set for an independent India, all but three princes (the rulers of Kashmir, Hyderabad and Junagadh) had signed 'The Instrument of Accession'. *Private Life of an Indian Prince* is about a fourth, a fictitious one (the ruler of Sham Pur), who holds out against the Union and is finally coerced into joining on the grounds that his administration has failed and has led to chaos in the state.

Though politically decimated, the princes have staged a come-back, if only in fiction. Since Independence we have seen, besides *Private Life of an Indian Prince*, Philip Mason's *The Island of Chamba* (1950), Manohar Malgonkar's *The Princes* (1963), Ruth Prawer Jhabvala's Booker Prize winner *Heat and Dust* (1975) and Gita Metha's *Raj* (1989). That is a lot if one considers that prior to Independence there was only one novel of repute – Dennis Kincaid's *Durbar* (1932); the others, scores of them, were mostly romantic pulp fiction which have long been forgotten. There was indeed Joseph Ackerley's unique *Hindoo Holiday* (1932) but, like E.M. Forster' more celebrated *The Hill of Devi* (1953), it is a memoir often passed off as fiction.

Private Life of an Indian Prince invites comparison with Malgonkar's *The Princes*. Both novels, through their respective heroes, concern themselves with the fate of the princes who vanished with Indian Independence; both are peppered with the prejudices and customs of the princely class; both expose the same regal ignorance, bigotry, false pride and total inability to come to grips with facts. The narrator in Anand's novel is the personal physician to Maharaja Ashok Kumar; the narrator in Malgonkar's novel is the heir apparent, Abharaj, and both these characters represent the voice of sanity that speaks out against the reactionary and medieval attitudes of the rulers themselves.

The differences between the two novels are equally marked. Anand's *Private Life of an Indian Prince,* as the title suggests, is the personal saga of one prince – though that does not prevent him from being a prime representative of his order. Malgonkar's title, *The Princes,* clearly indicates that he is speaking of the princes as a collective body. Malgonkar's purpose is to provide an accurate history of the princes, and he shows every evidence of having studied documents and prepared himself for the task. When dealing with the merger of the state of Begwad with the Indian Union, he mentions by their real names the major personalities involved in the drama and quotes voluminously from actual speeches and the newspaper reports of the day. For Anand, historical accuracy is not the main consideration. When I pointed out to him certain inconsistencies in his novel,[2] he hurled defiantly at me the reproach: 'I am not writing history, or even historical novels, but about the collective unconscious of various human beings in the novel form.'

Anand might not have thought of writing a historical novel, but he has written one that surpasses many – including Malgonkar's *The Princes.* To say this is not to minimize Malgonkar's achievement, for his novel makes engrossing reading – but chiefly as history clothed in fiction. The

---

[2] These inconsistencies were present in the 1953 Hutchinson edition of the novel and were corrected in the 1970 Bodley Head edition – of which this text is a reprint.

profusion of historical detail overwhelms the fictional, and the plot and characters occasionally seem to lose momentum. History there must be in historical fiction, but not history in the conventional sense. 'The best historical novels,' says Daniel Aaron, 'are loyal to history, but it is a history absorbed and set to music, so to speak, changed into forms akin to opera or theatrical productions.'

Anand takes care to be 'loyal to history' without becoming a hostage to it. He makes creative use of history: the events, when they are not real, are completely plausible. One such event is Vicky's interview with Sardar Vallabhbhai Patel, Union Minister of States, at five o'clock in the morning. The hour chosen by Anand is significant for it shows not only the bullying nature of the Sardar but also his power and astuteness. The Prince, already smarting from the humiliation of having to wait for an appointment, is scolded like a schoolboy for maladministration and ruthless oppression, and before he has had a chance to say one-tenth of the things he has rehearsed over the period of waiting in Delhi, he has signed the Instrument of Accession and the destiny of Sham Pur has mingled with that of the Indian Union. There is no exaggeration in Anand's epigrammatic summary: 'Sardar Vallabhbhai (Wishmark) Patel growled, like a big angry bull, twice or thrice from the rostrum in Delhi. And most of the sons of Suns and Moons fell into line as children of the earth.' But no historian would have dared to word it so, for the sweep and phraseology here belong to fiction alone.

Structurally, the novel, consisting of three parts and an epilogue, is expertly designed. Anand opens the story with a public scandal and immediately captures the reader's attention. Vicky has taken Bunti Russell to the ravines 'for the obvious purpose', and there is as much tension in the

Russell household as there is in the Maharaja's lodge. 'I have found no evidence of rape, but there has been an attempt at penetration,' announces the English doctor, much to the relief of the Prince's retinue. There is a scuffle with Bunti Russell's father, which the Prince wins with the succour of the strong arm of his ADC. But how dare a commoner lay hands on the sacred person of the Maharaja? Regal rage is now at its height, and so continuous is the monologue and so persuasive the campaign of denunciation that even the keen-witted and sceptical Dr Hari Shankar (the narrator) is inveigled into accepting the Prince's plan to lodge an official complaint with the Deputy Commissioner of Simla. But the Deputy Commissioner excuses himself from seeing His Highness, and on the trip back Vicky sees the need for a drastic remedy:

> As we drove away from the Deputy Commissioner's bungalow it impressed itself upon His Highness, in the quiet and cool of the evening, that things had gone very wrong, that he would have to do something very drastic to mend the situation into which he had got himself. For he asked his rickshaw coolies to come abreast of the rickshaw in which I was riding and told me, with more pathos than he had brought to his voice before in uttering the same truth, 'I am a rat in a hole.'

Anand is a master of the mock-heroic and the anticlimax. The passage just quoted reveals two of his chief characteristics: first, his sense of pity, not diffused or clotted, but tempered with an irony which bites an incident into the memory; second, his lyrical gift, which shows its full brightness when the author settles down to a clinical analysis of Vicky's character.

Having secured the reader's attention, Anand goes on to arouse his curiosity. What is Vicky doing in Simla when the fate of his state is in the balance? What are conditions like back home? Who is Ganga Dasi from whose grip the Prince cannot free himself? All this information Anand divulges to the reader during the royal party's return to the state, a journey which has become necessary because of the scandal, the exhortations of the prime minister, and the compulsions of Vicky's mistress. Had Anand opened his novel with the tangled history of the Prince's life and that of his state, the casual reader might have lost interest in the story. Anand wisely defers it till the homeward journey begins.

Part Two is almost twice as long as the other three parts taken together. Simla with its scandals was a paradise compared to what Vicky has to face in Sham Pur. There are three major forces working against him. The first is Ganga, whose emotional hold he understands as acutely as his inability to free himself from it. The second is the Congress Government in Delhi, actively encouraging upheavals in the state in order to force him into signing the Instrument of Accession. The third is the people of Sham Pur, the most powerful yet invisible actors in this drama, lying in wait to ambush the decadent prince and wipe out the feudal oligarchy that has preyed upon them for so long.

Vicky meets the dual challenge from his people and from the government of the day with foolish boasts and ill-conceived bravado. He arranges army manoeuvres near the Indian border, which he himself supervises in the uniform of an Honorary Major-General. It impresses no one and angers the peasants when his jeeps and tanks roll over their crops. He organizes a shoot for Mr Peter Watkins (nearly the Ambassador!) of the American embassy in Delhi in the futile hope of securing American intervention. The whole thing is an unrelieved fiasco (his mistress gets a chance to sleep with the journalist Kurt Landauer), and Sardar Vallabhbhai Patel, Union Minister of States, becomes alarmed and orders Vicky to report immediately to Delhi.

I have already spoken of the interview between the Sardar and the Prince – easily the most fateful episode in the novel. Anand also provides here a haunting picture of dawn in Delhi – 'the soulless capital of India' – with its eerie silence enveloping the long roads and the sequestered bungalows enshrouded in mist-covered foliage. Nature descriptions abound in the novel, each unforgettable, whether of Simla blossoming in summer, or the picturesque hunting lodge set at the edge of a wood, or the dense foliage with its suffocating heat on the banks of the Sutlej river. A painter in words, Anand's descriptions of nature are clearly visualized and are an integral part of his novel.

Anand could have ended *Private Life of an Indian Prince* with Sardar Patel forcing Vicky to sign the Instrument of Accession. From the perspective of an historical fiction, it would have been a fitting climax, and it would have been as easy to get Vicky to a mental asylum then as later. But history takes a second place to the story itself, and Part Three and the Epilogue deal with Vicky's tormented existence. The loss of his kingdom is followed by his mistress's desertion, and Anand now goes all out to impose upon the situation what he calls the 'Yoke of Pity – [the] compassionate understanding of the dignity of weakness, of even negative, broken-down people who struggle so hard to survive at some human level, and sometimes surpass themselves by doing things least expected of them....' Vicky, unable to bear the pangs of separation from Ganga Dasi any longer, has her paramour murdered and ends up losing his mind.

To prevent the novel from lapsing into sentimentality, Anand introduces the amusing episode of Vicky seducing the shop-girl, June Withers, during his brief exile in London. This the Prince achieves with consummate skill, and even his dim-witted ADC shows gumption by announcing Vicky's title to the beholders just as Vicky is about to panic. The campaign to seduce June Withers is conducted better than the struggle to preserve his state. On one flank she is besieged by temptations such as a Rolls-Royce, cocktails, dresses, dinners; on the other by the Prince's manoeuvres, which range from reading her palm to intimate confessions of the pain he has endured. June succumbs, but Vicky's passion for Ganga is genuine and June cannot replace her. In its pathos, this scene is reminiscent of another memorable scene: Vicky's visit to a courtesan in Delhi while waiting for an appointment with Sardar Patel. The singer and her song, far from offering the solace he seeks, merely reinforce his yearning for his mistress.

The Prince's madness on board the plane home is deftly handled. His utterances and gestures touch on the major chords of his past days. They have a coherence of their own and reflect the life he has lived and the passions that have wrecked him. The sight of a full-mustachioed Englishman throws him into a prolonged bout of hysteria, obviously a subconscious reaction to the British betrayal of the princes. His recitation from the epic *Heer-Ranjha* ('Your love, oh my Hiré, has dragged me through the dust of this world') is a confirmation of his love for Ganga and the price he has paid for it. His re-enactment of the drama of a man being murdered is the expression of the mental torture he must have undergone while conniving in the death of his mistress's paramour. The Prince's madness is no mere babbling; in his insanity he utters those truths which the external pressures of life had made difficult to express, even for one so accustomed to voicing his whims and fancies.

It is the characterization, however, that raises this novel to new heights. The two principal characters are the Prince and his mistress, Ganga Dasi. To this we must add a third — the cynical and troubled narrator, Doctor Hari Shankar, who becomes a character in his own rights as he goes about his business of dissecting his master's character and that of his master's mistress. Modelled on a Private Secretary to a Maharaja, there is as much of Anand in Dr Shankar as in the Prince, despite Anand's protest in the 'Author's Note' that 'the "I" in this novel is not to be mistaken for the author'. Dr Shankar is the rational side of the author analysing the irrational side as seen in the Prince. Though presented as the disembodied voice of sanity and good sense, he pursues his master as doggedly as his master pursues his mistress — and seemingly with no better results!

The Prince and Ganga Dasi defy facile literary definition: they are presented with a complexity and psychological insight rare in Indo-Anglian fiction. It is hard to put a finger on the spot at any given moment and say, 'This is it', for the very next moment the conclusion may be belied. The human mind is capable of strange contradictions, and a person can encompass deception, self-deception and honesty at one and the same time. Take Vicky's confession to June Withers as he tries to captivate her, 'I have lost my throne.... But that wouldn't have mattered. Only, only, the woman whom I loved also left me.' There is a sort of grandeur in this utterance — to lose a throne for love — even if the object is not worthy of the sacrifice. But coming to the point, is Vicky play-acting to win June's sympathy, or is he genuine about his feeling for his mistress? Is he indulging in one of his melodramatic gestures, or have the actor and the man now become one? There is no clear answer to any of these questions. The author's purpose is to reveal life in all its contradictions, not to explain it.

Anand spares Vicky no ignominy. Yet out of it all arises not a tyrant purged of evil, but a man who has loved and lost. Some readers might shudder to use the word 'love' in the context of this spoiled womanizer, but not to do so would be to deny the complexity of his nature and to lay down parameters as to what love is. What we encounter in this novel is not the delicate languishing of a Laila-Majnu or the less challenging offerings of a Harlequin romance. It is Love — the invincible destroyer, destroying everything in its path, and itself too in the end. Vicky is caught in the vortex of this love: the more he tries to free himself, the deeper he sinks. His plight, even if it is of his own making, cries out for pity and understanding. Not to sympathize with Vicky on moral grounds, as some Indian critics have done, is the madness of morality.

Anand in his personal life valued loyalty above everything else, and he knew that loyalty never fails a character in fiction. Early in the novel the narrator, Dr Hari Shankar, tells us that whatever Vicky's faults were, 'he was loyal to his friends.' And this loyalty pays him fair dividends, for his retinue stand beside him through all his travails. Only two persons in the novel betray him: his mistress Ganga Dasi and her paramour Bool Chand, the Prince's Political Secretary. Bool Chand is a despicable character with not a shred of goodness in him. He represents the hangers-on, the toadies and lackeys from which no Indian princely court was completely free. But Ganga Dasi's disloyalty is a different matter: its origin lies in her unhappy childhood and the incessant abuse and exploitation to which she was subjected by men. Anand is at pains to show that both Vicky and Ganga are the products of their respective environments, one hereditary – the other acquired, and to condemn them out of hand is to do them injustice.

In no other novel does Anand probe deeper into the human psyche than in *Private Life of an Indian Prince*. The task is overwhelming and Dr Shankar, for all his lengthy analyses to reach and reveal the well-spring of human actions, never quite succeeds in summing up either of the two as concisely as they sum up each other. Vicky describes Ganga as a 'bitch', and a 'consummate actress', whilst she calls him 'very clever', 'very cruel' and 'very jealous'. It is only later in the novel that Dr Shankar makes fewer attempts to dissect their relationship, and prefers terms such as 'sadist', 'masochist' and 'split personality' to sum up Ganga Dasi. After all, these terms are objective and safe and, for all their generality, as close to the mark as those of any clinical psychoanalysis.

Every character in the novel is drawn in sharp outline and with discrimination. There is the loyal but vulgar ADC, Captain Partap Singh, a giant Sikh 'with nothing in his head except a little white matter under the bun of his long black hair'. We have Munshi Mithan Lal, ex-tutor and now Private Secretary to His Highness, a ready victim of Vicky's perverse sense of humour, but a master of statecraft; Brigadier-General Raghbir Singh, who has enjoyed His Highness's mistress and his confidence, and now commands his army; His Highness's uncle, Raja Parduman Singh, a bully who is at least his nephew's equal in hurling abuse and epithets; Pandit Gobind Das, the provincial politician, not devoid of conscience but totally dead to other people's intrinsic worth; the new Prime Minister, Popatlal Shah, a cheap imitation of his chief, Sardar Vallabhbhai Patel, but strong enough to unnerve the Prince with his Anglo-Saxon economy of words; Maharani Indira, prim and proper, who lets her actions speak for her; the affable Mr Peter Watkins of the American embassy, whose ruminations in the jungles of Sham Pur hasten Vicky's downfall; the handsome journalist, Kurt Landauer, who finds Ganga an easier and more exotic quarry than panthers, and June Withers, who swoons to wake up in the Prince's arms and taste the life she has read about in the penny dreadfuls. All of them are intricately woven into the design of the novel, as intricately as the people of Sham Pur who hang like a dark cloud on the horizon and whose power is always felt even though their presence might not be visible.

Private Life of an Indian Prince has something to offer to every kind of reader. The historian will be fascinated by the intriguing relationship between the Prince and his subjects and the new Government of India; the moralist will find affirmation of his belief in Vicky's destruction; the romanticist will find consolation in the Prince's ultimate love for Ganga Dasi and his sacrifice; the realist will point at the futility of knowledge which is not bolstered by a will to act; and the psychologist will either agree with Dr Shankar's analysis or gleefully take issue with him.

The novel, however, will please most the committed reader who is also an artist. An order has been severely condemned, but the hereditary architect of the order retains our sympathy to the very end. This, in itself, is no mean achievement.

SAROS COWASJEE
Canada 2008   University of Regina, Regina

PART 1

I was deep in siesta in my room in the annexe of Sham
Pur lodge on the afternoon of a rainy day, when Munshi
Mithan Lal, ex-tutor but now Private Secretary to His
Highness, came in and twisted the toes of my feet to wake
me up. I came to, rather red-eyed and startled. I saw that
Munshiji was in a state of great perturbation. He was pale
and dishevelled and very tense. His usually immaculate, milk-
white, well-starched turban was wrapped anyhow on his head.
His thick spectacles were misted with the fumes of rain and
perspiration that flowed down from his quivering, pockmarked
face to his neck and the soggy clothes on his heavy torso. His
breathing was disturbed as though he had been running up
hill and down dale for hours.

'What's the matter, Munshiji?' I asked him as I waited for
him to recapture his breath. I vaguely guessed that one of
those things had happened to His Highness which always
happened to His Highness. I couldn't tell exactly what it
was this time, because anything, any of a thousand different
things, could have happened to our prince, especially in the
incalculable state of mind in which he had been ever since
he was asked to sign the Instrument of Accession to the 'free
India' a few months ago.

'Have you seen His Highness?...Has he been here?' Munshi Mithan Lal asked me in short gasps. His small, round eyes, behind glasses, were lit up with an abject terror.

'No,' I said, 'why?'

'His Highness cannot be found,' he said. 'He is lost.' And he waved his hand in a gesture of despair.

'He is lost all right,' I said cynically. Then I felt a ripple of tenderness for Munshi Mithan Lal go through me, as, indeed, I had often felt this tremor in my flesh in his presence, ever since I had first seen him in my youth. For there was something of Dostoevsky's 'Idiot' about him that made him a pathetically lonely person in Sham Pur State and certainly completely out of place in His Highness's personal entourage. 'Do sit down,' I said, relenting.

'I am undone! I shall be ruined!' began Munshi Mithan Lal, now with tears in his eyes. 'His Highness disappeared immediately after breakfast this morning. I thought he must have gone out riding. But Bhagirath, the bearer, says he hasn't seen him. Then I thought that he might have gone out for a walk on the Mall or the Ridge with Captain Partap Singh. But Partap Singh came back to lunch after shopping in Lower Bazaar without His Highness. As he did not turn up for the midday meal I began to worry. I wanted to come and tell you when you sent for your food to be brought here, but then I thought why should I spoil your bhojan. It has been raining heavily and he must have got drenched, because he went out without his mackintosh. Mrs Russell, in the flat below, is also frantic, because her daughter has not returned from school.'

'Oh, well,' I said sinking back into my pillow and smiling. 'There is no need to worry. His Highness has probably gone out for a little picnic with Bunti Russell.'

'Do you realize the seriousness of this, if His Highness has indeed gone out to "eat ashes" with her? Captain Russell has already rung up the police. And there will be a first-class scandal! What with the Praja Mandal people looking out for any excuse to damn His Highness, and this accession business not yet settled. Partap Singh has gone out looking for him in the khud, and the servants are out searching in all directions, towards Annandale, the Lower Bazaar, the Lovers' Lane....And the rain will not stop!'

'There are too many lovers' lanes so far as H.H. is concerned,' I said. 'Which one will they go to find him in? But don't worry,' I assured him. And I picked up a cigarette from the little plastic box on the bed-table.

'I am going to give up this thankless job and retire,' said Munshiji with one of those very rare shows of impatience that I had ever seen him express. 'That Sergeant, I mean Captain Russell Sahib, is threatening to shoot every one of us!'

There was the helplessness of a rather too self-righteous man about Munshi Mithan Lal, which made him seem even more ridiculous than he ordinarily was, with the pedagogic, parsimonious, religious boor in him, who had persisted in his 'thankless job' for years, though he knew that he could not make much of an impression on His Highness's mind, which was set on other, more pleasant, things than holy men and their wise maxims. To His Highness, Munshiji had been a great figure of fun, the proverbial court fool in disguise, and he had, with characteristic mischievousness, distorted his name and nicknamed him Mian Mithu, an appellation usually given to a parrot, because he was always repeating things parrot-wise from textbooks, such as he had learned for his BA degree, and from Emerson, Thoreau, Ruskin, Gandhi and from Bhagwan Krishna as reported in the *Gita*, all of whom he had read for what he called his 'extra-mural' studies. Ever since I had been away from the state, first at Medical College, Lahore, and then in London for my post-graduate studies, I had thought of the difficulties in the way of Munshi Mithan Lal coaching the Maharaja into grace and knowledge; and, especially when I myself entered His Highness's service as his personal physician, I had begun to appreciate the peculiar and intricate problems facing this good man in tackling his job. The old man had three sons who were being educated: one as an engineer, another as a lawyer, a third as a doctor, all in England, and he had to earn enough money to pay for their studies, even at the cost of those perverse humiliations which His Highness showered on him in the guise of his peculiar sense of humour. The fate of Munshi Mithan Lal at the hands of His Highness frightened me and I felt nervous to be in state employ. But then I had to work off the sum of the scholarship which the state had provided for my three years' research in England. And, anyhow, there were hundreds of unemployed medical men in the country. So I accepted my position, and even felt my vanity tickled when people complimented me on being lucky enough to be occupying so exalted a rank as that of the personal physician to a maharaja.

'Acha, brother, get up, put your clothes on and come and help me to find this naughty boy,' said Mian Mithu. Then his gaze fell on the menacing clouds, which were rolling across the valley beyond the window, and he got up, wringing his hands and repeating under his breath: 'Hey Ram! Hey Ishwar! Hey Parmatman!'

'Don't worry, Munshiji,' I said as I got out of bed. And, as I began to dress, I repeated the phrase with which he used always to dismiss the Maharaja's philanderings: 'After all, it is the sport of children, all this playing about in the zenana. And even Sri Krishan Maharaj had his gopis!'

'Son, don't mock at me and insult my religion,' Munshiji said rather priggishly. 'Relieve me of my anxiety and tell me if he told you where he was going.' And, with the strain, he belched and pressed his protuberant belly even as he writhed with a resurgence of his chronic nervous dyspepsia.

'He didn't tell me anything,' I said. 'But I think he must have taken Bunti down the khud to the waterfalls for the obvious purpose. He has had his eyes on her for some time, and she has been pursuing him, hanging around upstairs, dressed up like a gypsy, with a snake coiled round her arm… She is a nymphomaniac!'

'What is a nymphomaniac?' asked Munshiji.

I felt an irresistible impulse to shock Munshiji by analysing the behaviour of a typical nymphomaniac and by spilling the beans about His Highness. I wanted to tell him of how Mrs Russell herself had slept with her 'Dear Maraja Sahib' right under Munshiji's nose. I wanted to describe to him how the romance between His Highness and Bunti Russell had been encouraged by Captain Russell with all his unctuous talk, because the latter hoped in a short while to be able to blackmail the Maharaja and extort some money from him. I felt like telling Munshiji how he had been humbugging himself, talking of guarding His Highness against evil influences when he, Captain Partap Singh, the ADC, Mr Bool Chand, the Political Secretary, and myself indulged every whim and fancy of His Highness, in order to curry favour with him, and shut our eyes to what we did not want to see about His Highness, even while we pretended to be so concerned when anything happened to His Highness. But I abstained from saying all these things out of the respect for age which is so strictly enjoined in our country and which, in spite of my education, I had not yet succeeded in giving up. Why argue with this pompous ass, anyhow? Why prick the bubble of his complacency by telling him that ever since the time when in the Augean stables of these robbers-turned-kings no chariots were harnessed for war, ever since they could not go and conquer each other's territories because the borders of their kingdoms had been fixed for ever by special treaties with Her Britannic Majesty, Queen Victoria, these princelings had not much to do, after their precocious childhoods in the zenana, their expensive boyhoods in the Chief's Colleges, and all the flattery and adulation of hangers-on like ourselves, except to set about to achieve the only other conquests left to them, the conquests over women, the easiest victories in our hapless country where the place of women was still governed by Manu Smriti and the Hindu Mitakshra Law.

As we emerged from the annexe on to the gravelled path, which led to the lodge, the rain was still drizzling in that peculiar way in which it drizzles in the Simla Hills. The floating cotton wool of the clouds rose from the sub-valleys and struck the mountains in the middle. The mist became liquid and fell like dew, while the tops of the hills remained dry except for the few high points against which small wisps of clouds rose in spirals, covering and uncovering the mixed English, Swiss and Far-Eastern style chalets and bungalows and huts, where once lived the officials, the potentates and the memsahibs, both English and Indian, of devoted husbands who willingly grilled in the sun-scorched plains of India in the service of the British Sarkar merely to be able to help their wives to retain their school-girl complexions.

'I am sure even a giant like Captain Partap Singh would get lost in Simla today – what with those overhanging clouds!' I said this to ease the tension as we proceeded towards the lodge.

Munshi Mithan Lal did not answer, but kept screwing his face even as he belched with dyspepsia. So I nodded playfully to the carnations, the pinks, the sweet peas, the fuchsias, the lilies, the poppies, the dahlias, the pansies, the scarlet geraniums, the gladioli and the forget-me-nots which stood droopingly along the shapely beds laid out by the broad drive to the lodge. The rain seemed to have dulled their lustre and they seemed not to be in the mood for exchanging greetings. So, perforce, I had to hold a colloquy with myself from which I had been escaping all this while through my attempts at flippancy. 'You went into the service of His Highness,' I said to myself, 'knowing exactly what you were doing. You knew that the Maharaja was, like most Indian princes, an eccentric, who may do to you, to others and to himself any of a hundred strange things. But apart from the obligation you owed him, because he lent you 20,000 rupees for your studies in England, you were quite elated at the idea of being a favourite, a 'friend, guide and philosopher', because you were ambitious and saw prospects of achieving power over him, and through him, in the state. And although you kept your suitcases packed ready to quit within twenty-four hours, that being the time allowed for you to make good your escape from the state, you thought that it was a needless precaution against this maharaja. For, whatever his other faults, he was loyal to his friends. Now, however, you may have to get your suitcases really well packed and ready, because anything may happen after His Highness's latest escapade. This is really the culmination of that passion for his Brahmin mistress, Ganga Dasi, which, being thwarted by the various petitions to the British Government of his consort, the Tikyali Rani, Indira, as well as by the tantrums of Ganga Dasi herself, has led him to seek consolation for his will to lust and happiness in one desperate and mad sexual adventure after another. And knowing, as only you do, that His Highness is ill and will behave like this again and again, you should, if only because you have learnt to relish the thought of personal freedom and social justice as elementary needs of your mind and body, not be abject like all the other state subjects, but resign before you get involved any further in the tentacles of that courtesy and affection which the Maharaja seeks to weave round you, with his all-absorbing ego that knows no bounds.' But the other voice answered: 'If you owe the money and cannot pay it off immediately and have accepted the position which you are in, it is not easy to get out of it, especially because you still believe that you may be able to help the Maharaja to get well and to divert him from the path on which he is travelling. At any rate, it is your duty as a doctor to enable him to regain his confidence in himself, which has been shattered by Ganga Dasi, and to see him adjust himself to some kind of balanced social behaviour.'

Before this colloquy had finished, I saw Bhagirath, the bearer, running up towards us from where the drive turned sharp left towards the veranda of the two-storeyed pagoda-style lodge. As Bhagirath reached us, he leaned his head over his joined palms, made obeisance to us and, in a panic-stricken voice, whispered, 'Maharaj has come back.'

A sub-inspector of police came chasing after Bhagirath and shouted: 'Ohe, come here! Don't you know that no one is allowed to leave this bungalow?'

'He is a palace servant,' Mithan Lal said to assure the officer.

I saw that the lodge was surrounded by a posse of policemen, who clustered together in knots and whispered to each other as they stood by the servants, some in the veranda of the ground floor which was occupied by Captain Russell, others on the balcony projecting from the second storey of the house, with its large gables and french windows. The whole atmosphere seemed to be electric with cross-currents between the upper storey and the ground floor of the house, with two sets of people breathing furtively into each other's ears. And to the oppressive silence of the exalted house, usually only heightened by the impatiences and the rages of His Highness, was added a certain grimness. It was a kind of urgency, as if there lay an unexploded bomb somewhere between the two layers of the building. The bomb was sizzling and would not burst, lest it should outshine the burning refulgence of the Divine Light in the aura of power around the head of His Highness, descended, as he was supposed to be, from the God Indra via the God King Rama, and capable, by his mere presence, of putting into the shade any alloy of magnesium, or other physical or spiritual combustibles, except the Paramount Power.

As I waited for a moment while Munshi Mithan Lal talked to the sub-inspector of police, I caught a glimpse of Mrs Russell in the veranda of her flat, calling shrilly, 'Bera! Bera!' I believe she saw me, but she deliberately averted her eyes from me. I nearly thought of going to inquire after Bunti. But the usually unctuous, charming and flirtatious smile on Mrs Russell's plain face was absent, and her polly-tip-up nose sniffed the air haughtily while a scowl of fury sat upon her hard jaws and forbade any exchange. 'Bring hot water for Miss Sahib's ghusal,' she shouted. And I sensed that Bunti Russell was certainly suffering from exposure, whatever else she might or might not be suffering from, since her escapade with His Highness in some lovers' lane or other.

'Ohe hurry, ohe what are you looking at that bahinchod memni for?' I heard Captain Partap Singh's raucous Punjabi voice calling me. 'Leave the stale bitch alone and come and feel His Highness's pulse!'

I walked up as though in a hypnotic trance. For I had never quite recovered from the first shock of this giant Sikh's vulgar tongue, and I had always felt a certain fear of the loutish bully in him. He hailed from the Mhaja district of Central Punjab, the scion of an old landlord family. He had failed to take the Bachelor of Arts degree at the Khalsa College, Amritsar, six times, but he had captured all the sports prizes for the high jump, the long jump, the hundred yards, the cross-country run as well as javelin throwing. And, being a remarkable freak of nature, about seven feet tall, and a splendid decorative companion to have in court, in mufti or in uniform, His Highness had been persuaded by the Principal of the Chief's College (who was a friend of the head of the institution where Partap Singh had failed in all the exams but where he had captured all the sports championships) to engage him as an ADC. Uncouth, lusty, a good boozer, a voracious eater and with nothing in his head except a little white matter under the bun of his long black hair, he had all the qualities which would recommend him to that side of His Highness's nature which had been trained in the ideals of sportsmanship, inculcated into him at the Bishop Cotton School, Simla, as well as in the Chief's College, Lahore. Captain Partap Singh's rough-and-ready methods and manners embarrassed us all; though, I must confess, his hearty laugh, his generosity and the prodigal warmth of his uncivilized nature, were contagious and compensated for a great deal of his boorishness. I knew that he was as stubborn an enemy as he was a loyal friend. So I had decided after a few minor brush-ups with him to give him a long rope to hang himself with, and I generally laughed away his vulgarity.

'Where had His Highness disappeared?' I asked him as I ascended the steps to the balcony from the drive.

'Ohe bewakoof – he took that little bitch to the khuds!' Partap Singh said this in a loud enough voice for all to hear. And he continued without lowering his tone: 'Last time I had to rescue him from the hands of that washerman by Annandale, because the dhobi caught him red-handed with his wife. This time matters have reached beyond my arms to the quills of the babus!...Perhaps a nimble-witted bania like Bool Chand, or a learned doctor like you, can handle the authorities!' And he slapped me on the back with that terrific bonhomie of his, which was so back-breaking an abomination that I nearly fell while he guffawed with laughter.

'"Death to us and you indulge in blandishments."' I quoted a Hindustani verse at him.

'Captain Sahib!' Munshi Mithan Lal said with a scowl of admonition on his face, while he still stood talking to the sub-inspector of police.

'Of course, you haven't heard, have you,' said Captain Partap Singh, turning to me, 'that Munshiji's mother has died?' And he laughed again his obscene boorish laugh.

I gave him a cautionary look and proceeded towards His Highness's bedroom.

When I crossed the large dining room into the Prince's bedroom, His Highness sat up in bed impetuously and, throwing his torso forward, caught hold of my approaching legs like a child. Then he looked at me with the most abject appeal in his eyes. He knew that this worked with everyone because of the extraordinary fascination of his big brown eyes, studded like two moonstones in a face that was otherwise plain enough, with its narrow forehead, its almost sunken cheeks, sharp nose, thick lower lip, weak mouth, pointed chin and rather long ears.

'Now I suppose you are going to scold me just like Munshiji?' he said disarmingly.

I kept a non-committal silence, and he was nearly panic-stricken.

'Tell me,' he continued, 'that you are not angry with me. You know I am ill....Don't look so solemn!...' And then he smiled nervously and said to the ADC: 'Captain Sahib, look what an ass Dr Hari Shankar becomes when he falls under the influence of that great ass Mian Mithu. I am sure he too is going to exhort me to tread the right path like the rest of them.'

'I don't know about the right path, Highness,' I said, 'but certainly I am going to ask you not to go down the tortuous tracks of the Simla khuds in the rainy weather: you might slip and fall.'

'Only asses slip!' he said.

'Han, of course, obstinate mules can negotiate their way through the khuds!' I said ironically.

'I am not a eunuch of a mule!' he protested as he recollected himself.

'All right, Highness, you are a high-mettled horse!' I said, reaching for the thermometer in the pocket of my sports jacket. 'Let me take your temperature.'

'I am afflicted with a disease for which you will have to feel my heart rather than thrust a thermometer into my mouth,' he said, waxing sentimentally poetical. Then he added with a pout, which seemed rather ridiculous on the lips of a man well past his twenties, though he looked much older because of the pace at which he had been living: 'I wish you wouldn't go on "Highnessing" me all the time. That shows you are angry with me and are intriguing with Mian Mithu against me.'

'All right, Vicky,' I said, calling him by his nickname. This nickname had been given to him by the wife of his Principal at the Chief's College. The Maharaja's full name was Victor Edward George Ashok Kumar: Victor after Queen Victoria; Edward after Edward VII; George after the Emperor George V; Ashok after the ancient Indian Emperor Ashoka. The Principal's wife, Mrs Berry, abbreviated Victor into Vicky. And all his intimate friends preferred to address him thus informally. As this name had been recently familiarized in Simla by Bunti Russell, it found an echo in His Highness's mind.

'Ah,' he said, 'she went on calling me "Vicky, Vicky" for months, and even encouraged me with all kinds of blandishments. But when I came to the point, she shrieked and wept — the sali, bahinchod!'

'And in spite of that her father is making all this fuss!' said Captain Partap Singh. 'Sali! She-ass! Deceitful bitch! And the way she used to come here, dressed up like a doll!'

'You mean like a gypsy,' I said. 'Rings on her fingers and bells on her toes, rings in her ears and rings in her nose.'

'The whore!' said Partap Singh.

'Chup raho, Captain Ooloo Singh!' His Highness burst out in a rage, evidently because he considered that he alone was entitled to abuse her.

And, for a moment, the pale wheat blonde of his face flushed a vivid pink, his large brown eyes spat fire, the nostrils of his aquiline nose trembled, the sleek, well-oiled hair fell on the lobes of his ears, the Adam's apple of his long, syphon-like neck thrust forward. It seemed as if he would burst with rage. But the ADC retired and, as I brought the thermometer towards his mouth, he lay back docilely and smiled.

While I waited for the mercury to register to the timing of my wristwatch, Munshi Mithan Lal came in and, touching His Highness's feet, began to fuss:

'Oh Maharaj! You gave me such a fright! I didn't know what to do! Where to look for you! Your hair is still wet. I hope you haven't caught a chill....It is all the fault of that bahinchod girl!...'

His Highness was going to burst out again at the reference to the girl, but, as that would have meant chewing up the thermometer, he abstained from speaking, though he raised his torso impatiently. I immediately sat down on the bed and held him back. Then I turned to Munshi Mithan Lal and asked him to withdraw from the room till I could take the temperature without His Highness getting too excited. His Highness nodded approvingly. But, of course, Munshi Mithan Lal's solicitude about his monarch was always prone to express itself through the servile ministerings of his lumpy hands rather than through any sensitiveness to the Maharaja's moods. And he was not to be shifted now that he sat pressing His Highness's feet.

'You gave me such a fright, son,' he continued. 'I have had dyspepsia all the afternoon. You can ask Doctor Sahib if you don't believe me....And what are we to do about the authorities – the police and the Sarkar?...Mrs Russell has rung up Colonel Jevons of the Civil Hospital to come and see the girl. And the news will spread. Hai, what shall we do? Why did your Highness? But you are our mother-father – what right have we to say anything?...'

I could see the blood mounting to His Highness's face, and now I was really afraid for the thermometer. So I snatched it out of his mouth.

'Has he got high fever?' the Munshi asked, overshadowing me like a clawing bear.

'Please go out, Munshiji!' His Highness ordered.

'Only a hundred point one,' I said, speaking aloud to myself but so that the others could hear. Then I turned to His Highness and advised him to rest after he had taken a sleeping draught which I would send him by the bearer Bhagirath.

'But what are we going to do about the authorities?' Munshi Mithan Lal insisted. 'I wonder if I should go down to see the Deputy Commissioner about removing the police from the bungalow.'

'Munshiji,' I said, 'if the police want a statement from us we can give them one. As for the rest, I presume they have already got Bunti's story.'

At that instant, Captain Partap Singh came in and said:

'Colonel Jevons Sahib is downstairs and wants to see a responsible person.'

'Tell him to go to his mother's!' His Highness roared. 'Who does he think he is! Sala! Monkey-face! Doesn't he realize who I am? Ask him to get out of my house....Get out! Get out!...' And now he was hysterical, his voice rising to a shrill querulous height, his face livid and tense and contorted into an ugly expression, his lithe, bony body waving like that of a viper.

We all rushed towards him, whispering hoarsely: 'Highness! Highness!'

He lay down frothing and struggling, his eyes looking upwards with a look which was distant and forbidding.

'Arré, son, calm yourself!' Munshi Mithan Lal begged him with joined hands, not realizing that his servility was only exasperating His Highness the more.

'Come, come, Highness, you are a Rajput Surma Bahadur!' Captain Partap Singh was saying. 'Come, don't you care for anyone?'

I stood by the Maharaja's bed for a moment. Then I was disgusted by the whole business and turned to go.

'Oh, Hari, Hari, don't go,' His Highness cried in a voice that seemed to be woodenly artificial in its sentimentality. And then he uttered a weird rasping howl and began to weep, beating his head with his hands and burying his face in his bed-clothes and whimpering mawkishly and quoting a mixture of Hindustani and English lines: 'Oh, Bunti, why have you dragged me into the dust?...Oh, I fear thy kisses, gentle maiden....'

'Highness, Highness, calm yourself!' I almost shouted, as a certain hardness came over me at the sight of his desperate grovelling. 'Calm yourself, otherwise I won't be responsible for your health....I will go and see Colonel Jevons. That may prevent him wanting to see you. But if he hears you, he might do anything – "certify" you or anything....Now, please keep calm and go to sleep...I shall come and see you in a moment.'

As I came down to the ground floor, Bhagirath, the bearer, and Badri Nath, the Brahmin cook, and the other servants stretched out their joined hands to me with a special servility, obviously eager to know the news and yet not daring to ask for it. I had been very embarrassed by their servility when I first joined His Highness's service, but had later come to accept it as part of the ritual of the prince's court, except when men seemed to crawl abjectly before the Maharaja or members of his entourage.

The sub-inspector of police was still standing in the veranda of the ground-floor flat with his bevy of constables, and the atmosphere was charged with a greater sense of gravity than when I had come up the drive with Munshi Mithan Lal. The faces of the policemen, hard and mute with that disciplined brutishness which characterizes the Indian police, depressed me. It was as if they were saying to us: 'You preened yourself on being members of the Maharaja of Sham Pur's entourage and we had to salute you, but now your Maharaja's fate itself is in jeopardy, and you must grovel before us.'

As Colonel Jevons was still in Captain Russell's flat, I had to wait about in the veranda. I felt small and self-conscious and forlorn when I came to a standstill by a carved wooden pillar. For, in spite of my deliberate cultivation for years of a feeling of self-respect, I could not help considering the police constables as superior beings. I suppose the first fears of childhood are indelible, and I can never forget having seen the swaggering state police of Sham Pur beat up a servant of our household for alleged stealing. In the present circumstance, my fear of the police was mixed up with a vague horror of having to meet Colonel Jevons in this awkward situation. For the fear of the Englishman on the minds of us Indians, ingrained through generations of kicks and pricks, is more obsessive than the fear of an Indian official. The Englishman in India had always remained, in his role as the superior white sahib, an unknown quantity. He was silent, remote, non-human, and his behaviour in any given situation was unpredictable, being inalienably mixed up with the hauteur of authority. Also, he was for so long the symbol of the unlimited power of the Sarkar. Besides, he possessed that incredibly anaemic complexion, which in the tropics exudes, at its pinkest, none of the mellow charm of the brown face with its tincture of the malenim pigment, but oozes instead, to the people of India, the strange, parched, dry-as-dust indifference of contempt as well as the uncanny touch-me-not of a leper's wound, frightening in all its malignant potencies.

I shook my head and looked out before me. The hollows above Annandale were clearing. The wisps of cloud and fog had lifted. And a soft breeze stirred the dark boughs of the pines and deodars, across the rhododendrons and the other deciduous plants, above the mountain slopes towards Constitution Hill, aptly called the 'Roof of the World'. The nullahs in the deep valleys and khuds seemed to rush down through little waterfalls towards the nether worlds of the plains, where the fires of hell would be raging on midsummer days.

The lovely fresh greenery ahead of me did not take my mind away from the anxiety about the consequences to all of us if Colonel Jevons found evidence of rape on Bunti Russell's body. So I kept looking towards the dressing room of Captain Russell, tensely waiting for the surgeon to emerge. I had not long to wait, however, before he came, his round face beaming with a smile while his almost Scandinavian blue eyes twinkled with a knowing mischievous look under the platinum blonde eyebrows, his heavy torso surprisingly agile over the stumpy legs, modelled into smartness with tall boots and breeches.

'Mr Harry Shankar,' he said cordially, shaking hands with me as he evidently recognized me from the time I had gone with His Highness to consult him a few days ago.

'I am the doctor to His Highness of Sham Pur,' I said just to confirm his recognition of me and to get over that first tense moment which I always feel in meeting people with whom I am not familiar.

'How is Maharaja Sahib?' Colonel Jevons asked me in a tone which was friendly but patronizing.

'He is very good, sir,' I said.

'I don't think he is very good,' Colonel Jevons said, leaning conspiratorially over to me and giving me a broad smile and a wink. I was in a panic now.

'I meant...he is quite well, Colonel,' I hurriedly put in. 'He has a slight temperature and is suffering from exposure. Otherwise, he is all right.'

'His Highness doesn't seem to take much care of his health, does he?' Jevons said with a pout. And he gave me another sly side-glance, before assuming a confidential manner. 'Too much of this kind of thing,' he continued, shaking his head to emphasize his words, 'isn't good for him, you know!'

I surmised at once that 'too much of this kind of thing' referred to the Bunti Russell incident as well as the question of the constant love dreams that the Maharaja Sahib had been having and about which he had gone with me to consult Colonel Jevons recently. I wished the surgeon would put me out of my misery and tell me straightforwardly whether he had found evidence of rape on Miss Russell's body or not.

But before I could screw up courage enough to ask him he adjusted his stethoscope in the pocket of his jacket and began to walk towards the drive. I followed him disconcertedly.

'Er, how much truth is there in these rumours about His Highness?'

'There has been some difficulty,' I said, 'in his relations with the Tikyali Rani on account of the woman Ganga Dasi, who seems to have a hold on His Highness....The Tikyali Rani has, I think, petitioned the States Department about herself and her son....'

After I had said this, I was torn between my sense of loyalty to His Highness and objective truth. So I began to rationalize the Maharaja's role by invoking a comparison. 'It is like the love of the Emperor Jehangir for Nur Jehan, Colonel Jevons....His Highness is an intelligent man as maharajas go, but his development has been very uneven. And he seems to have an obsession about this woman....'

'Now, this Miss Russell,' Colonel Jevons said. 'Well, you know, this matter is serious....Of course, I have found no evidence of rape, but there has been an attempt at penetration!' And he pursed his lips, paled and stared straight ahead of him as if he was too embarrassed and angry to bring himself to speak about such things.

I was immensely relieved that Colonel Jevons had found no evidence of rape. Immediately I felt easier and more assured.

'Would you care to look at His Highness?' I asked.

'Well, no,' he said. 'I must rush away....You say there is nothing much wrong with him. Give him my compliments. And...well, I know you will look after him.'

This refusal of Colonel Jevons did not surprise me because, ostensibly, the incident about Bunti Russell had thrown him back on the defensive. The girl was, after all, possessed of a white skin, though she was a Eurasian. I was surprised that he was not tempted by the consultation fee, for he could have extorted any money he liked from His Highness, especially after this affair. But maybe he sacrificed the possible gain because he didn't know how far Captain Russell would go in order to redress the wrong done to his daughter. I was sure, however, that when he expressed the wish for me to convey his compliments to His Highness, Colonel Jevons's mouth must have watered with the lasciviousness he had displayed during His Highness's consultation with him, for he had been very eager to listen to all about the private life of the Maharaja.

'Rickshaw!' Colonel Jevons called.

But, before he had stepped into the beautiful vehicle, which the uniformed men-horses brought up from the drive, Mrs Russell could be heard shrieking: 'Bunti dear! Bunti! Don't be a silly girl!'

And then she could be seen chasing her daughter up the wooden stairs towards the balcony.

'Oh, Mummy, leave me alone, I want to see Vicky,' the girl shrilled as she ran, her dark, almost Eton-crop hair glistening, her face with its regular, well-chiselled features lit up, as though through her adventure she had suddenly blossomed into a pink carnation.

'Come back, Bunti! What will your father say?' Mrs Russell cried.

But the girl seemed to be unheeding.

'Now then, Miss Russell,' said Colonel Jevons, turning round from where he sat in his rickshaw. 'Now then, this won't do!...You are to obey your mother, young lady, and stay in bed....Come on, then, down you come!'

There was something very fatherly and peremptory in Colonel Jevons's voice. The girl slipped back like a child, reluctant and yet hypnotically obedient to the paternal command.

'That's a good girl,' said Colonel Jevons sternly, and looked away, his face red, his platinum eyebrows sharp like daggers, and his whole manner charged with confusion.

The rickshaw coolies gave a call and began to heave the carriage up the drive.

His Highness was pacing agitatedly around in his bedroom, dressed in a loose tunic and tehmet, when I came upstairs. He preferred this style of dress in bed to the English striped pyjama suit. His face seemed to be wrought by the high tension of his nerves, knit like a violin of which the strings are ready to burst. For a moment he ignored me, and only paced up and down the room more studiedly, the tremor of a smile on the corners of his mouth, which betrayed the histrionic nature of his wrath. I had often suspected that a great many of His Highness's rages were deliberately assumed because of an innate exhibitionism, a strong desire to show off at all costs, though I should have thought that being a prince and a high personage and thus the centre of all interest he would have had no need to attract attention by his posturings. But Vicky was a complex personality, and it was only towards the end of my association with him that I succeeded to any extent in disentangling those elements in his nature which were deliberate play-acting from the neuroses which possessed him.

'I am a naughty boy who ought to be whipped,' he said, lifting his head towards me supplicatingly. But then, as though he had realized that he was losing his rigidity, he turned defiantly and snapped, 'What did Jevons say?'

I hadn't even begun to answer when he continued: 'Why did you go to see Jevons?' And his face twisted as though he had just swallowed a bitter pill, like one of those which Colonel Jevons often prescribed to him. 'What does he think? I could buy off twenty of these Jevonses if I cared to!...Only the other day he was hinting about an invitation to visit Sham Pur. He asked me how I proposed to spend the hunting season!...What do I care about what Jevons says? Where have they sprung up from, the sweepers of somewhere!...

And what is their status anyhow?...My father never shook hands with these outcastes without gloves on. And even then he had a bath in Ganges water afterwards. I am not afraid of him....What did he say?'

I knew that in spite of his assertions to the contrary he was afraid. Always, before the transfer of power from the British to Indian hands, His Highness had paid encomiums to the Britishers he met, and to the Angrezi Sarkar which was the paramount power, rather than abused them. He had spent pitcherfuls of money on giving lavish banquets to the Viceroy and the other English officials when they came to shoot in the hunter's paradise which is Sham Pur. And he had loaded the various vicereines with presents of jewellery and precious stones; given gifts, in fact, to any Englishwoman with whom he came into contact. In his speeches he had always paid the conventional glowing tributes which the Indian princes were addicted to paying to their masters, though it is true that in private, when the Resident was hostile, or things did not go his own way, he had talked of the courage of Netaji Subhash Bose, the Rani of Jhansi and Raja Mahendra Pratap. After the transfer of power he leaned more and more towards nationalism, though his reluctance to accede to the Indian Union, in spite of Sardar Patel's exhortations, showed that he preferred the British Paramountcy.

I hesitated to answer his question. So he began again:

'I didn't like the bitch, anyhow! I don't like these white girls.' And he made a wry face. 'They nauseate me with their silly talk. And they stink because they don't bathe. That Bunti is a tomboy rather than a girl. Give me an Indian woman every time.'

'I suppose because we can take advantage of our own women more easily,' I put in.

'Aji, you have been spoiled by Europe,' His Highness said impatiently as he sometimes did when he was angry. 'You know how much I respect my mother!'

I wanted to add, 'and how much you humiliate your wife, and how much you really despise your mistress Ganga Dasi.' But I was afraid that the rage, which was directed against Englishmen and Englishwomen, might be turned against me if I dared to question his conduct in any way. So I held my tongue.

'Sometimes, I feel I ought to throw all you fools out of my state, donkeys that you are!' And he struck another posture. 'I think I shall go crazy if you people...' And he wrung his hands and shook his head in a despairing gesture.

'I think Your Highness should go to sleep,' I said.

'Oh, Hari, I am like a rat in a hole,' he cried abjectly, as he walked round and round. 'Here I am tied to that Tikyali Rani, who sends petition after petition to the Viceroy full of malicious lies. That dossier must be before Sardar Patel. And she has been to Delhi, contacting the States Department.... Now, how can I help it if I don't love her? She is a shrew, a trollop, a magician with evil influence in her control....I shall lose my mind if I don't get out of this hole!' He seized his head in both palms and shook it and then burst out again: 'She is after me, hounding me from pillar to post, from corner to corner. I tell you I am like a rat in a hole....And she has brought me to this. I would never have gone with this girl if the Tikyali Rani hadn't been forcing me away from Ganga Dasi. I should have had Gangi with me here if so many petitions had not gone everywhere against me and her! And now....Oh, what will happen to me? Where shall I go? What is your advice? Give it to me now. I need it. Tell me what to do. They will not understand me. No one will understand!...'

And he walked about stamping on the floor and then suddenly began to intone a stanza from Shelley in a peculiarly passionate sing-song manner:

> I never was attached to that great sect,
> Whose doctrine is, that each one should select
> Out of the crowd a mistress or a friend,
> And all the rest, though fair and wise, commend
> To cold oblivion, though it is in the code
> Of modern morals, and the beaten road
> Which those poor slaves with weary footsteps tread,
> Who travel to their home among the dead
> By the broad highway of the world, and so
> With one chained friend, perhaps a jealous foe,
> The dreariest and the longest journey go.
>
> True Love in this differs from gold and clay,
> That to divide is not to take away.
> Love is like understanding, that grows bright,
> Gazing on many truths; 'tis like thy light,
> Imagination!...
>
>   Narrow
> The heart that loves, the brain that contemplates,
> The life that wears, the spirit that creates
> One object, and one form....

'That is my motto!' he said, as he finished the recitation. He seemed to have got the verses by heart, very well indeed!

I was fascinated by His Highness's recitation, because I could see behind the clumsiness of his outward behaviour the reasons for his hopelessly ill-adjusted personality. For his intelligence seemed to have run riot through the large gaps in his education and experience. And this made him pick up many things, with which he was trying to form a single thing but which made him a bundle of ill-assorted fantasies and facts, whose incongruous collection into one personality made him a strange, wild creature. And yet he was not so ill-assorted as his mistress Ganga Dasi, because he was comparatively constant while she was absolute promiscuity. So it was touching to see the clashes between the poetry and prose of his life, the contradictions that arose from his reflection of the feudal, aristocratic idea that all excellence is inheritance, and the sense of direction which dictates integration through the discovery of values in the new society. The spirits of his dead ancestors were pulling him towards the old virtues, prowess, splendour, firmness, dexterity, generosity, heroism in battle and the other duties of the high-caste, superior, Kshatriya prince, while a number of new demons, the fashions of the hour, were pulling him into another direction, on account of the shameless schooling through which his childhood in his father's zenana, and his boyhood and youth in the hands of the Angrezi Sarkar, had put him. For he had learnt all the filth that his retinue of servants in the palace could teach him, and been spoiled by his doting mother, always anxious to save his life against the homicidal fury of his father's concubines. And he had been put through his paces at Queen Mary's School, Lahore, at Bishop Cotton, Simla, and Chief's College, Lahore; made to adopt all the postures, from that of a boy scout as well as the train-bearer of the Viceroy, of a bad cricketer, and an indifferent polo player, to a little tin god, from an unctuous, slavish speechifier, eulogizing beefy old burra sahibs of the Residency and the Political Department as well as the majestic proclaimer of new firmans and wielder of the power over the life and death of half a million or more of his people....All the old values and the new demons had been increasingly at war with each other in his soul. And there was no knowing where they would take him, since the will through which alone such powers could be harnessed had been sedulously crushed by the Angrezi Sarkar and his own parents a long time ago. He had few resources left after these two heredities had done their work. Except that he had an uncanny gift of perception, an almost convalescent abjectness, which was the opposite of his extraordinary cruelty, and a violent energy for voicing his fads and fancies, whether they took the form of naive outbursts, mere flippancy, or the more balanced rationalizations of poetry, which was always like someone else's confirmation of his own complaints. All his scandalous behaviour, therefore, was due to the incongruity of the various strains in him that were trying to unite and become one person, but only made him a kind of montage man, a pathetic creature, a spoilt child.

'No one will understand me, no one,' he was repeating as he fingered the plastic gadgets he had bought for his dressing table lately. 'No one....'

'Oh, I understand, Vicky,' I said, 'I understand. I think everyone knows you are unhappy. But you seem to have no instinct for self-preservation. And your danger is that you are weak and don't discriminate between your real friends and enemies. You —'

At that instant, there was a loud growling on the balcony and the rattling of the window panes under the hammer blows of a hand which was obviously that of Captain Russell.

'Who is that?' I said.

'Come out, you and your Maraja!' Russell shouted as he forced open the door and burst in.

'What is it?' I said, rushing into the drawing room. 'His Highness is resting.'

'There he is, the black bastard! He is not resting!' Captain Russell said, his colour a light purple with a kind of overall deathly pallor, his pug-dog face hardening, his nose snorting, though his eyes were humid with obvious grief.

'Go away,' I said. 'I shall come and talk to you in a little while.'

Captain Russell brushed me aside and proceeded towards the bedroom, saying: 'I can see him; he may be a bloody Maraja, but I don't care!' And he turned to His Highness, who had walked into the drawing room by now.

'What have you done to my girl? Eh, you....' Captain Russell shouted, his eyes flashing and his face tightening into a knot. 'What did you do to her? Your Highness! Tell me before I wring your neck!'

'Get out, get out of here!' His Highness ordered, trembling but drawing himself to his full height.

And then, without more ado, the Maharaja sprang lithely like a tiger on Captain Russell and, gripping his neck, pushed him over.

Overpowered by the surprise of His Highness's assault, the Captain retreated a little, but then pushed forward with the sheer weight of his heavy body, driving the Maharaja a few steps back with his clenched hands. But Vicky still gripped his neck with a tigerish grip and did not yield even though Captain Russell was trying to shake him off.

I tried to disengage them, shouting: 'Stop it! Stop it!' And I sought to wedge myself between them, but I am a frail person and could do no more than protect the Maharaja with my raised arms.

The noise of the scuffle brought Captain Partap Singh and Munshi Mithan Lal out of the ADC's room, where they had been exiled by His Highness. The police came crowding towards the door from the balcony but did not enter. Also, I could hear the voices of Mrs Russell and Bunti on the balcony; for, apparently, they had heard the noise of stamping footsteps above the ceiling of their flat.

'Please stop it,' I said again. 'Captain Russell, have some sense!'

But neither would let go, Russell growling, and Vicky hissing and shouting by turns, as he was overpowered by the burly frame of his opponent, but grim, with his fingers well dug into the Captain's neck, holding his opponent at bay, tears of triumph and anger in his eyes. The police had now entered the drawing room and were on the point of intervening.

Captain Partap Singh came and asked the policias to go. They obeyed. Then Partap Singh, seeking to spare Russell a fight, asked him to let go.

As Russell didn't listen, the ADC pushed the Englishman away with his long, strong arm, even as he dislocated His Highness's grip on Captain Russell's neck.

Captain Russell tottered and nearly fell on the dining table but recovered his balance and rose with the help of his wife, who was all remonstrances, sweet nothings and 'dear dears' while her daughter stood by the doorway, weeping.

'Get out! Get out of here!' His Highness was shouting, pale and pathetically undignified as his frame was unequal to carrying the pride of his warrior's soul, except with the help of Captain Partap Singh's arms.

Munshi Mithan Lal was brushing His Highness's clothes and calming him with pats on the back.

I felt the misery and shame of this humiliating scene spread into the atmosphere, as the ugly words and looks of the opponents charged the air, for each of the adversaries was fighting now in the void, to impress the peacemakers with the claim that he had won, while the police, headed by the sub-inspector, stood at the door ready to pounce on either or both of the participants in the quarrel if they should assault each other again.

'Come on, John, come,' Mrs Russell was saying as she restrained him from charging at His Highness again.

Bunti was weeping shrilly now.

Captain Partap Singh towered over the whole scene like a self-satisfied giant who knew he had found an occasion when his services were badly needed.

'Get out!' His Highness shrieked. 'Get out!....Partap Singh, throw them out!...'

Upon this Munshi Mithan Lal went towards Captain and Mrs Russell and the police and, like a good shepherd, gently chasing the sheep away, he spread his arms and signed them to leave.

Captain Partap Singh and I followed him into the balcony and asked the sub-inspector whether he had a warrant against any of us. As he answered that he had no formal charge to make, we asked him to leave the lodge with his followers. For a moment, he hesitated, hoping that Captain Russell, who had called him there to search for his daughter, would say something. When Russell walked down the stairs without a word he was persuaded to go.

Inspired by his regal rage, His Highness decided immediately to go and seek the help of the Deputy Commissioner of Simla, who had always been friendly to him, in the matter of Captain Russell's assault upon him. The rickshaws were ordered and Munshi Mithan Lal and myself were asked to accompany him.

I have often wished that I had dared, at some time during my association with His Highness, to tell him frankly and at length what I felt about him. For instance, I had a hunch that he was wrong in wanting to go and see the Deputy Commissioner. But so all-enveloping was the aura of his presence, built up through the hereditary privileges and prerogatives wrapped up by traditional practice in his person, that he always succeeded in involving everyone around him in the things that affected his outsized ego. This had developed in him the megalomania of a complete egocentric, which, though patent enough to his retinue, was impossible to break, both because certain laws of courtesy and good behaviour prevented us from being so rude as to interrupt his monologue and because we were his paid servants. I know that he had not a leg to stand upon in his complaint against Captain Russell, but I was swept off my feet and transported towards the Ridge through the campaign of denunciation which His Highness kept up uninterruptedly while he was dressing, building up his wrath on the fact that a mere commoner should have dared to lay hands upon the sacred person of a Maharaja.

The Deputy Commissioner refused to see His Highness. And, of course, the chaprasi of the Deputy Commissioner got it in the neck for bringing back the message that the sahib was 'not at home'. His Highness stormed and raved against the impertinence of the Deputy Commissioner Sardar Sant Singh, ICS, as he paced up and down the waiting room and declared that he would take up the matter with the States Department at the Centre. Apparently, Sant Singh knew about the nature of His Highness's complaint and presumed that the Government of India would give no quarter to a prince whose personal peccadilloes and recalcitrance about

31

signing the Instrument of Accession had already created a very unfavourable impression on everyone.

As we drove away from the Deputy Commissioner's bungalow it impressed itself upon His Highness, in the quiet cool of the evening, that things had gone very wrong, that he would have to do something very drastic to mend the situation into which he had got himself. For he asked his rickshaw coolies to come abreast of the rickshaw in which I was riding and told me, with more pathos than he had brought to his voice before in uttering the same truth, 'I am a rat in a hole.'

I suggested to His Highness that he should wire Srijut Popatlal J. Shah, the new Prime Minister, who had replaced the Englishman, Mr Horace, at the instance of the States Department in Delhi, to come to Simla for consultation. This seemed to His Highness the best thing to do under the circumstances, and we stopped at the telegraph office on our way back and sent the wire.

But when we got back home there was a wire from the Prime Minister for His Highness, asking him to return to Sham Pur as soon as possible for urgent consultations. The wires had obviously been humming all the afternoon, because there were many prying eyes from the unusual stream of rickshaws that went up and down the road by the lodge, with much talking in hushed whispers and guffaws of laughter. The scandal of His Highness's adventure with Bunti Russell had spread, and all the Messrs and Mesdames Hawkesbys of the summer resort wanted their ounce of malicious pleasure out of it.

His Highness's wrath knew no bounds and he was almost crazy with distress at finding himself in such a tight corner. He went on drinking steadily through the evening, helping himself to the liquor with his own hands in order to make sure that we didn't cheat him by putting more soda than whisky into his tumbler. And he refused to eat or to go to bed, and it was with the utmost difficulty that I persuaded him to sit back in the armchair and rest. But all my work was undone because Munshi Mithan Lal came fussing over him, and His Highness reacted to this affection by being more cussed than ever in his refusal to calm himself. At length I deceived him into taking a sleeping draught and he went off in the armchair, from where we lifted him on to his bed.

Afterwards, Partap Singh, Mian Mithu and myself partook of the elaborate, highly greasy meal that was usually cooked in the royal kitchen, and that had already given dyspepsia to Munshi Sahib and was also giving me a chronic indigestion: parathas fried in ghee and a rich pilao, with ten different dishes from chicken curry to dry brinjal burtha, papads and pickles of various kinds and halwa – they were all so tasty that I was sure that we were destined ultimately to die of overeating. Only Captain Partap Singh seemed as if he might be proof against such a disaster, for he swept the thalis and the katauris clean and had second portions of almost everything.

Hard upon the telegram which had arrived in the evening came His Highness's Political Secretary, Mr Bool Chand, our fat, almost pigmy-sized colleague, whom none of us could bear because, among other bad habits, he had a way of snorting every second minute like a horse who gets a piece of straw stuck into his nose and can't help clearing his snout. He told us in a few words, interrupted by many snorts, that the Prime Minister had sent him specially to fetch His Highness back. He tried to pump us for the reasons which had led the Diwan to send him on this mission, but we had formed an open conspiracy to tease him and wouldn't let on. It was always best anyhow in such matters to play for safety and let things come direct to people from His Highness, but particularly in the case of Mr Bool Chand, who was a manoeuvring minion of His Highness. The Political Secretary was the son of a rich bania grocer of Ferozepur, whom His Highness had picked up on a visit to Oxford some years ago, and the man had, in spite of his snorting, which annoyed the Maharaja, ingratiated himself into the favour of the prince in such a way that he was easily the most powerful influence on him and the state until I came to Sham Pur. I knew that he had been sent down by His Highness with a special message for Ganga Dasi. So I asked him what 'the first lady', as we called her among ourselves, had said. He evaded my inquiry and we felt that, by not telling him about His Highness's adventure with Bunti Russell, we were just about even with each other.

It didn't take long for Mr Bool Chand the next morning to get to know all about His Highness's difficulties, and it took him much less time to persuade the Maharaja to decide to go back to Sham Pur. Apparently, the message from Ganga Dasi was of a more imperative kind than the telegram from Diwan Popatlal J. Shah.

As we boarded the special train that afternoon en route to Sham Pur, via Kalka, His Highness waited tensely for the salute of thirteen guns to which he was entitled on arrival or departure. The guns started, but after barking seven times, spoke no more.

'I am like a rat in a hole,' he said, mortified at the insult implied in the reduction of guns in salutation to him. Coupled with the whispers of the crowd at the railway station, and the howls of the 'wolves' of society, which reached his ears through Mr Bool Chand, the reduction of guns came as the greatest shock to his pride.

At the first opportunity I could get to have a word with His Highness, when Mr Bool Chand had gone to arrange for tea at Kasauli station, I suggested to him to try and make a clean breast of the whole position about his affair with Ganga Dasi to the States Department in Delhi so that all the evidence that had accumulated against him, through the petitions of the Tikyali Rani and other complaints, could be sifted and some settlement arrived at about the heir-apparent to the gaddi, and the resulting unsettledness in the life of His Highness could cease. Also, I told him that he must not delay the accession of the state to the Indian Union any longer. In that way I thought he might be allowed to make a fresh start. Inside himself, I was sure he felt that that might be the best way, but he was too panicky, with the suspense of not knowing what would happen to him at the hands of Ganga Dasi after the Bunti Russell affair, to think of other matters seriously.

As I retired to my own compartment and settled down to the contemplation of the eternal twilight beauty of the Himalayas through which the train was passing, looking at the high peaks and the steep valleys, I tried to recapitulate in my mind the facts about the quarrel between Vicky and his Tikyali Rani to see if he had any chance of escaping the consequences of his past follies and of making a new start in his personal life.

Unfortunately, however, from whatever angle I looked at the story, from whatever angle I seized it, the consequences to His Highness of his past conduct in regard to the Tikyali Maharani and the accession issue seemed to me to spell disaster. I shall put down the narrative of his early life here, so that what follows may assume some kind of perspective.

His Highness's marriage to the Tikyali Maharani, Indira Devi, took place in 1935, when he was twenty-five years of age, and his new bride, who hailed from the small native state of Malati Pur in Bengal, was eighteen. This union had been arranged because the Maharaja Sahib had no male issue from his two previous Ranis, though he had had a daughter by the second Rani. Since two years before his third marriage, His Highness had been consorting with the Brahmin woman, Ganga Dasi, who was about five years older than he. And he had a son and a daughter by her. But as the kept mistress's son could not be acknowledged as an heir to the gaddi, the first two Ranis were anxious that he should have a son to succeed him. So the third marriage had been arranged. To the misfortune of the would-be Tikyali Rani, Indira, the fact that His Highness was carrying on with Ganga Dasi was not revealed either to her or to her parents.

The Brahmin woman, Ganga Dasi, had led an unhappy, vicarious life ever since she had been a girl, and, as she was the daughter of a state priest, she used to come to the various palaces as a saheli to amuse the two Ranis and, later, to act as a kind of nursemaid to His Highness's daughter by his second Rani. At one time, she went as a companion to the second Rani when she visited her brother's state, Badaun, in the Simla Hills. Here she contracted an illicit relationship with the Raja, the second Rani's brother, who had begun to neglect his wives. As she was suspected of having conceived a child by this Raja, public opinion rose and forced her out of Badaun, back to Sham Pur.

When Ganga Dasi returned home, it so happened that His Highness was just spending his summer holidays, away from the Chief's College, with his mother, who was his protector in the Court of Wards established since his father's demise in 1920. He was being taught some of the essential duties he would have to fulfil when he ascended the gaddi on attaining his majority next year and also enjoying the company of the two wives to whom he had been married off by his doting mother. As Ganga Dasi came to the palace frequently, the young prince saw her and fell in love with her. At first his connection with her remained a secret, but then she became with child by him and rumours about the love affair spread in the state.

Of his two legally married Ranis, the first one was older than him by ten years, while the second one was about the same age. In consequence, the older princess had no influence on him and, being of a religious temperament, she led a retiring life in a wing of the fort palace of Sham Pur, though the younger queen had continued to have conjugal relations with him and thus to wield some influence over him. But after the birth of a son to Ganga Dasi, this Brahmin woman began to possess him body and soul, to dominate him to the exclusion of all other things and interests. It was under these circumstances that His Highness's old mother, the Dowager Maharani, and his two Ranis encouraged the idea of a third marriage, so that he could have a son from a legally wedded wife. This marriage was obviously anathema to Ganga Dasi.

After His Highness's marriage to Indira of Malati Pur in 1935, his relations with his new wife were at first fairly cordial. And the two previous Ranis treated the newcomer with affection, especially as a son was born to the Tikyali Rani. Of course, Ganga Dasi was very upset and determined to regain her power and influence over His Highness.

It is customary in the states for the Maharaja to hold a durbar on the birth of a Tika, son and heir to the gaddi, and the occasion, which is made a public holiday, is marked by great rejoicings. Unfortunately, to everyone's astonishment, no such durbar was held on the birth of a son to the Tikyali Rani, Indira, and it seemed that Ganga Dasi had regained control over the Maharaja. And since she was manoeuvring for her own son to be accepted as heir to the gaddi, she naturally prevented His Highness from celebrating the occasion. The then Diwan, Rai Bahadur Laik Ram, advised His Highness to hold the ceremonial durbar; but as the Maharaja evaded the issue, the Diwan resigned, and the Finance Minister, Chaudhri Ramji Das, took his place.

After the arrival of the Tika, Ganga Dasi became obsessed with her design to get her own son accepted as the heir, and began a hate campaign against the Tikyali Maharani Indira, poisoning the mind of the Maharaja against her and trying to achieve her ends by fair means and foul. Thus she sought to win over the new Diwan, for instance, to her side. But as Chaudhri Ramji Das was a relatively honest man, and as he knew that Ganga Dasi was neither married to the Maharaja, nor, being a Brahmin woman, could ever be acknowledged as his lawful wife, he would not help her to have her son accepted as Tika. This turned her against the Diwan.

The Maharani Indira, though a well-educated girl, was young in years and as yet completely inexperienced in worldly matters, and she lived in blissful ignorance of the lengths to which her rival could go. Suddenly, one day, when her child was about eight months old, he fell ill, with a high fever. She was very troubled, especially when, on asking His Highness to get some medical advice, the Maharaja treated the matter casually. Later, as the child's fever continued unabated, a mysterious man, said to be a great yogi and sanyasi, was called. He prescribed the child some herbal medicine and the baby's condition deteriorated. The Tikyali Rani was in a panic, but a sudden stony silence greeted her from His Highness's camp and no doctor was fetched. The child was in an agony of pain after the administration of herbs and he died. The Maharani Indira suspected foul play, but as no direct proof except neglect to get medical advice could be adduced, her pleas for an inquiry into the death of the Tika remained unheard. But there were three facts which pointed irresistibly to the conclusion that Ganga Dasi had engineered the death of the child. Firstly, the yogi disappeared from the state after giving herbs to the sick babe, and no efforts were made to trace him. Secondly, there were rejoicings after the death of the Tika in the old palace where the Maharaja lived with Ganga Dasi. Thirdly, His Highness held a durbar after the death of his son and there openly declared Ganga Dasi's son to be the heir to his throne.

The Government of India did not accept his declaration. And this brought the wrath of Ganga Dasi and His Highness upon Indira, particularly because she had written to the Political Department about the death, in mysterious circumstances, of her son, and they presumed that the Government's non-acceptance of His Highness's nomination of Ganga Dasi's son had been inspired by this complaint.

Now His Highness refused even to see Indira and absolutely discarded her, and there were so many rumours afloat of what Ganga Dasi intended to do to her that she became frightened for her own life and went to live with her old mother-in-law in the Sham Pur fort palace. She had no opportunities to meet His Highness and to explain her point of view to him, because even when he came to the fort palace, Ganga Dasi accompanied him. What is more, His Highness openly insulted and abused Indira, charging her with treachery because she had written to the Political Department complaining about the death of her son. And her life was intolerably miserable. For even the servants, taking their cue from His Highness's mistress, began to behave very insolently and refused to carry out her orders. The Dowager Maharani loved her son far too much to take sides with Indira, though she sympathized with her.

In a little while, all except one or two servants, who were in attendance upon the Tikyali Rani Indira, were withdrawn, notwithstanding the fact that four of these were servants who had come at the time of her marriage from Malati Pur State with her.

At this stage, the second Rani, who was very fond of Indira, and still seemed to have some influence on His Highness, passed away. And this made Ganga Dasi more powerful than ever. For the first Rani was now mostly away at Haridwar or Mathura, visiting the holy shrines with the Dowager Rani, and there was no one to restrain His Highness from falling in with all the schemes of his mistress. And this made for the complete isolation of the Tikyali Rani. And there were days on which she didn't even have a domestic servant to do her shopping. The guards and the sentries, at the gates of the fort, prevented even women from coming to see her. And soon she was treated virtually as a prisoner, till she made representations to Delhi again and His Highness relaxed the conditions for fear of a scandal.

As the Maharaja was unable to bestow any legal status on Ganga Dasi, he began, by direct and indirect means, to buy property in her name. He sold some property belonging to himself as well as the state. He sold silverware and gold jewellery and other precious articles from the old palace, such as chairs and paintings and howdahs of elephants. Apart from this, he began to extort money from the people of the state by various illegal means in order to build up a fortune for her. The Diwan, Chaudhri Ramji Das, tried to dissuade His Highness from adopting such methods of obtaining money. But it was Ganga Dasi who was the real power behind the throne, and the illegal exactions continued. There were revolts in several parts of the state in consequence. These were suppressed by the state police with bloody violence and through a series of mass arrests and detentions. The people's movement gathered force and a Praja Mandal was formed which obtained the moral support of the Indian National Congress in British India.

At length an inquiry was instituted into the causes of the rebellions in the state. And it was proved beyond question that His Highness had oppressed the people in various ways. For instance, illegal dues, known as nazaranas, were taken from people; money was extorted from reversioners or heirs of those who died childless, from people who adopted children and even from people who arranged rightful succession. The penalty for disobedience to these decrees was the confiscation of the subject's property. And in many cases this penalty was exacted, and even applied retrospectively. Thus those who had money to pay actually paid and earned a little peace, and those who could not pay had the sword of Damocles hanging over their heads, that they might any day be deprived of their ancestral rights and properties.

Undoubtedly, all these oppressions, extortions, deprivations were primarily conducted under the influence, and for the benefit, of the Brahmin woman, Ganga Dasi. But that was not the only cue for passion which inspired His Highness. For, at this stage, he was, through his constant quarrels with Gangi Dasi, who was taking lover after lover behind his back, bursting out into mad furies of love-making and was going to a number of women who were supplied by agents appointed for the purpose of procuring them in different parts of the state. Not a virgin or a rupee was safe in his realms during this period. There was no question, of course, of His Highness bringing these women into the palace, as Ganga Dasi, who could not even tolerate the Tikyali Rani, would have had these new rivals murdered. So the Maharaja created other opportunities for the satisfaction of his lusts, by frequently going out on camping or hunting expeditions, when he was undisturbed by any watchful eyes. Except that, now and then, Ganga Dasi herself provided him with one of her female companions and there were secret orgies of which the nature is more myth and legend than fact, for no one could guess the exact nature of the perversions practised in the Brahmin woman's palace.

The maladministration of the state and the high-handedness of His Highness were the subjects of a further inquiry set up by the Government of India, and by an order of the Central Government some of the powers and prerogatives of the Maharaja were made subject to restrictions and supervision. The first condition in this order was that His Highness's Brahmin mistress, Ganga Dasi, and her two children, be banished from the state.

In an interview he had with Colonel Burton of the Political Department, His Highness accepted all the restraints proposed except the first one, which he begged should not be enforced. Colonel Burton told him, however, that the first condition was the most essential, for the irregular influence and interference of this woman had been the chief cause of the misery of the people of Sham Pur State, and, therefore, it could not be waived. His Highness was, in fact, asked to report within two months that Ganga Dasi had been banished.

Later, Colonel Burton came on a shooting tour to the state, and somehow or other the proposed exile of Ganga Dasi never happened. It was rumoured that His Highness had presented a precious necklace to Mrs Burton and had feasted her and her husband on roasted peacocks and some of the oldest French champagne he had in stock.

During the time when His Highness's conduct of state affairs was being inquired into, and the brief period during which it seemed that the order for Ganga Dasi's banishment might have to be carried out, the Brahmin woman was unable to pursue him and keep vigilant guard on him. The Maharaja began to frequent the old fort where the Tikyali Rani lived. He played upon her sympathy and showed himself very contrite. Indira relented and consoled him and performed her wifely duties by him. And they became intimate once again.

This return of His Highness to some degree of normality was encouraged by the Diwan, Chaudhri Ramji Das, who was keen on carrying out the instructions of the Government of India with regard to Ganga Dasi. The Prime Minister also tried to extract from the Brahmin mistress four lakhs of rupees, which she had collared from the sale of the State House in Haridwar. The efficiency and honesty of the Diwan was naturally much resented by Ganga Dasi. It was not surprising, therefore, when one fine morning the news came of the death, under mysterious circumstances, of the Prime Minister Ramji Das.

After the demise of Chaudhri Ramji Das, a cousin of His Highness, Chaudhri Raghbir Singh, was appointed as the Diwan. He was a profligate young man who had been Private Secretary to the Maharaja, a willing tool in his hands as well as Ganga Dasi's lover. At the instigation of the latter this new

Diwan sought to compromise with the Tikyali Rani by making overtures to her of a nature which she could not accept with any integrity. When he could not get a favourable response to his verbal wooing, he took advantage of her discarded and helpless condition by audaciously writing to her a love letter couched in the most flattering as well as the most threatening terms. As Indira refused to reply to this or to see him, he became her sworn enemy.

A trifle guilty at the thought of having thus improperly expressed himself in a letter, and afraid lest the Tikyali Rani should show the communication to the Maharaja, the Diwan began to ingratiate himself into the favour of Ganga Dasi by actively taking sides with her, so that he could get complete control over His Highness through the Maharaja's mentor. And the trump card of this new combination was to throw doubts on Indira's character! His Highness was only too amenable to the rumours which were floated about Indira's affairs with certain army officers of the Fort Guards, because the allegations which became current gave him the assurance that he alone was not guilty of excesses of the flesh. And, as it is the easiest thing, especially in a state, to give a bad name to a woman and hang her, these stories of the Tikyali Rani's misdeeds came to be widely believed.

Indira took the occasion, during His Highness's visit to the fort one day, to give him the letter written to her by the Prime Minister and to denounce his misbehaviour. But Vicky was not inclined to listen to her protestations and accused her of trying to frame-up a case against his trusted Vizier and cousin. And he disgraced her by abusing her in the presence of the courtiers.

After this, when Indira was allowed to go for a little holiday to Simla, His Highness disgraced her more publicly by issuing a parwana, an order to the Home Member, who forwarded it to the head constable in charge of Sham Pur Lodge at Simla, to the effect that no stranger be allowed to see her and that she be vigilantly guarded on her walks and rickshaw rides and not be permitted to go wandering on her own, without an escort. The result was that the Tikyali Rani came to be known to everyone as a bad woman, and became the subject of much scandal-mongering in the hill city, and untoward attacks began to be made on her by the fashionable heart squanderers who thought that she was easy game. And the fact that Indira had, during the brief spell of renewed intimacy between herself and His Highness, conceived another child made for all kinds of loose talk and conjecturing around her person.

In the third quarter of 1941, His Highness's mother, the Dowager Maharani, and the Senior Rani, knowing that Indira was with child, secured the Maharaja's permission and took her on a pilgrimage. They went to Haridwar and Mathura and Benares and Puri and to the temple of Rameshwaram at the southern tip of India, praying and doling out charity, in the hope that the expected child might be a son.

This was, of course, a very anxious time for Ganga Dasi, because she was frightened that the Tikyali Rani's womb might prosper and yield forth a new Tika to occupy the throne of Sham Pur. So she began to spread the rumour that Indira had run away and just disappeared.

The Tikyali Rani heard about this when she had come back, with the Dowager Maharani and the Senior Rani, from the pilgrimage and was resting at Dehra Dun, where she had decided to have the child in a good nursing home under expert medical advice. One day, a police inspector came with orders to hand over the Tikyali Rani to the Sham Pur police. This was the crowning humiliation for Indira.

She sent urgent wires to the Viceroy, the Governor of Punjab and to Mr Williamson of the Political Department. Mr Williamson wired back asking her to come to Simla at once, where he promised her full protection and medical advice.

Accordingly, she proceeded there in the company of her mother, who had joined her at Dehra Dun. On arrival she was examined by two IMS surgeons, who advised her to rest in Simla and take it easy in her advanced state of pregnancy. But Mr Williamson communicated to her the wish of her Maharaja that she should return to Sham Pur, and this officer curtly advised her to obey her husband's wishes. She was afraid of a miscarriage during the journey. But His Highness's orders were imperative and she left.

Indira was again consigned to the little palace in the fort and lived in constant terror of foul play, as she had had the bitter experience of losing her first son and knew that Ganga Dasi had contrived to have her brought back for no good reason. But fortunately, the presence of her own mother warded off the designs of the Maharaja's mistress and one fine January morning Indira gave birth to a son.

Again, there were no rejoicings in the kingdom of Sham Pur on the birth of the new Tika. And the Maharaja never even went to see his son and heir and refused to visit the fort palace for fear of Ganga Dasi.

Some months after the birth of her son, when her mother was going back to Bengal, Indira moved to a small palace on the estate in the village of Garhi, which had been given to her in her dowry; and here she remained for the next three war years.

The health of the child was very delicate. So, after much agitation, Mr Williamson got the Maharaja to provide a nurse for the Tika and regulated the grant of an adequate allowance of servants and a motor-car to Indira. And, when this officer came to visit Sham Pur two years later, in connection with further troubles in certain villages of the state, he made it a point to take the Maharaja to see the Tika, a visit which His Highness conceded with the greatest show of reluctance, owing to the consequence of such favouritism if it came to the notice of Ganga Dasi.

In the confined life which Indira was living she heard that Ganga Dasi was preparing a plot to have the new Tika murdered. She could not get any proof of this. But there must have been sufficient grounds for suspicions. For a new order was passed by the Political Department for the banishment of Ganga Dasi. Needless to say, this was not carried out because of His Highness's particular friendship with the Resident, Sir Hartley Withers, and Lady Withers.

When the Tika was four years of age, the Tikyali Rani began to plead for his education in a small kindergarten school at Simla. This was conceded and she was herself allowed, after many frivolous objections from His Highness, to go and live in the annexe of Sham Pur Lodge to be near her son.

Immediately after this there had been more trouble in the state and His Highness was forced to change his ministers, Chaudhri Raghbir Singh being made Commander-in-Chief and replaced by Rai Bahadur Pandit Shiv Nath, the Home Minister. But a change of horses in Sham Pur did not mean that one could cross the river of life any better. The affairs of the state did not improve to any extent.

So far as the Tikyali Rani was concerned, things went from bad to worse. For Pandit Shiv Nath was himself a Brahmin. Naturally, therefore, he was partial to the Brahmin woman.

Meanwhile, Indira began to feel the impact of the new regime very soon. It so happened that about a month after her arrival at Simla with her son, and the boy's Anglo-Indian nurse, Mrs Burrows, the nurse came and told the Tikyali Rani one morning that she was going out shopping to the Mall with the Tika. Indira casually assented to the outing. But as the morning wore on, and Mrs Burrows did not return, and lunchtime came and there was no sign of the nurse, she was in a panic. She sent her servants in every direction, but no one knew about the nurse or the child. She rang up the police, wired to the Viceroy and the Governor of Punjab, but could not get any news of Mrs Burrows or her ward. That evening Indira received a letter from the Resident of Sham Pur State that if she wanted to say goodbye to her son at the bungalow, Abergaldia in Chotta Simla, she could do so, because Mrs Burrows had been ordered to remove the Tika there, so that he could reside there and be out of the orbit of his mother's influence; and that she, the Tikyali Rani, should proceed to Sham Pur. The next morning Pandit Shiv Nath himself arrived to advise her to return to Sham Pur. His Highness had apparently been persuaded that the only way in which Indira would part with her son would be if the boy was kidnapped and the mother was presented with a *fait accompli*. The Tikyali Rani refused to leave Simla at the instance of the Diwan and told him that she would only go back under orders from the Political Department, with which she was in touch. The Diwan got the wind up on hearing that she had approached the Political Department and, after he had left, the child was brought back to her, of course without Mrs Burrows. Indira's representations to the Government of India bore fruit and she was allowed to stay with the Tika at the small hill station of Kasauli and a new Scottish nurse, Miss McQueen, was appointed to look after the boy.

The other consequences of Indira's representations were that Pandit Shiv Nath had to yield place to a Mr Horace, an ex-Director General of Police from the Punjab. Also a Mr Richards, a professor in the Government College, Lahore, was appointed Education Member, while a Major Nash was appointed to the Home and Finance Ministry. But the key to all power, Ganga Dasi, remained, though the question of her banishment became the subject of renewed negotiations.

Under the directions of the Praja Mandal, much strengthened by the post-war feeling of revolt current everywhere, and especially by the struggle for fundamental rights in the states, the people of Sham Pur became more than ever vocal. And the suppression of civil and political liberty by the new ministers only added fuel to the fire that had been smouldering for years.

Then came the transfer of power from Britain to India, and the attempt of His Highness Maharaja Ashok Kumar of Sham Pur to take advantage of the prevailing chaos, to strike out on his own and assert his independence by not signing the Instrument of Accession. This brought him into odium all over India.

Ultimately, he was forced by the agitation of the people in his state, said to have been engineered by the Communists, to sack his English ministers and to promise certain reforms. And Srijut Popatlal J. Shah, an ex-ICS official from Central Province, was appointed Prime Minister by the new Government of India.

It was after the appointment of the new Prime Minister that His Highness, not knowing the mind of the Government of India about him and about the action it would take either about Ganga Dasi or about his hesitation to accede, had come for a brief respite to Simla.

The separation from Ganga Dasi had troubled his spirit. And he had sought comfort in a flirtation with Bunti Russell, of which the consequences had been the violent scene with Captain Russell and our sudden exodus from Simla. And now, neither His Highness nor anyone in his entourage knew what would happen to him. We only knew that we were going downhill into the valleys and the plains, where either the implications of the Maharaja's rage would work themselves out immediately into a final debacle or he would get a chance to make a fresh start. Which of these two things would happen we did not know. But we knew that we were part of a destiny in which he had played very high stakes, higher than in any gambling house in the world, and that, with all the fates ranged against him, it was from now on a question of make or break.

PART 2

Although we had telegraphed the Prime Minister, Srijut Popatlal J. Shah, about our expected arrival, neither he nor anyone else turned up at Sham Pur railway station to meet us. And the usual salute of thirteen guns was not fired; not even the seven which had been fired at Simla. So His Highness got into another one of his passionate regal rages and everyone, from the stationmaster to the coolies, became reacquainted with certain unmentionable words in the Dogra hillman's vocabulary which they had not heard since the Maharaja had been here some months ago.

As always on such occasions, Munshi Mithan Lal showed his mastery of statecraft by whispering into His Highness's ears some kind of magic formula. I was so amazed at the calm which now suddenly possessed the Maharaja that I asked Munshiji how he had achieved the miracle. He told me that he had told His Highness that the mahurat for entering the palace had not yet been discovered. My amazement knew no bounds and became vulgar curiosity as I contemplated His Highness's hypocritical face with a continuous stare while we were being negotiated into the hallway. He accepted the make-believe about observing this superstition as a practised master of play-acting. We entered the special waiting room, with its Mughal towers and minarets, which had been constructed on the railway station for the use of the Royal House and the distinguished incoming and outgoing guests of the state.

I must explain at this juncture the reasons for the curiosity which will be aroused in the reader throughout this narrative about the many oddities of the Maharaja's life and the quaintnesses in an Indian state. Even before I went to Europe to do my post-graduate studies in medicine, I was aware of the survival into our twentieth-century world of the dasturs, the customs and conventions, of all the past centuries in an extraordinarily acute state of preservation. But, after three years of the West, I became more intensely aware of the jostling of our old habits and ideas with the new fashions we had acquired under the impact of Europe. So that all the religious and social taboos, inhibitions, prohibitions, which I had more or less accepted, if under protest, in my youth, began for a time, after my return, to irritate me until I had to work up a deliberate cynicism in myself as the necessary measure of self-preservation, in order that the strange facts might lead to amusement in me rather than to a nervous breakdown. I did not think things strange because I am a silly modernist, for whom everything European is good and everything in our own heritage bad, but because I have begun to see that the confusion arising from the clash of all the centuries with our own, in India, is bound to become worse unless we seek a synthesis of Europe and India, unless we evolve a new sense of values to live by and generally know the direction in which we are going. Unfortunately, the Indo-European contradictions in the life of the Maharaja of Sham Pur were too glaring not to admit of rude stares on my part. For here was a prince who had been educated in the English public school tradition and yet whose home background encouraged the darkest superstitions and the

most obscurantist ideas. The most barbaric impulses of both
civilizations dominated him and he played fast and loose with
life without asking himself any questions about himself.

It seemed to me quite ridiculous that we should be
waiting at the station for the discovery of the mahurat, or
the auspicious moment, to enter the state. I knew, of course,
that the discovery of the mahurat by the state astrologer was
a necessary and inevitable part of the ritual of our prince's
life. But the convention seemed to me to be carried to
excess, for not only the major comings and goings of His
Highness, but sometimes even the shopping expeditions or
visits to the club were preceded by the ostentatious
reckoning by the state astrologer of the position of the stars
vis-à-vis the day, the hour and the minute of His Highness's
toings and froings.

Furthermore, it appeared to me even more ridiculous
that we should be sitting on uncomfortable plush chairs,
built in the best tradition of the Imperial Czarist style,
watching the temperature rise in the barometer of each
other's faces to the highest points of Fahrenheit, while the
messenger was on his way to fetch Pandit Dhanpat Rai and
sort out the planets and the stars. It looked to me absolutely
outrageous that, in spite of my awareness of all the absurdities,
I should still be the willing slave of this pattern of behaviour
without a protest.

To complicate all this, Munshi Mithan Lal, Captain Partap
Singh, Mr Bool Chand and myself were sitting with our backs
to each other on the four-chairs-in-one which stood in the
middle of the hall, while His Highness was walking up and
down with a measured gait, as was his wont in moments of
acute tension. And I felt a fool in having to be a quadruplet,
so to speak, with my three colleagues.

I bore it for nearly half an hour, cowed by the refulgent aura of His Highness's prestige, which was always an omnipresent reality to us all. Then, for the first time in many days, I let the irritations of the courtier life express themselves in a comment which, though deliberately humorous, did not conceal the inner curve of bitterness beneath it:

'Why are we waiting here, when we know that Pandit Dhanpat Rai can persuade the stars to get into an auspicious array any time he likes?' I asked.

His Highness, whose nerves were on edge, seemed to find confirmation for his own feelings in my suggestion, as he said: 'I have two horoscopes, based on two different dates of birth. So the mahurat which may not be right according to one may be very auspicious according to the other. Let us go.'

'Yes, there are two or three different alternatives anyhow in the position of the stars,' said Mian Mithu gravely, realizing that His Highness was determined to leave.

'Chalo.' Captain Partap Singh beckoned to the coolies as though he was driving a herd of donkeys.

And the exodus began.

I was nervous that having initiated the movement homewards, I might get it in the neck if we went out of the waiting room, found no cars outside and had to expose His Highness to the sharp rays of the late morning sun. I hurriedly stepped out and was relieved to find that the silver Rolls-Royce was just drawing up with three Buicks and a station wagon between rows of policemen, who were lining the compound at intervals of twenty yards from each other all the way towards the town. What was more, there emerged Pandit Dhanpat Rai from the last Buick, with his white-bearded visage looking more like Rabindra Nath Tagore than ever before, except that his homespun kurta and dhoti, and the saffron caste marks on his forehead, shattered the illusory comparison immediately. I joined my hands to him in obeisance, putting on the most hypocritically reverential look that I could command.

'Asirvad, may you live long,' said the old man, casting the benediction with raised hands.

'Is the mahurat fixed?' I asked.

'Son, the auspicious stars in the horoscope always tally for His Highness.'

'Bravo!' I shouted, unable to restrain myself from bursting into English. And I ran towards the waiting room, but stopped short to see His Highness appear.

The astrologer joined hands to the Maharaja, a courtesy to which His Highness responded with compound interest, bending low in spite of his stiff trousers and touching the toes of the priest and taking the imaginary dust off the astrologer's feet to his forehead.

'Maharaj, you are blessed,' said Pandit Dhanpat Rai. 'The hour and the moment is ever auspicious for you. And your path is strewn with flowers all the way.'

I could not suppress an inner smile at the flattery of this unctuous ass. And, as I negotiated His Highness towards the door of the car, I whispered to him: 'Please look out for the few thorns that might have got mixed up with the roses.'

His Highness smiled good-humouredly and entered the limousine.

The State of Sham Pur can boast of beautiful street signs, even though the roads which they decorate are rather the worse for wear, being broad stretches of dusty, rutted highways, flanked by narrow byways and gulleys, along which travel the few motor cars of the nobility and the many horse-

driven carriages familiar in North India, the tongas and the
yekkas, the bullock carts and man-driven rickshaws. The main
street, stretching from the railway station to the principal
bazaar, is called Victoria Street after Her Gracious Majesty
the first English Queen Empress of India, in whose reign the
special treaty was made with His Highness's great-grandfather,
and the other roads are named after the various maharajas
and viceroys. The supreme touch of Victorian grandeur,
which puts the running sores of the capital into relief, are
the white-globed double lamps, specially made in London,
which reflect the sun's rays off their marble sheen during the
day and burn like the echoes of Czarist splendour in the night.

The traffic came to a standstill as the police van in front
of the entourage proceeded through the Victoria Bazaar, the
carriages and pedestrians fluttering away like hens as if at the
approach of a mad dog. The sentries on point duty came to
automatic attention; while the shopkeepers emerged on to
the doorsteps of their narrow, confined rabbit warrens and
bent their heads over their joined hands. And our awe-
inspiring presences passed halfway up the mile-and-a-half
stretch of the road. Then we turned sharp left through the
wooden gates of the splendid arched hallway, which led into
the main palace of Sham Pur, past two mounted cavalry sepoys,
who always stood like stone statues in full uniform on their
magnificent chargers, even like the Horse Guards with
busbies on their heads in Whitehall. The pigeons fluttered in
the alcoves of the ochre-coloured air houses on top of the
inner gateways and woke up the Rajput retainers, their lion
beards shining whiter than their tunics, decorated with red
cummerbund and ancient sword scabbards. And there was
a great bustle of shuffling feet in the marble-paved corridors
of the red sandstone palace.

Our cars stopped under the porch of the lovely ancient-style building with its magnificently carved pillars and cornices and network. And while we were alighting I felt a queer elation in my being. I always felt this under the shadow of the discreet grandeur which the palace reflected, a feeling heightened by the beautifully laid-out garden in the courtyard, where the many-coloured flowers stood in marble-cased beds, drawing life, against the sheen of the torrid glare of the cruel summer sun, from the huge fountain which played in the middle of the courtyard.

The palace formed a rectangular structure, in the wings of which we, the personal staff of His Highness, had our suites of rooms, flanking the main English-style living rooms of the Maharaja Sahib himself. Beyond an interior courtyard, paved with marble, stood a file of three-storeyed terraced buildings, which were the vigilantly guarded inner sanctums, occupied by Ganga Dasi and her female attendants.

The inner glow in me subsided as soon as we were in the hall, because His Highness, tense and preoccupied as he was, began to shout at the retainers to clear out of his way until one of them out of sheer fright fell across the head of a tiger skin which lay near the entrance. I was always aware of the influence of the jungle in this atmosphere, because of the silly association of ideas which the many tiger skins and the other trophies of the hunt, that hung from the walls or lay about on the floors, started in my mind, evasive and impalpable and yet strong enough to confuse me with unknown fears. And this confusion was worse confounded by the irritations set up through my awareness of an incongruous array of mechanical birds which used once to twitter when they were wound up but now stood in two large cages in the veranda, silent because their inner springs had broken, mocking at the droves of beautiful green parrots which flew from tree to tree, shrieking their song across the ochre-coloured buildings. We had fallen with a bang from the heights of Himalayan splendour to the sordid modernity of the bazaar, filled with cheap American gadgets.

As we entered the hall, we were aware of a presence which could neither be seen nor heard, but whose impress could be felt in the shifting, anxious eyes of the retainers. Then two female attendants darted in, their faces covered with their dupattas, and fell down and touched the feet of His Highness.

'Maharani Sahiba,' they whispered, and pointed in the direction of the living room.

We realized that His Highness's mistress, Ganga Dasi, was waiting for him. Although she was not a maharani, she was styled as such under orders given by His Highness two years ago when she had made scenes in order to achieve this recognition. Anyhow, the other two maharanis, as well as the Queen Mother, known as Raj Mata, lived in the old Fort Palace of Sham Pur, three miles away. So it could be no other than Ganga Dasi. We discreetly withdrew to our various suites.

As I passed by the living room, I caught a glimpse of Ganga Dasi through the slightly drawn curtains. She was dressed in a muslin kurta and salwar, according to the Punjabi style which had become fashionable, with her dupatta thrown carelessly across her neck over the shoulders. And her vivid, small wheat-blonde face, with the high cheekbones, shone with good health, though there was an anxious glint in her heavy-browed big eyes, which, in the flashing moment of my vision, seemed to suggest the usual hysteria which I associated with her. She averted her face from me coyly, though she did not keep purdah before me. And, as I passed by another door on my way to the left wing of the palace, I saw her withdrawing towards the mirror over the magnificent carved dresser on which stood personal photographs of His Highness, his family and his friends.

About half an hour later, while I was in my bath, Jai Singh, the chief chowkidar of the palace, came and knocked at the door.

'Maharaj has called you urgently,' he said.

I was irritated at the summons and yet, if the truth be spoken, I glowed within me with excitement at the thought that he depended so much on me. Immediately beneath this reflection there was an inordinate curiosity welling up in me about how the drama of His Highness's life, which had suddenly come to a head in Simla, would develop.

'Acha, I am coming,' I answered. And I hurriedly lifted myself from the comfort of the lukewarm water in the beautiful green-coloured Roman bath and turned on the cold shower. The gentle rain from the jet soothed my spirit, till I felt calm enough for any disaster.

I dressed in an embroidered muslin kurta and baggy, long-cloth pyjamas, several pairs of which His Highness had brought me from Lucknow, and which Francis, my bearer, had put out for me. And I proceeded towards the Maharaja's suite, taking my own time about it.

'My life is lapsing and you indulge in blandishments!' His Highness repeated a hackneyed Hindustani phrase to see me come ambling along.

As I entered, I heard a significant cough from behind the curtain which separated the bedroom from the drawing room. I instinctively lifted my eyes towards the curtain, and saw a pair of eyes peeping through the slits. Ordinarily, Ganga Dasi did not keep purdah from me, but I realized that she might want to envelop her new quarrel with His Highness with secrecy, although she knew that I knew everything about the Maharaja's past and present life, that I was his special confidant.

'I told you I am a rat in a hole,' His Highness said, deliberately. 'Well, I *am* a rat in a hole!'

His face was flushed and though he had cast off his serge jacket and his necktie he still had his warm trousers on.

Before I could make a comment, Ganga Dasi's black, middle-aged maidservant, Rupa, entered and, joining hands with His Highness, said: 'Maharaj, you are wanted inside.'

'I think I am in the way,' I said.

'Nahin, you wait and take my temperature,' His Highness said. And he waved Rupa aside with a flourish of his hand, saying, 'I shall come in a while.'

I took the thermometer from among the pens and pencils on His Highness's table and began to attend to him.

There was now a furious rustling behind the curtains, whispers, then one or two more coughs. Now my nerves, too, were on edge, because I felt that I would be courting Ganga Dasi's displeasure if I did not clear out at once.

'Vicky, come inside, I want to talk to you,' Ganga Dasi said in a stern, hurt voice, emerging from behind the curtain. Her round face was livid with rage and the heavy eyebrows above her green eyes were twisted into a frown, exaggerated in its severity by the straight, black hair which lay tightly plastered on the two sides of her forehead.

His Highness kept his face averted.

'Victor,' I said, '*they* want you inside.'

The whole situation seemed to have come to boiling point in him.

'Get out. Go away, Gangi!' he shouted as he turned towards Ganga Dasi. 'Get out!...'

'Acha!' she snarled, her face twitching with fury at this insult. And she rushed out, her whole body quivering with impatience and chagrin.

'Highness, you are tired and should rest,' I said sheepishly.

I took his hand in mine to soothe him and muttered in my embarrassment:

'Your temperature is normal, but you should calm down and rest.'

'The bitch!' he shouted. 'After having encouraged me to go to other bitches, she is —'

'Highness! Highness!' I whispered.

But he was shaking with anger and weakness, his face torn with the contrary emotions which seemed to go through him; the anger he felt and the fear of the consequences of defying his mistress.

I turned to go almost on tiptoes, hoping that my absence would make him retrace his steps towards the bedroom.

'Don't go, Hari,' he implored even as he sank into an armchair, and sat holding his forehead in his hands. 'Please wait, I want to talk to you.'

During this talk His Highness admitted me more deeply into the orbit of his private life with Ganga Dasi than he had ever done before. As, however, most of what he said confirmed the vague guesses that I had made about his association with the Brahmin woman, I listened with sympathy. Of course, he was finding it difficult to begin. His head hung down and his lower lip trembled a little before he could muster the courage to take me into confidence. So I tried to make it easier for him by making a beginning myself: 'Why do you feel so attached to her, Vicky?'

'I don't know,' he answered, his face assuming a grimace. And he writhed silently for a while. Then he said: 'Somehow she is bound up with my entrails....I suppose it is sex....And she was very devoted to me at times. It is awful, but my heart drums to think of her past lovers.'

'Jealousy?'

'It might be jealousy, but I long for her when she is not there.'

'What does she want now?'

'Oh, nothing new. She wants to marry me and get her son recognized as Tika and heir to the gaddi.' He said this with sighing whispers. 'And she wants me more completely in her grip without promising that –'

He couldn't go on, and I understood what he was referring to, though my curiosity about her past was aroused and I probed him: 'You seem to know all her subterfuges.'

Victor got up from the settee and walked towards the bedroom door to see if Gangi was eavesdropping. He adopted a casual gait as he did this. He did not want to arouse the suspicion that he was spying on her in case she should be inside. But he came back in a moment, moving his head to signify satisfaction.

'She is a consummate actress!' he said as he began to walk to and from the bedroom door.

'I don't think that she is deliberate,' I ventured. I wanted to say that I did not think she had a mind with which she could contrive designs to serve her diabolical genius. For she had seemed to me neither devilish nor angelic, but just a bundle of ill-assorted nerves, impulses and fancies bound up into a knot, as is the peasant woman's bundle, the knot being symbolic of the sharp, instinctive sense of mastery she had of all situations.

'You are nearly right, Dr Shankar,' Victor said. 'She is without design, except that she has always had an instinct for getting her way. She pretends to be a child, wanting protection, but she knows what she wants. She is clever....'

'That is the way with some women who preserve their "babyness" to get what they want,' I said. 'But, apart from her put-on helpless girlishness, she has charm.'

I was afraid that the tone of irreverence in my voice might annoy him. But he must have been feeling very bitter that day. For he burst out and said the most intimate things about his relations with her.

'The bitch!' he exclaimed. 'She comes to me with so many love words, shrieks and hisses that I – well, I like to sleep with her, you see! And she has got me....I am trapped, I tell you, I am like a rat in a hole!...Sometimes she is so wonderful. And yet for periods she drifts away from me and is quite separate, and I feel she is not with me, though she is living in the same house with me. You see, she wants other men. Even while I am having her, she is often telling me of the sexual feats of my cousin Raghbir Singh or someone else. She has never been satiated, although she has had so many men.'

After saying this he peeped into the bedroom again to make sure that we were still alone.

'I think she will not come here now,' I said to assure him. 'She must have taken umbrage and gone into the "dark room" to sulk.'

'There will be hell to pay, I know.'

'Where did you pick her up?'

'Oh, she comes from Hoshiarpur district. Her father was a priest in the 41st Dogras Regiment and her mother a whore. Pandit Piara Lal, the father, lived mostly in the Frontier with his regiment and could not take his wife and daughter to the cantonments with him. And he suspected his wife. He used to beat her up when he came home on furlough....Gangi told me she liked her father, because he brought her fruit and clothes when he came, but began to be frightened of his voice when she heard him shouting at her mother. As the whole village knew that her mother was a prostitute, and the children teased her, she became attached to her mother, did not play with the children and wandered about alone. And several of the village herdsmen had her in the hills before she was fourteen. And then she became addicted to self-abuse and pleasure and matured beyond her years.'

I could understand the pattern. Gangi must have been torn between the fascination for her father, the hero, and abhorrence for him, the tyrant. And perhaps each man in her later career came to symbolize these two aspects of Pandit Piara Lal.

'In spite of the relations she had with men,' continued Victor, 'she is a very lonely person, unhappy at heart and very frightened of what the world would say. She is secretive. Also, she tells lies as easily as most people tell the truth.'

I could imagine that she had always had to turn in upon herself and indulge in dreams and fantasies.

'There is something private I can't tell you,' Victor said with effort, 'but she is not normal in sex – she abuses her body and also –'

I did not force him to reveal what he could not tell me easily. And I tried to shift the ground for him.

'I hear she was married.'

'Han, she was sold in marriage to a Brahmin peon in the office of the Deputy Commissioner of Hoshiarpur. His name was Shiv Ram. She told me that she was very lovely at that age and everyone admired her green eyes, though the neighbouring women called her a "green-eyed witch". Shiv Ram was a drunkard. And, though she has been wild in her sex adventures, for some curious reason she still dislikes drink. She nagged him about it and he turned into the most highhanded of wife-beaters in a land in which this species abounds. She seems not to have liked him in sex either, because he took her as and when he pleased and then left her without saying a kind word to her. So she ran away with a professional wrestler and gambler, named Motilal, to Amritsar. After a few months, when Motilal became bankrupt, she lived with an accountant of the Imperial Bank, named Kishen Chand, who had been Moti's friend till the wrestler lost his money. As Kishen Chand has a wife and did not want to take full responsibility for her, he shared her with a few gallants from the Amritsar business and professional world: lawyer Balmukand, Professor Advani, export-import merchant Mulraj and the cloth merchant Munilal. Her fame as a courtesan, with the green eyes and a hill-woman's body, spread. And, as she had a good voice and sang hill songs, a film magnate of Lahore, Seth Ranchod Das, gave her a part in a Punjabi film based on the story of Heer and Ranja —'

'And thus she became an actress!' I said, fascinated by the story.

'Han, and after this she went from one lover to another,' Victor said, now almost worked up to a frenzy, hurting himself with the truth, his face pale but taut with hysteria. 'And she learnt all the tricks of the trade. But there was still a little innocent charm left in her, I suppose, and the babyish helplessness. And she longed for someone to protect her. So she got hold of an old Parsi gentleman called Homi Mehta, a retired sixty-year-old confectioner, who had made money in Lahore cantonment, but whose wife had run away with an army officer. Mr Mehta had met her at the house of Seth Ranchod Das, while she had been engaged in an offensive against the film magnate. And this Parsi idiot took pity on her because Ranchod Das, who was afraid of his wife, seemed not to be yielding to her tantrums. She turned her X-ray eyes, which penetrate right through the nerves, tendons, fibres and the marrow of men, to their bones, on poor Homi. The old man softened to her and took her under his care. He bought some land on the Canal Bank in Lahore and built a house for her, hoping that she would marry him and settle down. But just then she met a film writer, Indar Nath, who had written the songs for a picture called "Maya" and made a hit. Now she became part of the arty crowd in Lahore and took English lessons and became fashionable. At this stage the old Parsi proposed marriage to her. But Gangi pretended that she was in love with Indar Nath. The Parsi contented himself by accepting the platonic friendship she offered him and did not withdraw the gift of house and land he had given her.'

'I am surprised,' I said, 'that if you know so much about her past, you —'

'So am I surprised!' Victor exclaimed, pausing by the door to listen before uttering the next words with a bitter deliberation in his voice. 'She is a bitch, but I can't do without her!'

'Did you know her in her Lahore days?'

'No, no, I met her later, here in Sham Pur. You see, her father had retired from the head priesthood of his regiment and taken up residence in Sham Pur. She came to see him. And once she had entered the precincts of this city, she never looked back towards Lahore again.'

'I suppose she had the scarcity value of a film star in the provincial atmosphere of the state capital!'

But Victor did not interrupt his confession:

'She enraptured the sardars and officials of Sham Pur with her charm. And she began to frequent the palace as a saheli of my second Rani. And then, well, the mischief began.'

After saying this Victor suddenly stopped. I waited for him to go on. But his lips were sealed and the look of frenzy on his face disappeared.

'What about the Badaun affair?' I asked.

'How do you know about that?' Victor asked me, turning angrily from the writing table to which he had paced up.

'I am afraid everyone knows these things,' I said. 'If you imagine that these things remain secret, you are mistaken.'

'I don't know why I am telling you all this if you know already,' said Victor haughtily.

'I am sorry, Highness, if I am intruding on your secrets,' I replied. 'I only want to help. After all, who else can you tell all this to? If I know the details, I may be able to offer some advice.'

'Well, she went with my second Rani to Badaun and had an affair with the Raja Sahib of Badaun, who is my Rani's brother. There was a scandal and she had to leave Badaun for Sham Pur. On her return here she met me....' Victor paused for a moment, fixed me with a glare and then said: 'This is a secret I am entrusting only to you. I don't know if her son is by the Raja Sahib of Badaun or by me. That is why I have hesitated in acknowledging him as the Tika. She was probably pregnant before I met her. Though I don't think so. She fell in love with me after the very first moment she saw me in the zenana. And she was so warm and became so devoted that I could not go back to Chief's College after that. And when I ascended the gaddi she appeared at the durbar and I

nearly acknowledged her son as heir on that day, but my
mother was against it and, of course, Indira was very angry.'

'I still can't understand how you can trust her and live
with her.'

'I had behaved badly to my wives, and she had been bad,'
he answered, coming to sit on the arm of the settee. 'So I
thought that two bad people might make a good pair.' He
smiled, and then, turning very serious, said: 'She understands
me in a strange kind of way. And sex....'

'I feel that all this emotional insecurity is a heavy price to
pay for brief moments of pleasure.'

'I must not be unfair to her, Dr Shankar. You see, I can't
tell you of the happiness she gave me when she first came
to me. You will laugh at this. But I felt that someone had
come into my life, someone who knew the life of a town
like Lahore amidst all these yokels, someone to cling to in
the midst of all the artificiality of the state where I was a
kind of tin god. To have a private life with someone devoted
to you after all the ballyhoo of pomp and splendour! And
she was a lovely companion and gave me such assurance. I
could work ten times harder because I had a satisfactory
personal life. She used to bath me with her own hands and
fuss after me a good deal in the beginning. And so I
surrendered to her more completely than I have ever
surrendered to any other woman. She told me all the secrets
of her affairs and wished that she had met me first when she
was nearly a virgin....'

From what I knew of him, I sensed that there must have
been a certain satisfaction in the feeling that she preferred
him to any of her previous lovers.

'Then what went wrong? When did you first begin to
suspect her of...?'

'You see, she was by turns gentle, vicious, kind, cruel, loving, angry, generous, but always impatient. And she turns her green eyes on other men as and when she likes. Even while having sex she is thinking of others....' His eyes lowered and there was a tremor on his lips, as he repeated himself.

'All women are vain and seek admiration,' I said. 'But what exactly happened to rock your faith in her?'

Victor contemplated me with a glare as much as to say 'Can I trust you?' And then, breathing a little heavily, he said: 'If you will keep this strictly confidential, I will tell you. No one must know. You see, Gangi had had an affair with my cousin Chaudhri Raghbir Singh soon after she came to live in Sham Pur. When she met me she was still carrying on with him. And she proposed that I should share her with Raghbir Singh. I accepted this at first, but then I couldn't bear it and ordered her to drop Raghbir Singh. After a few quarrels she accepted this. And during the next three or four months she spoke more love words to me than any other woman has ever done. Then... well, one night when I returned here from the hunting lodge, some hours earlier than I was expected, I saw a light in my bedroom. At once, the thought came to me that Gangi was betraying me. As a matter of fact, I had deliberately returned earlier than I was expected. So I entered the suite from the side door in the veranda and peeped through the chinks in the curtains drawn over the half-open window. I found her standing in a passionate embrace with Raghbir Singh, kissing him and being kissed by him. Five times I saw their mouths come up to each other.... And I can never forget this scene, much as I try! You see, I felt it deeply because, sensing that she might do this, I had tried to persuade her the previous day to come to the hunting lodge with me. And she had lied and said that she had important business to talk over with Raghbir Singh. I had tried to win her away from her lover by being extra nice to her before going to the forest. But she had been withdrawn and slightly brusque with me, and I had gone away to hunt, unhappy in my mind....I tiptoed away from the window, but they heard my footsteps and disengaged themselves from each other. Gangi went into the bathroom, while Raghbir Singh retreated into the drawing room.... Well, the storm of hell raged in my heart. My body shook. I entered the bathroom by the outside door, which was unlocked. Gangi shrieked and nearly fell back, pale with fear. I brushed her aside from the washbasin roughly and began to douche my face with water. Then I dried myself and just walked past Raghbir Singh, there, into the hall. I drove back to the hunting lodge unhappy and angry and wept bitterly....'

Victor paused and averted his face from me obviously because tears had come to his eyes again. He was breathing hard and moved his head back to shake off the oppression which had suddenly descended on him. It seemed to me that the image of Gangi in the embrace of his cousin Raghbir Singh had made a shattering impression on him.

'Didn't you think of giving her up then?'

'That night I almost decided to do so.' Victor blew his nose on his white silk handkerchief. 'But both Gangi and Raghbir Singh came to the hunting lodge. My face was swollen, as I had been unable to control my misery all night. And I refused to see them. Raghbir Singh came in, however, and began to apologize to me. He said that he had given up Gangi, but she had insisted that he should see her just once to say farewell, and that when he met her she had proposed that he should sleep with her. He had refused to do so and told her never to think of him again, and they had just been saying goodbye when I had seen them. Raghbir Singh warned me that the woman was dangerous and that neither he nor I should have anything to do with her. My inner doubts about Gangi were confirmed and I apologized to my cousin for the situation, and we parted on good terms, though my friendship with him was broken for ever because I can never really trust him now.'

'I am surprised that you did not accept General Raghbir Singh's advice.'

'I refused to see her,' Victor exploded, 'but she insisted on seeing me. She came into the bedroom and began to kiss my feet and weep. Naturally, I relented a little. She kissed me and embraced me and craved forgiveness. I fought against myself and brushed her away. She came back, abject and grovelling and broken, and then I could not control myself. I took her in my arms. I rebuked her and scolded her and told her how she had destroyed my confidence in her and in the whole of our life together....I was furious and even hit her for doing this to me. She cried and cried, and I was overcome by tenderness for her and took her in my arms. And then – well, you know how it is....'

'I know,' I said with a slight irony in my voice.

'But, Hari, everyone in Sham Pur knew that I was living with Gangi. To break up the thing would have created a scandal! And, to be fair to her, Gangi did try after this incident to be extra good to me. Perhaps, however, I became more suspicious. And the whole of our life together has been poisoned by my fits of jealousy and Gangi's inability to suppress the harlot in her.'

'I must say you are brave.'

'I will tell you more but you must give me sound advice,' he began with a fresh frenzy. 'There were other incidents, small ones –'

When he was just resuming his narrative, there was the sound of footsteps in the bedroom, and his face went a ghastly pallor. He got up angrily and shouted: 'Who is it?'

I felt that he would lose his temper now if it was Gangi, because he had worked himself up to a rage with the recapitulation of his story.

'Rupa,' came the voice from inside. 'Maharani Sahiba —'

'What is it?' he snarled.

'Maharani Sahiba wants you,' the maid said.

Victor ground the bitter taste in his mouth. Then his face relaxed and he shrugged his shoulders, saying: 'That is Gangi all over! Excuse me, I will have to go, otherwise there will be hell to pay.'

I sat silently contemplating his elegant body as he walked into the bedroom on the way to the zenana. For a while, my mind was blank. Then I found myself muttering to myself, 'That's that!' And I began to walk towards my suite.

On the way I felt that, after all was said and done, we were back to His Highness's dilemma of the last seven years. In spite of the fact that he felt no security in Gangi, he found in her general amiability and charm, consolations such as he could not get from the company of his chaste, rather too proper wife. And while he suffered the agonies of hell from the ups and downs of Gangi's incalculable temperament, he was fascinated by the challenge of her moods, by the excitement and thrills of those changing colours, of which her vanities, frailties, ficklenesses and cruelties were the secondary hues as against the lush splendour of the primary colours of her lusts and passions. It was really the call of one chameleon to another, for they had both emerged, with similar temperaments, from the orbits of their respective affairs and mistaken their fatigue for the urgent need of each other. In the aura of the atmosphere that prevailed between them through the long-drawn miseries of days, the nights were relieved by the high-powered love-making and the reaching out to an insouciance where both of them felt calm and assured, having touched the ultimate limits of sex which held them both prisoners of each other. But during the days, away from her, Victor was racked. And, in fact, it seemed to me that His Highness craved for these tensions now, if only because the pleasure of making up and beginning afresh put a new zest into his otherwise banal life, tempered only by the artificial excitements which he was always seeking to create in the political and social relations of the state to feed the vanity of his enormously enlarged ego, even as he was creating these in his personal equations. The complex of his present position was, however, too intricate to admit of any simplification, and in the game of hide-and-seek which he and Gangi played they were approximating towards desires and impulses in themselves and each other which were wild and boundless and inchoate, the urgings of capacities which had been perverted and thwarted by the unreality of their lives, by the substitution in their careers of 'felt wants' for 'real wants'.

There is no rest for the wicked, they say in the trite English phrase. Certainly, being part of the amoral world of Sham Pur State, and being therefore wicked, there was no rest for any of us. For I had hardly awakened from my siesta on the afternoon of our arrival and had my cup of tea when I was recalled to His Highness's august presence again.

As if the crisis which was reached between Vicky and Gangi on our return from Simla (though I didn't know how exactly it had been fought out) was not enough, another crisis, a more obvious one, had been forced on him by Srijut Popatlal J. Shah, the Prime Minister, who had been appointed by the States Department at Delhi after His Highness had shown reluctance in acceding to the Indian Union. Srijut Popatlal J. Shah had sent a message through Mr Bool Chand to His Highness to come down from Simla for consultations. Unfortunately, immediately on our arrival, Victor had had a showdown with Gangi and did not even acknowledge the Prime Minister's message or send him any greetings. What was more awful was the fact that when Srijut Shah, having heard of our return, called at the palace, Victor was in Gangi's rooms and refused to see him. Upon this, the Prime Minister was incensed and left a caustic note for His Highness with Munshi Mithan Lal. Victor saw this letter when he emerged from the zenana and got into a panic and sent for me.

By the time I got to His Highness's lounge, Srijut Popatlal J. Shah had also been fetched, Victor having sent both Munshi Mithan Lal and Captain Partap Singh to bring him.

The atmosphere was very strained as I entered the room and Victor tried to ease the situation by flippantly making me the butt of conversation.

'Diwan Sahib, our English friends call Dr Hari Shankar "Hurry" Shankar, but he is the slowest tortoise that ever lived out of water.'

Srijut Popatlal J. Shah ignored the joke, swept me with a piercing glance from his shrewd brown eyes and sat in the armchair, solid, with his massive set face, a handsome, dark, round visage, with a broad forehead which gave the Gujarati banias the impression that the Diwan had an intellectual distinction not usual among his class. Popatlal had been in the Indian Civil Service, having retired just before the British left and, after serving on the Textile Board, had been suddenly lifted by Sardar Vallabhbhai Patel to be the Diwan of Sham Pur State, so that he could bring order into the chaos which spread in this little state and persuade the Maharaja to accede to the Indian Union. He was more un-Gujarati still in that he wrote poetry in his spare time and valued literature only second to money, a trait which is not so obvious among the middle class of Ahmedabad, the textile centre from which he sprang.

Since Victor's humour did not break the ice, or rather cool the heat of suppressed anger which the Prime Minister's presence extended, I tried to be amusing.

'Maharaja Sahib likes tortoises all the same, Mr Shah,' I said. 'And the advantage of being a tortoise is the tough outer layer on one's back on which one can bear all the "slings and arrows of outrageous fortune".'

I had really wanted to immolate myself. But the salt on my tongue made my words into a kind of unintended repartee. Even this did not excite Srijut Popatlal J. Shah. He was an experienced diplomat, trained in the British Indian steel frame tradition, where an Anglo-Saxon economy of words, combined with the bluff of authority, had been patented specifically for the purpose of breaking down the nerves of the ruled by the application of a power always held in reserve and yet reflected through benign condescension. Against this stern, immoveable and somewhat arrogant deity, the nerves of the heir to the proverbial gallantry of the Rajputs, the stamina of our prince, could not last out.

'I am very sorry, Diwan Sahib,' Victor began, 'that you thought it fit to withdraw the salute of thirteen guns on my arrival here.'

The Maharaja's lower lip drooped, and there was a significant dwindling of his ancestral pride visible in the lean face, while his big, shining eyes, sentimental like that of a spaniel dog, dimmed with a mist near to tears. I had never realized before how much the pride of being saluted by the thirteen salvoes, every time he left a station, was part of His Highness's person. For from the intimacy and familiarity of my daily contact with him he had come to seem so informal. But then I recalled that often when important guests came to a meal Munshi Mithan Lal was not allowed to sit at table with His Highness as he was an old-style Private Secretary, and that Captain Partap Singh and myself were only accepted round the main table because of our education and general snob value.

The Prime Minister still did not react, though the colour mounted to his face and made it darker.

And, after a prolonged silence, Vicky began again: 'I think Sardar Vallabhbhai Patel is angry with me, because I am known to have been an admirer of Netaji Subhash Bose, whom the Sardar always hated. Also, the petitions of Rani Indira have poisoned his mind against me.'

At this insinuation against his chief, Srijut Popatlal J. Shah felt it necessary to say something. Guardedly, he swayed his head to one side to signify negation and murmured: 'Your Highness, there is no question of personal animosity towards you. The issue is the accession of Sham Pur to the Indian Union.'

'Well,' said Victor, hedging as he got up and began to walk about. 'This question needs some thought. I have to consult my mother. You must remember, Diwan Sahib, that Sham Pur borders on Tibet and touches Jammu and Kashmir. As such, it is, like Nepal and Bhutan, a buffer state. And my forefathers were not even conquered by the Sikhs, except when some of the nobles in Sham Pur betrayed us. Our dynasty dates back to antiquity. And, long before Gandhiji preached the philosophy of Ram Raj, we have been practising it in this state. Besides, I must ask my people....'

At this Srijut Popatlal J. Shah flushed a vivid coffee colour and shuffled in his armchair, till his tussore trousers became crumpled and his bright necktie, with a lovely mango pattern on it, began to choke him. He passed his forefinger through his white collar and eased the mounting pressure of blood in his swelling arteries. Then, adjusting himself rather pompously into a dignified position, he rested back and began politely:

'Maharaja Sahib, I am here in Sham Pur to fulfil the orders of the Sardar. I am an administrator and I have been sent here on duty. I am willing to send a memorandum, which you may give me, to the States Department. Only, if I may advise you in your best interest, I think you should consider acceding, because most of the princes in India have already done so. After all, these accessions are intended to promote the unity of the country. And, as a patriot, I am sure you will consider it your duty to come into the family. Also, there are some personal advantages for you in taking this step.'

'Nonsense! What is the personal advantage to me, Mr Shah?' burst out His Highness impatiently. 'I lose my independence and my state. Is that the advantage?'

'Your Highness has no independence to lose,' interrupted Srijut Popatlal J. Shah brusquely. 'You were subject to the British paramount power.'

'But when the English left....'

'You are living in a fool's paradise, sir!' said the Premier, angry at being engaged in a constitutional discussion by a mere boy, who was obviously using newspaper arguments and ignoring the realities.

'Sir C.P. Ramaswamy Iyer,' ventured Victor, 'is a great legal brain. And he…well, he also stood for the independence of Travancore.'

'And where is he now?'

The Diwan's answer shattered the amateur politician, until Vicky went pale and bit his lips and looked towards Munshi Mithan Lal and me for support.

Munshi Mithan Lal sat with his head bent, breathing like a tired rhinoceros. And I considered discretion the better part of valour in a quarrel so ultimate as this, where I knew the Maharaja would lose hands down. Without attempting to dominate the scene, and with the help of the merest adjustment of his body, Srijut Popatlal J. Shah was master of the situation.

For a while, the wills of the two adversaries were engaged in a silent battle. And the quarrel would have petered out, I knew, by the acceptance, by the weaker of the two personalities, of a provisional truce on the basis of the postponement of the discussion, which was the usual method of His Highness in vital matters because he lacked the ability to decide an issue. But, at this stage, there intruded upon the scene Ganga Dasi, who had been eavesdropping in the dressing room of the Maharaja Sahib.

'Who is he?' she said, turning to Victor, demurely drawing the edge of her dupatta over her face.

Srijut Popatlal J. Shah did not take umbrage at this rudeness, but remained seated calmly in his chair, his face cushioned upon the palm of his left hand.

'Queen Bee!' Vicky exclaimed, disapprovingly, calling Ganga by the English nickname he had given her. 'Mr Popatlal Shah is the new Diwan.'

'What did you say?...Popatlal Shah?' Gangi played upon the name with the naive amusement which a naughty child seeks by a play upon odd words and names.

Srijut Shah's eyes spat fire at the insult, but he had long since disciplined himself into self-control, and the fire in his eyes soon turned into a mellow liquid, through which one could see the heights of condescension that he deliberately brought to the contemplation of this ignorant woman.

She winced under the effect of his gaze and looked up to Vicky, who, however, turned away and did not support her. At this she got into a panic and protested indignantly: 'All day people are coming and going in this palace, and we are not left alone even for a second. Every time I come in here there is a conference going on. Now what is happening?'

'Queen Bee, we are discussing some important state matters,' Victor said, with a cautionary glance to silence her.

'What are these important state matters?' the Queen Bee whined. 'You men consider yourself so self-important. Tell me, and I, a mere hill-woman, will settle the matter at once.'

The resentment in her voice compelled attention. That was what she had wanted. For, always she strained to be the centre of attention, the sun towards whom all the sunflowers must turn. Only, this egotism became ridiculous because of the gap between the ignorance and vulgarity in her nature and the seriousness of the occasions and issues into which she barged where the proverbial angels would have feared to tread.

Srijut Popatlal J. Shah could not bear it any longer. He heaved himself out of the armchair and, with his impassioned face set into a serious and grim mould, got up to go.

'Sit down, Diwan Sahib, and have some sherbet or tea,' Ganga Dasi said, exerting the light of her green eyes on him in that ogling manner of the harlot with which she was always able to win every argument. And she accompanied this seductive glance with a charming side movement of her head, an obviously coy gesture which was supposed to subdue the Diwan completely.

The surprising thing was that Srijut Popatlal J. Shah reacted with the tremor of a smile, yielding in one corner of his soul, so that his breathing became noticeably heavier. But the outer steel frame round his nature had been tempered in many a battle. And he said emphatically: 'I don't want to discuss anything with you.'

'Vicky!' she cried. 'Do you hear this? Am I to be insulted in my own house!'

His Highness's face quivered with contrary emotions. He was grateful at the joint front which Gangi had established with him against the Diwan, because it would heal the private quarrel between them. On the other hand, he noticed how she had exerted her charm on Srijut Shah and seemed to feel uneasy, as he had told me he always did, for fear that she may use her sex not only for the ends of power but for pleasure. He extended his hand towards her in a protective gesture.

Meanwhile, Srijut Popatlal J. Shah got up, joined hands in formal obeisance to His Highness and walked away with slow, measured steps. Munshi Mithan Lal and Captain Partap Singh walked out behind him.

The silence of doom spread on the drawing room.

I got up to leave after the other members of the entourage had gone, but, curiously, Gangi asked me to stay for a while. The need to know more about what had really happened since our return from Simla persuaded me to accept the invitation.

I felt a little embarrassed and out of place as Gangi went up to where Vicky was standing and put her arms round his neck, because, in spite of the fact that in Europe I had got used to lovers and husbands and wives kissing and cuddling each other in public, a slight self-consciousness at open love-making lingered still in the demure Indian parts of my nature; and my awareness of the tension between this couple, underneath the surface reactions, made the outer display of tenderness seem sentimental.

Vicky readily accepted the affection Gangi offered him, because he had sensed the little flutter she had excited in Srijut Popatlal J. Shah. And though she was ostensibly using her sex for his benefit, this kind of histrionic display always made him jealous, because it made him uneasy about her. Now, the assurance which her embrace brought him, seemed to soothe him.

'Let us have a drink,' he said. And he called: 'Koi hai? Whisky lao!'

Bhagirath, the bearer, came in, soft-footed, joined hands to do obeisance to Gangi, and went to the sideboard to get the drinks out.

'I have some American friends,' began Vicky. And then, with a flourish of his right hand, he continued, putting as much significance into his words as possible: 'I shall call them here for shikar....Actually, one of them sounded me about making a pact, for Sham Pur borders upon Tibet as well as Kashmir and India. I will show this Diwan a thing or two.'

'Your Highness, the Diwan has been sent here by Sardar Patel and has to carry out his orders. And I feel that the Government of India wants a strong united India. And even Sir C.P. –'

'Sham Pur is not Travancore,' said Vicky impatiently. And by now he was striking postures which obviously belonged to the clever, clever part of his nature. 'My forefathers maintained the freedom of Sham Pur for generations by keeping a well-trained army. We hillmen are still fit and in good condition. In our strength lies my hope of lasting out against Patel's bullying. And I am more than a match for this Gujarati bania, Popatlal Shah.'

'What a name — Popatlal Shah!' mocked Gangi. 'You were very rude!' said Vicky in a tone of admonishment which showed that, for all his boasts of strength, he was frightened of Srijut Shah.

'I can handle him!' Gangi said. 'You leave him to me. He will be eating out of my hands soon.'

This challenge, offered as a reassurance, did not settle Vicky's mind, but, instead, started an awful panic in him. And he tried to work off his fears with a show of greater cleverness:

'I can make Popat's life difficult here. And I have a few friends among the princes of the Simla Hill states. So Vallabhbhai won't find it all so easy in this area as he did in Gujarat!'

Against this kind of boasting my courage seemed to fail. I knew that if he really meant to carry out any part of this mad programme out of a self-will bolstered up by his lack of happiness in his home life, and the panic resulting from it, he was destined to end up in disaster.

'I am afraid the situation in the state is very explosive. The Praja Mandal....'

'Don't talk like a coward, Hari! Just because you are a hillman who has been educated, it should not mean that your ancestral pride and strength should have been weakened.'

'It is the way with these babus,' Gangi said. 'They get frightened easily.'

'I only want to tell you, Highness, that perhaps you don't know how grave the situation in the state is. You see, no one dares tell you —'

'And you dare to be impertinent!'

I felt a wave of anger go through me. I was itching to blow up the bubble of his complacency, but I controlled myself.

For a moment, the oppression of our opposite wills shimmered in the close atmosphere of the drawing room. But Bhagirath was already serving drinks, and His Highness raised his glass and said, 'Cheers.'

'Doctor Sahib,' Gangi said as she settled felinely into a corner of the settee, 'Maharaja Sahib is tired, especially after the quarrel we had yesterday. So please don't take his harsh words ill.'

'As a matter of fact,' said Vicky impetuously, 'I am glad Gangi has told you of this quarrel, because I want you to help to settle it. She wants me to sell some state houses here because she needs money, and also settle one of the houses in Simla on her. Now, Hari, how can I do it? The Praja Mandal is already agitating against me for selling the houses in Haridwar and some of the state property here.'

'But these houses belonged to your ancestors, Vicky, and are not public property,' said Gangi.

'To be sure, but I have no deeds to prove this,' said Vicky. 'Raj Mata has the documents and she won't show them to me for fear she will never see them again.'

'You are a weakling, Vicky, to let your mother dominate you like that,' said Gangi. 'I resent that deeply....Don't you think, Doctor, he is wrong to be influenced by the two women who have always intrigued against him? It was his mother who urged that awful Indira to send a petition against him to the Sarkar. And like a fool he can't see through them!'

'I have nothing to do with Indira, as you know,' Vicky said.

'But you are still subservient to the will of your mother!' she said shrilly.

'Oh, hell, everyone is against me,' raved Vicky, striking his forehead. 'The Sarkar, the Raj Mata, Indira, Gangi, the people, they are all against me – and now even Dr Hari Shankar is sulking.'

'So you see for yourself, Vicky, that people are against you,' I said. 'I think you can get them on your side, if you give orders to stop the repression that the police are carrying out against the Praja Mandal. And if you release the political leaders, both Sardar Patel and Diwan Popatlal will become much nicer to you.'

'You leave Popatlal to me,' said Gangi, almost in a furtive whisper, as though she was listening to some inner voice which arose from a deep faith in her instincts.

'What are the other grievances against me?' Vicky asked.

In order not to upset His Highness with the truth, I too preferred to play the Machiavellian game.

'You see, Vicky, one must keep some friends, who may stand by one in time of trouble. Now, even your cousins, the sardars, are up in arms against you, beginning with your half-brother, the Commander-in-Chief. And the jagirdars, whose lands have been confiscated, are intriguing against the gaddi. The people are still loyal, but there are interested parties who will exploit their grievances against you.'

'Do you think the people are really loyal?' Victor asked, partly because the traditional slogan of the ruling house was always in his mouth (that the Raja had the welfare of the Praja at heart), and partly because he wanted cleverly to use the people's will as a bargaining counter in his quarrel with the States Department.

'The people are born loyal and die loyal,' I said, lending myself to cynicism in order not to give the straightforward, truthful answer: that they were not bearing their misery as silently now as they used to do in the past.

All this statecraft was boring Gangi.

'Give me some more sherbet,' she said, referring to the whisky.

'Koi hai?' Victor shouted.

Bhagirath came in and began to help us to some more whisky. He had been trained in the conventional etiquette of ladies first, so he bent over Gangi's tumbler.

'Bhagirath,' His Highness shouted suddenly, 'would you die for me if the need arose?'

Bhagirath nearly dropped the whisky as he shuffled on his feet automatically, put the whisky bottle aside, joined the palms of his hands and fell at His Highness's feet.

'Vicky!' Gangi protested. 'He nearly threw the whisky all over my clothes!'

'Get up! Good slave!' said Victor with an imperious grace.

And while the servant resumed his work, Victor orated: 'I will form a solid alliance with the people against all my enemies. I will teach the sardars and the jagirdars the lesson of their lives. I will dismiss the officers who oppose me. And then I shall be strong enough to stand my ground against the States Department. I will offer the British and Americans the use of some strips of territory if need be. Later, I can turn them out.'

'I could achieve all that you want without stirring out of this palace,' boasted Gangi, half mockingly, half seriously. 'And rather than give away territory to the monkey-faces, you need only give me two or three houses.'

'Dr Sahib, we must organize a shikar and ask some of the Americans here,' Victor said, ignoring Gangi's remarks and putting on a patently clever diplomatic manner.

I wanted to tell him that another charge which was always being brought against him was that he was a spendthrift, extravagantly squandering his own privy purse, as well as state money, on any fancy that possessed him; that every hunt meant more expenditure on champagne as well as cigars; that it also meant employment of begar, forced labour. But my courage failed me. I only shifted responsibility from myself for the arrangements for the projected hunt by saying: 'Highness, Captain Partap Singh is the man who always makes the arrangements for shikar. I shall call him.'

'Han, Partap Singh,' he agreed, and he shouted: 'Koi hai — call Captain Partap Singh.'

'You have just returned from Simla and you will be off again,' Gangi complained with a genuine note of concern in her voice.

It seemed to me that though she was a harlot and wanted ever new sensations, exploiting each absence of His Highness to look for fresh prey for her vanity if not for her hunger, she was attached to him with the natural possessiveness of the chief, though unacknowledged, wife.

Vicky seemed to become impatient as she curled up into a sulk, and he raved: 'Where is this Partap Singh? Koi hai?'

There were whispers and pat-pats of rushing feet in the hall from the veranda and utter silence in the room, for the shadow of that absolute power, which was enshrined in His Highness, spread out through the reverberations of his voice, pregnant with all the potential terror and force in which lay the ultimate sanctions of his position as hereditary master of all he surveyed. I sensed the reality of this power and felt that no human being could escape corruption if such unlimited rights were given to him or acquired by him, because the will to power entails a belief in the superman even in the weakest person; and the weaker the person, the more tyrannical and irresponsible he becomes. The glint in the eyes of His Highness, which usually made them sparkle, became murderous, and his face was livid with a rising fury, as though a madness was beginning to possess him.

As Partap Singh did not appear he took it out on Gangi. 'I won't have you sulking here, she-pig! If you are annoyed with me, go and hide your face in the "dark chamber"!'

'Look, Doctor, he is being angry and nasty,' Gangi appealed to me. 'And I haven't done anything.'

'Go, get out!' he shouted.

At this Gangi burst into tears and began to sob, wiping her eyes with the palla of her dupatta.

It was strange but her tears only seemed to harden his heart.

'Get out! Get out!' he shouted. 'You only want something from me, either money or jewellery or houses! Everyone wants to exploit me, fleece me and rob me! Don't think I don't know you all! I haven't a friend in the world!'

He was fuming with anger and bitterness and fear and frustration. He swallowed the whole tumbler of whisky-and-soda at one gulp and threw the glass aside bad-temperedly.

Once Gangi had started there was no stopping her, and her sobs became hysterical.

And Victor, in his isolation, shouted the more shrilly: 'I will fix you all up properly. I will throw bones before all you dogs! I will appease the hunger of all my flatterers. Don't think, any of you, that I don't know what you really think of me! And what you want from me! Dogs and bitches! I can cope with you all!'

Over and above his stentorian accents, I could hear some gong-like notes beyond the outer courtyard of the palace, a kind of vague cloud of voices which seemed to approach nearer. I applied my ears, but the noise remained like a dense but resonant thunder without any strokes of lightning. I got up and rushed out into the hall.

'Long live the Sham Pur Praja Mandal!'

'Down with Maharaja Ashok Kumar!'

'Long live Pandit Gobind Das!'

'Long live Praja!...'

The slogans were clearly audible from beyond the outer deohri. And Captain Partap Singh was holding the crowd back from breaking into the garden by wielding a big stick.

'I am afraid the Praja Mandal crowd is trying to break into the palace,' I said, running back to the drawing room.

'Where are they? I am coming!' Victor said. And he ran.

But Gangi sprang at him and, arresting his feet, fell in a huddle as he had advanced halfway to the door. Victor kicked her and tried to get free of her. She clung to him and whined: 'For my sake, Maharaj, for my sake, Vicky, please don't run into danger like that. You are precious to me. You are —'

'Yes, Victor, please don't risk your life,' I said.

'I am not a coward,' he shouted. And, with one terrific push, he thrust Gangi aside and ran.

On the way to the garden, he snatched a rifle from the sentry.

I followed, shouting: 'Please don't do anything rash.'

I thought he might kill someone and I was in a panic. I ran behind him, but he was more nimble on his feet. In despair, I could only shout and utter cautionary calls. Luckily, the words that came to my lips were: 'Shoot in the air. Shoot in the air, if shoot you must.'

And, by a miracle, the suggestion affected him in a Couéstic manner.

He pointed the rifle to the sky and pressed the trigger.

All the pigeons and the doves in the niches of the palace gateway fluttered away.

The people began to fall back before Captain Partap Singh's big stick....

The 'hoom' of the hot, oppressive nights of Sham Pur in the late summer is certainly not conducive to sleep; and the violences of the previous afternoon, followed by the strain of calming His Highness down, had left a hangover of tension in my nerves, which overtired my body, so that I had rolled about in my bed, wrapped up in the coils of a prolonged insomnia, till the very early hours of the morning, when my eyes closed against my will. But it seemed to me that I had hardly yielded to this half-sleep when I noticed the pressure of a presence on a chair by my bed. At first I thought that it was my bearer, Francis, who had come with the morning cup of tea. Then the peculiar aura of a woman's body made itself felt, accompanied by the exhalations of the Lanvin scent which Gangi preferred, and I woke up with a start.

'I am sorry I have disturbed you so early in the morning,' she said.

I could not see her clearly because of the blur created by the mosquito net, so I lifted the curtain to look at her.

Francis, who had been waiting to fetch me my tea, came and adjusted the end of the net to the pole above.

I saw that Gangi's eyes were swollen with sleeplessness and tears, and I felt rather sorry for her as she was obviously distressed. On the other hand, I knew that her sorrow was merely skin deep, the surface index of a feeling for Victor which was genuine enough, even though it was the sugar coating on the bitter poison of opportunistic possessiveness which was underneath. Therefore, I felt curiously detached, an attitude encouraged by the fear that her presence in my rooms might excite unnecessary suspicions in the exacerbated mind of His Highness.

'Bring tea for the Maharani Sahiba, Francis,' I called out to the bearer, who was disappearing.

'Have you any brandy?' Gangi asked.

'Yes, yes, of course,' I said. And I called out to the servant, 'Francis, fetch some brandy, also.'

It was obvious that her distress was acute enough for her to feel the need to drown it. I knew she was an insidious creature who tried to hide much of the disruption in her nature, probably from the habit of her early childhood, when she had been left alone so much and had developed secretiveness to conceal her wild and uncontrolled desires and impulses against her own better nature and the taboos of the elders of the village. And I realized that even though she had come to seek my advice, she was not going to confide in me any more than she thought suitable in order to win my sympathy and support.

'Have you a cigarette?' she asked.

'Han, han,' I said, fumbling eagerly for my cigarette case under the pillow. 'Please forgive me for not offering you one. I must be still sleepy.'

I sat up, offered her a cigarette and lit it for her with my lighter. I knew that, like most hill-women, she smoked, but I did not expect from her the sophistication which tries to cover the gaps with the incandescence of rolled tobacco.

She puffed at the cigarette and dramatically ejected smoke from out of her nostrils. Usually, I am always the first to speak, so that ease can prevail, but this morning I felt constrained to wait, because I did not want to say something, anything, so that she could retain the pride of her secrets and only tell me what was strictly necessary to her purpose. I had begun to feel lately that only by going deep down and tracking the surface emotions to the ultimate motivations can people become clearer with themselves and each other, and that whereas, in spite of many hindrances, the process of revelation had started in Victor, Gangi's inner world was full of too many sores to be exposed either to her own view or to the gaze of other people. I believed that it would do her good to let a little fresh air in.

Unfortunately, however, the pride of her putrid emotions was too blind to even prepare a declension, and I waited in the yawning emptiness between us in vain for her to say something. Her nostrils quivered and she turned on the light of her green eyes at me with a slant obviously calculated to soften me. I felt scared of the temptress in her and began to squeal.

'After the incidents of yesterday, we have probably all slept badly,' I said. 'I wonder whether the Maharaja Sahib had any sleep at all.'

'Don't worry about him,' she said. 'He was drunk by the time he went to bed and you yourself gave him a sleeping draught. He is still asleep. At least, I left him asleep.'

'I am worried about him, though,' I said. 'He is not at all well. And ever since our return from Simla he is surrounded by a sea of troubles.'

'He will float,' she said with a cruel smirk on her face.

'I don't think he is such a strong swimmer as to weather the storms that are mounting.'

'You don't know him,' she said. 'He is very clever and – very cruel....'

At that moment, Francis came in with the tea tray and she stopped, her round hill-woman's face, with the small flattish nose, knotting up into a scowl of suppressed fury.

I helped her to a cup of tea.

'The brandy!' she said.

'Oh, forgive me – of course, the brandy,' I said. 'Will you have it in your tea or shall I order coffee?'

'Neat,' she said in English.

I poured the brandy for her into a rather inelegant tumbler which Francis had brought on the tray. But I was not too ashamed of the tumbler, for it seemed to suit the strain of vulgarity that was obvious in the leer on her mouth as she looked at me pouring the liquor.

She drank the brandy in a gulp and made a wry face.

'You were telling me about Vicky,' I said.

'I don't know what to do with him,' she began. 'He is so incalculable. He may do any of a hundred different things, and he says anything that comes into his mouth. And all the time he is so jealous of me, while he goes off and does what he did in Simla – eats the ashes!'

'Maharani Sahiba, he may do a hundred different things because he has so much nervous energy,' I said, 'but he is devoted to you and you can't give any other meanings to his actions than those which arise from his love for you.'

This seemed to flatter her, and she picked up the cup of tea and sipped it with lowered eyes which reflected a half-complacent light and the seductive manner.

'Then why doesn't he make a will and settle some money and houses on me?' she said with lips pursed to give finality to her utterance.

I felt a wave of anger sweep over me, and I tried to swallow the bad taste in my mouth with copious draughts of tea. It made me mad to feel that she was so obvious in her opportunism and the attempts to win me over to her side. And yet I was surprised at her plain speaking, at the kind of brutal honesty about her selfishness, unrelieved by anything except the sanctions of sentiment with which she covered it, and the genuine fear of being left alone and bereft in her old age. She had lived so many lives, and covered these lives with so many lies, that I felt that this frankness on her part might be the beginning of a process of regeneration. But I only had to look at the furtive green eyes to realize that my last surmise was erroneous in the extreme. For she was looking for something she could not find, and even wanted to make me her prey because she did not know what to find. And the spiritual void in her was only compelled by the hectic blaze of each transient desire, which fell like rose petals, faded and discoloured, away from her, leaving the gaps in her nature yawning like pits where nothing can grow, and covered on the sides by the fungus growth of coiling manoeuvres which could never be uncoiled.

'I think Vicky feels cornered,' I said. 'He is being attacked on all sides. And he needs sympathy.'

'Then why doesn't he come to me and open his heart out to me?' she said with a blandishment of her head. 'Why doesn't he?'

Now, I could not help marvelling at the basic downrightness of her instinct, the woman's instinct which had spotted the fundamental weakness in his nature. She had put her finger on the ventricles of his heart, as it were, and felt the essential feebleness of his inner pulse, the source of cowardice in his nature.

'Maharani Sahiba, he is in the grip of his mother. He has not cut the navel string which binds him to her. And he cannot surrender to any woman completely. And the people are against him.'

Put in this way, my explanation was beyond her. She could not comprehend the meaning of the words I had used, and looked blankly at me.

'He is very weak-willed,' I said to help her, 'and he is easily dominated.'

'He is very cruel,' she said. 'I am frightened of him.' And as she talked, tears came into her eyes, and she sobbed: 'He gets drunk and he is so hard, so hostile to me. And no one understands me!'

What she said only proved my point about him. It was because he was weak that he was cruel, for a strong man reserves his strength; and the fact that he was drinking heavily and beating her showed that his nerves were bad and his patience was easily exhausted. At any rate, I was sure that in all this he was reacting to her actions, and what was true about him was more than true about her. For they were very similar in their temperaments, both highly emotional and easily inflammable. She too was essentially weak-willed and cruel in consequence, with the added ruthlessness of the woman always able to take her revenge on man for all the hereditary wrongs done to her; and if she did not get drunk, she resented his attempt to dominate her because of an inordinate love of power in her own being. But as all this would have been difficult to explain to her without imputing blame to her, for which she might have reacted against me, I kept my own counsel.

'I am sorry to hear this, Maharani Sahiba,' I said consolingly, though her tears were hardening me against her from my knowledge of her hypocrisy. 'Please have a good cry. You will feel better.'

'You are a strange doctor,' she said, crying and smiling at the same time. 'You want me to cry so that I can feel better!'

At this I felt that, in spite of her apparent worldliness and instinctive manoeuvring skill, she was innocent like a child in many ways, and I softened to her and even contemplated her face with desire. Ultimately, her worldliness and cunning were the worldliness and cunning of a child, or of a completely ungrown-up person, so obvious and patent that the desperate liar and cheat in her was likely to be found out all the time. And she seemed very lovable.

'You see, you are already smiling,' I said lightly.

And she coyly turned on the bent-head charm of her face at me again and repeated the words 'Strange Doctor!' significantly.

Now I was in a panic. I did not want to get involved or entangled in this complex any more than was necessitated by my official duties and my natural sympathies for all the actors in the tragi-comic play that was being enacted before my eyes. And I knew that, so far as she was concerned, her way of getting sympathy or friendship was to absorb one to herself sexually, not necessarily by giving herself but by captivating and surrounding one in the aura of the warmth that she exuded, until one was her willing slave and did her bidding. But how was I to get rid of her from this embarrassing contiguity?

'Sometimes I feel,' she said, demurely wiping her tears with the end of her dupatta, 'I shall end my life. I am so unhappy, Doctor Shankar. I think Vicky despises me, because I am an illiterate hill-woman and because I deceived him once or twice. And he won't trust me. And I feel that he really prefers that woman Indira just because she is a BA. He has recognized her son as Tika, and my son has no chance because I am not even his wedded wife. And I have done so much for him. While his mother and his Ranis have only spat poison all around. And still he won't recognize me or my son. Why can't he marry me? There is no other way out for me — is there, than to get rid of myself?'

She put such an intensity into her utterance that, for a moment, I believed that these words represented the deepest urges in her. And yet, as I reflected on the speech, I knew that it was a mixture of half-honest impulses with a histrionic attempt at martyrdom, a sentimentally tragic declaration which arose from a temporary weariness that did not blot out the dominant obsession with the will to conquer that underlay her simulation of defeat.

'I have some arsenic,' she said.

'Maharani Sahiba!' I protested, as I was suddenly shaken out of my complacency by the feeling that an ignorant hill-woman, with the rudimentary sensations and blind impulses of an upstart, without any sanctions on her mind higher than the guile and the lies with which she sought to win her way to power and possession, may, in a moment of aberration, really take her life. And then Victor would be sunk indeed!

'Don't be frightened,' she said. 'I won't tell anyone that you gave me the arsenic!'

If this was intended as a joke, it arose from a cruel kind of wit. And my head throbbed with the momentary fear that she was quite capable of blackmailing me with the imputation that I had procured the arsenic for her. I tried to control the hysteria which was working in me by a deliberate attempt to laugh.

'You must help me, Doctor,' she said, thrusting the knife into my divided spirit at last. 'You must take my side. Please advise Vicky, without telling him that I have said anything. He is a child and he doesn't even know what is good for him. I could help him so much in settling his difficulties in the state.'

'I am sure His Highness appreciates you,' I assured her.

I think she expected me to say more to comfort her and to give her confidence, because she seemed, from the emptiness in her own nature, not to believe in others mainly because she did not believe in herself. But I could not say any more than I knew.

'Has he said anything to you, lately?' she asked, grabbing at the remnants of reassurance with mellow, sad eyes.

'No, but as His Highness's doctor, I know what he really feels,' I said. 'He is devoted to you.'

'Did he say so?'

I smiled. I wished I had had more true words to wave before her greedy senses. But as I knew that not only was he attached to her with the maximum degree of finality that is possible in so unfinal a thing as love, but suspicious of her and frightened of her, I did not wish to say anything which, in its truthfulness, would make a treachery of some words of mine against the others. Then, on the impulse of the moment, I thought I would extract from her what she really felt about him.

'Tell me, Ganga Dasiji, why do you torture him so by making him jealous and by making scenes about little things?'

'Doctor!' she said indignantly, 'how can you say such a thing, when you know that for seven long years I have loved him and have borne him two children? He does not see that I am a warm and affectionate person, and I can't stir an eyelid without exciting wild rages of jealousy in him! I don't even mind how many women he has! And it is he who likes scenes!

He is always making little things into big things. I think he likes being unhappy really. Whereas, I am happy-natured and never want rows. How can you accuse me of torturing him?'

This eloquent plea of self-justification convinced me of the complete impossibility of ever convincing her that there could be anything wrong with her. The facts about her several affairs of the last seven years were known to me, and here she was covering up her defaults by a disingenuous show of warm-hearted innocence, not knowing that I knew the facts. Somehow, she believed that she could bluff everyone into a credulous acceptance of her integrity. And I was now in despair about advising her or advising Vicky on her behalf. For her pride would not allow her to admit anything about the nature of her bias for herself, and she was merely using her sex appeal to excite pity in me to force me on to her side in a quarrel which she seemed to regard as the curse of a cruel fate.

'You must help me,' she pleaded finally, bringing pathos into her voice.

I got up from my bed in order to shake her off.

She took the hint and got up.

'I will do my best,' I said conventionally. Then I felt a violent urge to be honest about the whole thing and really try to help them both if I could. 'Acha, I think it will be best if all of us three have a talk and thrash out the differences between you two. Only, you will have to accept my advice....'

'Try and persuade him to do what I want,' she said like a child wanting the moon.

I smiled.

Immediately, her face went pale with desperation, and I knew that she knew that I was biased in Vicky's favour.

'You are all ranged against me!' she cried.

And now her face was blank as if she was bereft of all confidence, and her eyes glared into the emptiness blindly with a dazed look of horror, such as I had seen before when she was in a tight corner.

There is something compelling about Monday morning, with its serious and straight face, compelling even to a Maharaja. About eight o'clock on Monday morning, Vicky sent orders for the whole entourage to get ready to go to the office with him at 10 a.m.

When I went to the hall at the appointed time, surprisingly enough, he, who was always late through his procrastinations, was there on the tick of time. This very alacrity imported that he was tense. His eyes, too, were bloodshot, obviously from sleeplessness and, I suspected, tears. He seemed to be trying to offset the evidence of his inner discord by a histrionic smartness of manner, for he was dressed in the uniform of Honorary Major-General of the British Indian Army. But though this ostentatious display of military grandeur seemed to impress Captain Partap Singh, Mr Bool Chand and Munshi Mithan Lal, I could see that, behind the façade of smartness, there were disturbances bordering upon panic. At no time during the past few days, when he had been saying to me that he felt 'cornered like a rat', did this phrase seem to apply more aptly than on that day. For he was encircled on all sides, besides being involved in a series of vicious circles inside himself.

As we got to the deohri, I found that there was an armoured car standing ahead of the caravan of cars. I realized that this was a necessary precaution taken by His Highness after the arrest of the Praja Mandal leaders yesterday. For it was likely that there might be demonstrations by the angry people, in spite of the increased precautionary measures that had been ordered immediately after the dispersal of the crowd by the shooting in the air and the club-work of Captain Partap Singh.

'You come into the armoured car with me, Hari Shankar,' His Highness said. 'Also Partap Singh. And let Mian Mithu and Bool Chand travel in the Rolls.'

I saw Bool Chand's face fall.

'Highness, I want to report to you on the negotiations which you ordered me to carry out,' Mr Bool Chand said. And then he snorted involuntarily.

'Don't snort!' His Highness said sharply. 'I shall hear you later.'

Apparently, the negotiations with which he had been charged were some parleys with Indira, to see if she could be persuaded to withdraw her petitions against His Highness from the States Department at New Delhi, and the feeler to Srijut Popatlal J. Shah to see how much conscience money he would want to come over to the side of the Maharaja. As a shrewd, greasy bania, Bool Chand was the ideal agent for such negotiations. And, from his eagerness to report back to His Highness, he seemed to have had some luck. However, the coward in him was frightened of travelling in the Rolls rather than in the armoured car. Still, he joined his hands in obeisance to the Maharaja and, with a ghastly pallor on his dark face, turned towards the unprotected car behind Munshi Mithan Lal.

'Captain Sahib,' His Highness began as we settled down into the armoured car, 'what did General Raghbir Singh say about the army manoeuvres?'

'To be sure, Highness, he is ordering them.'

This was the first I had heard of army manoeuvres. Apparently the only counter to the States Department at

Delhi, or to the States People's Movement, he could think of was to hold manoeuvres in Sham Pur to demonstrate to all and sundry the real quality of his might as an independent ruler. And so involved was he within his own subjective power urges that it all seemed pathetic. For he was not even concerned with the fact that there had been a great deal of discontent in the villages through sporadic manoeuvres. The peasants were requisitioned always to do forced labour in the areas in which the manoeuvres took place; and poultry, eggs, butter, milk, fuel-wood, etc., were taken free of charge, or for merely nominal prices, by the soldiers; while whole fields full of crops were crushed and laid bare by the tanks and the artillery.

'What did he say?' His Highness probed. 'I mean what was his attitude towards me?'

'Very cordial, Highness,' said Partap Singh. 'Unlike the other sardars, he is loyal.'

'Han, han!' said Victor, seeming to listen and yet not listening. For he was absent-minded, thinking of some deep game. And his weak, sensitive face was darkening with thought.

I looked out of the window of the armoured car and saw that the main Victoria bazaar was copiously sprinkled with bunches of policemen. Most of the shops were shut, because business did not begin in Sham Pur till nearly midday; though the suspicion crossed my mind that the Praja Mandal may have called a hartal, a complete cessation of work, for not many people were about.

'I will fix them all, one by one,' His Highness boasted naively. 'I think Diwan Popatlal Shah can be won over and...'

From behind the shadows of his visage there was reflected a glint in his eyes, as though the hidden universe was suddenly being lit up by flashes of insight. But as there was a trace of sadness in the tones of darkness in the lines beneath the eyes, I knew that his strategy in tackling the Diwan, the Commander-in-Chief, the rebellious sardars, the Praja Mandal leaders, and almost everyone else, was based on the insecure foundations of his relationship with Ganga Dasi, and that, deep within, he knew he was doomed, that the thinking points in him were merely a number of cold, deliberate and mechanical tricks, beyond which he was enmeshed in a cloud of unknowing.

He sought to protect himself from the awareness of coming betrayals by building up a bluff of heartiness. Thumping Partap Singh on the back, he said in the proverbial Punjabi phrase: 'Don't you care for the limp lord!'

As I looked away, while His Highness was building up this bonhomie, he began to feel a little uneasy.

'Why so solemn-faced?' he asked.

'Monday morning!' I answered.

But this did not satisfy him. And he looked quizzically at me, and was going to say something, but then controlled himself.

As we got out of the armoured car and proceeded towards the annexe of the Huzuri Bag Palace, which served as the office, he leaned over to me and asked: 'What did Gangi say to you about me this morning?'

I was slightly taken aback at the fact that he knew his mistress had been to see me. But I surmised that nothing remained hidden in the palace. And I was glad that I had resisted all Ganga Dasi's assaults on me and controlled myself when I felt a little slippery.

'She wanted to enlist my support to get a settlement out of you.'

'I suspected her. She is trying to be clever.'

The sentries were saluting us; the chaprasis of the office were bowing and scraping and making obeisances with hands lifted to their foreheads; the clerks were bustling to and fro; and Brigadier-General Chaudhri Raghbir Singh came out and gave his cousin a military salute.

'Chaudhri Sahib, come in and we will have a brief conference.'

Brigadier-General Chaudhri Raghbir Singh bowed and followed.

His Highness encompassed the inner sanctum of the modernist office, with its large, steel tube table and the plastic gadgets which decorated it. Then he took off his belt and handed it to Captain Partap Singh, significantly asking the ADC: 'Captain Sahib, please keep those asses, Mian Mithu and Bool Chand, away from here. They are under your guard.'

I took the precaution of taking this hint and started to drift away.

'Don't go, Dr Shankar, just in case I fall ill in the middle of my conversation with Chaudhri Sahib.'

At this we all smiled and sat down, Chaudhri Raghbir Singh and myself facing His Highness across the table.

His Highness spread his hands out before him, almost as though he did not know where to put them. Or was he groping for something? From the way he kept his eyes bent before Chaudhri Raghbir Singh, I guessed that the shadow of Ganga Dasi was still between them, in spite of their cordiality for each other.

'Acha, Chaudhri Sahib, I hear that our uncle, Thakur Parduman Singh, is up again,' His Highness began. 'The son of a swine! The thief! The harbourer of dacoits and petty thieves! The robber!...If only the Angrezi Sarkar had crushed him and the other rebels when they rose against my father! I know that my Bapu's life was embittered by the leniency they showed to the rascal and his friends Mahan Chand of Udham Pur and Shiv Ram Singh of Hukam Pur. That is why Bapu died an early death.'

His Highness paused, not so much out of remorse or sorrow at the memory of his father's death as to see what measure of sympathy he could get from Chaudhri Raghbir Singh. Of course, everyone knew that the old Maharaja's bitterness with the rebels did not kill him, but that his death was hastened by TB resulting from debility caused by complete promiscuity. Chaudhri Raghbir Singh's face remained impassive. His Highness drummed the table nervously with the fingers of his right hand and then continued: 'The Sarkar had no business to intervene and advise lenience.'

Then he got up agitatedly and, taking long strides away from the table, shouted: 'That the nobles who bore arms against their own Maharaja should have been let off so easily under the Resident's advice – wah, what clemency was that?...People like that ought to be taught the lesson of their lives! Instead, they came out rather well from the rebellion, because their sons were put in nominal charge of their estates. That is why they dare to raise their heads now! But they don't know that, unlike Bapu, I will deal ruthlessly with them. Never mind the batichod new Sarkar and their demand for our accession!'

'It is difficult to inculcate in them the spirit of *noblesse oblige*.' And the General looked up at me naively to see the effect of his use of this big word on me. As my head was hung down at hearing of these new troubles of His Highness, Chaudhri Sahib continued: 'But if we see from our side that their just claims are met, and their dignities and privileges maintained, then they will have nothing to go on in asking the States Department to intervene.'

His Highness suspected a certain leniency in Chaudhri Raghbir Singh's attitude towards them. In fact, this lingering bias was obvious in the Commander-in-Chief's restraint. And yet the Maharaja did not want to alienate his cousin.

'The robbers! They resent the fact that I made you, and not one of their sons, Commander-in-Chief!'

'I think,' said Raghbir Singh, persuaded now to be a partisan of the Maharaja, 'that they have been accustomed to ruling the roost in the countryside and to defy the gaddi from their hill forts and castles. And they are restive because they fear your Highness.'

'I shall bend them to my will!' said His Highness, grinding the words under his molars. 'You will see! I am not my father's son if I don't! Just let them try! I shall see to them, the illegally begotten!'

Now he had worked himself up to a rage, till he looked slightly ridiculous, and his mixed English, Hindustani and hillman's Punjabi speech became twisted:

'Parduman Singh is a dacoit! Mahan Chand is a dacoit. And Shiv Ram, sala, is the helper of dacoits!...How dare they lift their heads. We shall see if they come to the durbar for the Dusserah or not!'

'I think we shall get them in hand before Dusserah!' Chaudhri Raghbir Singh said, warming up to his cousin on the curve of the feeling for intrigue which seemed the main impulse for action in state affairs. He seemed to be straining every nerve to put the Prince's mind at ease, which showed that he had conquered the slight jealousy he felt for His Highness on account of his own affair with Ganga Dasi. Except that he did not give any indication of what he really thought; but then, I knew that he did not think much, because he could not think much.

'I tell you I shall clear every one of these fools out of the way!' His Highness continued, pacing up and down and talking aloud to himself, as it were. 'I shall drive out all the hypocritical counsellors of our brotherhood, who come crowding round the assembly hall and show themselves as my devoted subjects but are in fact rebels! I shall build my state on the loyalty of the ryots who are devoted to my house. But I must have no interference from the States Department. And this I can secure if only I can get Indira to withdraw her petition. As for the Praja Mandal crowd, I can buy them off. At any rate, they agree with me, because if they believe in Gandhiji they believe in Ram Raj. I too want a state in which the Raja and Praja can live as father and sons. I want to renew in the people the belief that I have their interests at heart....I am not like the other rulers who despise their people!'

These words were like romantic gestures and I could feel the hollow ring about them. I felt irritated listening to him.

'To impugn the morality or politics of your enemies does not prove anything against them,' I protested.

'But His Highness is talking of the ideals of Ram Raj,' General Raghbir Singh put in.

'Dr Shankar is anglicized, Chaudhri Sahib,' His Highness said, 'and he does not understand our ancient ideal of kingship.' And he began to recite, in mellifluous Hindi, the classic formula of the Hindu Raja:

Between the night I am born and the night I die,
Whatever good I might have done, my heaven, my
Progeny, may I be deprived of it, if I oppress you.
I shall see to the growth of the country, considering
It always as 'God'. Whatever law there is here,

> And whatever is dictated by ethics, and whatever
> Is not opposed to polity, I will follow. I shall
> Never act arbitrarily.

I felt a slight hardening of my jaws at all this. But His Highness continued to recite what he knew by rote, almost like a fourth-form schoolboy, specially for the instruction of his Commander-in-Chief.

> To thee this state is given, thou art the director
> And regulator; thou art steadfast and will
> Bear this responsibility of the trust so
> Given for agriculture, for well-being, for
> Prosperity and for development.

The highfalutin oration did not conduce to the spiritual betterment of the handsome, empty-faced brute that was Brigadier-General Chaudhri Raghbir Singh.

> To thee this state is given, thou art the director
> And regulator;...

His Highness repeated the phrase with distinct emphasis, seeming naively proud from the way his head was cocked to one side even though he looked furtively at his cousin, as he was unsure of the effect of the oration on him.

It seemed to me clear that Victor had been straining desperately to win over Chaudhri Raghbir Singh to the completest loyalty and friendship, but felt that the more he had tried the bigger had become the chasm that divided them. The self-conscious look on his face proclaimed his frustration. And from his big, shining eyes a ghost peeped through, the figure of Gangi, whose shadow was between the two cousins, having parted them finally and irrevocably through her embrace with the Commander-in-Chief.

There was an unwholesome silence in the room for a while. His Highness could not bear it. He hissed at me with a deliberate smile: 'Cassius, you have a lean and hungry look! Why don't you speak? Say something!'

'I was thinking that you defined the powers and privileges of a monarch, but did not say anything about the limits and responsibilities of kingship.'

'I am not sure whether you are a friend or a foe!'

'I am somewhat by way of being a democrat,' I said, laughing nervously because I was taking an opposition attitude.

'People like you and the Praja Mandalis keep shouting, "Democracy, Democracy". What is Democracy? Where is it practised?' His Highness came to the attack, his face reddening. 'To attain equality with the ignorant rabble, to reduce everyone to uniformity with the stupid herd! Wah, what barking is this? Haven't you ever read Plato's *Republic*, in which he defined the ideal of the philosopher king? Sir Malcolm Darling, who did such good work in the Punjab, gave me a copy of this and suggested that I should follow the precepts laid down in it.'

I kept my mouth shut. This seemed to enrage him.

'Of course,' he continued, relenting, 'I think there should be some kind of legislature of men chosen for their good sense. As the sage Manu says: "Learned men who know the traditional history and the customary law of the land, men who will be alike to foe and friend, distinguished for their rectitude and fearing God and Religion."'

'God!' I said ironically in a soft voice, deliberately softened to suppress the anger I felt at the insult to my self-respect in having to tolerate such humbug. And I continued: 'I was forgetting the old boy. He has not shown up in these parts lately. For an old friend of your family, He seems particularly disloyal to you. But, for all I know, He may be round the corner. And He may come along and help. And, of course – what am I saying?...He is very constant. Why, men pass away! Empires rise and fall! Even the stars grow old! The earth prepares for the coming of the Ice Age! And yet God remains, always the great pillar of strength to humanity!'

The bitterness in my voice was so obvious that I thought my end had come. But, curiously, His Highness smiled as though he was highly amused. Then, after a moment, he said quietly: 'The trouble is that I am a genius whom nobody understands. But I shall make you understand. I shall make everyone understand! I shall show you the stuff I am made of! I...I...I....'

He could not finish his sentence and the last accent petered out into the occasional stammer that affected his speech. It seemed that he had no words to express the violence of the emotions which quarrelled in him, only clinging to the 'I', the egotistical self in which he had not much faith even though he was always very assertive about it. Perhaps this histrionic 'I' was the only word in which he could, in his isolation, find a refuge, the only chimera he could cling to with any degree of tenacity in the elusive world which was slipping beneath his feet.

As he could not find words to express himself, he veered round, sweating, and, with his brows knit in anguished awareness of his isolation, he turned to Brigadier-General Chaudhri Raghbir Singh.

'Acha, then, the manoeuvres are to be held as soon as possible, Raghbir Singh. Choose an area near enough to the territory of the Indian Union.'

'Ji Maharaj,' assented General Raghbir Singh.

There was complete silence after this historic decision. And in the next few seconds a grimness settled on the atmosphere. His Highness paced back to the table with a bent-head seriousness. Then he relaxed and said to Raghbir Singh:

'Let us have some polo this afternoon.'

'Acha, huzoor.'

'Acha, on your way out send Bool Chand in,' His Highness said, politely indicating his wish for the General to leave.

I too got up with the thought of slinking out.

'Where are you going, Hari? You know that I am not feeling well,' he said impatiently.

I sat down with a weak smile.

After Chaudhri Raghbir Singh was out of audible distance, His Highness asked me in a whisper: 'Do you think he can be trusted?'

'Han, I think so.'

'In spite of his affection for Gangi?'

'Yes, it seems to me that he has genuine affection for you also.'

'I am not sure....'

But by this time Bool Chand had entered.

'What did Indira say, Bool Chand?' His Highness asked, with an abruptness which obviously showed his contempt for the Political Secretary.

'I am afraid she wouldn't see me, your Highness,' Bool Chand answered.

'You mean you took "no" for an answer!' shouted His Highness.

Bool Chand kept silent. Then he snorted. 'Incompetent fools! And what about Popatlal, Mr Snorter-donkey-Bool Chand?'

'He gave me an appointment for tomorrow morning.'

'Fool! Fool! Fool! Get out of my sight! Get out!'

Bool Chand withdrew sullenly, with his head bent over his joined hands.

'We shall have to go and see her ourselves,' he said to me with disgusted despair.

'Perhaps in the evening,' I said.

'Yes, after polo,' Victor answered. 'Get Sharma to bring me any letters there are to sign and wait outside. We will go back to the palace after a tour of the town.'

I felt relieved at being ushered out of his frenzied presence.

The sun makes a ghost of one in India, melting one's flesh and eating into one's soul; it surrounds one with a mist, from behind which one's parched tongue moves towards the lips with a hollow rasping sound; it makes all the animate and inanimate objects seem foreign to the touch, as though one discerns them from the orbit of another, more ethereal world; and it creates those intangible layers of warmth, in which one lives and moves and has one's being, as in the graded, fiery regions of the seven hot hells of the Buddhist conception. One is always poised in the aching attitude of yearning towards the cool, green as the grass, liquid as running water, and soft as the breeze which comes from the mountains covered with snow.

In the atmosphere created by the sun, the only escape is the shut eye and the recumbent posture, known as siesta. That is why I am always talking of either going to bed in the afternoon or of rising from it. And while I do not apologize for this frequent reference to an operation which resembles death, I want, nevertheless, to prove that it is life-giving,

regenerating and renewing. The proof of this is that one feels
very much dead, very much like an extra-planetary ghost, if
one cannot sleep in the afternoon, if one cannot indulge in
the siesta.

Usually, of course, I am able to sleep well, being a young
healthy animal of the Punjab hills, except when I am specially
worried about a patient. For instance, for the first six months
after my return from London I made up for all the arrears
of sleep which a medico has on the debit side of his ledger
through living in a country where everyone takes it out of
himself. But I have not had many overdoses of sleep, specially
since I began to be actively associated with Maharaja Ashok
Kumar as a consultant. Private Secretary, friend, or whatever
my relations with him may be called. All my siestas have since
then been disturbed, either by being prematurely broken
by a sudden and peremptory order to attend His Highness's
presence, or by worrying about him and his ménage.

That afternoon, when I returned from the office by the
long route of an aimless drive through which Victor wanted
to reconnoitre the position and to get to know what his
subjects in Sham Pur were feeling, we had an elaborate,
soporific lunch and retired to our rooms. But while Victor
probably succumbed to the slow fumes which rise to one's
eyes after overeating, I found no peace, in spite of the breezes
set up by the powerful electric fan from the ceiling, specially
cooled as these breezes were by the copious water which
was sprinkled on the straw tatties outside the two doors of
my bedroom. For, just before the midday meal, Ganga Dasi
had appeared, dressed up to the nines in a colourful sari
with bandhini work of white spots on red background, and
casually announced that she was going out to eat the midday
meal with a saheli, the wife of the rich merchant, Lalla

Sadanand. I saw that there was a certain studied deliberation in her casualness, and her eyes were looking furtively this side and that, like two little birds hopping about in a cage. But though Victor seemed disappointed, because he preferred to eat the midday meal in the zenana with his mistress, he did not seem to notice the shifty look in her green eyes, believed her and let her go. I was, however, unfortunately poised near the window of the drawing room which overlooked the courtyard, while Victor and Gangi were embracing each other, and saw that the car which was waiting for her had, seated by the chauffeur, a chaprasi from the office of Diwan Popatlal J. Shah, the new Prime Minister. And my suspicions were aroused.

Throughout the meal I had kept very solemn, until Victor divined my mood and said, 'Are you worried about Gangi?'

I refrained from being honest for the reason that one is inclined to make superficial responses in conversation and also because I did not want to be serious and upset the Maharaja when he was already in the grip of so much inner and outer disruption.

But when I returned to my rooms and changed into a pair of shorts to go to sleep, the basic flaw in the relationship of His Highness and his mistress began to obsess me. There was no stabilization of his temperament, or his state affairs, possible, unless the cancer of doubt about a possible, or rather inevitable, betrayal of him by Gangi could be removed. And this cancer, beautiful like most real cancers, because of the element of masochism which was an important part of Victor's make-up, could not be removed easily, because, apart from the difficulties of making the cancer worse before performing the major operation, one had to consider the fact that Ganga Dasi, the symbol of doubt, was herself the loveliest part of this cancer. Nothing short of her removal would end this disease. And that seemed, under present conditions, from my knowledge of the intricate way in which he was bound to his mistress, an impossible task for Victor to perform.

I rolled on my bed from side to side, first in an effort to see how the cancer of Victor's suspicions, confirmed by my own prognostications, could be removed.

I had tried to analyse the couple's actions and reactions, and found that she had no creative sense with which she could associate Victor, except the art of making love, which revenged itself on her through its excesses and wild-woodedness and which destroyed him by enslaving him to her.

And now I surmised that Victor was in danger again through the stirrings in her to go to Diwan Popatlal J. Shah, even though this affair would be merely an opportunistic manoeuvre to ward off harm from coming to Victor under the axe of the States Department in Delhi, so that she could get the necessary time to secure her own position in Sham Pur.

These and similar thoughts plagued me as I lay in bed, sometimes with my eyes shut and sometimes with them open. Like slow-burning phosphorus, they sizzled on the surface of my mind, sprouting like little globes of heat on my body, silent, half-expressed words, bandied from tongue to lips, rising to my mouth without being uttered. And they were stored up somewhere behind my ears, as though I had heard someone else tell me these things about Gangi by way of gossip and I had saved them for later use as rare and precious pieces of information, curios in the museum of knowledge about human affairs that I was building up, or, to put it in medical terms, an important case history for my files.

About half past four in the afternoon, I got up and soaked myself in the Roman bath which Francis always kept ready filled with cold water. I was relaxed from the tension somewhat and let my fingers trek on the map of my body, almost as though I was soothing an invisible itch.

Francis came and called out that His Highness had sent a message that Dr Shankar Sahib was to come to the polo ground pavilion, to pick him up before going for a drive in the evening, according to the arrangements made at the office this morning.

I came to, towelled myself and began to dress. I was irritated slightly with Francis, because there were no buttons on any of the four muslin tunics which had come from the dhobi.

'Look, Francis, you might see that there is at least one kurta with buttons on in my wardrobe!'

'Sorry, sir,' Francis said. And he immediately went to look for thread and needle.

I was digging into the drawers and found a longcloth tunic. 'You'd better get it done later,' I said peevishly. 'Now go and get the tea.'

And when he disappeared I began to ruminate on the extraordinary facts about Francis: that he was probably the laziest and the least hard-worked of bearers in the whole of Sham Pur; that nothing I could say to him, or do, had altered his easy-going, lackadaisical manner towards his work or myself; that he stole money, finding out all the new hiding-places where I tried to conceal my purse; and that if I could not, in spite of my analysis of him, change him, I could have no hopes of changing Victor or Gangi, or the state of affairs in Sham Pur, unless I could go out and help to smash the whole fabric of this feudal-cum-bourgeois society and get together with people who wanted to rebuild it.

Francis brought the tea tray and, as a special concession, after my rebuke about the buttons, poured me a cup, letting the tea brim over into the saucer, a thing which he always did and which, he knew, irritated me, and about which I had always shouted at him.

I controlled my bad temper and proceeded to right the wrong done to me with my own hands, rationalizing Francis's default by thinking that the relationship of a master and servant was the most humiliating and that the basic defect lay in me for employing a bearer on the modest pay of thirty rupees plus board and lodging, when the actual worth of Francis's human personality was much higher, for he was intelligent and could probably learn and do a skilled job and get more money.

In this reflective mood, I walked out of the palace and, refusing a lift in the car, proceeded towards the polo ground.

I had hardly walked up to the main deohri, through the quadrangle of the garden, when Jai Singh and the hall chaprasis came running up to me with joined hands, asking whether I had forgotten that the car was waiting in the inner deohri. I told them that I preferred to walk. Unable to comprehend such an attitude in so exalted a person as the Maharaja's physician, Jai Singh asked if I would like the durban to yoke the horses to the phaeton. And he and the others were rather disappointed when I merely waved my head in negation and walked off.

As I crossed the stretch of the deserted Sham Pur bazaar I realized that the hartal of the shopkeepers in the capital, which was partial this morning from the number of shops that were still open then, was now nearly complete. Congeries of people stood about under the arcades beyond the shops or on the shady portions of the pavement. They whispered, or I imagined they whispered, as they saw me walking along

instead of riding in a car as usual. And I supposed that they
thought I was mad. I knew that they had grave doubts about
Victor's sanity, and I had heard rumours that the people
considered the Maharaja's entourage equally affected. And,
for a moment, I amused myself by giving the populace the
benefit of the doubt in this regard; for, as a medical man, it
was easy for me to believe that we were, indeed, all more or
less affected. I realized that the classification of the varieties
of mental illnesses is very unsatisfactory; that the classes
overlap; that individual judgements vary too much in the
use of these; and that they are largely based on symptoms
observed after a breakdown rather than on the mental
constitution of the patient. It seemed to me that not enough
emphasis had been given by those concerned with minds
and their illnesses, on analysing the characteristic traits which
the patients show before mental illness, as is frequently done
after the onset of the illness.

These professional speculations of mine were disturbed
by the ringing bells of two tongas, which came galloping
towards me in a neck-to-neck race, accelerated by the lifted
straps with which their drivers lashed the horses. I jumped
aside, irritated by the red dust kicked up by the chariot race,
and wondered what was happening. I saw that the tongas
were occupied by groups of policemen with uplifted rifles.
And, before I knew where I was, they were firing over the
heads of the stray groups of people, who sat around smoking
the hubble-bubble, or getting shaved by the barbers, or
douching their faces with copious sprinklings of cold water
from the street pump after their siesta. Most of them scattered
in a panic, shrieking and moaning as though they were dying;
while some, with more presence of mind, lay down flat on
the ground; and a few stood dumb-stricken, immobile and

ghastly pale. The scourge passed quickly enough and I realized, for the first time in many days, what it meant to be a human being of the pedestrian variety in Sham Pur State. The grapeshot which had been sprinkled over the heads of the crowd yesterday had shocked me out of the complacency with which I had been accepting Sham Pur. Then I had thought that there was no way out of Victor's predicament in facing the Praja Mandal crowd but to overawe it. Now this cold-blooded attempt of the police to spread terror among the people, who had struck work in protest against the previous day's shooting and arrests, spread the darkness of confusion in my mind, already burdened with the weight of His Highness's private life in which I was involved. My heart beat fast, involuntarily, and a queer rage filled me against the bestial, unhappy life in the whirl of which I was caught. And yet, even as I began to walk along towards Curzon Road, beyond which spread King George's Gardens, on one side of which was the polo ground, I realized that there was no escape for me because of my debt-slavery. Especially if, realizing how ill Victor really was, I could restrain him from the high-handedness with which he was leading himself and his state to unforeseen disasters.

The arcades of the bazaar finished when I reached the Elephant Gate of Sham Pur in the old city wall, and I had to emerge into the still, hot sunshine. A strange nervous energy possessed me, born of revulsion against the stupid, brutal life which I lived, and my veins swelled with the heat and the anger. Mimic suns danced in the shimmering sheen before my eyes. And the varied emotions of the day concentrated in idiotic circles in my body.

I found some relief in the cool glades of King George's Gardens, where two swans floated majestically on the small pool fed by the fountains, which punctuated the length of a waterbed, descending in tiers from a marble baradari, or air-houses, built by the grandfather of His Highness. I went up and stood by the pool, looking at the images cast upon the water by the swans, and I marvelled at the limpid grace of the birds which expressed itself in their lassitude.

I had to move on, however, for fear that the match might finish before I got to the grounds and Vicky might be upset at my lateness. I had hardly gone past the tennis lawns, with their faded blue curtains, when I saw pickets of policemen on the road leading to the polo ground. The one nearest to me, as I approached, came up to me and said: 'No one is allowed to go this side.'

I was dumb in the face of this insolence, because I presumed that everyone in the state knew me as His Highness's personal physician. And I impatiently tried to brush him aside. At this his eyes became bloodshot, his jaws hardened, and he thrust the strong arm of the law before me to bar my way. I lost my head and struggled, trying to push my way forward. And this roused the policeman's ire. He pushed me back. I struck out, even as I prevented myself from falling. My palm more than brushed his head, and he retaliated now with his uplifted stick, which, however, I caught in my hands.

While we were struggling over the stick, two of the nearby policemen rushed to the scene and fell upon me, raining blow after blow, until my velvet cap fell away in the dust and I cowered and nearly collapsed, abusing the roughs and shouting.

The noise of the scuffle brought the head constable from the gateway of the polo maidan running towards us. He recognized me even a hundred yards away and shouted to the policemen to stop. But a sadistic joy in punishment had now got hold of the policemen. They were oblivious to his orders in their mad fury. At length he came and wrested me from their grip, and he began to abuse them at the top of his voice for showing such lack of discrimination.

Apart from the humiliation of receiving this treatment I was full of fear at my completely unpresentable appearance if I now ventured into His Highness's presence. Fortunately, I was not bleeding anywhere and was sure I had received no black eye. So I brushed my hair with my hands and, arranging my clothes with nervous fingers, proceeded, escorted by the head constable and the now abjectly servile policemen, who were falling at my feet and asking for forgiveness and vying with each other in handing me back my cap.

I shook them off with a peremptory gesture and walked towards the pavilion.

The polo match had finished. His Highness, his cousin, the Commander-in-Chief, and the other eminent players and spectators were standing round the champagne table, being served drinks by the white-liveried khansamahs.

'Hello, Mr Late Latif!' His Highness greeted me. 'And why are you looking so pale, as though your mother has died?'

I tried to smile, but I must have looked very sheepish, for I was badly shaken by the beating I had received.

'Come and have a drink,' His Highness said in a high-spirited voice.

'Khansamah, give Doctor Sahib a drink.'

I readily accepted the tumbler of champagne which Bhagirath offered me. I knew that this would soothe my nerves and restore me to the illusory eminence and respectability from which the policemen had so rudely brought me down to earth. But, inside me, my confidence in this set-up was very badly shaken. For I realized that all this magnificence, the flash and pageantry of the gentry, the polo and the champagne, etc., was the decorative outer surface, the appearance, of a crude reality, underneath which all the decencies of life were symbolically or really crushed and ground in the dust.

Flushed as he was with champagne and boisterous to the point of a back-slapping bonhomie, it was difficult for me to detach His Highness from his friends by any signs or gestures I could make, such as moving my head to indicate that we should go. So that ultimately I had to pull him aside and remind him that we had to go and see the Tikyali Rani Indira. He liked the flattery and the adulation and the talk, and it was difficult to wean him away from the crowd, even when he had decided to start off. My face began to twitch, waiting for him to cover the last lap of his conversation with Raja Sansar Chand, a young landlord and nobleman, who was pressing with an invitation for His Highness to come to dinner with him. My blood tingled with the sparks set up by the champagne and I was on edge, with the hangover of the resentment against being beaten up and insulted by the police.

At length Victor extricated himself from the somewhat abject Raja Sansar Chand, the pince-nez on whose nose were covered with the fumes and the sweat of the effort he had had to make to ask the favour of His Highness's company, and we proceeded towards the silver Rolls-Royce.

'I suppose I had better come as I am,' he said. 'I can't go home and change now.'

'You look very handsome,' I assented, with the slightest strain of irony in my voice.

The sun had gone down and the sky was luminous as though we were going towards the regions of hell, where the blood of victims in the temple of Kali on Siva's hill, and their shrieks were shooting up to the heavens, for the pink and orange streaks of pain limned the horizon.

I yielded to the five fingers of the night as I relaxed to lovely landscape of the small bare mountains into which we emerged after the railway level-crossing, half a mile away from the polo ground. There is an incredible mystery about the Indian evening, especially before the moon's dawning, that absorbs one, body and soul, to the uneasy rhythm of the beetles which churr in the marshes. And the wonder of it all ties one's tongue, making one hollow above the neck, so that one's eyes stare out as though from an antique mask. The fumes of the drink inside both of us had also risen to our heads and for once we were silent as though in the temple of twilight.

A pariah dog howled away as he was surprised by the sudden approach of the Rolls near the small village, which straggled below the giant walls of the Sham Pur Fort. And the shopkeepers and the peasants from nearby houses, who sat with indistinct, dark, mellow faces in the light of small earthen saucer lamps, all got up with joined hands and obsequiously bowed before the passing limousine.

The car swerved through the serpentine bazaar, up to the vast courtyard of the fort beyond the giant doorway of the hall, and made its way to the steps of the little red sandstone palaces and halls that crested the hill.

There was much bustle and activity and the chowkidars and attendants ran swift-footed in all directions to spread the news of His Highness's arrival.

The semi-nude priests from the temple of Kali, which stood in the inner courtyard of the lower palace, came crowding round us with waving tuft-knots and begged His Highness to visit the temple. Victor pointed to his tall leather boots and they accepted that answer, for, much as they respected him and expected a bounteous gift, they could not allow the temple to be defiled by cow-hide.

'The Raj Mata and the elder Rani are at prayers,' one of the more impetuous priests said.

'Also Rani Indira?' Victor asked.

The priest silently waved his head in negation as though he thought Indira was a lost soul, because she did not attend the temple.

His Highness, whose attitude to his mother, as well as his two wives who lived here, was one of an ambivalent love and hatred, because he had resisted their possessiveness, was not particularly concerned with any of them but only wanted to get an assurance out of Indira that she would not prosecute her petition to the States Department at Delhi any further.

So we walked grimly up, past the magnificent pillared dewan hall, up some narrow steps, flanked by the loveliest jali work, into the inner sanctums of the old-world palace, with delicate frescoes on the walls and small mirrors studded on the ceiling in mosaics of the most haunting quality.

Impulsively, I went to sit at the window-seat, decorated with cow-tailed cushions from which the whole valley below the hill fort was visible, calm and placid in the oncoming evening after the murderous heat of the day.

Victor wanted to do the same, but his tall boots made it impossible for him to sit down on the floor and he went and occupied one of the plush chairs with which the room was vulgarly furnished.

'Just like Indira to furnish this place in plush,' Victor complained.

'I don't like her taste,' I said. 'In this old palace the old Indian furniture would look very appropriate.'

'It is things like this that used to irritate me about Indira,' Victor said, a tone of regret in his voice. 'And we used to quarrel about these little things. And she was so self-righteous!'

At this juncture, Indira appeared, a demure, handsome young woman with chiselled, even features, marred by deep shadows of suffering under the eyes. She was clad in a simple white cotton sari and immediately created that feeling of uprightness and simplicity which was what Victor had in mind when he had spoken of her self-righteousness. She swept us both with a hurried glance and then, dipping her eyes coyly sat down on a low indigenous chair near her husband's feet.

'It is a very auspicious day for our household,' she began. 'Vicky, the moon seems to have risen.'

'The moon is always about,' Victor said.

'No, to me every night seems a dark night,' answered Indira sadly. There was a pause brought about by the truth of this utterance. Then, aware of the congealing impact of her self-pity on Victor, Indira added in a brighter tone: 'We were all talking about you – the Raj Mata was saying that you had not called to see her ever since you returned from Simla!'

I saw that Victor was feeling more uncomfortable than ever after this.

'His Highness has been very busy with state matters ever since we came down,' I put in hypocritically.

'Yes, I have been working twelve to fourteen hours a day,' Victor said.

I knew that this was Victor's cover for the guilt of neglecting Indira; for, as long as she believed that he was immersed in statecraft, she would think that he was not paying any more attention to Gangi than to his wedded wife.

'To a mere mother,' said Indira, 'each domestic detail appears so big that she tends to forget the business of the world. But you do exaggerate – twelve to fourteen hours a day!'

'You are a leisured woman and cannot understand that my work never ceases,' said Victor with a slight note of impatience in his voice.

'I suppose polo is also work,' Indira said with a smile.

'Of course,' said Victor priggishly. 'I have to keep up the prestige of the state by producing as good a team for matches with outsiders as possible.'

'That is very clever!' I said humorously.

But, just at that moment, there came a maudlin, childish voice from the next room: 'Indira – is that my Bapu who has come? And can I come and see him? I am not at all sleepy.'

'Now see,' said Indira. 'My work never finishes.'

And she got up to go and attend to her son.

But the boy had not waited for permission to appear. He was already on the threshold, a rather cherubic little fellow with a fair face, modelled upon his mother's, dressed in a muslin kurta and pyjama and without any slippers on his feet. And, recognizing his father, he ran towards Vicky and collapsed in his lap.

I saw that Vicky was as moved by the affection of his son for him as he was embarrassed that some servant might see him in this tender relation with his child by Indira and report to Gangi. But the paternal feelings triumphed and he stroked his son's sleek hair as the boy buried his face in his father's hands, seemingly through a pent-up feeling of love for Vicky, whom he saw so rarely.

'Sit up and show me your face, Aji, son,' Vicky said.

The boy felt inhibited more than ever at this show of affection.

'Come, son, talk to your father,' coaxed his mother. 'You have been asking for your father all these days. Now that he is here, why don't you say something?'

This irritated Vicky as it reminded him of his defaults. He pursed his lips and tried to lift his son up.

But the boy would not show his face.

At length Vicky forcibly held him up, hardening his jaw and his heart in the process.

Indarjit's eyes were full of tears and he covered them with his hands.

This made Victor very impatient. And he shouted: 'Be a man, don't cry!'

'Come, my son,' Indira said, running towards the boy. And she rescued him from her husband, afraid that Victor might become harder towards the boy.

At this moment there were shuffling steps on the stairs, and the weary, whining voice of Raj Mata, Victor's mother, percolated into the room.

Victor got up, furious that he had let himself in for all this.

'What is this I hear,' the Raj Mata was saying, 'the moon has risen over our palace? Moon-face, Ashok, my love, where are you? The eyes of your old mother are tired of looking in the direction of the hills from which you come....And...oh, I feel so hurt, my son, that you did not come all this time....' And the rest of her words were smothered in her sobs, as she came with tremendous vigour and put her arms around him.

The first Maharani, Uttami, a plain hill-woman, came in and stood self-effacingly with the edge of her dupatta drawn over her face to hide it from me, the stranger, as well as from her husband.

'Don't cry, Ma,' Victor said as he stood, erect and unbending, towering over the old woman.

'I am crying out of happiness, son,' the Raj Mata whimpered, 'not out of sorrow.'

And now the contagion of happiness had caught everyone. For Indira began to wipe the tears out of her eyes with the palla of her dupatta, and her son sobbed the more vociferously to see his grandma affected, and even the hill-woman, Uttami, hissed from behind the curtain of her dupatta, obviously convulsed.

'I am not dead, I am alive! Why are you all crying?' said Victor with suppressed rage.

The sentimental women shook themselves like hens at the cruel indifference of the cock, and, smoothing the ruffled feathers of their emotions, they sat back in a kind of decorative array by their hero.

'What is your news, son?' asked Raj Mata, making an effort to appear cheerful. 'I hear they have appointed a new Diwan – Popatlal. What a name!...A bania, I hear! A Poorbia! They are not as kind as the Angrezi Sarkar, I am told. Is that true?'

'Raj Mata,' said Indira, 'Sardar Patel was Gandhiji's right-hand man. And they all went to jail for the country.'

'But, my little one, they are mean, low people, sprung up from nowhere,' said the Raj Mata, with the hauteur of her feudal contempt for mere commoners. 'This Sardar – of what state was he a sardar? He looks like an angry bull from the pictures of him. And his dhoti is much too short for his legs!'

'Raj Mataji!' protested Indira.

'Acha, mother, I must go. I have not even bathed and changed after polo.'

'There is some sherbet coming,' said Indira.

And, turning towards the inner chambers, she called, 'Sudarshan!'

'Ay a ji,' came the obedient servant's voice.

He was on the way and entered with a silver tray, decorated with seven silver tumblers, full of sherbet.

'I want some sherbet, mother,' Raj Kumar Indarjit announced eagerly.

'Wait, son,' his mother cautioned him. 'Your father doesn't come here every day.'

This *faux pas* on the part of Indira seemed to irritate Victor still more. Embroiled in guilt feelings by his neglect of his family, he was morbidly sensitive to any explicit or implicit reference to his defaults.

'Give it to him, Indira,' he said. 'I don't want any sherbet.' Indira looked daggers at him, for she seemed to think he was contradicting her injunctions to the child. The latent hysteria discoloured her face. But she gave her son a tumbler full of sherbet.

'Do have some, son,' the Raj Mata said. 'It is the sherbet of Khas with the arec of Keora in it. We get it specially made. For, in the hot weather here, it is the only cooling thing, because we cannot get any ice as you can in the town.'

'Ma, I have had some sherbet of another kind,' Victor teased her.

'Oh, son,' she said, shocked at his open avowal of the fact that he drank. 'You must remember the fate of your father. I dread to think what will happen to you if you take after him. I can see with my dim eyes that you look more and more like him every day. And when I pray for his soul to the mother Kali, I always say, "Please Kali Mai, save my son from the habits which ruined his father."'

'Acha, Ma, I must go now,' Victor said, oppressed by the whole atmosphere and the talk, with its insidious recriminations, moralizing and sentimentality.

'Wait, son,' the Raj Mata insisted. 'At least wait till Doctor Hari Shankar has had some sherbet. Doctor Sahib, have a glass of sherbet. It has good medicinal properties, even though you were taught in Vilayat and perhaps despise our Indian things.'

I smiled sheepishly and took up a tumbler out of politeness.

I could see that Victor was perspiring profusely with anger and heat. I gulped the liquid down in order to keep myself in readiness for departure.

Victor got up as soon as I had put the tumbler back onto the tray and signalled me with a movement of his head.

'Acha, Ma,' he said, making a formal obeisance to her with joined hands.

'Ishwar bless you, my son,' said the Raj Mata resignedly. 'May you live long.'

The two Maharanis kept a demure silence.

Indarjit let go his tumbler so that it fell and the sherbet spilt, even as he came and caught his father's legs.

'I won't let him go, grandma,' he said. 'I won't let my Bapu go.'

'Come, child,' coaxed Indira, 'your Bapu has important work to do.'

The cutting bitterness of her utterance aroused Victor finally.

'You have spoilt him utterly!' he shouted. 'He whines and sulks and is stubborn like a donkey!'

The tone of anger in his father's voice suddenly frightened Indarjit and he began to howl.

All the three women fluttered around him, fussing with soft, coaxing words and remonstrances. Victor turned his back on them and proceeded towards the stairs. I followed him.

As he reached the doorway he turned to me and whispered: 'You talk to her and ask her if she is prepared to withdraw her petition for a consideration – I will settle the income of some villages on her.'

And he hurtled down the stairs.

I retraced my steps and, embarrassedly, asked Indira if she could come down for a minute.

Indira seemed highly incensed at Victor's behaviour, and was on the verge of tears, but, making a desperate effort to control herself, she nodded her head in assent and followed.

Strangely enough, Victor was waiting in the courtyard at the foot of the stairs, and, impetuous, impatient and downright, his hands on his waist and legs apart like a man playing at being a colossus, he began immediately:

'Indira, I really came to discuss something very important with you. But mother won't leave us alone and we can never talk....Look, I want you to know that, though we are temperamentally so unsuited to each other that we can never live under the same roof, I have the deepest friendship for you. After all, it is better that we should not give Indarjit a background of scenes and recriminations. I don't know how to say it...but you see, what I mean is – well...I am not such a worthy person as you. I believe, though, that we can rescue some understanding from all the muddle into which we have got ourselves. And we can be deeply united. I shall give you all the money and comfort you need. I don't know, but I am trying hard to change myself; to transform this state into something stable and real. But I realize that I have started too late. And our marriage too — well, our downfall was not brought about by any deliberate desire on my part to break it, but through my weaknesses and your strength. Still, I want to assure you that I am not all that bad.'

There came a certain moving sincerity into Victor's voice as he struggled towards the boundaries of truth from the chaos in which he had been plunged for months. And the quality of his soft voice reflected itself in Indira's face, in a tenderness which moved from her silent mouth to the tear-blurred lines under her eyes. But the inexplicable despair of Victor did not reach into her, in spite of the struggle he had made to communicate with her at a higher level. And his plea scattered on the indifferent atmosphere, while Indira gazed uncomprehendingly as though she could only see the agony on her own face wherever she looked. His solicitude had touched her deeply, but she had so hardened herself against him for years that now when he was about to make a demand on her, the proud walls of her emotions were impenetrable even against her will.

'What is it you want from me?' she said.

'I need support in my fight against the States Department,' Victor said. 'And you could relent and —'

'Oh, you don't know how I have suffered!' she said. And her voice broke, and her face quivered in the effort to control the flood of tears. 'I have been eating my heart out for you bit by bit, until there is no more of it left, even to give to you!'

'I am sorry,' Victor said.

At this one of the walls of her ego seemed to yield and she inclined towards him and put her head against his chest.

But he stiffened involuntarily with a jerk, though, realizing what he had done, he began to stroke her head. Only, for all his professions of friendship, he had cut himself off so completely from an organic sexual relationship with her that his recoil held him back in the very act of expressing his tenderness.

Indira realized this even as she lingered on his shoulder.

'Do withdraw the petition you had lodged with the Sarkar, then,' he said, taking advantage of her woman's weakness.

'I suppose I will do what you say,' she said. But then added, 'I will think about it.'

And she disengaged herself from him as soon as she realized that she must not yield and surrender and be used up completely, so that he could throw her on the scrap-heap afterwards under pressure from Gangi.

I stood by, the witness of this tense scene, with an unknown mouth that seemed never to have talked, and I swallowed my breath to calm the panic, the confusion and the embarrassment which the situation caused me.

'You are right,' Victor said to his wife. 'You are quite right to guard yourself against me. I have given you no proof of my honesty in the past. So why should you believe me? And I am a very bad man. You are right not to trust me.'

'Oh, Victor, I can't, I can't!' she cried as the tears broke through her big brown eyes and her being flooded with the waters of sympathy for him, which had always been brim full in her. The conflict of joy in his humility and sorrow for herself was too intense, however, and she swayed to and fro till she could not even bear to be human and ran away up the stairs like a frightened little animal.

There was nothing for it but to move away, empty and blind in the face of a struggle that I felt could never be resolved in the mechanical way in which Victor had sought to resolve it.

About half past one that night, Victor strolled up to my room and called out from the veranda in a mock-respectful voice, 'Doctor Hari Shankar, has your exalted self gone to sleep?'

'No, no, I am not asleep,' I lied as I woke up from the first slumber of the night and switched on my table lamp. And I shuffled about in an unnecessary panic of politeness and said, 'Please come in, Highness.'

Victor was dressed in black silk pyjamas and looked very much like my idea of Mephistopheles with his pale, lean face, as he entered.

'You know, Gangi has not appeared for the evening meal. I don't know where she is. She went to eat the midday meal with the wife of Seth Sadanand, but I understand that she came back and went out again for the evening without leaving word about where she was going.'

I had a shrewd guess about where she had gone, but tried to bluff Victor by a hearty invitation for him to sit down and have a drink.

'Yes, yes,' he said boisterously, so that I knew he had been drinking already.

'Will you have coffee?'

'Coffee! — that is cheating.' And he began to recite a hackneyed Hindustani verse: 'O Saki, bring the cup of wine....'

'Francis!' I shouted.

But there was no answer. My guide, friend and philosopher had apparently gone to his well-deserved rest for the night.

'I know where the whisky is, though,' I said. And I got up to fetch it.

For a while Victor sat silently with his right hand under his chin and stared emptily before him.

'You look sad,' I said as I handed him the tumbler of whisky.

'Torn open by these women and —' He did not finish his sentence.

'Anguish, remorse, guilt — all these spring from the birth trauma and childhood,' I said, waxing philosophical.

'However they spring, they lead to misery,' Victor said, impatient at my detachment. 'The thing is that one suffers!'

'It is the uncoiling of the ego from libido and mortido tensions,' I said, persisting with my abstractions, half ironically.

'In me it is the regrets of the past, of what might have been, that are causing the heartaches now.'

'Why, have you been reading some old love letters?'

'No, but seeing Indira this evening revived all the memories of the early days of my marriage with her. She was a good Hindu wife, in spite of the fact that she had passed BA. Especially when I was ill, she looked after me. And, after all, she bore me two sons. And she had a wonderful sense of humour.'

From the catholicity of Victor's taste in women I had not expected this confession about the single-heartedness that possessed him at one time. But it was obviously due to the strong hereditary belief in the conception of the devoted Hindu wife that he felt this nostalgia for the few months during which he had lived as man and wife with Indira. And perhaps the note of regret in his voice was encouraged by the vague fear he had of Gangi's inevitable betrayal.

'You know,' he continued, 'I was so attached to Indira, until she began to be possessive and jealous of other women, that whatever I did, whoever else I had, I looked on her as my greatest friend. And often I felt that in this Rani I had found a twin soul to whom I could confess everything, reveal all my secrets. We used to lie in bed late into the night talking about life. She told me everything about her family and her childhood friends. And I told her of all my urges and desires, even of my wildest desires. And I believed at last that like a compassionate mother she would understand everything, so long as I delivered myself to her body and soul, with all my strengths and failings. But unfortunately she was too good for me, because I was so bad. And she was always self-righteous and indignant even when I looked at another woman. And she began to scold me and nag me and find fault with me till she made me ashamed of looking into her eyes and taking her into my arms. If only she had not been so jealous, I would never have gone away from her. But she was afraid that I would spend all the money on other women and there would be nothing left for her. And she began to spy on all my movements through the servants, and I hated the idea that I was being watched. It oppressed me to be enslaved like that. So I broke away from her in my mind and felt a great relief when I met Gangi, because she was as bad as I, and the two of us could perhaps make a good bad pair....'

'Until Gangi also began to be possessive.'

'Yes, and worse, because she retained her habits while expecting me to remain faithful to her. And then she wanted marriage with me to legalize her two children, which the Sarkar would not allow. And she wanted more money than even Indira, and jewellery and also property.'

'Poor Vicky!' I said, with a sympathy disguised behind the irony. 'It is your Calvary to suffer at the hands of women.'

'I know I am a weak man. I am like pulp in their hands. They can do what they like with me.'

'I think this weakness would be a good thing if it arose from understanding and not from defeat,' I counselled. 'The trouble is that you will not really accept. And as you like your conflicts, and your women want what you cannot give, all of you suffer. Each of you punishes his or her own self and those nearest to you.'

'I don't understand such subtleties.'

Now I was impatient with him because, somehow, I felt clarity in my thoughts about him in the middle of the night.

'You are not so weak as you think, Vicky,' I said, combining flattery and courtliness with truth. 'You are the least neurotic of all the people in this tangle. Otherwise, you wouldn't be talking to me about yourself and have me always by. At least you are aware of your difficulties. And your desires, which is the root of your troubles, are elemental. And Indira, too, is strong, because she has faced up to her own loneliness and conquered her fears enough to defy you. The only misfit is Queen Bee. She is not only helpless, but powerful and destructive. And there is no limit to her desires, even as there is no limit to her ignorance.'

'You are talking like a sage. But I am caught, trapped!… Why does one have to marry or be attached to a woman?'

'Of course you had to marry. Everyone has to marry. Only a puritan resents the vulgarity of the mundane experiences which occur in the daily life of a man and woman together. There is no such thing as being unbound, except for a split mind, which is incapable of forming any stable attachment and wanders from place to place, dreaming daydreams which have little or no contact with the realities of life. But in a wise marriage the ordinary life is transformed from the trivial detail to some exalted purpose which is the secret wish of both the partners. And then the couple see their reflection in the mirror of this higher personality to which they are always aspiring.'

'Then there is really no escape?' Vicky asked in a whisper.

'No, we are all captured.'

'What about the Buddha's ideal of non-attachment?'

'It remains an ideal. But where Buddhism failed Hinduism succeeded, because it made concessions to the weaknesses of man. "Live in action," said Krishna to Arjuna in the *Bhagavad Gita*. Only, there has been some confusion in our minds, because Gandhi borrowed the European Christian belief in original sin and introduced an element of guilt into the Indian soul, thus emphasizing the old Indian idea of ascetic withdrawal from life, the denial of all sexual intercourse. And he exalted prohibition, penance, fasting and prayer. Whereas life in the pagan Hindu sense is immanent: truth is immanent: God is immanent. The whole universe is a kind of Lila, sport, in the expansive mind and heart of Brahman. The manifold world began when desire arose in the heart of the One Absolute, and now there is the constant desire on the part of mankind to break duality and attain absorption in the One. So that desire is an essential element in us and all our actions are motivated by it; and we feel that we can choose to do this or that freely; that is to say, we feel the illusion that our will is free. And thus we go on, until we realize that, though there is free will in a limited sense, we are really bound by responsibilities, duties, even as we have a certain number of rights – and then we are freed in a higher sense by the recognition of our responsibilities in a universe which is determined by the acts, thoughts and feelings of other peoples both in the past and the present.'

'It is all very difficult,' Victor said, his thoughts wandering with the congestion of ideas in my speech and resentful of my lecturing tone. 'Surely, it is not all so logical. What about all these silly things that women do?'

'All their capriciousness, all their failings, revenges, hates and loves are the index of their desire to grow,' I explained. 'But in many people the infantile pulls are too strong to allow all-round development and they remain helpless neurotics, selfish, vain, cruel, heartless, ungrateful wretches, immersed in their unhappiness and liking it, lying on a sick-bed, and receiving sympathy and admiration, but really at heart not desirous of getting well at all!'

'Do you believe in Darwin's idea that we are all descended from the apes?' Victor asked, suddenly going off at a tangent.

'I suppose everyone believes in evolution of one kind or another, nowadays,' I said, 'except the nihilists, who think that humanity is so wicked and barbaric it ought to be wiped out and —'

There was a sound of footsteps in the veranda and a knock at the door.

We were both rather startled and breathless.

'Maharaj,' came the voice of Rupa, the old maidservant of Gangi. 'Maharani Sahiba says, are you not coming to sleep?'

'Acha, acha, I am coming,' Victor said, startled. And, turning to me significantly, he added, 'So she has come back wherever she has been!'

'Please go, Vicky, otherwise she will be annoyed.'

Victor lingered in his chair, apparently in the grip of fear, ennui and drink. And I waited silently for him to move or say something.

'My heart is thumping wildly,' he said at last.

'You love her and fear her,' I said. 'Go to her.'

He rose from the chair and, without looking me in the face, walked sheepishly away.

I could not sleep though I switched off the light and lay down on my bed. I was sure that Gangi was up to some trick to summon him like that into her presence. I was sure that she had drifted away from him for a while. Equally, I was convinced that like 'the thief turning sheriff' she would put the blame for everything on to him and humiliate him.

For it was obvious to me by now that this woman was at once sadist and masochist. She wanted to torment him and be tormented. A compulsion to conquer the members of the opposite sex and to change lovers dominates the nymphomaniac. And yet, as most men and women exhibit the same traits to some extent, no one noticed that she was a schizoid, or split personality.

What was the moment of her unhinging? And where did the unending traces of the disturbances in her soul lead to? How far between the earth and the sky would one have to go to learn the truth of her being, the sources of the conflict in her? And how many gaps would there be in one's understanding of her, if one did not know anything but bits gleaned from Victor's revelations about her and from one's own scanty observations? And how was one to measure the span through which she had come to despise him and yet have him constantly in mind? Did the secret lie in the undermost, entangled roots of sex, the concealed source of many things, which one never sees?

Perhaps there lay the trouble. Since every man had been a kind of cruel father to her, she loved and hated men in an ambivalence which resulted in the woman's amazonian revenge against man.

How shocked and insulted she would be if all these questions were raised in her presence and she was told that her sufferings could perhaps be eased by a confession of her

139

difficulties to me! But few people understand their sufferings. Nor has love been learned. And what remains in our lives are the husks of emotions and ideas, dimly perceived and allowed to fester in the cesspools of the hells beyond redemption, through a kind of liberal non-interventionism encouraged by the selfishness which prevents us from holding each other's hands.

I was ruminating on these things when Victor returned and collapsed in the armchair by my bed in the dark. I put on the light, more startled by this visitation than I had been by his earlier entrance, because I saw that he was dishevelled.

'Forgive me,' he said. 'My legs feel weak under me and I don't feel well. She has locked me out after a scene. She accused me of having gone back to Indira!'

'That is the kind of justification she must give in order to go away from you herself,' I said.

'Oh, what are you saying?' shrieked Victor. 'Do you mean...?'

'Yes, I think she is having an affair with Popatlal J. Shah,' I said.

'God!' Victor said, beating the temples of his head with his palms. 'Oh, my God!...' And he began to weep like a child, his cries flying past any words I could speak to soothe him, till I had to close the doors to prevent the reverberations of his shrieks from penetrating into the thick night, dense with the sleep of the innocent and the guilty alike.

There is a wise saying of Leo Tolstoy that man gets over everything, everything except the tragedy of the bedchamber. Of course, the sage of Yasnya Polyana might have added that the well-known healing qualities of time make a difference though the scars of love remain.

Long-range considerations apart, however, there is the awful pain of the immediate hurt, which arises at frequent moments suddenly like shooting stars in the sky of one's soul. And, in the soul of Victor, harrowed by his invidious position as a non-acceding, unpopular, autocratic ruler, other comets were also bursting, and whole planets were in a state of ferment. So the descendant of the Suraj Bansi clan, who were supposed to be descended from the sun, tried to seek out the sun and find comfort in the heart of nature.

He sent me a message early in the morning to get ready to go with him to inspect the hunting lodge in the forest and also to see if the army manoeuvres had started.

Victor looked very sombre and glum as he came up to the hall where I was waiting for him. He had ordered the Cadillac this morning and that meant he wanted to drive himself, for he always used this car when he was in the mood to take the wheel. The chauffeur, Haider Ali, opened the doors for His Highness and me to enter, and then went into the back seat past the small space behind me. Impetuously, Victor started the car and, with a sudden jerk, we were off.

As we drove across the main Sham Pur bazaar, which was still seemingly under the grip of the hartal, I reflected on the fact that Victor had not asked Captain Partap Singh, Munshi Mithan Lal or Mr Bool Chand to accompany us. Obviously, it was because I was privy to all the most intimate details of his relations with this woman. And a man with a broken heart seeks in such a friend the images, feelings, memories and anecdotes of his beloved. Almost instinctively I supplied the place of a woman in Victor's life by becoming a kind of *tabula rasa* in which everything was mirrored.

This realization, though somewhat flattering, was also humiliating. But a medical man learns to bring those little

mothering ways, those delicate attentions which may give
the patient confidence in himself and in life. Nevertheless, I
came to know a few things about myself which I had hitherto
only vaguely glimmered: that I was weak, vain and timid;
that I did not have the courage of my convictions and could
not act in a crisis with the single-minded zeal of a good moral
person; that, substituting psychology for morality, I had
dissolved the values of my inheritance and was experimenting
with the new and tentative hypothesis of liberal individualism
which concedes free will to every person, even though that
person may be determined by his or her own subjectivism.

But because I had been shifting the emphasis from value
judgements to psychological understanding of the causes
which led people to act in certain ways, I felt a curious
affection, bordering upon compassion, for Victor, and an
understanding of the process by which the violation of his
genuine weakness and sensitivity by his bad upbringing had
transformed decency in him into an evil and revengeful will.

The dusty roads of Sham Pur had already given place to
the rutted, pitted paths, strewn with stones, that led to the
jungle of Parma, where one of the many hunting lodges was
situated, nearly at the foot of the lower Himalayan ranges.
The thin, drawn face of Victor quivered with every big bump
in the road, almost as though the Cadillac had become a
substitute for his mistress, for whom he felt a tender
sympathy. A creaking sisterhood of bullock carts, proceeding
at a snail's speed right in the middle of the narrow road,
impervious to His Highness's hooter, did not improve the
Maharaja's temper. Further up, there was a herd of goats,
which displayed the manners of their own native hills and
plains by fanning out in fear and terror in a half-circle
between two hills. And when they were cleared by the wild

lashing of the herdsmen, we soon came across a series of bridges over small nullahs at the approaches of which the Public Works Department had put notices closing them to all motor traffic except state cars.

'I wish they would strengthen the bridges,' I said, just to break the monotony.

But it was an ill-considered remark. For, as the first bridge had creaked under our weight as we crossed it, Victor's fear of a bridge collapsing turned into guilt at the neglect of his PWD. He said irritably: 'You want modern luxuries in the heart of the jungle, don't you?' At the turn of a small hill, which the road was cresting as it reached out towards the slopes of the Terai, there was a veritable witches' sabbath, because the Cadillac ran over one dog among a troupe of pariahs who had been squatting over their mangy hams. I turned and saw that the wounded dog did not die but dragged itself with shrill, sad yelps towards the wayside and collapsed. But Victor drove on with a hardened jaw and shut-mouth obstinacy, obviously controlling himself from feeling remorse for this murder. And the crunch of the gravel beneath the car was the only sound between us during the next mile. At that stage, however, we had another fright because a young boy ran across the road from behind a hamlet and just missed being run over.

'Doctor Sahib, you take over,' His Highness whispered, obviously nerve-wracked and worn out by the strain. And he brought the car to a standstill under the shade of a tamarind tree. And, getting out of his door, he made room for me and came into my place from the left.

We drove peacefully enough for the next quarter of an hour along the circuitous, uneven road, more deeply rutted than ever, as it penetrated deeper into the forest. I took the

car on to the dusty tracks by the edge of the road as long as
these unpaved stretches lasted in the valleys which we
traversed, but had perforce to swerve on to the gravel where
the road was narrow. I kept a steady, slow pace and did not
rush. And, after the first nervous twitches, Victor began to
relax and have confidence in my driving.

'What really happened last night?' I asked him softly.

'She jilted me,' he said with a tremor on his lower lip. 'She
scolded me about having seen Indira and she turned me out
of her room. She seemed insane with jealousy. Something
has come over her.'

'She is only pretending to be jealous of Indira,' I said, my
eyes riveted on the rough, serpentine road ahead of me.

I laughed a little and added: 'I think you are exaggerating
there. You really mean that her emotions towards you are
changing, not –'

'Han, I have been feeling that there are certain currents
in her....She is going away from me. She did this at the time
of her affair with my cousin. She maintained the outer
relations with me, but inside she was with him. I could see it
in her eyes and in the way she hung on his words, teasing
him and being teased by him. And then she would become
impatient and irritable with me over small things. And
sometimes she was furious with me and looked at me with a
hard glint in her eyes. And I felt so surprised to see her
change, because there had been no occasion for a quarrel.
And I wondered why she had suddenly begun to hate me so,
and why she was being so cruel to me. I looked at her
appealingly, asking for pity. And she would relent a little.
But then she would begin to harden herself against me once
more and thrust me away into the mire of suspicion and
uncertainty....I feel she is doing the same now. I think she is

scheming against me. I know she is drifting. That is why she would not let me sleep with her last night. But I wonder why she sent the ayah to call me if she only wanted to drive me away. I am beginning to believe that —'

'I think your difficulties with her have just begun.'

Victor seemed rather shocked when I said this, though he knew that what I said was only a confirmation of his own familiar feelings. The surprised anguish in his face reflected, I felt, his dread of the fact that she might leave him.

'Do you really think that she might leave me?'

I did not answer this question, because I knew it would torment him for days if I answered in the affirmative. I tried to soothe him by asking him another question instead.

'Why do you care for her so much?'

'You know, there have been times when she has been dependent on me, so possessive that I could not even breathe. I was all in all to her. And during those days I could not be free of her. In fact, even now, in that way I know she is still possessive and would like to keep me firmly in her hold. But somehow, somewhere, she has also decided to resist me and throw me away. And the two feelings are quarrelling in her.'

'And I suppose that though you did not worry when you could take her for granted, you are now unhappy that she wants you and yet doesn't want you. You are both evenly matched in this war.'

'But you don't see, Hari, that I can't do without her. I can't rest without her. I need a woman. And she is that woman. I need her support. What with all the troubles of the state I need her by me now especially. And it is terrible that she should treat me as she did last night. I could have hit her for insulting me like that. Oh, I feel mad at the very thought of her rejection of me.'

Victor's voice rose as he said this. And I could sense the bitterness that was rising like a flaming fire in him. In all his explanations he had not mentioned that he wanted her physically also, and I knew that there was a strong pull of the wanton in her for him. So I asked him: 'Is there any residue of sex which has not yet been appeased?'

'Of course,' he answered. 'As I have always been ailing, I have not even begun to give free rein to our love. At first her children came. And then it took me some time to forget about Raghbir Singh. And she is so highly sexed that she would approach me all in a mad passion and not have the patience to prolong our pleasures by talking about things and adjusting ourselves together.'

'Well,' I said, embarrassed by his revelations and yet marvelling at his honesty, 'from the dust out there, I guess the infantry of Brigadier-General Chaudhri Raghbir Singh is ahead of us.'

'You know, I would not like to lose her,' Victor continued. 'And yet an appalling fear grips me, the fear of a life without her, as though I am swimming in a sea without a raft.'

'Hullo,' I said. 'I hear the sound of firing. The convoys seem to have come to a standstill.'

'What do you think is the matter?' Victor asked, nervous and impatient.

I slowed up a little but kept driving steadily across the incline of the hilly road and soon we emerged past the sarcophagus of the jungle, away from the funereal halls of tall shafts and tendrils of dense greenery, interspersed with small clearings and cool bowers.

Presently two sepoys put up their hands to stop us at the head of a bridge. As soon as they recognized His Highness they stood at attention and saluted.

'What's happened?' His Highness asked.

'Don't know, Maharaj,' one of the sepoys said, looking straight in front of him as he still stood at attention.

'Son of don't know – why don't you know?' shouted His Highness, angry at the stupidity of the sepoy.

But an officer – a Captain, from the pips on his shoulder – came running up from the other end of the bridge and, saluting perfunctorily, said: 'There are some Communist guerillas, sir, sniping from the two sides of the hills beyond the village of Panna there. And they have held up our convoy.'

'But we want to get to the Panna hunting lodge,' His Highness said.

'It is not very safe, Highness,' the Captain said.

'We must go! What is this?' His Highness's Rajput blood was up.

'Well, sir, you can make a detour by the track from Panna which emerges near the hunting lodge; but we will have to give you the escort of a platoon. I will go and detail off a platoon.'

'These Communists must be wiped out!' His Highness burst out like an angry boy. 'It is a good thing I ordered the manoeuvres....Captain Sahib, where is General Raghbir Singh? Please ask him to meet me by the crossroads before Panna.'

The Captain saluted and about-turned with a dramatic alacrity.

But he did not need to go and inform General Raghbir Singh. The invisible wireless, which is rumour in India, had already communicated to the Commander-in-Chief news of the arrival of the Maharaja, for his car was hurrying along towards us across the bridge.

We got out in time for General Raghbir Singh to come out of his car and greet us.

'I congratulate Your Highness on your sagacity in ordering these manoeuvres, because there is trouble in the villages,' General Raghbir Singh said in a flattering tone.

'I shall not rest till every Communist is destroyed!' His Highness said histrionically.

'Of course, the sardars are also behind the disturbances,' General Raghbir Singh said to sober His Highness. And then, realizing that Victor might feel he was trying to create differences between him and his cousins, the noblemen, the Commander-in-Chief added: 'I think they are themselves divided. And yet all of them are inclined towards the Congress Praja Mandal. And the Praja Mandal seems to have Communists in it, though the two parties hate each other.'

'I shall destroy the sardars too! What do they think they are, to defy me! Swine!'

Victor was working himself into a rage. But he saw the strong, relatively undisturbed face of his cousin, Raghbir Singh, and felt a little abashed about his hysterics. So he changed his tune:

'I should like to see Thakur Parduman Singh. After all, he is an old man and in the position of an uncle to me. He may see that the States Department is threatening the very existence of Sham Pur!'

'Han, Highness,' said Raghbir Singh. 'We must see all the three sardars: only, we must see them separately. I shall send a message to Thakur Parduman Singh. I hear he is at Udham Pur, which is only seven miles from the hunting lodge.'

'Acha, we will proceed there,' Victor said. 'It is all the same to me whether they come together or singly.'

'Huzoor, it is easier to settle them one by one,' suggested Raghbir Singh with instinctive cunning.

'Han, it is easier to destroy them one by one,' agreed His Highness.

'I shall go and order an escort for your car, Highness,' said General Raghbir Singh.

He came to attention, saluted and turned.

Already a procession of armoured cars, tanks and jeeps was advancing towards us. So General Raghbir Singh walked up towards the bridge to give the necessary orders.

The hunting lodge was about a mile and a half away from the village of Panna, a majestic wooden bungalow in the Nepalese-Chinese style, situated on the edge of the wood, a kind of last outpost of human existence before the vegetable and animal world took over. The walls of the ample veranda were covered with tiger, panther and cheetah skins, interspersed with the heads of stags and deer, all trophies of the hunt of the last two or three generations. And somehow, after the miles of wilderness of matted thorns and weeds and flat paddy fields around Sham Pur, one felt suddenly ushered into the tangled web of scrub and shrub and a dense green hell which was frightening as well as fascinating to me for the dangers it might hold.

Actually, I knew that there was no possibility of a tiger walking in. Rather, I felt that one might be surrounded by the guerillas here and be cut off from all contact with the world and be heard of no more. For, the luxury of this lodge, with its beautiful oak furniture and its chests and, what was more important, its arsenal of guns, made it an obvious target for the armed bands composed of the discontented villagers who were in revolt against poverty and forced labour, which took thousands of them away from their fields to serve as beaters and camp-followers during a hunt at the summons of any lackey of the Maharaja.

I also realized that the three noblemen, who were in league with the Praja Mandal, seemed determined to destroy the Maharaja, considering that they had joined hands even with the Communist guerillas in open armed rebellion against the state. And our escort of one platoon was nowhere near enough, should the guerillas attack us.

I roamed around warily on the beautifully kept lawns of the lodge, while Victor finished his toilet. And then, while he went out looking for pigeons and wild doves in the niches and gables of the beautiful roof of the hunting lodge, I went and bathed.

When I emerged I was suddenly accosted by a dishevelled young man who said: 'Dr Shankar, leave the Maharaja and come over to us – you know your heart is with us!'

And, saying this, the lad made off.

I was unnerved for a moment and followed his slouching gait, trying to remember his features. But he had fled.

His Highness was a good shot and had felled six big and beautiful pigeons by the time I returned to the veranda.

I found that his morale was up with his success with the birds, and he brought an enormous zest to the breakfast which was served to us by the permanent cook-bearer, Khuda Bux, who was attached to the lodge.

'Tell me, then, Khuda Bux, how are things with you?' Victor asked the benign old man with the broad, flat face. 'And what has happened to your henna-dyed beard?'

'By Allah, I am loyal to your Highness, even as I have loyally served your father and grandfather. Only, being a Mussulman by birth, I seem to have come under suspicion of the Hindu villagers. And for the last few months, Huzoor, ever since the riots, I have been living in continual fear of being murdered. There is much that goes on in Panna and Udham Pur that does not reach your ears, sire. But when the headman, the Jagirdar himself − forgive me, Maharaj, already I have become impertinent!...'

'No, no, go on, and tell me everything.'

'Huzoor, almost all the Muslims in Udham Pur were murdered, some months ago, except those who ran away. And to tell you the truth, Maharaj, that is why I had my beard shaved off. And, Huzoor, how shall I tell you?...But I saved myself by falling at the feet of your uncle, the Thakur Sahib of Udham Pur. I told him that I would become a convert to the Hindu faith and − tobah! tobah! − by assuring him that I − oh, I can't even tell you the truth! That I, who have eaten your salt, should have uttered those words! Please forgive, Maharaj....'

'Tell me, tell me, Khuda Bux.'

'Maharaj, I told him I would tell him all about you. But I had every intention of getting to know all about him and telling you, my sire!'

'So you betrayed my salt!' said Victor teasingly.

I was surprised that he was not angry or suspicious about Khuda Bux, in spite of this khansamah's revelations about his treachery. But I knew that Victor had an instinctive love of intrigue and was waiting to judge to whom Khuda Bux had been more loyal.

'Maharaj, how can I ever betray your salt!' continued Khuda Bux. 'To be sure, these murders made one lose one's izzat! I had to have my beard cut, and crawl before a fanatical Hindu like Thakur Sahib, and even to get converted! But I could never betray your salt. In fact, I have gleaned enough about the real feelings of Thakur Sahib about you to tell you, Huzoor, to be careful of him.'

'And what have you gleaned?' asked Victor. 'But, look here, khansamah, I wanted to have those pigeons curried for breakfast and you are here talking away....'

'Huzoor, the pigeons are being done by Damru,' assured Khuda Bux. 'I will go and fetch them.'

'Oh no, you leave them now for lunch and tell me about my uncle.'

'What shall I say, Huzoor,' apologized Khuda Bux. And he looked aside as though unable to record any unpleasant facts about His Highness, lest it be inferred that he agreed with the Maharaja's enemies.

While Khuda Bux was making up his mind, Victor sighed heavily and, with a sudden gesture of his head, said to me: 'I don't know why Gangi is doing this to me. She doesn't realize that I would do anything for her.'

'Cruelty is a fundamental habit with a neurotic,' I said. 'And it is precisely because she knows that you would do anything for her that she is doing this to you.'

What I said seemed to carry conviction with him and he hung his head down.

'Thakur Sahib is after those lands by the Sutlej river which he says were to be divided between your father and the Thakur Sahib's wife, your aunt,' began Khuda Bux, as though he was talking on his own. 'He says that there is a document somewhere in the Sarkar's office which proves his claim. And, according to him, you say the document cannot be found....'

'Does the swine accuse me of stealing it?' Victor snarled as he got up. And his eyes flashed even like those of the tigers and panthers who stared out of the walls.

'The other two thakurs, Mahan Chand and Shiv Ram Singh, used often to come down to the house of Thakur Parduman Singh, Huzoor. And they all drank hemp together and abused your sacred person.'

'I know, I know. I know that every man's hand is turned against me!'

'What is their complaint?' I asked Khuda Bux.

'Sahib, it is heard that they claim the right to the Sham Pur Palace in Benares and to the properties in Delhi, Lahore, Amritsar, Haridwar, Bombay and some part of the lands on the Sutlej – according to the same missing document.'

I reflected on the nature of the heritage over which these cousins were fighting like dogs over a bone, and the ironic fact that all that they were fighting for was threatened not so much by the Praja Mandal but by the Communists. It was strange how the privileged fought over their position and power even in the face of disaster, right till the end, in a mad scramble to which they were driven by urges, desires and fears, which were only heightened by disruption.

'All this shooting is being helped by the thakurs, Huzoor,' said Khuda Bux. 'And it is a good thing that you are here, and the Jarnel Sahib, and the foj....The innocents will get heart....'

'Acha, acha, clear the table!' ordered Victor impatiently. Khuda Bux bowed, salaamed and proceeded to clear the breakfast things.

Victor walked up to the door of the magnificent dining room and looked out expectantly. Then, beaten back by the glare, he withdrew and came towards me, wringing his hands and saying: 'The unrest in the state has coincided with my difficulties at home. Why did this have to happen to me? I feel cornered!'

'All one's difficulties,' I said, 'arise from the greed of a weak stomach and the longing for women of a weak heart.'

'Philosophizing won't help,' Victor said.

'But concealing the truth won't help either,' I said. 'Certainly, this is no way to get rid of fears and sorrows.'

'How can I be free of them?'

'I suppose if one limits one's demands on life,' I said without any conviction in my voice, 'and faces the roots of one's conflicts, one may become more or less free. Not by continually deceiving oneself, by being selfish, unjust, dissolute, discontented, envious and afraid....' I realized the harshness of my dictum and checked myself.

'Go on, speak your mind. I deserve all this. So long as you don't scold me too much.'

'You were made too luxuriant a tree long before you were even a sapling. You grew to an awareness of sex before the proper season....'

But there were voices in the veranda and I could not go on.

'Where is this rape-daughter?' came the shrill staccato hillman's accent of Raja Parduman Singh's voice. 'I want to tell him that while he goes about womanizing, his subjects are in revolt. The whole praja is in revolt! And, rape-sister, he is not ashamed!...'

A wiry, dark little man, with a brave, upturned moustache, the Raja Sahib was a typical white-clad, feudal nobleman in his muslin robes, tight pyjamas and big turban.

'His Highness is there,' counselled General Raghbir Singh from behind the old man to calm him.

'Han, Raja Sahib, don't be so angry,' said Thakur Mahan Chand, the replica of his elder brother, except that he was fairer and taller.

'Han, uncle, let us at least hear what he has to say,' advised Thakur Shiv Ram Singh, the youngest of the three noblemen, who was dressed dandily in an English sharkskin suit which was belied by the gold rings he wore in his ears.

'Ohe, keep quiet, fools!' shouted the old Raja. 'Let me take this boy to task for ruining his patrimony. He has been spoilt! All of us have been too kind to him. He deserves a shoe beating! What a scandal he has created in Simla by raping that memni! And his carryings-on with that Brahmin whore, Ganga Dasi...! I wonder if he has brought her here. I should like to drag that woman by the hair and throw her out of the state!'

'Jayadeva, uncle,' said Victor, coming forward and bending to touch the symbolic dust off his feet.

During the ceremonial greetings, Raja Parduman Singh kept a stern silence. But as soon as Victor stood back, his uncle began the attack again:

'Ohe, darkness has come over the world! – Darkness! Brazen young man, you lose the deeds about our property and then have stupid little brown-paper letters sent to me from your office, ignoring my just demands! Do you think that you can evade the issue?'

'But, uncle, I am willing to talk it over with you.'

'What is the use of talking now?' said Raja Parduman Singh, stalking up to the veranda and studiedly sitting back into a cane chair. 'What is the use of repentance now that the sparrows have eaten away the grain from the fields? You first write little chits to us. Then you ignore our letters and refuse even to see our emissaries.'

'I was at Simla, Raja Sahib,' apologized Victor.

'Han, han, we knew how you were eating the ashes in Simla. You had spoilt your religion already by eating beef.

Now, after sleeping with a beef-eating memni, not even the waters of Ganges can purify you. I don't know what the world is coming to! Our family was known for its purity and grandeur. You have reduced the prestige of our house and dragged our good name into the dust!'

'Nowadays, young people are rather free about their taste in food and women,' I said, to lighten the conversation.

'Acha, I agree that princes and noblemen will rape women,' the old man said with a twinkle in his eye. 'But to pollute one's religion by eating beef! And to lose one's head completely!'

'Brother,' said the young Thakur Shiv Ram Singh, 'you yourself went across the black water in the First World War and spent some time in France.'

'Chup raho, you young dog, you are no one to speak. I know the direction in which you are going!...And are you not concerned with your rights that you are taking sides with this pup?'

'Let us discuss the real question, then, rather than religion,' said Victor, summoning all his courage to face his enemies.

'There is no talk,' snarled Raja Parduman Singh, his eyes flashing like that of a mongrel dog. 'We have presented our demands for the restitution of our rightful properties. As you did not do anything about them, we have appealed to the Sarkar at Delhi. And, as the Praja Mandal is out for your blood, your only chance is to concede our demands and have one enemy the less.'

'I won't be bullied like that!' said Victor, averting his face and trying to suppress the anger in his voice.

'Well then, we shall show you!' raved Raja Parduman Singh, standing up and striking his huge stick on the cement floor of the veranda of the lodge.

For a moment the abundant greenery of the forest outside seemed to be ablaze with the heat of the argument, which had ignited the broad glare of the day.

'Leave me alone for a month or so, and I shall call the whole brotherhood and settle any just claims you may have according to the documents,' said Victor.

'But you say the documents are not to be found,' said the young Thakur Shiv Ram Singh.

'Son, you can't evade the issue for ever with your promises,' said Thakur Mahan Chand.

'There is no question of waiting for a month,' shrilled Raja Parduman Singh. 'There is no talk with a blackguard like this...'

'Uncle,' said Victor. 'I have borne your abuse patiently enough. But I shall not be responsible for the consequences if you go on like this!'

'I for one am not talking to a lecher like you!' shouted the old Raja. 'Come, boys, let us go. This illegally begotten has no intention to settle with us....'

At this Victor leapt, like the lithe tiger he was, to attack his uncle.

General Raghbir Singh came in between them and held him back.

'You see the rascal, he is not above attacking his old uncle! The swine! The idiot! The lecher! The good-for-nothing scoundrel!' Raja Parduman Singh yelped like this even as he walked away with frightened, shaky legs towards the garden.

Victor's face was red with patches of white on the forehead.

'I knew it was no use talking to this bastard,' continued the old man. 'He is like the English, evasive, and he tries diplomacy on an old rogue like me! I knew before we came that we would get nowhere with this swine!'

'Uncle – stop your foul tongue!' Victor shouted, stretching himself to his full feeble height and frothing at the mouth.

'I shall say what I like, you pup!' shouted the old Raja, brandishing his thick stick at him from a safe distance.

The victoria in which the three noblemen had come moved away.

The frenzy of the quarrel rose across the air, burning up and shrivelling everything, until the dazzling yellow glare shimmered before our eyes like the sheen on the top of a huge jungle fire.

On our arrival at the Sham Pur city palace we found Ganga Dasi waiting anxiously for Victor in his drawing room.

'I hear of trouble all over the state,' she said. 'And where have you been? I have been so worried about you. Vicky, you might have left a message for me as to where you had gone. I have sent messengers all over the place to look for you!'

Victor was hot with the mounting suffocation of the Sham Pur late summer afternoon, irritable with the hangover of his quarrel with his uncles and cousins, and hungry, as we had not stayed for lunch at the lodge after the awful scene. And as we had heard the sound of spasmodic firing near Panna village, His Highness had been worried all the way, even though General Raghbir Singh told him that the army would clear up the trouble in no time. His face was rigid, as though a sort of nullity had come over him, a kind of hopelessness, or even the sense of some impending disaster. He had not said much on the way back.

'What is the matter?' she asked as though she had forgotten about turning him out the previous night and was blissfully unconscious of anything wrong between them. And she went up to him with a swinging of her hips and, making eyes at him with the most charming of blandishments, tried to melt him.

He stood away, confused and angry. Then he looked at her, uncomprehending.

She laughed at him with a mellow look in her eyes, and purred like a cat full of the bliss of her own exuberant sex, radiant. He was afraid to be drawn, for he seemed to realize that she would only bring him to herself and then throw him over again. He looked agonized even as his lips puckered into a smile.

Suddenly, she touched his harrowed face and stroked it. And, instantly, he bent towards her and looked into her green eyes and her face, and, catching hold of her, buried his face in hers, kissing her gently, with a soft, tender movement of his lips, and with ever so delicate an abandon. This gave me time to withdraw discreetly away.

'My life,' he was saying, 'my dearest life! Why did you turn me away last night? Why? I will do anything for you. You know that, my darling, don't you? I will gladly wear a peasant's torn clothes and go and work in the fields if the States Department doesn't let me marry you and make you my Maharani. Only be good to me, and I will sacrifice myself for you....My beloved....'

My curiosity had made me stand long enough outside the door and eavesdrop on this declaration. But I was scared to be seen thus listening and went towards my room. I knew in my bones, however, that this was only a partial reconciliation. And that she was playing tricks with this fool, in order to exact from him the full measure of the security she wanted, and that, while he would really surrender to her because she seemed to him the only tangible, secure thing in the world he could hang on to, there was much venal greed in her callow soul above the genuine core of the affection she had for him.

During the whole of that day, I did not see Vicky. Apparently, the homecoming had been very cordial, the warm greetings having transformed themselves into the play function of sex. And I was glad enough of a respite until, on coming home from a swim in the river Sutlej on the morning of the next day, I found a letter waiting for me with a strange, impatient scrawl on the envelope. Francis, my bearer, friend, guide and philosopher, told me that he had been handed the letter in the Sham Pur bazaar, where he had gone to buy a packet of cornflakes for my breakfast. When I sat down to breakfast, I opened the letter and read its contents. My mind eagerly yielded to each word as though it came to my ears like a sigh of despair uttered by some distant voice at the moon's downing, when the earth is engulfed in a deep dark night.

Dear Dr Shankar,
I write this letter to you in the vain hope that it might reach you and touch your half-dead conscience and make you influence the young tyrant under whose autocratic rule I and several of my comrades are counting the days of our likely sojourn in the living hell of Udham Pur Jail.

I was arrested with six others on the fourteenth of August, 1946, for leading a procession of villagers into Sham Pur to demand a moratorium on debts and the abolition of various illegal taxes like Elephantauna and Motrauna, etc. Since then, without any charge being made against me and my comrades, without a trial, we have been detained here. We have protested to the Maharaja, to the Diwan, and to the Government of India, against our detention without trial, but there is no answer, and we have begun to feel that perhaps the outside world does not exist. I hope you will acknowledge this letter if only to make us believe that the conscience of the world is not quite dead.

While you may not be able to help us by persuading the stubborn Maharaja that we should either be tried in a court of law or released, we feel that you could at least bring to his notice the barbarous and inhuman conditions that prevail in this jail so as to relieve the agony of our detention.

On our part, in order to touch any bit of conscience that may have survived in the ruler, we are beginning today a hunger strike and we shall go on fasting till our demands begin to be considered.

Before I tell you of our demands, I want to acquaint you with some of the facts of our existence here.

The two leaders, Devi Prasad and myself, are kept in a Class I cell, which is a small black hole, continually stinking with the smell of our own urine in open pots. The heat of the Udham Pur summer chokes us, till every breath we take seems to be our last without being the last. As we move about in the congested space of nine feet by six, all our movements are watched through the strong iron bar gates, by the armed warder who is always parading up and down.

All the other detenues, about twelve, are now being kept in a Class III dormitory, which is thirty foot by ten. Here they are huddled together, and, as there is no lavatory in this dormitory they have to relieve themselves at night in one corner, which has caused all of them to go down one by one with malaria, hookworm, anaemia and TB.

As none of us are given any bedding or blankets to spread on the cement platform on which we have to sleep, two détenues died of pneumonia last winter, while one succumbed to colic, and the rest complain of rheumatism.

The jail doctor seldom visited us till one of the sick détenues assaulted the jailor and threatened to kill him if he was not given medical attention. And though this détenu died, the jail doctor began to visit our cells once a week.

We have to cook food in turns. Each of us gets a quarter of a seer of rice per day and we have all become skeletons of ourselves. We eat out of iron pots, which lie about in the cells after the meal is finished, so that flies fester round us all day.

As the kitchen is about ten yards away, the smoke of wood fuel spreads to our cells in the evening, and, through the absence of a drain, the kitchen water flows into the small courtyard before us, seeping ultimately into the open well about twenty-five yards away, over which there is the continual drone of mosquitoes, our deadliest enemies.

The concentration camps of the Nazis may have been worse, but this jail of ours certainly is not better than the Lahore and the Delhi forts, where the British tortured the détenues during the war. And, from the proportion of people who die here, this jail compares with the notorious Newgate and Dartmoor jails of the 18th century, in England.

Day and night our necks, hands and feet remain fettered with heavy iron chains, even while we cook or work, until the flesh of some of us is bruised and full of pus.

No books, no papers, or writing material, is given to us. I am writing this letter on paper which the convict warder stole out of the jail office for the bribe I gave him of the silver ring I had smuggled in.

In the evenings we are made to hold compulsory prayers, during which we are made to chant – 'Maharaja Sahib ki jai!' 'Sham Pur Raj ki jai!'

The jailor has established a fifth column among convicts, which informs him against any other prisoner who does not get his relatives to pay a bribe, that is shared between the jailor and the convict warders. And the whole hierarchy of officials and warders resembles the big flies who suck the blood of the little flies, with the little flies encroaching on the littler flies, until men begin to lose all faith in each other.

In view of all this, I want to put forward before you the following concrete demands which I would like you to put before the Maharaja for speedy action. Only if these demands are conceded are we willing to break our fast.

1. All prisoners detained without trial should either be tried in an open court or immediately released unconditionally.

2. The classification of détenues should be abolished, and the same food, clothing and medical treatment should be given to all.

3. All détenues must be given access to books and newspapers.

4. All détenues should be given adequate family allowances by the State.

5. An inquiry committee should be set up to look into the jails and improve conditions in these Belsens and Buchenwalds, so that the light of humanity and justice might prevail.

Yours faithfully,

Som Nath.

I contemplated this letter in a state of perturbation which can only be described as utter confusion. For, the appeal of the note to my conscience was immediate, even as the threat of the guerilla who had accosted me at Panna Lodge had been immediate. And yet the invidious position which I occupied in the service of the Maharaja was pulling me in the direction of caution and restraint. From the floating lightweight, who skipped from one emotion of the Maharaja to the other, I suddenly felt I had become a massive weight of misery, overburdened with the sense of guilt at my ineffectual life, while these fighters were fasting and sacrificing themselves for their ideals. I felt the shadows thickening over my eyes, my blood pulsed darkly as if it was mounting to my head in a fury from the welter in my soul. Again and again, I tried to fix the central theme of the détenues' demands and the core of the whole problem of Sham Pur before me. But, apart from the gleams of half-truths and certain aspects of the whole, there was only a vacancy in my mind. I could not think consistently. I could only feel the vague cloud of fear hover over me about having to take a radical decision. And yet the very sources of my being, where I could take any decisions, were corroded by the sloth that I felt in the face of life.

At last I tried to make the effort to get back to the essential things about myself, and to begin to think anew. Though the thoughts I thought were not uttered, I was really talking aloud to myself in a colloquy which went somewhat like this:

'Who are you?'

'I am a man. That is to say, I have the gift of reason and speech and can choose and select what to do. I have free will and am not enslaved or subject to anything.'

'But you are talking of an ideal man. Actually, you are enslaved and have little free will. Of course, you have reason and, through that, you are distinguished from the beasts and cattle. And you are a citizen with certain rights and responsibilities.'

'Yes, there is the rub. I am capable of considering the connections of things and can comprehend some aspects of the universe, but I am limited. And yet my hands and feet can't move except in the interests of the whole of my body. I can't really live without considering all the claims the world has on me.'

'But, most of the time, your hands and feet do move without considering the whole of your body. And your body is seldom in the control of your mind. And the mind never wholly aware. So that though the whole may be superior to the parts, in fact you act from partial knowledge and unascertained motives. And usually you do things which are more immediately agreeable, whatever the misery that may come afterwards.'

'Then I fall short of the ideal man?'

'Yes, indeed, you fail to live up to the ideal all the time.'

'Then there is really no difference between me and cattle, who chew the cud of complacency and pursue the pleasures of resting in the slimy mud?'

'That is inevitable.'

'And do you think that by yielding lazily to the pleasures of the moment, or the immediate future, that is to say, by not considering what might happen to other people in the world through your sloth, you do not lose anything?'

'I only become slightly insidious, hiding my faults cleverly, behind the facade of my vanity, and get along fairly well because most other people are doing the same.'

'So you make no effort to fight the demons in you. If you were a student and did not work to improve your knowledge of a certain science you would fail in the examination, wouldn't you? Would you rather fail or would you try to remove your ignorance and come through the test?'

'I am not sure whether it is worthwhile to get to know things and pass exams and become aware. Where does it get you, if other people remain ignorant and stupid?'

'What would you feel like if you lost your job and had no money?

'I would be miserable if I were destitute.'

'Then you don't feel miserable and destitute if you lose your self-respect, your honour, decency and gentleness? Does not the debauchee lose his manhood? Does not a coward lose something essential of himself?'

'If you put it so bluntly, then I must confess that I have already lost my self-respect by my continued association with the Maharaja.'

'And what are you going to do about repairing the damage?'

'Well, I am aware of the differences between myself and Victor.'

'Then you must discover what these differences are and thrash them out with him and either change him or leave him.'

'What about the conflicts in him? As a doctor I have to understand him and not to judge him.'

'From understanding, certain values can be born. He can't escape responsibility merely because he is ill. Other people who are also ill with hunger are involved.'

'Acha, I will try and evolve some such understanding as may serve like a balance for weighing up matters, some test for distinguishing between what is straight and crooked.'

'If you do so then already you have begun to think. You have become a philosopher. And you may thus be able to decide on a way of life....'

Before this colloquy was finished, I had a message from Victor, through Munshi Mithan Lal, to ask me why I was so late in attending on him that morning, and would I come over to discuss arrangements for the hunt. I told Mian Mithu I would be along presently. There went my decision: I did not even have the opportunity to think for myself in this capricious atmosphere where I was on duty all the twenty-four hours.

The sun was already fairly high in the heavens when I walked up to Victor's rooms. And there was that extraordinary silence which sometimes comes on the Indian scene before noon in the hot weather. Only a few sparrows shrilled across the lawn in the courtyard, and a crow alighted from the dome above the deohri, caw-cawing for food, but was shooed away in mid-air by the chaprasi in the hall. And then the silence, the awe-inspiring silence, which had always been deliberately built up in and around the palace to supply the aura of grandeur, reverence and unreachability, added itself like a weight of oppression on to the quiet of the garden.

I had been asking myself how, exactly, I could communicate the inner thoughts which arose in me after reading the détenu's letter. I realized, as I drew nearer Victor's rooms, that I could only feel a certain remorse for my weakness. And yet I felt calm in the heart of the storm, detached as though I was standing on an island, looking on at the violent battle of wills and bodies that was going on in Sham Pur, with all the enemies of His Highness ranged around this palace, as it were, together in their minimum aim to bring him to heel, but separated by ideological conflicts from each other. Victor was nearly drowning in the well of his own loneliness, seeking desperately to keep afloat and clutching at any straw, but an indifferent swimmer, and doomed to go down to the bottom, to come up again as a corpse, of which the ashes would later be suitably cremated and adorned with a tombstone, as the remains of the last Maharaja of Sham Pur. I knew that he too surmised that he was heading for disaster, in fleeting glimpses of the shape of things to come, but that he hoped that his cleverness might help him to survive.

As against the depression from which I suffered, Victor's mood was extremely buoyant that morning.

'Hallo, you misanthrope!' he said to me as I entered. 'Now what is troubling you?'

I smiled sheepishly and stood by Munshi Mithan Lal, who was poised before His Highness with joined hands.

'Mian Mithu is another one of the same kidney,' Victor continued.

'Please forgive me, Maharaj,' Munshiji said abjectly, 'I have erred.'

Meanwhile, Mr Bool Chand sat in an armchair, with an inanely gleeful smile on his face, witnessing the humiliation of Munshi Mithan Lal.

I could not guess what could have happened to bring Munshiji into such disfavour. But while I was pondering on this, Mr Bool Chand snorted, according to that ugly habit of his which he could not overcome, and His Highness turned on him.

'I think you are a bigger ass than Mian Mithu himself, a real ugly ass, the way you snort!'

'To what do we owe this excess of good humour?' I dared to ask.

'Ah,' he said, 'all of you are such dunces that you can only see the dark side of life! And none of you know the ecstasy of union....'

'Han, han, I understand now,' I said, significantly cocking my head to one side. 'But why this displeasure with poor Munshiji?'

'The fellow keeps a most important telegram from the American Embassy in his pocket for two days and doesn't even tell me about it until I ask him!'

Victor said this working up a mock anger.

'But, Maharaj, you were in the...zenana,' Munshi Mithan Lal whined.

'You are like an uncle to me and the Queen Bee,' Victor answered. 'Oldie, why didn't you come in?'

'Is the telegram very urgent?' I asked.

'All telegrams are by their very nature urgent!' Victor answered.

'That is true,' I agreed, humbly accepting my defeat. 'And they tend to make one angry,' I added in order to get my own back.

'Sometimes they make one glad,' he said quick-wittedly.

'And what is the glad news in this telegram?' I asked.

'Mr Peter Watkins of the American Embassy in Delhi is coming down to hunt tomorrow with a party.'

'Is he the Ambassador?' I asked.

'Nearly the Ambassador,' Victor said. 'He is an important secretary. Actually more important than the Ambassador, because the real power is always in the hands of the underlings.'

'Your Highness,' said Bool Chand, 'we should really have asked some people from the Home Department for the hunt. What use are these Americans?'

'Fool!' said Victor. 'You don't know anything about statecraft. The Americans are the coming power in India. And if they back my claim for an independent buffer state of Sham Pur, then I will have some more cards up my sleeve to play against the Home Department.'

'The Americans are certainly the coming power in India,' repeated Munshiji.

'Han, han,' agreed Bool Chand weakly, because, from the blank look on his face, the subtlety of the stratagem had really not quite dawned on him.

'Don't you see, idiot, that Sham Pur is so placed strategically that an aeroplane flying at a sufficiently high altitude can reach Samarkand in seven hours!'

'I understand, I understand now, your Highness,' said Bool Chand enthusiastically.

'But Mian Mithu can only mechanically repeat my words,' rebuked Victor. 'He did not understand how important this wire was.'

'Highness, you were inclined to plump for the Communists yesterday,' I said. 'After your quarrel with your uncles.'

'You are also thick-headed!' said Victor. 'You people have learnt nothing from the British. But my Principal at the Chief's College taught me that the safest and surest rule in diplomacy is an ambiguous foreign policy. You always apply two lines and see which one will win!' I tried to wear an air of casual indifference.

'Acha, now go and get the arrangements ready, Mr Mian Mithu,' ordered Victor. 'We will not go in the direction of the Panna hunting lodge where the guerillas are, but go twenty miles to the north, to the Dharam Pur Lodge. Lalla Chottu Ram knows all that is to be done. Only, I suppose, there will be some European ladies in the party and Maharani Ganga Dasi. So we must send all the cars from the Sham Pur palace garages there immediately. Bool Chand, you help Mian Mithu and ask Captain Partap Singh to exert himself also. You will all be rewarded if the hunt is successful. Doctor Sahib, I want you to come and see the Queen Bee. She is feeling slightly out of sorts. And I want her to be well enough to come to the hunt tomorrow.'

We headed towards the courtyard which led to the inner sanctums of the zenana, but we had hardly traversed the veranda when we saw Gangi approaching.

'But you must not strain yourself, childling,' Victor scolded her. 'We were coming to see you.'

'I was lonely and couldn't stay up there,' Gangi said in a petulant child's voice. 'I wanted you near me.' And, with a charming blandishment, she coyly drew the end of her apron on to her forehead and advanced towards Vicky's drawing room. We followed her.

As we entered the room, Gangi walked briskly with a deliberately exaggerated swaying of her buttocks and went and sat cross-legged on the ample settee.

'Listen, listen, boys,' she said. 'I have something to tell you. I have a hunch we can trap the new Diwan....'

'What makes you say that?' Victor asked.

'I feel I could make him dance on my palm, if I liked,' Gangi said. 'You will see what I can do to him if you ask him to the hunt.'

A sudden pallor came on Victor's face as he listened to these words. Then he hung his head down. It seemed to me that he had sensed that there might be something between her and Popatlal J. Shah.

Myself, I was certain that she was already having an affair with the Diwan.

'He seems to be a bore,' Victor said. 'And I am not sure that he will want to come to the hunt.'

'He may be old, but he seems to be impressionable,' said Gangi. 'And you may be able to get more out of him than out of those American idlers!'

'In terms of sheer diplomacy you are right,' said Victor. 'But...'

He did not complete his sentence. She was laughing with her eyes, blind to him, and full of the power that she had acquired over Popatlal J. Shah, which, in turn, would help her to increase her hold upon Victor. She was radiant as she sat there, amused at the cleverness with which she could manipulate the lives of men.

With a swift, desperate impulse to possess her soul and body, to get confirmation of his hold on her, he went and clasped her hand, saying boisterously: 'We shall have fun at the party, but you must get well and come.'

And he stroked her hand with a soft, insidious movement, seeking to intoxicate her sensuality with the tender caresses of his own body.

In the tentative gestures of affection between them, I was conscious of the strange sense of dramatized sentimentality that seemed to characterize their mixings.

I wanted to withdraw and leave them, so that Victor could extend his grasp over her elusive mind and body and wean her away from where, I was sure, she had been straying for the last few days.

I walked up to the window and stood gazing emptily at the garden, a gossamer film between my eyes and the outside world, while my inner vision turned terrified on the resolve I had made to tell Victor about the grievances of the détenues. I felt frustrated and impatient in the face of the superficial, elegant and polished atmosphere of statecraft which I always had to experience even when I wanted to do or say something serious. A violent hatred surged up in me against Gangi, who seemed to me to be the cause of much of the putrescence of the court. In everything she did, whether she laughed or cried, she was instinctively manoeuvring and intriguing to acquire greater power. Even now she was obviously playing a game, yielding to Victor, accepting his caresses, when she had only betrayed him yesterday and would betray him again and again. She was pitilessly involved with herself, and would draw him on, only so far and no further than it suited her. And then she would thrust him away. I stood motionless, timeless, like a skeleton, harrowed by the subtle tension of a half-dead, sick body. 'Shall we go and have a look at the stable, Hari?' Victor said. I turned and nodded assent.

'Oh, Vicky, don't leave me alone,' Gangi whined in a maudlin voice. 'Stay with me, will you?'

'I shall just go and come back, Jan,' Victor said. 'I will be back in half an hour only.'

'Acha, I will go to sleep here for a while,' Gangi said, shuffling sulkily and averting her face from him.

'All right, you go and order Chottu Ram to speed up the preparations,' said Victor, turning to me. 'The hunting lodge at Dharam Pur must be got ready and all arrangements made to take the guests there direct from the station. We shall go by motorboat upriver and join them there tomorrow evening.' And he sat down by his mistress.

The hunting lodge of Dharam Pur was accessible both by road and by the river Sutlej. And while the Americans had been taken by the land route, His Highness decided to take the party by motorboat.

After about an hour's steady run upriver, through fields, we began to enter the jungle.

Like a sharp sword the boat tore its passage against the current of the Sutlej. The foliage became dense as soon as we left the main river and went up the tributary stream, so that, though the afternoon sun had been omnipresent when we left Sham Pur, we seemed already to have entered the twilight. And, with this gloom, we also seemed to feel a kind of dementia overtake us, a kind of craziness produced by the suffocating heat, by the heavy smell of the trees and bushes, and by the eerie expectancy which the atmosphere produced. And yet, even though we felt oppressed as we gnawed our way into the heart of the jungle, we were also fascinated and drawn by the thickening, clammy vegetation. And while the light filtered, a greenish blue, through the dense bushes and the interlaced boughs, we contemplated the water hyacinths and the deathly yellow sponge-like bells which hung down from the trees.

While Victor was at the wheel of the motorboat, Srijut Popatlal J. Shah had been sitting, set and impassive, in his chair, in the cabin of the launch, and Gangi lay felinely curled up on a small settee. Munshi Mithan Lal, Mr Bool Chand, myself and the various attendants were lounging about on the boat.

'There is something in the souls of men which draws them back to the jungle,' Mr Popatlal J. Shah said pompously after he had been contemplating the dark forest for a long time.

Gangi was half asleep and oblivious of everything outside her, so long as she held the souls and the bodies of the men she wanted securely in her hands.

'Why is it that the jungle draws one?' Victor asked with a bored cynicism in his voice.

'Perhaps because life is elemental here,' answered Popatlal. 'Everything in the jungle preys upon everything else and the survivor is not always the strongest, bravest and the most godly.'

'I think that is so not only in the jungle but also in the whole kingdom of Sham Pur,' I said from the bitterness which had been welling up in me since I had received the letter from the jail.

The remark was greeted with silence, because whether Popatlal's generalization about the forest was true or not, certainly it was true about Sham Pur State.

'The jungle is a good escape,' said Bool Chand, trying to be smart. 'If one's feet have pounded for a few years on the hard safe pavements of civilization.'

'I hate it,' burst out Victor. 'It frightens me. I feel there is something sinister in the air. It is choking me....'

I realized that, under the effect of the dark suffocation around him, the inner discord in the Maharaja's soul, due to his suspicions about Gangi and Popatlal, had fermented into a kind of hysteria.

'I will take the wheel if you like,' I said.

'No, I am all right,' said Victor with gritted teeth.

'Whatever you may say,' began Popatlal again, his dark face glowing with the sense of power that arose in him not only from his position as Diwan but from being Gangi's paramour, 'man has to be eternally on guard here against things he seldom sees, for fear that when he sees them it will be too late.'

'So has man to be vigilant in Sham Pur,' I said.

'To be sure!' said Victor.

'Diwan Sahib means snakes and pythons and tigers and insects,' said Mr Bool Chand brightly.

'I mean the same thing!' I said, emphasizing the ambiguity in my previous observations, though I could see that the emphasis fell flat on Bool Chand.

Srijut Popatlal J. Shah continued, however, as though having understood the oblique reference, he was now trying deliberately to camouflage the actual situation by mere rhetoric.

'Can you hear the hum of the jungle? The forest is never quiet. It pulses with myriads of lives. The earth and vegetation are full of living creatures. Things climb and creep and crawl. The bigger insects eat the smaller ones. Treachery always wins.'

'And guile, Diwan Sahib,' I added. 'I have seen the lovely full-blown death-lotus trap a humming bird's beak in its sticky heart and slowly close its tender petals round the fluttering body of its victim.'

The parallel was not lost on the Diwan and he looked at me with bated breath, and even Gangi half-opened her eyes and, sweeping us all with a sleepy glance, said: 'The butterflies alone are happy.'

'Yet I have seen a jaguar smack a butterfly in a fit of sheer wantonness and crush its lovely wings beneath its paws,' I said. 'So not even butterflies are safe!'

'Everything has its enemy,' said Bool Chand, butting in again. And he snorted.

'Certainly you are our public enemy number one!' exclaimed Victor.

And everyone smiled. And the situation was eased. All the talk we had been having seemed like empty sound in the face of the sheer insidious beauty of the jungle, the secret exhilaration that seemed to arise from the eerie glow of the sunset, which was spreading itself over the placid mirror of the greenish, black water, lit up here and there by the fading lances of the dying sun.

After a few long, seemingly endless miles, the stream opened out into a lake, and the creepers and water hyacinths gave place to lotuses, which were folding on the placid waters on the approach of the night from the steep mountains that rose to the north.

As we veered towards the left of the lake, little thatched huts became visible at the foot of the biggest pine-clad mountain and some tracks leading to a magnificent pagoda-style building which was obviously the hunting lodge.

Some village women were filling their pitchers with water on the edge of the lake, but fled as soon as they saw the motorboat approach, ostensibly because Victor's reputation as a seducer had not been forgotten here since the days of his teens, when he used to demand any woman who came within the orbit of his lustful vision.

But an old liveried chaprasi, apparently the caretaker of the lodge, showed up and began to do obeisance to us with joined hands as though worshipping his gods.

Vicky shut off the engine and steered the launch towards the small wooden pier which had been built specially for the Maharaja and was profusely covered with barnacles and moss.

We all alighted and were soon surrounded by a crowd of supplicating men and boys.

'Get away, get away!' shouted Munshi Mithan Lal. 'Where is the palanquin for the Maharani Sahiba? And where are the horses?'

The greeting population scattered with abject smiles and the palanquin and the horses became visible.

We male folk walked away behind Vicky towards the horses, while the palanquin was taken up to the launch under the charge of Munshi Mithan Lal. A cursory glance revealed the miserable condition of humanity in the narrow, confined little thatched cottages, as skeleton after skeleton showed up and salaamed. We ascended our horses and made off towards the bridle path behind the red-liveried watchman.

The bridle path was the roughest track, and in order to afford easier passage for our entourage, the forced labourers from the village had cleared the undergrowth for two or three yards on either side by burning the bush. The acrid reek of the still smouldering shrubs made for a certain amount of haste in our climb, and this haste was made dangerous by the high-spiritedness of the Maharaja, who touched off the black horse on which I was riding, and the white mare on which sat Srijut Popatlal Shah, with his cane. Both the beasts bolted with a suddenness that was nearly fatal for me, though the Diwan's weight saved him. My head whirled as the straps fell out of my hands and the coolies on the track scattered hither and thither, and I thought I was done for. Fortunately, a daring villager ran up alongside my horse and, trampling barefoot through the burning bushes, brought my mount to a standstill.

I was dishevelled and indignant. And as I looked back I saw that Popatlal was red in the face.

But just at that moment Victor had set off the pony on which Munshi Mithan Lal was riding with the same trick with which he had started us off, and as poor Mian Mithu swayed and struggled to control his pony, he looked so ridiculous a sight with his heavy torso that everyone laughed. Fortunately, the pony was not mischievous and Munshiji could control it.

The hunting lodge stood on the promontory of a hill in the foreground of higher mountains. Our eyes were refreshed when we ascended the track high enough to see the beautiful contours of the lodge in front of us and the silver-grey lake below us, with patches of rice fields on the wooded plateau on the sides, over which vapours of mist and smoke seemed to hang like pendants in fantastic shapes. In the far distance, the long-drawn cry of a peasant could be heard, frightening the birds over his field, but for the rest the landscape was empty save for the cattle which browsed in the swamps in the valley.

Victor cantered up the drive to the Dharam Pur Lodge like an eager boy and we entered behind him into the compound, from where arose a loud 'hurray' from the

American guests, under the charge of our stalwart Captain Partap Singh.

'I am Peter Watkins from the American Embassy, your Highness,' said a stocky man of about forty-five with a Charlie Chaplin moustache and pop-eyes, dressed in jodhpurs.

And he came forward and shook hands with Victor most cordially, with American informality. Then he proceeded to introduce his compatriots.

'This is Mr Homer Lane of our Embassy, and Mrs Lane, a Norwegian, as you can see from her blonde hair. And Mr Kurt Landauer, journalist. You know Major Bell from the British High Commissioner's office and Mrs Bell....'

His Highness bowed to each of the guests with truly regal grace. And then he began to introduce us all: 'Mr Popatlal Shah, the respected Prime Minister', as he put it; 'Mr Bool Chand, who snorts like a horse'; 'Munshi Mithan Lal, alias Mian Mithu, who repeats everything you say'; 'Dr Shankar, the brown-skinned Englishman'; 'my ADC, Captain Partap Singh, the Herculean giant, who often wrestles with Choudhri Chottu Ram, here, the chamberlain of the palace'.

The slight touch of humour was appreciated and there was exaggeratedly servile laughter on the part of the American democrats, who felt flattered to be talked to so informally by royalty. But amusement gave place to a certain amount of confusion when the palanquin, in which Gangi was being borne, showed up and His Highness, pointing towards it, said, 'Her Highness the Maharani Sahiba!' The two white ladies fluttered visibly and the gentlemen wondered whether to bow to the shroud-like phenomenon, join hands *à la indienne*, or shake hands if the Maharani should emerge. However, they were spared the embarrassment, because the palanquin was borne straight into the lodge.

And Victor led the way towards the veranda, saying to his guests: 'You must be longing for a drink! I know I am.'

Mr Watkins advanced jauntily abreast of His Highness. Mr and Mrs Homer Lane followed, Mr Lane limping with a slight Goebbels-like club foot. Mr Kurt Landauer, a bright moon-faced young man with auburn hair, palled up with me. And Mr Bool Chand made a trio with the short-statured but very cocksure Major Bell and the tall, flat-chested Mrs Bell, while Munshi Mithan Lal brought up the train with Captain Partap Singh and Choudhri Chottu Ram.

By the time we got to the veranda, Gangi had alighted from her palanquin and stood with inimitable grace and charm in the Punjabi kurta and salwar in which she had travelled, the dupatta drawn with a peculiar twist over her head, so that she seemed a demure young woman, the very opposite of the harlot that she really was.

The Americans were all taken in by this vision of loveliness and joined hands, even as she lifted her hands to greet them.

An extra hustle became noticeable at the appearance of the lady. And Captain Partap Singh, Choudhri Chottu Ram and Munshi Mithan Lal nearly knocked into each other as they raced towards the veranda to hurry Bhagirath, the bearer, with the champagne. This worthy was, however, already agog as he wiped the tumblers clean and placed them in order on the large table in the veranda.

The impact of the mysterious East, in the form of Gangi, on the inquisitive West was soon drowned in the froth of the lovely French champagne of 1905. And the address 'Dear Maharaja Sahib' and 'Dear Maharani Sahiba' punctuated the bonhomie that was sought to be worked up for the occasion.

After drinks the guests wandered on to the lawns of the lodge in twos and threes, while the villagers, particularly the shrivelled up old men, the large-stomached, naked little children and the wiry shikaris, gathered together on the fringes of the garden, admiring the exalted guests and nursing various hopes in their hearts for bounteous gifts of bakhshish.

But the art of getting bakhshish is not known to the hillmen of Sham Pur. They only know the art of doing forced labour, whether this is in their own fields, for the benefit of the local landlord, or for His Highness the Maharaja Sahib when he comes to hunt or when any of his minions are passing their way. This art of extorting money from the rich is an accomplishment which people only learn in the towns. And, lo and behold, I saw one of the jugglers of Sham Pur arriving at the gate, revolving his hand drum in his hand, and dragging a couple of bears and a couple of monkeys on the leads held in his left hand, with his son, the apprentice to madarihood, following close behind. The juggler had a shrewd instinct. He knew that the local population, who had seen the show often, were not interested in his antics, apart, of course, from the fact that children are perennially fascinated by all jugglers. But the white sahibs are a race apart, because they are always looking for the real India. And the madari, with all his mysterious mumbo-jumbo and tricks, somehow conduces to the feeling in the foreign spectators that they are, indeed, in touch with the very essence of the mysterious East when they see his tricks.

So the sahibs and memsahibs gathered round in the waning light and His Highness rudely ordered the madari to do a few tricks, 'but only a few tricks!' The servants brought chairs for the exalted. And, with the low hedge bordering the lawn to separate the exalted audience from the lowly performers, and the lowlier villagers and shikaris, the show began.

Girding his loins, rolling up his sleeves, and with a terrific aplomb, the madari began, to the tune of his hand drum, to celebrate first the wedding of the he-bear and the she-bear. The animals were both made to sit respectably on two small drums away from each other. The bride was shy and covered her face with her paw, according to the musical instructions of the madari.

'Come come,' he intoned, 'come and accept your mate according to the Hindu rites. Come and meet your lord and remain for ever his wife. Do not go away. Pass your lives together happy in your home and children!...The God Indra is pleased to bestow you on this stalwart man! May you have twenty children!'

The bride got up and shyly went towards the bridegroom, and there were wild guffaws of laughter, distinguished by a gurgle in the throat of Gangi, which showed her extraordinary interest in the formula.

'And now,' continued the madari, 'come come, ohe ladhia, ohe ladhia! Come, take the right hand of your bride and give her a pledge for your happiness together!'

The bear advanced gallantly and took the hand of his bride.

'Tell her,' goaded the madari, 'tell her, tell her, "I wish you to become my wife and to grow old with me." Tell her, tell her, "The God Indra has given thee to me to rule over our house together." Tell her, "May the lord of creation, Brahma, give us many children!"'

The bear grunted and growled to order, causing considerable mirth among the village children.

'Tell her, then, ohe ladhia, ask her, "Come, my desired one, beautiful one, with the tender heart and charming looks, come to your husband and bring forth heroes."'

The bear grunted and growled more loudly and, holding her hand, stood looking at the she-bear tenderly.

'Now then show us how you dance, ohe ladhia!' the madari directed. 'Show the sahibs your skill as the favourite son of God Indra.'

At this the bear led the she-bear into an ecstatic dance, a kind of jumping movement, in which the newly-wedded couple thumped the earth and swirled clumsily around in no rhythm at all, the very caricature of this graceful art.

The guests were highly amused, the ladies shrieking, especially when at the suggestion of the madari that he should 'play the part of Gary Cooper against Greta Garbo', the bear embraced the she-bear and kissed her snout.

'Is that really how Hindu weddings are performed, Maharaja Sahib?' asked Mr Peter Watkins.

'Actually,' said Diwan Popatlal J. Shah, 'the juggler was pronouncing the exact ancient vedic invocations which are uttered at the celebration of the marriage.'

'Yes, yes,' said His Highness. 'This juggler is a badmash. He knows a thing or two.'

'Now, Maharaj,' said the juggler, 'shall I celebrate the wedding of the monkeys?'

'No, no,' ordered Captain Partap Singh, 'one wedding is enough for an evening. Do something else!'

Reciting some more mumbo-jumbo, spitting on his hands and rubbing his palms, the madari called his son and got ready to do the basket trick.

The boy was put into the basket and the lid was put on top and daggers thrust into the basket from all sides and right through the lid. But when the lid was lifted and the basket tilted there was nothing in it. With a big dramatized howl of surprise, the juggler invoked the spirit of the boy to emerge from paradise. And lo! the body which incarnated that extraordinary spirit was discovered among the village children, unscathed and complete and without any wounds.

The white sahibs, who had been dazed with horror at the dagger thrusts, and the memsahibs who had shrieked, were relieved that the murder proved to be no murder! And they were all willing to pay handsome bakhshish to the juggler.

But it was against the laws of hospitality that the guests should have to pay for anything. So His Highness ordered Captain Partap Singh to tell the juggler to stay on in the village and be in attendance throughout the hunt, and assure him that he would be suitably rewarded.

When the show ended quite a little of the ice which stood between the exalted and the lowly had melted, if not quite broken. And the shikaris shifted on their haunches, near enough to the hedges to be within speaking distance of the sahibs.

The chief shikari, a middle-aged man, named Buta, came up to where I was standing, by His Highness and Mr Peter Watkins, and whispered furtively: 'Huzoor, there is a panther in these parts. It has been causing terror to the cultivators in the village. It takes away cattle in broad daylight.'

'And you pretend to be a shikari!' Vicky mocked at him. 'Why haven't you killed it already?'

'Maharaj, it is a difficult prey,' the man answered, 'one of the most difficult beasts I have heard of in my whole life as a shikari!'

Apparently, Buta was putting up his price for negotiating the hunt.

'The Tehsildar Sahib organized a big hunting party,' continued Buta. 'Only he did not ask me to accompany him. And when the Tehsildar Sahib and the men approached the garden, armed with guns, lathis and daggers, the ferocious panther fell upon one of the beaters, who insulted it by pointing his finger at it. So the panther almost mauled him to death. The Tehsildar Sahib and his men fled, leaving the beater there, and I had to go and rescue him, though I only succeeded in dragging his dead body back.'

'You are a very brave man!' said Vicky half ironically.

'But listen, Maharaj, the exploits of this panther did not end with killing his beater. It chased another man who was working in his paddy field. And it inflicted serious injuries on him and then fled to the hills, because the two villagers raised an alarm! On hearing all this, I decided to do something. I strolled up to the bluff of that hill there, with my "muzz gun", as you Sahibs call it. After a little prowl, I got to the spot where the villager had been attacked. The beast came to the scene of its triumph of the evening. I met it face to face. I stared at it and it seemed to bend its eyes down with shame at its follies. Then it growled defiantly at me. I said to it, "Now you have met your uncle!" The panther seemed confused and did not know what to do. Like a bad nephew, who protests when he is reprimanded for being mischievous, it rushed towards me. I fired the only shot that was in my gun. The bullet was true. It passed through its neck and entered its back and finished it for ever. I will present the Amrikan Sahib with the head and the skin, and he can take it home and say he shot it. I don't mind, Huzoor. To me a little cash is more valuable than a lot of prestige!'

Victor and I burst out laughing at the extraordinary cynicism of Buta, while Peter Watkins, not knowing that the joke was on him, asked us what the shikari had said, which made us laugh the more, until I concocted an explanation:

'He says he will do anything for money.'

'Now,' said Buta, 'there is another panther, the father of this beast I shot, which wants to revenge itself on me for killing its son. I think it lives in a cave in the hill above this palace. Tell the Amrikan Sahib that I will help him to collect another head and skin which he can claim more genuinely to be his kill than the previous one I was talking about. In fact, every Amrikan Sahib can have a beast.'

'At a price!' I said.

'How wise you are, Dakdar Sahib,' answered Buta. 'To be sure, in famine times even brackish water is sweet. And, nowadays, with rising prices, there is, indeed, a price for everything.'

Mr Peter Watkins, who had heard two or three references to the Amrikan Sahibs, was naturally curious.

'He is a bounder,' Victor said. 'An amusing rogue! But he knows his job.'

'He says,' I interpreted, 'that there is a panther on the prowl just above this lodge.'

'What are we waiting for then?' said Mr Watkins impetuously.

'There is a little intricate ritual which has to be gone through before a hunt,' I said. This gentleman here will insist upon it.'

'Maharaj, if it is your will,' said Buta, 'then I can get a goat tied to the post by the machan.'

'Apparently, great minds tally,' I said.

The American looked incomprehensibly at me.

'Of course,' said His Highness. 'What is the use of a vagabond like you? Go and get all the bandobast done.'

'I am for the hunt immediately,' said Peter Watkins, offering further proof of the fact that great minds tally. 'I know,' he continued, 'the boys are itching to get at this panther.'

'Won't the ladies be tired after the journey?' I asked.

'This is a man's sport,' said Peter Watkins with the bravado that oozed from his pugilistic frame. 'They can come and look at the moon for a while and then go to sleep.'

'The moon can do things to people,' I said.

'Oh, well, we are here for a good time,' said Mr Watkins. 'Aren't we?'

'Well then, it will be done exactly as you wish,' said His Highness. And he turned to Buta in the colloquial hillman's speech in which each sentence seems to become more intimate if accompanied by a little spicy abuse. 'Rape-mother, get along and see that the Amrikan Sahib bags the panther tonight.'

'Maharaj,' said Buta, falling with joined hands at His Highness's feet. 'Not only the white-leather ones but Huzoor and Huzoor's servants will have something to take home as a souvenir of this shikar.'

'Never mind us, you look after this Sahib,' His Highness repeated, and turning aside to me remarked: 'I want him to believe that he has a strong arm. His arm is going to be useful to me.'

'To be sure, I understand,' Buta said. And he ran fleet-footedly on his wiry legs towards the machan in the jungle.

As we turned towards the lawn, the guests were strolling about and already the disposition of forces was fairly obvious: Mr and Mrs Bell were walking up and down, arm in arm, as only an English couple can do with their tremendous athletic energy. Mr Homer Lane had settled down to a whisky-and-soda and was holding Mrs Lane's hand almost as though he was frightened to lose her. Srijut Popatlal J. Shah and Mr Landauer were walking up and down with Gangi between them, both trying to talk cleverly in order to hold her attention, forgetting that she only understood basic English. This was a game in which, I knew, the Diwan would be the loser, because he was essentially a bore and would take conversation towards metaphysics and big words, whereas Kurt's young, sleek presence in itself fascinated Gangi, particularly because she was a brunette and he was a blonde and the polarity of opposites presented a challenge. Mr Bool Chand seemed rather tense as he watched this trio from where he sat with Mian Mithu waiting for His Highness's orders.

'We get ready to go to hunt this very night, boys and girls,' announced Mr Watkins with much gusto.

'Oh hurra!' shouted Kurt, running up to us.

But his was the only enthusiastic response. The rest looked askance at the leader of the hunt in the manner in which one looks at a too energetic master-of-ceremonies on board a ship.

After we had had a hurried meal out of tins which the Americans had brought as their contribution to the house party, both out of consideration for His Highness in the days of food shortage and also to avoid having to eat hot curries, we got ready to go to the hunt.

The flowers around the lawns of the palace sent up exhalations of perfume as the evening thickened into night, the rich scent of the 'Queen of the Night' rising to a crescendo of triumph above the more discreet airs. And the trees stirred with a cool breeze that came from the slightly tempestous lake. And I wished that I was resting with my own thoughts and going to bed early rather than rushing out to the machan for a possible all-night wait for the panther to show up.

But Buta came to collect us and we trooped up behind him, by the light of primitive torches carried by the villagers turned shikaris.

Up the mountainside we went, under the canopy of trees which blotted out the stars, and across a narrow track bordered by wild scrub, pomegranate bushes, cactus and headier, until we got to the scene of operations, the machan, about a quarter of a mile away from the lodge.

The machan was a forty-foot-high structure made of bamboo poles, hollow at the base, with a shooting-box on top, which was open on all sides and from which the hunters could shoot down on the beast below without any danger of retaliation from the hunted prey. The beast was drawn towards the machan by tying a live goat in the middle of a clearing below the shooting-box. The hunters ascended the box by means of a rather precarious bamboo ladder.

Naturally, the ascent to the box caused a lot of amusement and concern to the guests, the ladies shrieking as they went up the dizzy heights, step by anxious step, while the gentlemen laughed and tried chivalrously to help the fair sex towards the box.

The panther must have heard the guffaws of laughter and the hysterics and, therefore, refused to oblige by coming along to offer more joy at his expense. So we sat in the shooting-box on hard, uncomfortable chairs, or stood about, waiting for the beast to appear, and tense because Buta, the shikari, had enjoined strict silence if we were to draw the panther on.

A half moon was shining in one corner of the sky, and the stars seemed to be brighter than our hopes for a successful shoot, and the hum of vegetation, spasmodically interrupted by the drone of the beetles and the croaking of the frogs, all conduced to a restlessness which soon showed signs of eruption.

The ladies were the first to give evidence of this state of nerves.

Gangi had, after a few maudlin complaints, collapsed and was asleep with her head on Victor's shoulder.

'My dear, I am for bed,' drawled Mrs Homer Lane with a husky reminiscence of Greta Garbo.

'So am I, darling,' said Mr Lane. 'I am very tired and sleepy.'

'It is best to go to bed early,' put in Srijut Popatlal J. Shah, 'especially after a long journey.'

'OK, those who don't want to wait had better go,' said Mr Watkins rather gruffly.

'And not so much noise either,' said Mr Bell. 'Otherwise, it's all up with the hunt.'

'It's a shame,' said Mrs Bell, 'now the panther will never appear.'

'You can go too if you like,' Mr Bell said, turning to her rudely.

'No, no,' she protested. 'I am for staying.'

'I will conduct the party down,' said young Kurt Landauer. 'I shall lift Her Highness on my back if she is too sleepy.'

Victor turned to him, breathless and rather dazed. In a flash he knew that Gangi must have fallen for him and encouraged him during the early part of the evening, though how she could do so with her indifferent English he could not understand. But he knew that sex needed no language but the body. She was at it again, even though she had inclined, seemingly so innocently, on his shoulder until a little while ago.

'One of the shikaris can carry her,' said Srijut Popatlal J. Shah, breathing heavily with the uncontrolled jealousy of an old man losing his grip on life.

'We will look after Her Highness,' insisted Mr Bool Chand, puffing and blowing with a strange energy.

'I think after all this talk the panther will never come,' said Victor with a regal deliberation in his voice. 'I suggest that we do the easy hunt which I had ordered as a second alternative. This will be over in half an hour. Then we can all go down together.' And, without waiting for assent or dissent, he asked Captain Partap Singh to see if the cheetahs and the buck were ready.

'Ji Huzoor,' said Captain Partap Singh, and rushed down.

Orders passed from mouth to mouth and soon we could see activity down below on the clearing.

About a hundred yards away, the shikaris were leading two bullock carts, on each of which sat a cheetah, docile and well behaved like a domestic cat.

'Where is the herd of buck?' His Highness shouted, standing to his full height on the machan.

Gangi woke up with a start from her half-sleep and nearly fell from her chair. Victor did not help to steady her, and she whined: 'Oh, Vicky, I was having such a sweet sleep.'

Kurt Landauer lunged forward and held her carefully by the shoulders.

'Where is the buck, I say?' shouted His Highness.

'Maharaj, Buta has gone to round it up from the enclosure,' answered Captain Partap Singh.

'Are the cheetahs still hooded?' His Highness shouted in a voice loud enough to wake up the whole sleeping jungle.

'Yes, Maharaj,' the assistant shikaris all answered with one voice.

And they got into position to remove the stiff cowls from the eyes of the cheetahs, which were tied ready to be released at a signal from the chief shikari, who had been rounding up the buck and driving them forward.

'There is Buta coming with the herd,' Captain Partap Singh shouted to reassure His Highness as he now stood by the bullock carts, on which the cheetahs strained at their chains on smelling their prey, the buck, coming nearer.

'Silence!' ordered His Highness as he sighted the black herd of buck come calmly across the clearing. And he turned to Mr Bool Chand and whispered, 'Go, one of you, and ask Partap Singh whether the cheetahs should go off now!'

Except for Mr and Mrs Bell, the white guests did not know what was happening, but, pretending that they knew, watched the show quietly, though with eyes strained towards the clearing.

Now the cheetahs on the carts were swaying and struggling like dogs on a leash after a rabbit.

'One cheetah off!' His Highness cried impetuously without waiting for Mr Bool Chand to deliver the message to Captain Partap Singh.

At once the attendants on the carts took off the hood of one of the cheetahs. The beast spotted the herd of black buck, growled and gnashed its teeth.

'Release him, son of a swine!' ordered His Highness with a mounting temper.

The attendants seemed to fidget a little nervously. Then they released the chain. The cheetah sprang forward like an arrow from a hunter's bow. The buck had a fairly long start, for Buta had not deemed it fit to give the signal for the cheetah's release yet. But the trained beast had been writhing in a pent-up fury and overtook one of the most delicate-seeming buck, seizing on its tender neck, while the rest of the herd scurried in a panic.

'Bravo! Bravo!' His Highness shouted with a gong-like voice. And the guests clapped, while the cheetah sat sucking the life-blood of the buck with the cruellest and most relentless grasp imaginable, pressing down on its prey with fiendish howls and growls. The buck sank back exhausted, almost dead before the cheetah, its horns standing useless but strangely, uncannily angry, with their points thrust against the wrath of its destroyer.

Buta, the shikari, ran and covered the cheetah's eyes with a hood again, while the beast had its teeth in the neck of the buck. With deft hands the shikari cut open the buck and, dragging out its entrails, offered the cheetah a meal more suited to its palate than the neck, which was to be reserved for His Highness's guests. The cheetah had to be forced to transfer its desire from the tender neck to the entrails. But once it tasted the second course it left the neck willingly enough.

At the point when Mrs Homer Lane saw the cheetah fall upon the entrails, she uttered one shrill shriek of pain and fell back in a faint.

Victor ran back towards her, full of rage at the spoiling of his fun, for the second cheetah had yet to go off, and yet chivalrous at the sight of Mrs Lane's weakness.

Mrs Lane was sinking, helpless, her white face, with its wide nostrils, transfigured with a ghastly green flush, her mouth frothing.

Mr Lane was fanning her with his hands and bending over her so as to prevent Victor from getting too near her.

All the guests stood still as they watched the scene with impatience and alarm.

In a moment, however, her eyes opened with a melting light and saw Victor looking at her and smiled.

As though not to be outdone by any other woman in commanding the attention of the men, Gangi also let out a deliberate shriek and fell limply on the floor in an obviously histrionic faint.

This was Kurt Landauer's chance to show his gallantry. He lifted her to the chair and fanned her with the lapel of his shirt till she came round.

Srijut Popatlal J. Shah's face wore a scowl of frustration at his inability to show the necessary chivalry.

Mr and Mrs Bell were angry that the fun of the hunt had been spoiled.

Mr Peter Watkins was in a rage that emotional complications had already begun to spoil all the joy of the shoot, especially as he had left his wife and kids at home just in order to have the pleasures of pure sport.

'OK, we go home and sleep!' he said in a disgruntled voice. 'We have had enough for one night.'

However vivid and beautiful the dawn in the jungle, it had no fascination for the white members of the hunting party in the Dharam Pur Lodge after the previous night's exploits. So that the chota hazri of tea and toast remained untouched by every bedstead and not all the insistence of Bhagirath, the Maharaja's cook-bearer, succeeded in persuading the bearers of the sahibs to go near their masters with the request that they come down for breakfast. The Indian members of the party, however, who were unused to sleeping after sunrise, all came down, except for Ganga Dasi, who affected a slight indisposition as usual.

I found Victor very silent at table, with black shadows under his eyes. For, apparently, he had slept badly. After breakfast I drew him away to the shady part of the lawn and, without much ceremony, accosted him with a brief, brutal summing-up of the whole position.

'The moon is in her blood again,' I said. 'And you must cut her out ruthlessly. Otherwise she will deceive you again and again and destroy you.'

'Will she never change?' Victor asked almost in a whisper, refusing to believe that he should ever have to give her up.

I moved my head in negation and added, 'No, I don't think so.'

Victor hung his head down. 'Perhaps I am unnecessarily jealous,' he said. 'She can't possibly fall for that hog Popatlal J. Shah. And as for Kurt Landauer, it may be only a passing fancy.'

'I don't think she will fall for anyone,' I said. 'I rather think that she despises men. Only, she is absolutely unscrupulous and wants to make use of them. Popatlal obviously seems highly useful to her, because she thinks she can secure the gaddi for her son through him and get an estate for herself into the bargain. And Kurt is a young man who pleases her vanity by paying attentions to her.'

'I have myself rather fallen for Mrs Lane,' said Victor. 'And I don't mind her flirting with Kurt....But do you think – she has already slept with Popatlal?'

He uttered the last sentence with some trepidation, as though he half knew the answer and realized that my confirmation would dishearten him by leaving no element of doubt in his mind, where hope for her return could flourish and luxuriate in an atmosphere of indecision.

'I think yes,' I said, putting some deliberation into my voice.

'When do you think she went to Popatlal? And what makes you say so? What evidence have you?' Victor asked, his face harrowed, his lips trembling a little.

'In Sham Pur, on the night when she locked you out,' I answered.

'Is there nothing that can cure her? Where have I failed her? What don't I give her that she finds the need to drift away from me?'

'It is her wayward temperament,' I said, 'a kind of habit now, after she has met and left so many men, a kind of weakness in her which she cannot control.'

Victor's eyes were fear-haunted and furtive, unable to settle on any particular thing. It seemed as though he would willingly cut himself up and throw the carcass of his love at her feet to trample on if she liked, because at least that would be more dramatic and concrete, and he would then have to believe that she was being cruel to him, really believe it, rather than be racked by the uncertainty that she might still love him in some corner of her soul. And as he put his fingers into his hair and pulled the forelock it seemed to me that his desire to torment himself, to rend himself, seemed to become an overwhelming passion, bigger even than his love for her.

'I think,' I said to console him, 'that she wants ultimately to be on her own, and alone, away from all the men who foul her, taking them and the others she needs, and thus active in life, but not to be absorbed by them. But what you are seeking is absorption with her. And this she resists, because she does not really want to be possessed, even though she wants to possess. It is this conflict in her, between being possessed and dominated, and the will to be *free*, that makes things different. She wants to run wild like a goat, from mountain to mountain, with a strange ambition to get there, she does not know where.'

Victor seemed to be overcome by the wonder and awe of this revelation about her. And yet he didn't seem to believe in this ruthless analysis. He had never quite forgotten her prostration of the first days of their life together, the passion she had brought to him and the strange, almost servile, devotion. She had been aware of his status as the Maharaja and she had exalted him as her lord and willingly reduced herself to the position of a slave. She had kissed his feet, and touched his body with reverence and tended him with loving care. And, during the first few years, when she had his two children, she had gone on being his slave, kissing his feet and worshipping him as her lord and master, while he was her king, as well as ruler of the state, with his responsibilities. From having a split mind himself, incapable of any permanent attachments in his youth, he had become rooted in her and hardly ever craved for other emotional relationships, except when she drove him to a frenzy of desperation. Now she had begun to demand her rights and to assert herself with complete licence, and to give herself to his inferiors. That she could leave him, the great Maharaja, hurt his pride. And now how could she revolt against him, especially when he was cornered on all sides? Somewhere in his nature, in spite of a dim awareness of the discord between them, he could not accept *this* rejection. It would be like accepting failure, the failure of his whole life's effort at finding a base for his emotions; it would be the death knell of all his hopes of fighting for the independence of his state; and it would leave him utterly destroyed, joyless and dead.

I realized all this on that morning, seated by Victor on the veranda of the hunting lodge, and I knew that His Highness also vaguely surmised that I had come to this awareness. But he felt that I wanted to talk to him and he did not want to listen.

'Don't you think she will ever...?' Victor insisted again, but did not finish his sentence.

'The thing is to cure oneself,' I said. But realizing how priggish an answer that was, I added: 'I know how agonizing it is to be attached to a person, to have lived with her and grown into her and then to have to contemplate rejection by her. I can guess....Only in the casual affair does this pain not arise. But once one is bitten by affection for a person, and this affection has become sex, and passionate sex, capped by the mental habits of marriage, then only the more stupid and insensitive of the partners can destroy it. For, already the joy of such a relationship has become a kind of super reality, an illusion, an infectious illusion.'

'It is not an illusion to me,' Victor said desperately.

'I said "infectious illusion",' I answered. 'It is like a contagious disease: once one catches it one has to suffer it. But you can take it that people like the Queen Bee, who are promiscuous, always suffer each time they go and satisfy their vanity, because age makes an important difference. At thirty a woman becomes richer with giving herself in sex, but at thirty-five or forty infidelity does not really rejuvenate her. It only nourishes the illusion that she is wanted and pleases her vanity. And soon the illusion wears thin. And then either women pursue the illusion again or give up.'

'So they can give up the illusion, sometimes?' Victor said, looking for any ray of hope.

'The pitfall in the psychology of a nymphomaniac is that she will believe that her next victim will be the last,' I answered. 'Whereas there is an infinite regress in this business.'

Victor got up with evident disgust and cleared his throat. His eyes were averted from me as though he was too hurt to be able to bear to look at me. I felt tender towards him because I realized how he was harrowed by suspicion. And I sought to console him with a platitude.

'You know, in a marriage of love, both the partners have entered more or less equal and free. Otherwise, the one who loves will be hurt and destroyed by the other who doesn't love deeply. And resentments will set up curtains of bitterness and dissatisfaction, and the poison will seep through the partners. It is best in such a situation to let the promiscuous one run wild until the fascination of adultery is exhausted by misuse of body and mind and depth returns to the wild one.'

'Soothing syrup!' Victor said with a troubled smile.

I thought I would now take the occasion to broach the matter of the détenues. And I paused to gather strength enough to begin.

'Let us have a drink,' Victor said impatiently, depriving me of my chance to say anything serious. And he shouted, 'Koi hai?'

At lunch that day the venison from the shikar of the previous night formed the main curried dish. And Victor dispensed hospitality with a warmth which was heightened by the half bottle of whisky he had consumed since our talk together. The meal was, therefore, a somewhat raucous farce. Fortunately, the ladies were all absent, because they preferred to dine with Gangi in the zenana.

'Ohe!' he shouted on seeing the chamberlain, Chottu Ram, taking a third helping of the venison curry, 'we should have remembered your appetite and let off the second cheetah to get some more buck! Look at him! Look at him!'

The white guests turned to look at Chottu Ram. His cheeks were, indeed, puffed up like balls with the morsels he was swallowing.

'I don't know how he can do it!' said Mr Watkins. 'I find it very hot.'

'Yes, a real hot curry this, for once!' opined Mr Bell with a knowing air. He was red in the face, though he pretended to like the curry.

Mr Lane's glasses were dim with the steam of the perspiration from his face as he looked up.

'Gosh!' said Kurt Landauer.

'We have a large variety of dishes in India,' said Srijut Popatlal J. Shah. 'Only today, His Highness preferred to treat us to an English-style lunch on china plates, with forks and knives, and not in thalis, as is our usual custom.'

'Ohe!' said Captain Partap Singh to Chottu Ram, who was now sweeping portions of meat with each chapati and devouring huge morsels. 'Ohe, your stomach is your own, even though the food which you are eating has been provided by His Highness!'

Everyone laughed at this, because Partap Singh's mode of speech was as crude as Chottu Ram's appetite.

Chottu knew he would be the butt of all jokes now, so he dramatized his absorption in the meal. He took bigger morsels still and satisfied his greed and amused the guests at the same time.

'I wish for Chottu's sake,' repeated His Highness, 'that we had let the other cheetah do the work, because we should have been able to provide more game to our chamberlain.'

'One buck was enough, Maharaj,' said Chottu, 'if only Bhagirath had put more chillies into the meat.'

The foreign guests smiled at the reference to them, because they were, indeed, taking good helpings.

'You wouldn't think that such a little person as Chottu Ram could have such an enormous capacity,' said Munshi Mithan Lal, to wipe out the effect of Chottu's tactless remark.

'The exact size of a stomach is about the contracted fist of a hand,' I said, to contribute my quota of conversation to drown the possible ill effects of Chottu's vulgarity.

'If a tall man like myself ate so much,' said Captain Partap Singh, 'it would be all right, but this fellow Chottu!'

But Chottu only accelerated the devouring process.

'Actually, I could outdo him any day,' said Partap Singh.

'That's a challenge!' said His Highness, relaxing his face to admit a smile.

'I shall take the challenge!' said Chottu.

'I shall win!' warned Partap Singh.

'Take a bet on it!' said Chottu.

'Acha,' said Partap Singh. 'Let His Highness name the conditions and the bet.'

'I shall eat twenty hard-boiled eggs here and now and drink a bottle of champagne!' said Chottu.

'I shall eat twenty-five!' said Partap Singh.

'All right, whoever gives way will pay five hundred rupees to the other,' said Victor. 'And I shall give a thousand to the winner….Bhagirath, get forty-five eggs boiled at once!'

'Han, Maharaj, by tomorrow,' said Bhagirath.

'No, today, just now,' Victor ordered.

Bhagirath looked dubiously about and smiled as though he thought that His Highness was playing a joke on him.

'Why are you sniggering?' Victor shouted. 'Go and get the eggs.'

Bhagirath could not help sniggering even though he bowed his head and went to the kitchen.

Mr Watkins and Mr Lane had not quite understood this game and turned to Mr Bell for enlightenment.

His Highness explained to them the nature of the contest even as he got up and plied them with more champagne. He wanted to warm up the party.

'I shall show Chottu that I can outdo him in eating!' boasted Partap Singh after he had swallowed the champagne left over in his tumbler. 'I shall show you all! Why, I could have become the second cheetah last night! I could have sucked up its life-blood!'

'Some men only look human!' I commented to mitigate Partap Singh's animalist bragging.

'Domestication makes some difference,' said Victor.

'Huzoor, in captivity even a lion grows to be a goat. And I am by religion a Singh, a lion, King of all the beasts.'

'And you will never be tamed,' I said.

Bhagirath appeared with six hard-boiled eggs on a plate, saying: 'Maharaj, there are six hard-boiled eggs left over from the morning.'

'But we want fifty!' Victor roared.

'I have put twenty more on to boil, Maharaj,' Bhagirath said. 'I thought I would bring these to go on with.'

'Acha, meanwhile serve the halwa and the dessert,' Victor said.

The foreign guests signified that they had had enough.

'Only coffee for me,' said Mr Lane.

'Come on, Mr Lane,' coaxed Victor. 'Satisfy yourself even though you choke yourself, because then you will be free of desire. This is the safest rule, be it for food or be it for love.'

'Your Highness, you must know a great deal about both,' ventured Mr Watkins with an impish smile.

'I have never been untrue to any emotion,' Victor said, taking Watkins's light-hearted remark seriously. 'So I have had a lot of experience. I never deny any emotion, crush it or turn away from it. During my youth, I got everything I wanted. All the obstacles in my way were removed, so that I could have what I wanted. And I have become habituated to having things my own way. But, of course, I get trapped by the things I want and possess, and so I am, as Doctor Shankar would say, really the loser when I gain. Now I have been trying to develop the art of never being caught....'

'And yet, I am afraid,' I put in, 'His Highness always gets caught. His vanity is colossal and he doesn't know when he is being trapped.' I winced at my rudeness.

'Doctor Shankar may know me better,' said Victor. 'But, Mr Watkins, inside me I am really fundamentally free, unattached. All these things pass me by. I remain untouched and unmoved, though, on the surface, I know I am involved. That's the truth. Really, believe me.'

'Somewhat of a yogi,' said Mr Lane.

'More like a schizophrene,' said the canny Mr Bell.

'Yes, that's what he would like to be, a yogi,' I said. 'But he is not. Mr Bell is right. His Highness is incapable of permanent attachments – except that he has his fixations!'

'Bhagirath! Where are these servants? What about the eggs?' Victor shouted suddenly, in a frenzy at my rudeness. And he turned to Chottu Ram and Partap Singh. 'Get ready, you will soon be remembering your mothers!'

So we descended from the sublime to the ridiculous again.

Bhagirath appeared.

'The eggs! the eggs!' Victor shouted. 'Don't you see that the two giants are hungry? They will devour you if you don't look out!'

'Here, Maharaj, I have brought twenty more,' he said. 'The cook is boiling the rest. But the fires in the kitchen had been extinguished.'

'Chalo, begin!' His Highness said to Chottu and Partap Singh.

'After Captain Sahib,' said Chottu.

'No, you first,' said Partap Singh.

'Stop this war of courtesy and begin!' ordered His Highness.

The two giants began peeling the eggs.

'Salt, pepper, khansamah! And some more champagne!'

Bhagirath put the cruet-stand before the giants and went off to open another champagne bottle.

The giants began to eat.

'Let us help peel some more for them,' offered Mr Watkins, joining in the fun.

'You will both die of jaundice,' I said to the contestants.

They had polished off two eggs each already, and were reaching out for more.

'Have some champagne to wash them down with,' Victor suggested, pouring the frothing liquid from the bottle that Bhagirath had opened.

Both the giants merely nodded assent and went ahead with the competition. The atmosphere became more and more awful as their faces got redder and redder.

Chottu Ram had eaten ten eggs already and his eyes were bulging behind his glasses, his face looking gloomier than when he started.

'Fourteen,' said Partap Singh. 'I am leading. Bhagirath...' And he picked up his tumbler and swallowed the champagne in a mouthful.

'I should chew them slowly,' I said to him. 'I say this as a doctor.'

'I shall eat them as I like,' he said.

Bhagirath brought another dozen eggs.

Chottu began to look a little green.

'Stop it now,' I said to him.

'Of course not, this is a match!' said His Highness.

'I shall persist to the last,' Chottu said. And he began on the eleventh hard-boiled egg.

But somehow it wouldn't go down.

'Have some liquid,' I suggested, concerned for him.

He hiccupped, groaned, and brought up the eggs and the champagne on to the table before him.

I got up and walked away, unable to control the bile in my mouth in the face of the men. I saw that everyone turned away and left. The lunch party broke up.

After such a lunch a deep siesta became inevitable, and the four o'clock tea was served in the bedrooms of the guests.

As Victor had asked me to come in and discuss with him the exact way in which to broach the subject of American help for his independent stand, I knocked at his bedroom door, after Bhagirath had been in to put the tea at his bedside.

I thought that Bhagirath had awakened him, but it seemed that he had been sound asleep, and it was my knock at the door that broke his slumber.

As I entered, he looked somewhat startled and passed his right hand through his glossy, silken hair. But, suddenly, he was more than startled. He was in a panic. He looked round, open-mouthed, and said: 'Where is Gangi? She was asleep beside me!'

I knew what was in his mind. His face paled and I thought he was going to shout. His head swayed dizzily and he bit his lower lip in order to control himself.

'I guess she has gone to Kurt,' he said. 'As you said, "the moon is in her blood". When Kurt lifted her in the machan last night, I knew she would....That is why I was so worried this morning...' But he did not finish his sentence.

I moved my head despairingly.

He shot out of his bed and raced out of the room into the veranda and towards Kurt's bedroom.

I dared not call him back for fear of rousing the other guests, but merely followed.

With an uncanny instinct for manoeuvre, even in this mood of excitement, he applied his eyes to the jali which covered the window, and he stood transfixed. Then he beckoned me with a swift gesture of his right hand.

I got up to the window and saw the shocking reality; Gangi lay in bed with Kurt in a passionate embrace. She was still dressed, though her salwars were undone, while Kurt was naked.

I dragged Victor away to prevent him from seeing too much.

'Get away!' he growled at me. 'I shall kill them both!' His voice rang metallic and hard across the corridor and penetrated Kurt's room. There was an instantaneous sound of shuffling feet and anxious whispers.

I put my right hand on Victor's mouth, and holding him hard with the left, dragged him back towards his room. He bucked like a stallion and his eyes were red hot, spitting fire at me, while he wrestled with me to get free. I exerted all my strength and bent myself in the effort to extricate him from the scene which he wanted to create with that latent histrionic ability that he exercised to the full before believing the evidence of his senses. Nothing but foul abuse of Gangi would have sufficed to reassure him. His mouth opened and his hysteria spluttered across the tense silence of the veranda.

At that stage I lifted him bodily and took him to his room even while he shouted and protested.

'Vicky, you will ruin everything if the Americans hear you,' I whispered peremptorily. These words seemed to hypnotize him and he became docile in my hands.

I brought him to the room and flung him on his bed.

He burst into tears and, turning on his face, buried his head in his pillow and sobbed.

I sat down by him and stroked his back.

He seemed inconsolable and poured forth sentiment and abuse for Gangi in turns, with the refrain, 'Oh, how could she do it to me!'

I let him cry his heart out and he calmed a little.

After a while, he said, 'I know she can't help these urges.'

He paused for a moment and then continued, 'It seems so cruel that she should do this kind of thing and hurt me to satisfy a passing fancy!'

He lay back and rolled across the bed from side to side, evidently whipped up by the agony, thrown back to resources which he did not possess, for he had given himself up to her unreservedly for ever.

'I shall leave you to dress,' I said, embarrassed. 'You have to talk to the Americans.'

'Call Mr Watkins.'

I walked away silently.

'Ask Watkins to join us for a stroll in half an hour,' Victor called after me.

Victor did not keep a pretence of secrecy about the talk we were to have with Mr Peter Watkins. For, meeting the Premier, Popatlal J. Shah, in the garden, His Highness asked him whether he would care to come for a walk.

'I can see that wonderful swing there at the end of the garden, Your Highness,' said Srijut Shah. 'I would like to sit on it. I feel like a child. Come, there is a bench for you and you can talk while I enjoy myself on the swing.'

'Nero fiddled while Rome was burning,' Mr Watkins said. 'But we will let you have your little game.'

So we strolled up to the end of the garden where Popatlal occupied the cushioned seat at the base of the swing. Victor seemed absent-minded and racked.

'People are saying that Nehru fiddles while India is burning,' I said airily.

'And it is true,' said Mr Watkins. 'He has been saying that he believes in Communism –'

'No, no, no, Mr Watkins,' said Popatlal J. Shah. 'Panditji says many things. He was once a Socialist. But he has said on the radio that there is no difference between him and Sardar Patel on fundamental questions. And the Sardar has stated that he will see every Communist in India dead before he is finished with them.' And as he said this, the Prime Minister looked towards His Highness naively for approval.

'If the Sardar is out to destroy the Communists, then why doesn't he help me to put down the guerillas who have raised their heads to the skies in Sham Pur?' Victor said irritably. 'Even the noblemen of my state do not see the threat clearly enough and have combined with the Reds against me. And yet the Sardar is helping these cousins of mine.'

He seemed naturally to have become bitter.

'That is a different question,' said Popatlal. 'The issue of Sham Pur is accession or non-accession. Once the accession is conceded, the Government of India will help the state forces and the police to put down the Reds. The unity and integrity of the Indian Union comes first. And we are doing our best to encourage this unity.'

'I am not concerned with the inner differences of the various units in your country,' said Mr Watkins. 'But I do see that the position of Sham Pur State is a very important one, considering its peculiar geography. Especially in the days of the aeroplane. With the advance of the Chinese Reds to Sinkiang and Tibet, India will need to defend itself against the Communists from the north. And if there are guerillas already plying in the state, then the sooner something is done about it the better!'

'Of course,' I suggested, in a vein that I knew would obviously open me to the suspicion of being pro-Red, 'the one way of making Sham Pur proof against disaster would be to feed and clothe the people.'

'That is a platitude which is being put about in all the liberal and pro-Communist press,' said Mr Homer Lane, butting in from where he had come to stand by his chief in a shirt and shorts which exposed his feeble skeleton-like body in all its ridiculous Goebbels distortion. 'People don't realize the acuteness of the menace here. Soon, the Reds in China will be infiltrating across the mountains into India. In fact, I hear the Tibetan Communist Party is planning to conquer India!'

'What, the Lamas have turned Red?' said His Highness.

'I have heard an interesting story about the Tibetan Communist Party,' said Mr Lane. 'They sent a member of their party to Mao Tse Tung to get to know the latest line. This comrade travelled for six months by yak and pony to get there. He received his instructions and took another six months on the return journey. After he got back and reported to his friends they heard that the party line had changed in the meanwhile. So they sent him back to Mao Tse Tung again to get to know the new line....'

'And, I suppose,' said Mr Watkins, 'in order to make the story a little more interesting you might add that Mao Tse Tung referred him to Stalin.'

'And Stalin liquidated the Tibetan!' added Popatlal J. Shah.

'And the American press played it up as a big purge,' I added.

His Highness laughed like a child at the story. Then he turned and said: 'I have a feeling that the huge crowd in our villages will one day march on my palace and seize power! And yet I can do nothing about it, because the Sardar won't understand that to destroy my dynasty would make Communism inevitable!'

'There is such a thing as democratic rule,' said Popatlal. 'And the Sardar feels that those institutions must be created here which –'

'I am not sure that democracy is suitable for this country,' put in Mr Watkins.

'Is that an American democrat talking?' I said.

'Yeah,' he said, on the defensive. 'The East has changed my mind about the parliamentary system.'

'I would concede to no one my belief in the ultimate value of the democratic system,' Mr Bell added with some emphasis.

'Mr Watkins, you can't object to a dictatorship of the Left if you think that democracy is unpractical!' I said.

'I would rather have a dictatorship of the Right!' Mr Lane answered before Watkins could speak.

'Then why did you fight Hitler?' I asked.

'I think we were fooled into doing so by Roosevelt!' he answered.

'Certainly,' I said, 'Hitler has left a rich heritage of potential Fascism everywhere.'

'Would you rather have Communism?' Mr Watkins asked me.

I kept quiet.

'Silence means consent,' said Mr Lane.

'Doctor Shankar is rather a Red,' said His Highness, half apologetically.

'Anyhow, I feel,' said Mr Watkins, 'that this border kingdom ought to be prepared to meet all eventualities.'

I felt that His Highness must actually have given him to understand that he might let the Americans build some air bases here in lieu of support in his fight for independence, as against Sardar Vallabhbhai's demand for accession.

But, from the tightening of their faces, Mr Watkins's statement came as a thunderbolt to Srijut Popatlal J. Shah. I think he realized that all the preparations for the hunt and this house party had a significance beyond the mere pleasure principle which had seemed even to his deft ICS diplomat's mind the main reason for the shikar.

'Let us have a drink,' said His Highness, unable to bear it all any more.

I felt he had been very tactless in having this talk in the open, and I was sure that sinister developments would follow from his laxity in this matter.

All the guests had come down to the ample veranda of the hunting lodge by the time we had terminated our discussion on politics. And they all seemed rested after the siesta they had enjoyed; the ladies looked fresh in their new change of clothes, and every trace of the day's heat and emotional and political tension seemed to have evaporated. Bhagirath had arranged the drinks on the table and was busy mixing cocktails for the ladies, while the other bearers poured out whiskies-and-sodas for the gentlemen.

Kurt Landauer wound up the gramophone he had brought with him and led off safely by asking Mrs Bell to dance with him. Mr and Mrs Lane followed suit. And Mr Watkins asked Gangi, who was dressed in the most lovely sequins of a white silk sari, looking like the essence of purity itself in spite of her adventure with Kurt in the afternoon. His Highness was already flushed with drink. Srijut Popatlal J. Shah contemplated him disdainfully from the corners of his eyes as he sat talking furtively to Mr Bool Chand. Munshi Mithan Lal superintended the arrangements for drinks and provisions because Chottu Ram had collapsed from eating too many eggs in the lunch competition. Captain Partap Singh was manoeuvring to get more and more tumblerfuls of neat whisky into himself as the bearer went round. And I hugged my glass, while I listened to the staccato sentences in which His Highness jerkily delivered himself even as he sipped or swallowed his drink.

'She is completely oblivious of me,' he said. 'As if I don't exist.'

She was dancing badly and she seemed to be shrinking and afraid. Mr Watkins did not seem to be able to help her. Luckily, the record finished and he was able to negotiate her gracefully to her chair.

Kurt put on the reverse side of the record and quickly came towards Gangi with almost outstretched arms. She got up, looking the while in the direction of Victor with surreptitious glances.

A dark flush suddenly covered Victor's face; his brows knitted and his eyes spat fire.

'The bitch!' he exclaimed under his breath. But as his eyes lowered, he seemed ashamed of himself, ashamed of his anger against her.

'Why don't you ask her to dance the next dance with you?' I said.

'I can't bear it,' he said, and writhed, breathing heavily the while, almost panting. 'And I don't know what Popatlal is up to. I am beginning to suspect Bool Chand.'

'I think you shouldn't have talked to the Americans in the presence of the Diwan,' I said.

'All right, all right, damn you, always preaching!' he said gruffly, and moved away from me, making straight for Mrs Lane, who was sitting down for a breather. And, without so much as a 'by your leave', he lifted her and took the floor.

I could see Mr Lane's face change immediately, an almost perceptible revulsion going across it in a spasm of red blood that suffused it.

Strange and amorphous were my feelings at the way Victor had insulted me, crushed his own pride in his crude approach to Mrs Lane, and aroused the white man's prejudice. And a little way away from where Victor was dancing, with elegant steps only slightly affected by his inebriation, was Ganga Dasi close in Kurt's arms, her feet pattering awkwardly, as her lover moved like a French apache with her in a small space, but her face transformed by a flush which mirrored a curious exaltation in her, a kind of revival of the old familiar exaltation when a new man tickled her vanity and made her believe that she was being loved perfectly, sublimely.

The cumulative effect of the whole noisy evening, with the opposing wills, was to produce in me a repeated sense of the doom that was imminent in it all: the cruel, ugly inevitability of the disruption that was in store for us, the main actors in this drama, both individually and collectively. For impinging on my consciousness was the pressure of the people of Sham Pur, who, though absent from this scene, were yet perhaps the most powerful actors in the drama, the invisible mass lying in wait to ambush the intriguing, agonized, decadent prince and his courtiers, and ready to wipe out the whole putrescent order with a ruthless determination to clean up the Augean stables of the feudalist oligarchy.

The gramophone record came to an end and the pairs broke off and reverted to their places in that vague lull which is so tense with conflicting desires.

Mr Lane was apparently cross with Mrs Lane, and she sat shrinking from him as though through the fear that he might rebuke her.

Victor saw Gangi's face glistening and knew it was not for him, his mouth tight shut in order to control the storm of dissatisfaction that raged in him. It was almost as though he was grinding his heart in a desperate hatred for her.

Just at that moment came the shikari, Buta, running up the garden and shouting: 'Maharaj, the panther has come and killed the goat. I think he is waiting in a bush near the machan and will return to his kill.'

'Off we go!' said Kurt, stopping the gramophone. 'We will get him this time.'

'Come,' said Victor. 'Let us go together in case he smells the young blood of Mr Landauer and gobbles him up after he has finished with the goat.'

Everyone noticed that there was a strain of rancour in Victor's voice. And yet there came the faintest blur of ecstasy on his face, the feeling of release from the tension about Gangi. For now Kurt would be occupied by the sport and perhaps her fantasy would evaporate in his absence at the machan.

Gangi sat motionless, in the gloom of her passion and fear, absorbed in herself.

'The ladies had better stay here,' said Victor.

There was a silent consent to this proposal.

'I won't go either, darling,' said Mr Lane to his wife.

Apparently, Homer was full of a nameless dread of his own weakness in the face not of the panther, but of the tigress, his wife, who he felt was drifting away from him towards the Maharaja. And he knew that by being with her he could arrest the cravings in her, the reaching out of her dark, unsatisfied physical urges towards Victor. He exuded a chilly antagonism towards her, as though he was incensed at her, and yet he looked towards her from the corners of his eyes, waiting to appeal to her to pity him for his physical deformity and his weakness.

'Come on, Doctor Shankar,' shouted Victor. 'We might need medical attention in case one of the sahibs faints on seeing the panther!' The reference to Kurt was obvious in the maliciously humorous tone of his voice.

I followed the hunters towards the machan.

We waited nearly till nightfall for the panther to appear. But the beast was not on his best behaviour and did not oblige. So Captain Partap Singh had to be sent down to ask the beaters to do something to expedite the panther's return to the scene of his kill; and Munshi Mithan Lal was ordered to go and get some refreshments for the famished guests.

Soon the tomtom of drums began to be heard and the rattle, which peasants use to scare away the birds, punctuated the darkness of the jungle, and we were all bathed in the sweat of expectancy, panic and hope. The five of us, Victor,

Kurt, Mr Watkins, Mr Bell and myself, each had a gun poised ready to shoot. And, as we had been sitting in one position for at least three to four hours at a stretch, we felt cramped and ill at ease, waiting, watching, with dilated eyes and breath held back, till the blood seemed to mount to our heads and make us half-mad automatons, idiots, with nothing in us except our instinct to kill.

The jungle before us loomed like an inscrutable god from whose jaws seemed to issue the sound of the drumbeats, from where the panther would emerge at any moment.

I could not bear the oppressive weight of the atmosphere and asked His Highness in a whisper: 'Is there any certainty that the panther will emerge with the drumbeats? Won't it be frightened off?'

'It may roam around for miles before it comes back to its kill or it may emerge immediately if it is hungry,' Victor said.

'But won't the drums make it suspicious of the danger that lurks for it?'

'What danger,' said Victor mockingly. 'You have probably never hit a rabbit in your life!'

I was relieved at his good humour and answered: 'No, but I have dissected not only rabbits but human beings.'

'And there is Mr Landauer,' continued Victor banteringly. 'Look at the number of cartridges he has dumped next to him, though I doubt if he will get even one shot before Mr Watkins fells the panther.' He was obviously flattering the first secretary at the expense of Kurt.

'Oh, Highness!' exclaimed Mr Watkins. 'I don't know much about this kind of hunt. It will be your shot that will get it, I am sure.'

I wanted to say that it was most likely that it would fall to a shot of Buta's, but desisted from deflating the pride of the exalted by so cruelly realistic a comment.

And thus we sat longing for the panther to come and be slain by us heroes, the great unerring shots.

'Night after night I have sat up waiting for a tiger or panther to come,' Victor lied to impress the Americans.

'The machan is swarming with mosquitoes now,' said Mr Bell after his prolonged, patient and melancholy silence. 'I am off.' And he slipped away on tiptoe.

After Mr Bell was out of hearing, Victor began to fill the blankness of time with tentative probings about the American intentions to help him in his struggle to retain his independence.

'Mr Watkins,' he said, 'the English always knew the value of this state as a hunter's paradise. They also knew that it is a good buffer state. Mr Bell and his like are suffering from sour grapes, now that they have had to go. But as the Americans alone are concerned to stop the Red menace from the north, we could discuss some arrangement....'

'If you look at the history of the last two thousand years,' I put in hyperbolically, 'the Russians have never attacked India. It was the Huns, the Mongols, the Turks, the Tartars, the Portuguese, the Dutch, the French or the British, but never the Russians. Are we sure that we need to protect ourselves against them?'

'You may be a good doctor,' said Mr Watkins impatiently, 'but you are a very bad politician.'

'Some kind of collaboration between my American friends and myself is necessary,' said His Highness, ignoring Mr Watkins's and my comments. 'I am glad you came to Sham Pur, because you will understand the situation in my state. I hear that some millions of rupees are going to be spent on constructing air fields in India under the guidance of experts from your country. Before you go away I would like to show you one or two sites in Sham Pur which may be suitable.'

'We want the good will of all sections in this country,' said Mr Watkins evasively. 'We are not interested in anything but to help the war-shattered and backward countries of the world to get on their feet.'

I was itching to stop this fairy tale with a cynical gibe about China, Turkey, Greece, Germany, Korea and Japan, but was restrained from so doing for fear Victor would blame me for the breakdown of his negotiations with the Americans if, as was certain, nothing was done by them to help him keep the independence of Sham Pur.

'I say, I think we had better give up this long wait,' said Kurt. 'We will come back later.'

'That's an idea,' said Mr Watkins.

Just as they were going to get up, however, Captain Partap Singh returned and said that the panther had been heard to move from its hide-out and was probably advancing towards its prey. He said Buta was almost sure it would come and would we become alert, ready to shoot.

So the Americans settled down. But the whole thing happened before they had ever got into the position to shoot. For, from the uncanny silence, broken only by the whine of the beetles, there was a faint rustle in the bushes beyond the pole to which the goat had been tied. And there the panther was stealthily digging its claws into the flesh of the goat.

'Shoot!' the Maharaja whispered.

But before either Victor, or Watkins, or Kurt, or I, had taken aim and pressed a trigger, a shot rang through, apparently from Buta's gun.

'Shoot! Shoot! Shoot!' Victor shouted, as he wanted the Americans to do the killing.

Mr Watkins and Mr Landauer opened up, but both were wide of the mark.

The panther had received Buta's bullet in its head and was reeling as it groaned.

Victor fired and sent a shot into its belly. And he shouted excitedly again: 'Shoot, Mr Watkins, shoot!'

Mr Watkins took aim and sent a bullet into the panther's body.

Mr Landauer missed again.

I too was wide of the mark as I pressed my trigger.

There was an awful suspense as the panther remained on its feet.

Another shot rang through from Buta's gun.

And with this, the panther collapsed in its death agony, half its body lying athwart its own prey.

At dawn the next day we were awakened from our sleep by Captain Partap Singh, who said that Buta had come to inform us that the mother of the panther, killed last night, had come and sat mourning for its son, and would we come and bag it.

Victor felt that Mr Watkins must be given a chance of doing a kill on his own, as thiere was no doubt left last night that the young panther had fallen to a bullet of Buta, rather than to a shot of Watkins or Landauer. So the Americans were roused.

They were very eager and turned out in their striped pyjamas and dressing gowns.

Buta, who was waiting downstairs, saw the gaiety of our guests' attire and told us that though we were all unerring shots, to be sure, we had better take the precaution of not mounting the glorious heights of the machan, but take the more hazardous course of stealing up to the prey through the bush. And he led the way.

Our eyes were dilated wide in search of the beast as we followed Buta up a track on the hillside. We were nearly on tiptoe, and felt guilty every time a twig snapped under our feet or the bushes rustled. I think we were all rather afraid of the danger of this adventure, because the mother panther might make a frontal assault and, without the protection of the height on top of the machan, we would not stand an earthly chance of survival.

At last we got to a position behind some thick scrub, where Buta asked us to wait and look.

Our eyes strained to pierce the undergrowth before us, but we could not see the mother panther mourning over its son.

Buta then discovered an aperture in the foliage through which it was possible to see the beast.

Our faces paled visibly and I, for one, found my legs shaking involuntarily.

'Now then, take aim, Sahibs, and shoot,' said Buta.

Both Mr Watkins and Mr Landauer adjusted their guns and fired.

They missed their mark.

'Rape-mothers! Brothers-in-law!' cursed Buta, indignant and bad-tempered but fortunately speaking in the hillman's speech, which the sahibs did not understand. 'It is moving....'

And, forthwith, even without taking aim, he took a blind shot at it.

The mother panther gave a heart-rending yell and rolled over and fell without a struggle. Apparently, it had decided that life was not worth living after the death of its son.

'It is not yet finished,' said Victor. 'And it may attack us. So please have a pot shot at it!'

Mr Watkins found his target this time, though Mr Landauer seemed to be a purblind hunter, and failed to hit the panther.

'If he is the same in everything else,' said Victor to me in Hindustani, 'all enthusiasm and no go, then I have not much to fear from him.'

The tumult and the shouting had died down by the time we came down to breakfast that morning; and, not only because it was Monday morning, and we had to go back to Sham Pur, but because other things had happened to sober down the atmosphere, everyone was in that grey mood which makes for frayed tempers and disdainful sniffs.

For one thing, Srijut Popatlal J. Shah had already left without even saying goodbye to His Highness. And Mr Bool Chand had gone with him.

Furthermore, he had left a wire which he had received from the States Department at Delhi asking him to send His Highness to see Sardar Vallabhbhai Patel as soon as possible.

Srijut Popatlal J. Shah had not written a covering note to His Highness to interpret the States Minister's message, but had left the telegram, which had been brought by a courtier, to speak for itself.

Gloom descended on the bright, sunny morning as soon as the darkened brow of His Highness became visible over the heavy eyebrows. And silence, the sister of gloom, cast her shadow across the hunting lodge. And in the wake of silence arrived their young cousin, anger, lurking in the bloodshot eyes of His Highness and on his dilated nostrils. That telegram was the ultimate challenge, the final potential threat to his very existence, and thus to the continuance of his dynasty, which claimed descent from the Sun, the Moon, the God King Rama and many of the other supernatural powers, and weaknesses, who people the Hindu pantheon. His Highness's face contracted and he looked rather like the righteous mongoose which is setting out to kill all the snakes in the neighbourhood.

'I am going upstairs to lie down for a while,' he said to me.

And as he said this and walked away, I saw that his face relaxed. I felt that the stubborn self-will in him was giving way, that he would not fight the States Department any more, that he did not care what became of him.

Sensing the nature of the doom that had descended upon him, the guests also drifted away into corners, smoking their after-breakfast cigarettes and pipes on the veranda of the lodge or on the lawn below.

But the shikari Buta, came and disturbed the vague doom of the atmosphere with his effervescent and bumptious talk.

'I have asked the beaters to bring the panthers here, so that the sahibs can have their photos taken,' he said to me.

'Ah, yes, that is a good idea,' I said.

And I tried to work up a little enthusiasm by asking the guests to get ready to be photographed.

'It will be a little while, Huzoor,' Buta said.

'All right, I will go and get my camera,' said Kurt Landauer.

'Ask him why he became a hunter,' said Mr Watkins, coming up to where I was leaning on the balustrade of the veranda overlooking Buta's swarthy, half-clad, wiry, bare-footed figure on the pathway. I translated the query.

'I was enraged by the impertinence of a panther who attacked my friend Shibu and killed him,' began Buta. He only needed a very little encouragement to begin story-telling. 'I decided to kill that panther and all other beasts from that day.... This ferocious beast had pulled down a man from a tree and mauled him. Later, it came and attacked and injured a youth in a cattle shed and then disappeared in the paddy field by the lake. So I went for it and shot it.'

I explained Buta's yarn to Mr Watkins in a free English transcription.

'I thought you Hindus were a gentle, non-meat-eating race,' said Mr Watkins.

I communicated this sublimely ignorant statement to Buta. 'The Sahib does not know the laws of the jungle,' he said, with redoubtable logic. 'Tigers and panthers and other wild animals live in the jungle, Huzoor. And they don't trouble men or cattle so long as they can get other prey. But when they do attack humans, should we forgive them their sins like Mahatma Gandhi and be eaten up quietly? What philosophy is that? To be sure, they attack shikaris and villagers, mainly because of their instinct for self-preservation or for the protection of their mates or young ones. In the ordinary course of their lives they are of great help to man. They keep down herds of deer and of wild pig and rabbits which would ruin all harvests if they were not destroyed. A Tehsildar Sahib once said that the best way to protect the forests against theft of timber is to keep a tiger for every five acres of jungle. And the best way of preserving the balance of life and death in the animal kingdom is to keep shikaris well fed!'

I knew that Buta would contrive to bring the conversation round somehow to the question of bakhshish. I told Watkins everything the shikari had said. And the American was most amused by the dexterity with which the talk had been brought round to the question of bread and butter. Just at that instant, however, Victor came up and said: 'It is no use, I can't rest.... What is this scoundrel up to?'

'He naturally wants his bakhshish,' the American said before I could open my mouth. 'And he deserves it for the splendid work he has done.'

'Ohe, son of a swine!' His Highness shouted. 'Aren't you ashamed of asking these sahibs for bakhshish when you are going to be given something by Rai Bahadur Chottu Ram?... Shameless fool!'

'Maharaj, please forgive,' said Buta, bending his head over his joined palms.

'Go and get to your work, then!' His Highness shouted.

'The beaters have brought up the panthers there in the garden for the photographs,' I said.

'Yes, let us get the photographs done, Mr Watkins,' His Highness said. 'And then we must pack up quickly and go to Sham Pur. I will have to leave for Delhi tonight.'

Kurt Landauer was already on the lawn tinkering with his camera. But it took some time to round up all the guests for the photographs, especially the ladies, who went to powder their noses and kept the gentlemen waiting.

I suggested that while the ladies were getting ready, the guests who had actually taken part in the hunt should be photographed in one group, and all the gentlemen in another, and the whole party in a third. His Highness agreed to this. Only, he took upon himself to organize the groups so that Mr Watkins should be prominently in the centre of all of them. And Mr Watkins, though affecting a certain bashfulness which reddened his face, fell in with these arrangements, even actually putting his foot on one of the panthers at Buta's suggestion to symbolize the fact that he had been responsible for killing it. As Kurt had taken most of the pictures, I took over the camera from him while he joined in with the various male groups. Then the ladies came down, except for Gangi, who was still indisposed, and, amid much real and artificial laughter, giggles and nervous shrieks at contact with the dead panthers, the photographs were taken. Needless to say, the actual killer, Buta, was nowhere in the picture.

And then something ugly happened.

In the olden days, Buta would have accepted the rebukes of His Highness and not minded his exclusion from the pictures, but he had been caught by the spirit of the new times and could be heard arguing with Rai Bahadur Chottu Ram as he stood at the head of the beaters and other forced labourers.

'What is this buk buk?' Victor asked in a gruff voice.

'Don't talk like that, Maharaj,' said Buta, half gallant, half impudent, even as he bent his head and the joined palms of his coarse, black hands.

'What are you barking?' shouted Victor, enraged at the man's impertinence.

'I am not a dog, Huzoor,' Buta answered back. 'We want our fair wages. And Rai Bahadur won't give them to us.'

'Maharaj, I have given them what is customary,' said Rai Bahadur Chottu Ram.

Fierce and hard, seething with an anger with which seemed to be mixed all the indignation Victor obviously felt against the fates which were gripping him like a vice, squeezing his spirit dry and destroying him, annihilating the very roots of his personality, his kingship, the source of all his power and dignity, he burst into a storm of passion.

'Jao!' he raved. 'Chale Jao!...' His throat was hoarse with shouting, his eyes red shot and his whole frame shook from extremity to extremity.

'No more begar, Maharaj,' said Buta, his face still leaning over his hands.

Victor sprang forward like a tiger in a paroxysm of rage and struck his head, kicking him the while, till Buta fell back, bleeding in the mouth and nose.

Some of us pulled His Highness and held him back. Meanwhile, he frothed at the mouth and raved and shouted the foulest obscenities.

After the awful scene in which the hunt had ended up, the Americans cooled off, and sheepishly withdrew, going off to Delhi by the afternoon train. They seemed to be afraid that they would become involved in the storm which was gathering in Sham Pur, from the way our cars were pelted with stones as we passed through little villages, in spite of the strong police escort that we took with our convoy, and from the deathly silence that reigned in the capital, which was in the grip of a hartal when we got there. Victor hinted that if the guests would wait till the evening, he would come with them, but the sahibs pretended that they had important business to attend to.

'Perhaps you will come for a longer weekend,' Victor said, abjectly, merely because his instinct for hospitality could not accept his failure to have kept the guests for a longer spell. And he ordered Captain Partap Singh, Rai Bahadur Chottu Ram and Munshi Mithan Lal to arrange special air-conditioned compartments for them and to see to their comfort in every way.

When I returned to my rooms to rest a little before packing up to go to Delhi by the night train, as His Highness had ordered, I found, of all people, Mr Bool Chand waiting for me. I surmised at once that he had ratted on Victor and yet wanted to save face, even as he wanted to offer himself in the role of negotiator in the desperate situation in which the Maharaja found himself. He sat impassive in the armchair and pretended to be calm when he was frightened at his betrayal of His Highness.

'You are the one!' I said, taking the offensive. I was angry and could not sit down. So I took off my jacket and stood under the fan to cool down. Francis took my jacket and retreated.

Bool Chand looked sheepishly at me, with a faint smile on the corners of his lips.

Then he asked: 'Did His Highness say anything about my leaving with the Diwan?'

'No,' I said. 'But I am sure he noticed it and thinks that you are like a rat deserting a sinking ship.'

'You can abuse me if you like,' said Bool Chand, with that cool hardness with which he usually disarmed everyone. 'But the situation is serious for him, and I have been trying my best to persuade the Diwan to intercede on his behalf, to help to bring about a settlement by negotiation.'

'A settlement there will be,' I said. 'All wars end up in peace — on a conference table!'

'You will agree, though, that the negotiations are difficult,' Bool Chand said. 'His Highness's bid for independence and the States Department's demand for accession are incompatible. And it will require some manoeuvring to bring about a settlement. The Diwan did not like the idea of His Highness asking for American help.'

Bool Chand had stated the position clearly enough. He had inherited the hard-headed lucidity of his Marwari businessmen ancestors. But he seemed to be utterly lacking in that sentimental affection or regard or loyalty for Victor which obliterated my own reasoned analysis of the situation.

'What are things like in Sham Pur and the villages generally?' I asked. 'Have you heard anything?'

'The hartal is still going on,' said Bool Chand. 'You must have seen on the way that the shops are closed. The people in the city are now not only demanding the release of the Praja Mandal leaders, but they are shouting the slogan of "Quit Sham Pur" against the Maharaja.'

'And what about the military manoeuvres?'

'General Raghbir Singh is back in Sham Pur,' said Bool Chand. 'He was anxiously waiting for His Highness to return. I hear that the three sardars, Raja Parduman Singh, Thakur Mahan Chand and Thakur Shivram Singh, have gone to Delhi to see Sardar Patel. It seems that the sardars fell out with the Communists, because the guerillas began to divide up the land among the peasants on the estates of these noblemen. And, though the state army has taken control of some of the villages, the Communists and the peasants keep shifting their ground and go to other villages, divide up the land there, leave a small commune behind and go further afield, playing hit-and-run tactics with the army. They have looted a great many rifles and ammunition from the army. That is why General Raghbir Singh looked so seedy when I saw him this afternoon. And there are other surprises waiting for His Highness....'

I did not catch the meaning of the last sentence, but I realized that it was all up with Victor, finally and for ever; that, though it would still take him days to admit it, he was already defeated on all fronts and that the best thing was to persuade him to acknowledge it. And, against the sentimental basis of my stand, the ugly, blatant opportunism of Bool Chand seemed to be much more realistic, even though it left a bad taste in the mouth. With this realization, a kind of inertia seemed to come over me, the belief that it was all hopeless. And I was surprised that I had not seen the futility of the whole business with brutal clarity before, and that it had been left for this crook Bool Chand to reveal it to me. Why, Pandit Gobind Das, the Praja Mandal leader, who was no revolutionary, had been at the head of the processions which demonstrated against His Highness! The sardars, who were feudal chieftains, had openly revolted and, for a time, joined the Communists! The States Department had sent Srijut Popatlal J. Shah, and Victor had ignored his advice and sought the help of the Americans! Maharani Indira insisted on her rights. And, while demanding gifts of money and jewellery and land in lieu of the non-recognition of her son as Tika and the bestowal of the status of Maharani on her, Gangi was betraying him physically! And, beyond all these realities, stood, menacing, because more real, the people of Sham Pur State, the peasants from whom he had extorted nazaranas and begar; the small landlords from whom his officials had been exacting huge fees for adoption of children, the men whose property the state had often appropriated when they died without leaving heirs; and the big lords among whom he had discriminated on the basis of personal likes and dislikes! Not all the Machiavellianism of Victor could ward off the nemesis that was approaching. And when the full nature of all his difficulties would dawn upon him, when he would see himself really cornered on all sides, I knew that his disillusionment would probably break him. I could only see the darkness of utter gloom spreading around him on all sides.

'His Highness is a trespasser on the sacred soil of the Indian Union!' said Bool Chand as he got up from the chair. 'A criminal....There is no divine right of kings left any more!'

I looked at him open-mouthed.

'Sham Pur has no place outside the great Indian Union!' he went on. 'It has no sovereignty of its own. Sovereignty belongs to the people!...And everyone is against him, including his own household!'

Noble as these sentiments were, I was flabbergasted at the owner of the mouth which uttered them – the selfsame jackal who had once come insinuating himself into the service of His Highness with the soul of a boot-licker, a flatterer and a toady.

'Sham Pur is a wealthy state so far as its natural wealth goes,' he continued, confronting me full face. 'And yet Sham Pur has remained one of the most backward areas, industrially and economically. But its strategic importance is great today. Chaos and anarchy cannot be allowed to prevail here. And as the motives of His Highness in wanting to assert his independence are anything but altruistic, I am all for Diwan Popatlal Shah taking control, until His Highness sees Sardar Patel and signs the Instrument of Accession. It is your duty to persuade him to hand over control to the Diwan before he goes. Otherwise he will get nothing from Sardar Patel, not even his privy purse.'

The substratum of ugliness and vulgarity that was in Bool Chand's soul shone brightly as he waxed eloquent, an unhealthy, evil glow that transformed his small face into a spurious vitality. Even the horsy snort that might have ruined his declamation was kept in control and did not arise to demolish his new dignity.

'That is what I came to say to you,' he added.

Angry and stiff against Bool Chand, and full of self-disgust, I did not bend even as I said 'Acha'. I did not know how I would tackle Victor, because that would be a positive step, and, for the while, I was only full of negation, of rejection and refusal. A putrid bad taste for the whole of life filled my mouth at being part of this filth, and I felt myself an empty shell. And yet I knew that I ought to remain human for this last phase of my life in Sham Pur, the phase that would become recorded history. For, it was no good, having been a willing part of the putrescence, not to take the punishment of eating the dirt which one had helped to pile up, of going through the murky waters of the dark river of this hell, if only in the hope that somehow one would come clean at the other end.

'I must have a bath,' I said to Bool Chand. 'And then I will go and see Victor.'

He snorted like a satisfied horse and went.

Despairingly, I turned towards the bathroom, shouting, 'Koi hai?'

Brigadier-General Chaudhri Raghbir Singh was still with His Highness when I went in to see him. I retreated from the door involuntarily on seeing the two cousins together, but Victor beckoned me in, from where he was standing, listening to Chaudhri Raghbir Singh, who was walking about the room with a military stride.

'... They have never forgotten the old quarrels they had with your father. And now they are spreading the rumour that the deceased Maharaja Sahib was publicly humiliated by the British Sarkar, as you are being insulted by the Congress Government. They have dug up an old story. It is being said that, some years ago, the late Maharaja Sahib had gone to Delhi, accompanied by Thakur Parduman Singh and Thakur Mahan Chand, to attend a Durbar held by the Viceroy, where all the princes and nobles had been invited to discuss their part in the formation of the Chamber of Princes. At the Durbar, so they say, your revered father was placed below the rulers of Kapurthala and even Mandi. He took umbrage at this and walked out of the meeting. The Viceroy was angry and is said to have ordered him to return to the State and deprived him of his salute of thirteen guns. I think we were children then and did not know about the brave act of your father in defying the Sarkar....But the essence of the story is that the two Thakurs, our enemies, went sycophantly to the Viceroy, and it was thus that Thakur Parduman Singh got his knighthood; and it was then that Thakur Mahan Chand began to assert his right to carve an independent kingdom away from the suzerainty of Sham Pur. And they have egged on Thakur Shiv Ram Singh ever since. So that for years, as you know, he has led the band of primitive tribes, the Sansis, in daily raids on the villages near his own estates. Whole areas near Parma and Udham Pur have been in a state of panic. The ryots have been reduced to destitution. As Shiv Ram Singh paid good huckster's profit to Thakur Parduman Singh, he was not only left in enjoyment of his loot, but encouraged to intensify the banditry!'

'And I have been made to believe that I am responsible for all the discontent of the ryots,' said Victor with a suppressed indignation.

'I tried to persuade Your Highness to let me carry out a campaign against the Sansis two years ago! But instead you yielded more power in the Government to the old Parduman Singh by making him Revenue Minister!'

'I did not realize that, being a blood relation of mine, he would still want to oust me from the gaddi,' said Victor, his face glowing in the dark.

'They have been trying to oust the dynasty for two generations. And yet it was me against whom you were suspicious.'

Victor hung his head down. Then he turned from the window and said:

'Forgive me, Raghbir. I let a woman come in between us. She is a whore, anyhow And what if you have had her – I should not have let my love for you be poisoned by her....' He seemed to be choked by his words and his eyes were liquid with tenderness for his cousin.

'We must fight them to the last,' said Raghbir Singh. 'I can still destroy them!'

'Only if I can come to a good settlement at Delhi,' Victor said despairingly. And his lower lip drooped into a childlike pout and the words weakened in his mouth. 'They have gone to Delhi before me.'

'It is not easy to see Sardar Patel,' I said to console him. 'There may still be a chance if you can come to a settlement.'

'I want to talk to you about that,' Victor said to me significantly.

For an army officer, General Raghbir Singh was particularly sensitive and took the hint and made ready to go.

'I want you to consider yourself the custodian of all my interests,' Victor said. 'Don't let Diwan Popatlal do anything until the negotiations at Delhi are over. I will be back in two days....' And he came forward, with outstretched arms, and took the more tentative Raghbir Singh into his arms.

The General saluted after he had disengaged himself from Victor, and stalked out.

Victor did not notice the departure of his cousin. He stood aloof, visibly hardening himself. He looked grey and unreal even as his mouth quivered with the need to say something unsayable. Then he shook with tension, like a tree moved by the rumour of a storm.

'I can't even trust him,' he said at last. And he moved away from the window and came and lay down on the sofa, ghastly livid as though something in him had given way as he relaxed. He lay flat with his legs outstretched, and his eyes, strangely iridescent, seemed to wander across the ceiling. He moved his face first to one side and then to the other, looking vague and uncertain as though wrapped in a cloud. And a sigh escaped from his lips, like the last groan of a man who is drowning.

Suddenly, however, he sat up and said: 'I won't give up. I will fight till the end.'

'Has Your Highness given the order for your luggage to be packed?' I said.

'No, no.' And then he shouted, 'Koi hai?'

The chaprasi Jai Singh appeared. 'Get Maharaja Sahib's luggage packed,' I ordered. 'We go to Delhi by the 11.30 train.'

'Some warm clothes, Huzoor?' the chaprasi asked. 'Oh, get out and go and pack!' Victor raved.

There was a stillness between us for a moment, during which Victor seemed to be subduing the storm in his nature Then he stood up and went to the window again and, with his back towards me, said: 'I must come through this crisis. I will do so. I know that the States Department has won and that I must sign the Instrument of Accession and accept the limitation of my powers. But....'

It had taken an enormous subterranean effort for him to come to this recognition. For, all the pride, the hard core of his dignity, trussed up for generations by the conventions of absolute autocracy and the will to power, had to break down in him before he could admit such a thing. It was so difficult a truth to face that he became dumb as soon as he had uttered it. And he stood weak, helpless, his face averted from me, lest I should see the tears that dimmed his eyes and of which I had already caught a glimpse as he had turned round to address me.

For a while, he stood thus. And I thought that he was beckoning his soul to stand firm, taming all the lions in his nature, curbing his ambitions. But just when I felt that the battle was nearly over he reeled and came and flopped on to the sofa again, and, with a terrific howl of a sob, began to weep like a child, covering his face with both his hands so as not to be seen in this abject state.

I went over to him and sat down by his side, stroking his back, though I knew that any physical or spiritual comfort I could offer would only make him more distressed.

In a moment, he raised himself with effort and wiped his eyes with his handkerchief.

'I suppose,' he said, 'having acknowledged my defeat at the hands of the States Department, I ought to acknowledge my defeat at the hands of Gangi also.... You don't think she will ever change, do you?'

'I don't think she will change easily,' I said.

'You don't know,' he said, his face twisted by a bitter kind of tenderness, 'that she came out of the bath at the hunting lodge this morning with her strange eyes pathetic and sad, as if she was asking for forgiveness for what she had done with Kurt. She looked so frail and innocent, so lovely, that I did not know what to do except to take her in my arms. All my anger against her seemed to melt away. And she stood there, offering herself to me in her nakedness, as if she was all there for me and me alone.... But this afternoon when we returned here she was petulant and impatient. I slept by her side, but she had gone away from me again, I don't know where....I don't know what happens to her suddenly. I look at her but cannot understand her.'

'She is ill,' I said consolingly. 'She does not know what she wants. But she comes in the grip of a whim or a fancy and this possesses her like a jinn, as in one of the old tales, and then she goes ruthlessly for the person she desires. And, having attained her objective, she lapses into the vague, weak person she really is.'

'The strange thing is that for days, even weeks and months, she used to make me feel that she was a part of me,' Victor said. 'And she made me feel strong. She put courage into me!'

'For my part I would like to help you to be free of her,' I said, 'because she will destroy you emotionally, physically, spiritually. She is an untamed jungli. And she will suck your life-blood and then spit you out. Get rid of her! She is a completely unscrupulous woman.'

'But I don't know why I still love her!' Victor answered.

'I think we had better get ready for the train,' I said.

His Highness had booked a suite of rooms in the Imperial Hotel in New Delhi, and we would have been comfortable enough, under ordinary circumstances, for the summer heat was waning in early September. But all the elements seemed to have conspired to eke the last ounce of pain out of Victor. And the mounting hysteria, and the tension of weeks, now led to a collapse through which he found that lying down on his back was the most comfortable position in life. The breakdown came gradually, of course, and each major factor accentuated the symptoms, till Victor's mind and body shrank invisibly under the various strains.

First of all, from the moment of one's arrival one feels like a ghost, wandering about the long corridors of the

Imperial Hotel, or resting in the tall, spacious and empty mausoleum-like grandeur of its drawing room.

Then we learnt that Thakurs Parduman Singh and Shiv Ram Singh, who, we had previously heard, were staying in Maidens Hotel in Old Delhi, were staying in a wing of the Imperial Hotel, apparently also waiting for an interview with Sardar Patel.

As pride and confidence were an integral part of Victor's Maharajahood, he believed that Sardar Patel would see him immediately he rang up for an appointment. But he did not reckon on the fact that the States Minister had not only other Maharajas to settle with, but that he had to attend to his duties as Deputy Prime Minister and Home Minister, and that to get an appointment to see him was one of the most difficult tasks to perform in New Delhi. After Victor had officially written to the Sardar, Captain Partap Singh rang up the States Department to ask when the interview would be. He was told that the matter was receiving the Honourable Minister's attention and the time and place of the interview would be communicated to the Maharaja in due course. Victor asked me to ring up the next day, and the same formula was repeated to me. He asked Munshi Mithan Lal to go to the Secretariat and see if the interview could be expedited, specially by greasing the palm of one of the officials there. But he could not see anyone except a clerk of the States Department, named Khosla, who said that the Department would duly communicate with the Maharaja Sahib. When Victor realized after all these rebuffs that he was in no better position than his enemies, the thakurs, in the matter of the interview, he tried to save his dignity by going to the Secretariat himself to solicit a more favourable treatment.

But he was seen by the same clerk, Khosla, and told that though he might be given precedence over the two thakurs, since he was a ruling prince, there was no knowing what Sardar Patel had in mind and what he would do. Munshi Mithan Lal quietly slipped a token of a hundred-rupee note into Khosla's hand and that softened the little bespectacled man, but actually, Victor lost more face by going to curry favours from a clerk than if he had stayed in the hotel and waited patiently.

Of course, it was difficult to wait patiently in his present state of mind, or to be patient at all! For, all the time, like a continual toothache, was the dull pain of the feelings he had about Gangi.

I tried to assure him about her in such a way that he might accept her promiscuity as part of her mental illness. I said that it was strange that when a person was physically ill, the illness was attended to, a doctor called in and treatment taken seriously; but that when anyone suffered from an acute neurosis, this was supposed to be part of the temperament of the person, unalterable and permanent like a bad habit. I tried very discreetly to insinuate that he himself was sick.

Victor was rather irritated by this kind of analysis and said that he was now sure I was a Red. I confessed that perhaps I was. Upon this he gave me a lecture on Revolution.

'Actually,' he said, 'I believe in Revolution myself. I am true to the words of wisdom put in ancient times by the poet into the mouth of Shri Ram Chander, King of Ayodhya, of the Suraj Bansi clan, from which my family is descended: "There shall be no pain in my heart in having to resign for the sake of pleasing my subjects; every tie of affection, every feeling of compassion, every happiness, even the idol of my heart, my wife...."'

'Then you should have conceded the reforms demanded by the people of Sham Pur and accepted accession – if you believe in Revolution, you –'

'I believe not in Revolution perhaps, but in my people,' he said, shifting his ground. 'Revolutions are always brought about by the disgruntled well-to-do men.'

'I suppose you will mention Mirabeau, Chicherin, Robespierre, Marx, Lenin....'

'Yes, the people love their kings and are too loyal to revolt,' he said. 'But the middle-class leaders get their opportunity when the literate have destroyed the traditions of loyalty and good habit and weakened the people's will. In every land there are many disgruntled people, who are unfit for civilized life! Always ripe for revolt and eager to destroy. They were usually kept in control by the princes. But nowadays when there are wars and famines and newspapers, men like Nehru and Patel break loose and corrupt the minds of the praja, appoint their agents and bring about revolution, with Hitler's tactics, from within.'

'What Hitler did so often was not to bring about a Revolution but to enact a *coup d'état*, which is a quite different thing.'

'Whatever he did or did not do, I am against revolutionaries like him and Patel....'

'I am afraid you are mistaking the aspirations of a people for the desperation and energy of demagogues,' I said non-committally to terminate this argument.

For Victor, always confused and muddled in his political ideas, had now become incensed and crazy and was difficult to talk to.

And I sedulously tried to divert his mind from brooding both on his public and private problems by persuading him to come sight-seeing round Delhi.

We went and picnicked one day at the foot of the giant column of the Qutub Minar, built by the Slave King, Qutub-ud-Din, which overlooks the countryside up to the city of Agra. We visited the old fort built by the ancient Hindu king, Prithvi Raj, as well as the Red Fort built by Shah Jehan. And we toured the various mausoleums from the tombs of the Lodi Kings to Humayun's grave and Safdar Jang. All this tourism elated him a little, because every monument was some kind of tribute to the strength and sagacity of a king, and his belief in the capacity of princes to do heroic deeds was much strengthened. Unfortunately, however, graves, even though they be ancient and glorious, leave me with a feeling of death and decay, and as most of the old buildings of Delhi are graves, I felt depressed and did not hear, though I listened to, Victor's constant iteration of the values of power, prowess, splendour, firmness, dexterity, generosity and the like. And I don't know if the others felt this or not, but certainly I felt that, as I wandered about in Delhi, I was a kind of ghost wandering about in the vast graveyards of the hopes of India.

But if Victor did not feel this, he certainly looked it, a wraith, who flopped about from place to place, when he was not asleep or eating the awful English meals served in the hotel.

During these days I had occasion to reflect on the tragedy that seemed to befall the Indian princes.

There was a time when they could flaunt their wealth and spend their fortunes freely on the turf as well as in the gambling houses of Nice and Monte Carlo. And in the poverty-stricken countryside there was current the adage, 'Blessed is he who looks upon the face of his ruler.' And abroad the foolish shop girls read, with a curiosity made up of escapist romanticism, myths and legends as well as the 'true' stories, written by the hacks of the Yellow Press, about the dazzling Rolls-Royces from which this Maharaja shot 150 tigers in his jungle kingdom; and how that Maharaja had the most priceless jewels, pearls, with rosy sheens of supernatural qualities and emeralds and opals as big as hen's eggs, and how the other Maharaja had his drinking water fetched from the holy river Ganges all the way to the Savoy Hotel in London and how he gave 20,000 soldiers and £80,000 during the war to the British Government towards the war effort. The cynics among the princes were even then strong enough, for His Highness the Aga Khan had declared that 'it was no beer and skittles playing at being a god!' And not all believed that these kings, the sons of the Sun and the Moon, were really as handsome as they were made out to be, or their queens as beautiful. All the same, however, their prestige, bolstered by the British Sarkar, was gradually beginning to wane.

The whirligig of time brings the strangest revenges. A tough, feudal landlord from Gujarat, who fancied himself as Bismarck, was soon to preside over the destinies of the whole lot of maharajas and win them over to the idea of accession, while rewarding them generously with compensation by way of big privy purses and certain important jobs.

Sardar Vallabhbhai (Wishmarck) Patel growled, like a big angry bull, twice or thrice from the rostrum in Delhi. And most of the sons of Suns and Moons fell into line as children of the earth. They had loyally served the British in their day, but they saw the new stars and comets rise above their heads and began to claim descent from these. They saw advantages in the prolongation of the fortunes which were offered them and they fell in with the new array of forces, piously hoping that they would continue to indulge themselves to their hearts' content as long as the people in their states were kept from shaking them off their perches.

Of course there were some recalcitrants. My Maharaja of Sham Pur was one of them.

In order to while away the tedium of the endless wait for the interview with Sardar Patel, Captain Partap Singh suggested to His Highness that we should go to the bazaar, of an evening, and hear some music. As the suggestion was made in the presence of Munshi Mithan Lal, even the crude Partap Singh had to put it delicately, but what he really meant was that we should go out on the razzle one night to the house of some courtesan and enjoy ourselves. Curiously, Victor was not so enthusiastic about this as he usually was. For Gangi obsessed him and his spirit was further congealed by the fears and doubts about what would happen to him at the hands of Sardar Patel, though really in his heart he knew that the inevitable Instrument of Accession would have to be signed and he would have to say farewell to the power he had enjoyed in Sham Pur. So, for a few days, he did not listen to Partap Singh's reiteration of the plea for pleasure. Then, one night, after dinner, when we had had a good deal of drink, Partap Singh told us that he and Munshi Mithan Lal had gone and fixed up for us to hear a mujra and we must go. His Highness suggested that we give the slip to Munshi Mithan Lal in the corridors of the Imperial if, indeed, we had to go. We agreed to do this and escaped to Old Delhi.

'Are we going to Babban Jan?' Victor asked Partap Singh.

'Highness, there are no Muslim courtesans left in Delhi since the Partition riots,' Partap Singh answered. 'And Babban has gone to Lahore. But I have discovered a Hindu girl by the name of Lakshami, who is as beautiful as a goddess and sings like a nightingale.' And he directed the chauffeur through dirty half-deserted bazaars, full of the smoke of fuel fires, the coughings of tired humans, and the barking of stray dogs, till we reached the northern end of Chandni Chowk, beyond the Clock Tower. Alighting by a dark by-lane, we went up some narrow steps to the first floor of a house of ill fame.

Partap Singh knocked at the door on the first floor, and a middle-aged woman came out, demurely covering her greying hair with her dupatta.

'Come, come, Sardarji, our fate seems to have awakened that you have actually come,' she said, her fair broad face with its sensuous lower lip wreathed in the whore's forced smile. 'I thought you would never come....And is that the Maharaja Sahib? Come, Sarkar, come and grace our house with your presence. And where is that fat Munshi you brought with you when you came three days ago?'

'Where is Lakshami?' Partap Singh said, leading us into the old-style baithak, or living room, with its cow-tailed cushions and dirty white sheeted elegance. He ignored her inquiry about Munshi Mithan Lal, because he really had not wanted His Highness to know that he had brought that puritan here.

'She has gone to sleep,' the woman said. 'And so have the tabalchi and Ustad Durga Das. But I shall awaken them.... Come, Maharaj, come on our heads, come and sit down....'

We went up shyly and settled down by the cushions. Fortunately we were all wearing tight pyjamas and achkans, and it was easier to recline back than it is in English clothes. And Vicky seemed to relax.

'Does she really sing well, or is she just an amateur?' Victor asked Partap Singh.

'Huzoor, I made sure of all that when I came here the other day,' Partap Singh answered.

I looked around and saw the familiar paraphernalia of a courtesan's living room scattered about: the hookah, the betel-leaf carrier, the drums and the harmonium. And on the wall facing us was the inevitable calendar with the picture of a Japanese geisha girl dressed in a kimono, smiling broadly, a fan in her hand. But with all, the room was empty of content, as though it was the stage of that Shakespearian phrase where everyone came and played his part and went on.

Victor seemed to grow more and more solemn as we waited for the performers to appear. And I guessed that he was so much in the grip of his memories that he could not relish the prospect of pleasure in another woman as much as he used to do in the past.

'Still introspective?' I said lamely.

'I feel,' said Victor, with a frankness that was meant to bluff as well as to uncover his domestic predicament before Partap Singh, 'that I have descended into a dark night where the only thing I can see is the light she brought into my life.... You know when I first had her, I wanted my union with her to last for ever and for ever and wanted to shut out the whole world from my gaze. I wished to be with her in an unending life, in the living, palpitating passion I shared with her, as she came to me, a golden girl, shrieking with desire.... And yet I was afraid then that it might not last. And now I think of that moment and am imprisoned in the memory of it, and nothing seems to exist outside....'

Partap Singh was obviously enjoying the confidence, but

also had his own formula for distracting the attention of the Maharaja.

'You will see, Huzoor, how lovely Lakshami is!' he said.

But Victor went on grinding his soul for souvenirs from the past.

'You know Gangi can be very playful. She would deliberately play hide-and-seek with me before yielding up to my embrace. Or she would coyly avert her face to evade my kisses to draw me on. There were times when I believed that the sports of Krishna and Radha would last for ever.'

'Who knows they may last for ever,' I consoled. 'After all, Radha and Krishna had their quarrels as well as their minglings.'

'But she is very strange,' Victor said sadly.

'A snake,' said Partap Singh.

Victor did not accept the comment as it came from the ADC, whose opinion in such matters he did not respect. And he became aware that he had said more than he had wanted to say in the presence of Partap Singh. And he withdrew into himself again.

After a while, the middle-aged woman appeared with Lakshami and the musicians. They all joined hands in obeisance to His Highness. They were obviously refugees, amateurs at this game, for they seemed lacking in the graces of the traditional courtesan and her troupe.

'My name is Rukmani and this girl is called Lakshami, Maharaj,' the middle-aged woman began. And, turning to the girl, she said: 'Now, don't be shy with the Maharaja Sahib. He has come such a long way to see you.'

'Han, han, daughter, sit nearer the Maharaja Sahib, snuggle up to him while I tune up the tabla,' added Ustad Durga Das.

Lakshami's face was cast in a demure mould. She was a dark-complexioned girl with a well-chiselled, sharp, fine nose, big brown eyes and a strong chin, all framed by a white dupatta which set off the whole dusky visage as an evening is often set off by the moonlight.

She moved a little nearer but still remained outside His Highness's range.

He looked at her with an appetite that seemed to grow with the looking: the warm, dark flesh conduced to a kind of enchantment.

She became aware of his interest, but sat as though stranded, a little helpless as she bent her eyes before Rukmani, and forlorn, lost to the world.

'Acha, then get ready to sing,' said Rukmani in an admonishing voice.

Lakshami looked dumbly up at the taskmistress and then lowered her eyes.

'Don't force her if she doesn't want to,' Victor said. 'Let her just get used to us and she will talk.'

'You see how gracious His Highness is to you,' said Rukmani. 'I know he is as generous as he is gracious.'

'At first let her perform,' said Partap Singh brutally, 'before she can expect any generosity.'

Lakshami's face seemed heavy with disappointment. Her lips trembled a little and she looked pathetic like a young calf ushered up before her butchers.

'Sire, you must forgive her shyness,' said Ustad Durga Das, the tabalchi.

Victor's solitariness and detachment had disappeared at the sight of the girl. Now his face quivered. He bent forward and patted her on the head, saying humorously: 'Don't be afraid. I am not a cannibal. I won't eat you.'

With this Lakshami smiled through her tear-dimmed eyes and looked up.

'Now then,' said the Ustad, striking the drums hard on the sides to test them, even as he turned to his companion: 'boy, start up.'

Lakshami's head stooped again.

'Show your cursed face to the Maharaja Sahib,' ordered Rukmani peremptorily. 'He is so kind to you.'

The dread of Rukmani's wrath overpowered Lakshami now. She cowered, then shook her head and braced up to the occasion by a patently artificial put-on smile, in the light of which the tears in her eyes glistened. But her mouth would not open. Only her lips trembled and she seemed to be making a desperate effort to keep up appearances.

'Come, let us have a song, Bibi,' Partap Singh coaxed her, in case His Highness should get bored with her reticence and go.

'Han, daughter, sing for the Maharaja Sahib!' goaded Rukmani, her face wreathed in a frown.

'Han, do sing,' said His Highness. And in order to reassure her, he lunged forward and patted her on the head.

She moved her head away instinctively. But then she realized that he might be offended at her recoil. Drawing the dupatta over her forehead, she inclined her face a little, smiled genuinely for the first time, glanced coyly through the corners of her eyes at Victor and said in a mellow Punjabi accent: 'I will try and sing. I am rather out of breath, because I have just eaten.'

'There is no talk,' Victor said in Punjabi. 'Take your time.'

After this there was that awkward momentary silence which yawns before the singer actually starts to sing.

Lakshami cleared her throat, hummed like a blackbird, became silent and then began to utter the first accents of a popular film song:

'A heart broke into a thousand pieces...'

The refrain carried an air of foreboding about it, which was accentuated by the drum beats of the tabla, and the noise of the harmonium, and the verses became potent with meaning for Victor in his present state of mind. He swayed his head gently as though stirred from the depths. And he looked at Lakshami, regarding her as a kind of prophetess, who had sensed the impending disaster which was coming to him. Then he sat fascinated, inert and sad, listening to the lilt of her voice.

'A heart broke into a thousand pieces,' she repeated. And she added the next verse: 'Some fell here and some fell there...'

Now the words seemed to affect him so deeply that his face was set in the mould of agony, even as he sighed and moved his head slowly as though accepting the threatened break-up of the centre of his life.

'Wah! Wah!' the vulgar Partap Singh shouted the conventional appreciation of the heart-squanderer. Victor gave him a withering look till the ADC shrank into his shell.

But the damage had been done.

Lakshami's voice broke into a sob and the tears welled uncontrollably to her eyes. The thread of her song, which she had held fast in her throat, had snapped.

She covered her eyes with her hands, darted like an animal at bay and ran into the back room.

'Lakshami! Lakshami!' shouted Rukmani. 'Shameless one! What talk is this?'

'Hain! Come here!' shouted Durga Das.

'Let her go,' Victor shrieked, as though he had sensed, with complete sympathy, the girl's inability to go on with the song. Somewhere, deep down, there was an almost convalescent feminine strain in his nature with which he felt a strange weakness for women, a kind of fellow feeling that was morbid like the prolonged anguish of some reparation he had to make for past guilts. It was this feeling for atonement which had drawn his body always towards women: and it was perhaps through this that he was rooted in Gangi, the weakest member of her sex that he knew.

He collected himself after his display of bad temper, but sat in absolute hostility to the company. He seemed to be under the spell of Lakshami for the moment, as he could never have been in the power of a self-conscious whore.

'Please forgive us,' began Ustad Durga Das. 'Lakshami comes from a good home. She was abducted by the Pakistani Muslas from her Hindu husband, a vakil of Lahore, and she was married off to her seducer in Sialkot. Then Shrimati Sarabhai had her rescued and brought back to Jullundur, where her first husband was. He would not have her back, because she had been used by a Musla.... And Rukmani found her, hungry and homeless, at Delhi station, and brought her here...'

'The swine!' Victor hissed.

'These Muslas have done terrible things!' said Durga Das.

'Han, Maharaj, they tortured me and even spoiled me, an old woman,' said Rukmani. 'Until I had to take up this profession.'

Victor's face glowed with rage against the pimps before him. They had misunderstood him. I knew he had abused the lawyer husband of Lakshami and not the Muhammadans. He sat with his head hung down, as though he was sinking into the bottomless pit of despair. And he ground his teeth in an effort to chew the bitterness hard in his mouth and then he swallowed the dry husk of horror, in his throat mirroring the dread which was passing down into his system.

We were all dumb with fear at the incalculable elements in the situation. Would he rise and smash up everyone and everything? Or would he growl like a tiger at bay and frighten us all? What would he do?

I surmised that he had transferred his tenderness from Gangi to Lakshami for a moment, and then taken the feeling, enriched by compassion, back to his mistress. But, because Gangi was not here, he sat in the wilderness, suspended, unresolved and ignorant of what she, whose sex he adored, would do to him.

We waited patiently for a sign from him.

'I think a husband who turns a wife out, because she had been abducted by a Mussulman, is a swine!' Victor said, looking up and flashing like a sword which is suddenly unsheathed.

No one dared utter a sound, though I could see the confusion in Durga Das's sheepish eyes.

At that instant, there was a furious knocking at the door.

The boy at the harmonium sprang up.

'First ask who it is!' shouted Rukmani in a panic.' Then open the door.'

'Kon hai?' the boy asked.

'Is Maharaja Sahib here? I am Munshi Mithan Lal....Open the door.' He struck his stick furiously at the panel.

Captain Partap Singh ran up to the door and opened it.

'A call has come from Sardar Patel's secretary, Maharaj,' said Munshi Mithan Lal, panting breathlessly, his eye-glasses dimmed with the steam of perspiration. 'The Sardar has given an appointment for five o'clock at dawn for you to meet him.'

The red anger in Victor's eyes turned to a white fear. His warm face became pale.

Then he said: 'Five o'clock in the morning, did you say, Munshiji?'

'Han, Maharaj!' answered Mian Mithu in a voice which showed the kind of distress he must have felt when his mother died.

At this Victor laughed out loud, an artificial, hysterical laugh, which fell cracked and hollow on the abject audience.

'Chalo!' he said, lifting his hand. And then he got up and stood like a little stiff colossus in the middle of the empty, soulless room. 'Give them five hundred, Partap Singh,' he ordered. And, turning to the pimp, he said: 'Look, three hundred is for Lakshami. Give it to her. That is my order!'

For a moment, he surveyed the room with a blind, frustrated look. Then he made towards the door.

We followed.

A grey night was merging into a grey dawn as we motored up to the residence of Sardar Vallabhbhai Patel at a quarter to five. Dead Delhi seemed deadlier in the eerie silence which enveloped the long roads and the sequestered bungalows, enshrouded in the mist-covered foliage. Only the lamplights glistened like jets of life from the empty, soulless capital of India.

The sentry at the entrance of the bungalow told us to park the car on the roadside and wait by the lamp post fifty yards away. As we followed his directions, I couldn't help wondering at the oddness of the hour for which this appointment had been given, and felt both irritated and amused at the place of the rendezvous. I think all of us were thinking similar thoughts, though no one dared to say so. And I guessed that His Highness, who had been feeling humiliated enough at having to wait about in Delhi all these days, felt more humiliated when he realized that he, a prince of the Suraj Bansi clan, had to wait by a lamp post in order to see a mere commoner, who happened by good fortune to have become Deputy Prime Minister and Minister-in-Charge of the Indian States.

'It is cold,' Victor complained, shivering a little.

'Maharaj, take my muffler,' said the devoted Mian Mithu.

'No, no, let us walk a little and I shall get warm,' said Victor, proud and taciturn.

As we strolled up to the lamp post and beyond, I felt as though, instead of diminishing, the grey darkness was growing. I tried to distinguish the colours of the flowers in the rounder at the crossing of the four roads, and I could see the pinks and the blues and the reds clearly, so I realized that it was my black mood, arising from sleeplessness, the worry about the future, and the general strain, which made the world seem darker to me. We had all been so sunk in the morass of our own subjectivism, that everything outside us seemed to be contracting, withering, darkening.

We retraced our steps towards the gate of Sardar Vallabhbhai Patel's bungalow, our shoes getting soaked in the dew on the copious grass that grew here and there on the fringes of the pavement.

There was a stirring on the drive by the hall of the bungalow, and by the time we got to where the sentry stood we saw the Sardar walking up. His hard jaws were contracted beneath the dark brown refulgence of the serious, set mien, under the two small points of light which were his half-closed eyes. A simple homespun tunic under a shawl was on his compact torso and a shortish dhoti, going down to just below his knees, covered his legs. He had chappals on his feet and a stave in his hand. The moment of his approach was full of the most awful terror, as though his legend had overpowered us. We all made obeisance by joining our hands to him.

'Raja,' he said, nodding his head briefly.

Victor's face became abjectly pale, though there were streaks of livid anger across it at being called merely Raja, when his title was Maharaja.

But Sardar Patel's strong point was the scowl from which he seemed to frown contemptuously on all and sundry. And against the hard lines of that face, Victor's visage was comparatively gentle and mellow, in spite of the hysterical monarchical rages he used to put on.

The Sardar looked around cursorily and scanned the faces of the two plain clothes men who followed him. And it flashed upon me that even this arbiter of the destiny of the princes, the Deputy Prime Minister of India, the man of steel and iron, was slightly afraid.

'Walk with me,' he said, 'and we will talk your business over.' And he strode forward, a stolid peasant, with a shrewd glint in his small eyes, and the conceit of power seated casually upon his knotted forehead.

For a few moments, Victor, who walked abreast of him, tried to keep step with him – an awkward process, because the Sardar's tread was slower than his own. Then, after he had adjusted himself, he waited for the great man to begin. And the essence of the greatness of the great man lay in not beginning at all, in breaking the nerves of the person he was dealing with by not saying a word, until the victim fell a prey to the folly of words, always fumbling and stupid when they come out of a terrorized soul. If Victor had lived and moved and had his being in the dark night, the Sardar was not really very far advanced towards the dawn, in so far as he dared not project the blinding light of his convictions, without restraints and hesitations, on to his victims. Neither of them would throw a fire-brand into the darkness.

At last Victor, already reduced to half his size by the humility which the Sardar's grim silence imposed on him, began by saying, respectfully, in Hindustani: 'Sir, you have called me.'

'Yes,' the Sardar said firmly. 'I have called you to sign the papers for the accession of Sham Pur to the Indian Union.'

Brief and to the point, the conclusion was put by the Sardar peremptorily, without stating the major and the minor premises. The logic of power does not really admit of argument.

'Diwan Popatlal Shah did bring your message, Sardar Patel,' Victor ventured.

'And you ignored it!' the Sardar snapped. And he looked at Victor hard, and, turning round, swept us all with a glance that seemed to say: 'Fools, anti-social knaves, how dared you help this princeling to defy my orders!'

'Sir, I want to…say…that….' Victor began, but could not go on.

I guessed he wanted to say: 'Before your light and your new order came, I held sway over my people, the descendant of a long line of potentates.' But Victor had more than dimly recognized the force of Sardar Patel's logic and had really no answer to give except to sign.

The Sardar wheeled round with a sudden jerky movement. Victor, who was caught unawares, came to with a start and ran a step or two. He looked back and saw us following docilely, the silent witnesses of his humiliation. He signed to me with his dumb mouth to come forward; apparently he felt I could help him out.

I quickened my steps, but there was a sinking feeling of doom within me and the terror of the Sardar had penetrated deep beneath this awareness of nemesis. I advanced only a step or two beyond Captain Partap Singh and Munshi Mithan Lal.

'What have you to say about this — you ignored the new Diwan I sent you!' Sardar Patel growled in a voice which was half hyaena-shriek, half wolf-growl.

'The Diwan Sahib virtually demanded my abdication, Mr Patel! 'Victor said, nervous yet defiant.

'Accession is not abdication,' said the Sardar, stopping suddenly and breathing hard even as he inclined his torso to ease some spasm he seemed to have. There were a few knots of men ahead and the Sardar looked at them askance.

'After all, Diwan Popatlal is only an ex-ICS officer,' said Victor impudently. 'And he openly insulted the dignity of the ruling house to which I —'

'Diwan Popatlal was sent there by me, and he was under orders from the States Department to negotiate a peaceful settlement with you!' He resumed his steps again and Victor touched my arm for support and we began to walk.

'There was a man called Dhebar,' the Sardar proceeded, 'in Jamnagar State. He rented a house in the city of Jamnagar. He paid the rent of the house, put his luggage there and went away on business. In his absence the Jam Sahib's government sent for the owner of the house and persuaded him to turn out Srijut Dhebar from the house. The owner did so.... Today...justice has been done. Srijut Dhebar is the Prime Minister of a state ten times larger than the little kingdom of the Jam Sahib, which turned him out of the house he had rented. In the Bible it is said that "the beasts of the field have their lairs, the birds of the air have their nests, but the son of Man hath no place where to lay his head". Now, under the new conditions, it is becoming possible for any son of man to become the Prime Minister of the state which ignored his existence as a popular leader.... The old order has to go.'

'But, sir, there are certain political advantages for the Indian Union if Sham Pur remains independent,' ventured Victor. 'It is nearly a buffer state....'

'So you think we don't know what is good for the Indian Union?' answered the States Minister, stiffening. And then he became silent.

The procession walked grimly along. Sardar Patel's steps were more determined now that he had got into his stride. He did not look right or left, up or down, but seemed to look straight ahead, his face clear and hard, as though stuffed up with righteousness, ignoring the outer world, the half-revealed shapes and sounds that make up nature in the hours which precede the coming of daylight. It is possible that I fancied all this about the Sardar, that I was making up the kind of pattern about him which I knew would fit his legend. But any such meeting with an historical personage becomes personal-impersonal and somewhat symbolic, like a landscape into which one can read any meaning one likes.

The silence became oppressive. I could see Victor's face swelling as though the poison of bitterness which he was grinding between his teeth was accumulating in his mouth. And he seemed to walk with effort as though he lacked all faith in this squalid, banal activity, the morning constitutional of the arbiter of his fate, Sardar Vallabhbhai 'Wishmarck' Patel.

'I am not sure, sir, that India's leaders,' said Victor, 'are aware of the danger of Communism!'

The Sardar did not relax his set expression. Only, his narrow eyes swept the prince with a cunning elephant's glance. For the rest there was silence again.

A drove of parrots wheeled across the whitening sky and a few crows cawed.

The stern Sardar had led us almost round his bungalow, though we had not realized this until a dark man, dressed in an English-style silk suit, came walking towards us from the States Minister's residence. I recognized him to be Mr D.F. Verma, one of the assistants of the States Ministry.

'Hello, Mr Verma,' Victor greeted him as he too recognized the negotiator between the States Ministry and the princes.

Mr D.F. Verma was as taciturn as his master and merely nodded.

'Tell the other people I can't give any more interviews this morning,' said the Sardar to the plain clothes men. Then he turned to Mr Verma. 'We must finish this business and get the papers signed. Have you the documents ready?'

'Yes, sir,' answered Mr Verma, calm and unruffled.

I stepped back and yielded my place to Mr Verma.

'Shall I have to sign the Instrument this morning?' Victor asked, incredulous still about the doom that he knew was awaiting him in the bungalow.

'Maharaja Sahib,' said Verma, 'the facts which have come into our possession about Sham Pur State are very bad. Mr Shah takes a very poor view of the hand you took in shooting at the members of the Praja Mandal. The ruthless suppression that your Highness has been carrying on has antagonized everyone. Your own cousins are in revolt against you. And, the grievances of your Maharani apart, the administration has been neglected. The story of illegal taxes and begar and slavery is confirmed by your own officers. Mr Shah has recommended that the Central Government should take over the administration. But we have decided to be lenient and treat you as we are treating the other princes. Your privy purse will be assured and –'

'Mr Verma, I would like to put the real facts before you,' Victor said.

'We know the facts, Raja Sahib,' said the Sardar, inclining towards him condescendingly.

'Your Highness can rest assured,' interpolated Verma, 'that we have a full report on all that has been going on in Sham Pur State. It is a story of unbridled autocracy!'

There was a finality about Mr Verma's words which shut Victor up completely, cast a pallor on his face, as though he was smashed up. He walked along, accepting the whole thing coldly now. Stripped of all the illusions of regal vanity, he yet seemed calm. I knew that although he had sensed that he would have to accept the terms of the States Ministry, he had not known exactly how it would happen, and he had tried to see the hope of some formula in the very texture of his curiosity about the methods Sardar Patel would adopt to make him submit. Now he had gone through the much-dreaded interview, and the terror which the States Minister's studied silences had driven into him seemed to have overpowered him. He looked numbed as though he was suffering from a shock, the real incidence of which would not make itself felt till much later, like the pain of a surgical operation which comes long after the actual cutting and bandaging.

As we got to the gateway of Sardar Patel's house, the vast grey darkness which wheeled over New Delhi was yielding to a blood-stained white, and the shapes of trees were beginning to be limned clear and sharp against the percolating light. The sentry at the gate came to attention as the Minister entered the drive.

Hard and righteous, impersonal like a demon, the Sardar cast the shadow of an oppressive silence on the landscape against which the impertinent cawing of the crows was the only violation.

Victor too seemed to have hardened in the attempt to hold himself intact against the corrosions set up by defeat. Mr Verma was negative and dumb.

'The papers are inside, Verma,' said the Sardar. 'Bring His Highness in to sign them.'

We followed, docilely. Only the plain clothes men fell away into positions like the demons who guard the lesser gods in the Hindu pantheon.

Defeated, exhausted and disillusioned, Victor returned to Sham Pur with us, desperate but dumb. Inarticulate, like an automaton, he had moved about in the train, or lain inertly on the bunk, gloomy and spineless. And by the time we got to the palace he seemed dead beat, except that his eyes had lit up as he had said to me: 'Now, I shall be more or less in the same position as Gangi, one of the disinherited! Maybe, this will bring us closer together.'

On arrival in the palace, the first thing he did was to send Jai Singh to the zenana to fetch the 'Maharani Sahiba'. And he lay down on the settee, breathless from the physical strain of the journey and yet with tremors of excitement in his body at the prospect of meeting Gangi.

'Don't go till she comes,' he said to me.

And then he seemed to lapse into a kind of stupor, staring at the ceiling vacantly, and lying limply, with his legs and arms outstretched, in the way in which one does while one is airing one's body under a fan.

'Talk to me,' he said, turning round to me. 'Tell me about yourself. You have never told me the story of your life.'

'I have never thought myself important enough.'

'What do you think of the whole thing?'

I knew that by 'the whole thing' he referred to the happenings at Delhi. I was in a difficult position, because I felt at heart that the situation in which Victor had found himself was part of an historic transition that was by no means finished and would bring still more shocks and surprises to all in the next few years. I wanted to be as honest as I could be in explaining this to him. So I said rather abstractedly: 'You see, Victor, the world, and India, as part of the world, is in a "state o' chassis".'

'What is "chassis"?' Victor asked, opening his eyes wide and then closing them.

'It is an expression used by the Irish poet O'Casey to represent change. This change has come from the steady movement of mankind from the age of pre-history to our modern times. The vast knowledge accumulated by men through the European renaissance has led to it in a way. And it has been hastened by the French and the Russian Revolutions. Not to speak of the English Industrial Revolution. But, already at the end of the 19th century, the simpler, older world was going. The conventions of the past were breaking down. Our world has been like a volcano, slowly fuming away and erupting every five or ten years. One day it will burst finally and either destroy the earth with its lava or fertilize it for a long time to come. Meanwhile, the whole world is in a vigorous state of ferment. And, in spite of the criss-cross of ideas, the battle of concepts which arose from the enlightenment in Europe with the further ideas implicit in that enlightenment — I mean liberty and democracy and the rights of man, and man's relation to religion and the new knowledge – there has been arising a man, a new kind of human being. This kind of man is everywhere. He is like a point of light in the surrounding darkness. He is a universalist in his vision. I know of a few such men. Therefore, you see, I feel that I can see a unity in the changes that are occurring before us. And I do not want to resist these changes. I realize that there is vitality in the urges of men to harness science and to use it to eat and drink well. If only the few who are frightened of change don't use science to destroy mankind with an atomic war we should all come through to plenty. It is perhaps the contagion of this enthusiasm that enables me to steer clear of the schizophrenia which afflicts you, for instance. You are unable to give up your past and to accept the broadening of life, which is releasing the oppressed. And there are quite a few others like you. And their stubborn self-will makes them abnormal in our age. And hence the distraught atmosphere of our time. It is because some of us perceive the inner relations of the advance made by humanity, in spite of the many setbacks, that makes us hold on to some hope for a future. Of course, our far-sightedness in accepting change and even helping it to come about has to reckon with the fact that the owning interests are narrow-sighted and even blind, and they are on the offensive!'

'Then you believe that the ignorant can rule the world without experience.'

'I believe in men. They have a great vitality in spite of the humiliations they have suffered.'

'So far they have only been capable of suffering humiliations. Hitler could crush them and win them over. France subdued them. And strong men everywhere can control them. Your masses represent only blind energy.'

'I am afraid most of the strong men are really alienated from their own integral vision and sunk in the morass of darkness. Look at Hitler; he depended on mystical signs and symbols and on soothsayers and –'

'You don't believe in the soul, then?'

'I don't believe that there is a soul distinct from the body; the soul is body, the body is soul – and together they make a man.'

'What about the mystics – Sri Aurobindo, for instance? I was hoping to go to him.'

'Mysticism is the approach of a dying man. It is a blind alley, leading to God, from whom no traveller returns to tell what he saw at the other end.'

'You seem very sure! I did not know that you were so cocksure....One of my ancestors withdrew from life and became a sadhu and –'

He was interrupted by the footfall of the chaprasi's soft tread. He sat up.

'Maharaj,' said Jai Singh, 'Maharani Sahiba is not there. She has gone away to her mother's village.'

'To her mother's village?' Victor shouted. 'Why? When? To her mother's village?'

'I knew she was not in the zenana, Maharaj, because I put her luggage into the motor,' the chaprasi said. 'I only went to look, in case I had made a mistake.'

Victor got up and stood facing the chaprasi.

'Did she say anything? Any message?'

'Ji Huzoor, she said that she would not be back for some time.' And the old man fell at Victor's feet and laid his head there over his joined hands, his body trembling and shaking.

'Get out! Get away! Get out of my sight!' Victor raved, eyes flashing like a madman's.

As Jai Singh began to crawl away, the Maharaja followed him and shouted: 'What did she tell you? What exactly did she say?'

'Maharaj, she said that I was not to tell you that she was taking all her luggage. And she gave me a 100 rupees.' The chaprasi was weeping as he said this, because he too realized now, as Victor had realized, that Ganga Dasi had run away.

'How much luggage has she taken?' Victor asked desperately, looking for some ray of hope, some sign that it might not be the end.

'All her luggage, Huzoor,' answered the chaprasi. 'Ten boxes and a hundred years' luggage, Huzoor. Bool Chand Sahib was with her.'

'Bool Chand! Hain! Didn't you prevent her? Couldn't you stop her?' Victor shrieked, raising his hands towards the chaprasi. And now tears were streaming out of his eyes and he shouted: 'Get out, good-for-nothing fool! Get out of my sight!...Why didn't you stop her? Was it Bool Chand or Popatlal?'

'Bool Chand, Huzoor.'

'Get out, you treacherous dog! Get out!...' And he began to kick Jai Singh on his shins.

As the chaprasi retreated, Victor swung round, beating his head with his fists, in a mad, inchoate despair at being abandoned. Then he shook as though his legs were giving way under him and he fell back on the settee, weeping and sobbing, his face covered with his hands. It seemed to me that the pent-up clouds of misery of days had suddenly mounted to the peaks of his soul and crashed like a monsoon.

In a moment, he sat up suddenly and, wringing his hands in violent gestures of defiance against the malevolence of the world, he began to talk aloud to himself, not without showing in his histrionics the awareness of the fact that he had an audience.

'Where have you gone? Oh, where have you gone?...Why have you left me like this?...I want you! I am dying for you....Why have you done this? Why?...Why do you want to destroy me...?'

And again, after these protestations, he broke down and fell down weeping, his face buried in the cushions on the settee.

A revulsion came over me, a kind of hatred against myself, that I could not help him. But I found myself sitting still while he cried. I felt suffocated and choked with the feeling that I could not enter the inner core of his pain, the place where it hurt him most.

I went over to him and eased the strain of the necktie which was making the blood mount to his temples.

'Leave me alone – leave me alone!' he shouted. 'Go away! Get away!'

But I knew that that was the last thing he wanted me to do.

I decided to help him to get to bed and to keep a vigil by his side.

There is an apophthegm that in the multitude lies wisdom. Certainly, the people have a second sense. They knew that negotiations had been going on, between the Sarkar at Delhi and the Maharaja, for Sham Pur to become a part of Hindustan, and that His Highness had been resisting this. When Srijut Popatlal J. Shah had come to the state, the populace had rejoiced, because, under the outer, joined-hand politeness, they harboured resentments from whole eras of oppression, which needed just the confirmation that the big Sarkar at Delhi was on their side, to become vocal. And the Praja Mandal leaders, mostly small men with big ideas, had come to surface on the crest of this enthusiasm, and hartals had been called and processions held, and loud words spoken, ending up in the attack on the Maharaja's palace, which had been foiled by His Highness's use of firearms, the arrest of the Praja Mandal leaders and the establishment of police rule, of which even I had been the innocent victim on my way to the polo ground. But if the atmosphere abounded with rumours of all kinds emanating from the inner meaning of the big hunt and from the details of the miasmatic revolution which spread in the towns and the villages through the activities of the rebellious cousins of the Maharaja, as well as the Socialists, and the Communist guerillas, the principle behind the widespread disturbances was not open to doubt: there seemed to be an open conspiracy to curb the autocratic powers of the Maharaja and to achieve full responsible government, with a democratically elected legislature representing the people. This basic aim was, of course, the reflection, by and large, of the struggle of the peoples of British India which had got a quarter of the way to freedom through the transfer of power from the British Crown to the representatives of the Indian National Congress. It had taken its inspiration from the phrase in the oft-quoted text of the Independence resolution: 'We believe that it is the inalienable right of the Indian people, as of any other people, to have freedom and to enjoy the fruits of their toil and have the necessities of life, so that they may have full opportunities of growth. We believe also that if any government deprives a people of these rights and oppresses them the people have a further right to abolish it.' And though they had never self-consciously announced this slogan, this pledge had also dominated the mind of the people of the states, even as it had obsessed the population of British India. By the light of this they had been guided, by this right they had stood, and to secure it to themselves they had begun to struggle. Only, because here in the states the 4th century BC was linked much more intimately with the 9th, the 19th and the 20th than in British India, the path of progress was cluttered up with all the hangovers of history – the conceptions of absolute monarchy, feudalism, open banditry, neglect, mystic veneration of the kind which regarded princes as the descendants of God, liberal doctrines and the ideals of the French and Russian Revolutions, and even the idealistic anarchism of Bakunin. And the confusion was made all the worse by the personal entanglements of the Maharaja. Somehow, in the workings of history, the spicy bits of good-humoured conversation about the loves of princes and princesses constitute, in the mouths of the people, a more potent weapon of struggle than politicians admit. For the gossip of the bazaar is always the froth on the surface of realities to which a humanity, living at low pressure, resorts as a safeguard against the intensity which might kill everyone. Laughter at the inordinate cruelties and injustices rampant in society is a necessary precaution against adversity. The ultimate, final and irrevocable struggle was, however, destined, through the irreconcilable aims of the various factions, to go to extreme solutions. For the swiftness of tempo necessary to clean up the debris of 2000 years, through the limited aims of Sardar Patel to take the princes into collaboration, through the opportunism of the cousins of the Maharaja, and of the Praja Mandal leaders to grab power for themselves, and the revolutionary aims of the Communists to destroy the whole set-up and create a Bolshevik state, made variously for timidity, muddle and violence. At the moment everyone's attention was concentrated on the fact that the Maharaja had been forced to sign the Instrument of Accession. And, naturally, the joy of the populace knew no bounds.

On the morning of the second day after our return from New Delhi, the din and noise of shouting multitudes outside the palace awoke us. Victor came rushing into my room in his pyjamas and insisted that we should go and see what was up. As we climbed up to the rooms of the main deohri overlooking the Victoria bazaar and peered from the jalousied windows, we could see a thick procession advancing towards the palace a hundred yards or so down the street.

Victor shook as though the sight of the enormous populace advancing towards him seemed to constitute a threat to his physical presence. His face was pale, though he stared hard out of the apertures of the windows to try to see and understand what was happening. As he looked at me for a moment, I could see a strange horror in his dilated eyes, as though he felt that the universe was cracking and he was sinking into the caverns that were yawning beneath him. His breath began to come and go quickly as the slogans 'Praja Mandal ki jai! Pandit Gobind Das ki jai!' resounded back from the sky.

'Will they storm the palace?' he asked.

'No, there is no question of that,' I said. 'You are still the constitutional head of Sham Pur. You have signed an Instrument of Accession, but not of abdication! Sardar Patel was very cordial to you immediately the document was signed....'

Victor lowered his eyes, as he was slightly abashed at his weakness. The romance and dignity of the hereditary prince seemed to have dissolved from his person and he sat, shrunken and dishevelled in his silk dressing gown, as Louis XIV might have sat, witnessing the victory of the people over him.

'I say, Pandit Gobind Das looks rather seedy,' he commented bitterly.

It was true that Pandit Gobind Das, the Praja Mandal leader, looked pale as he sat quietly like a god on the throne-like dais of the rath, drawn by ten pairs of bullocks, behind the advance guard of richly caparisoned elephants.

'I suppose he is yellow with the fear of victory, or maybe it is his inverted vanity.'

'He is dead! He seems dead! His five senses may be about him, but just look at his fat, flabby body. The ass! How can he rule? Brother-in-law, sprung up from nowhere!'

The bitterness and abuse sprang, it seemed to me, from the death in him of the nobility which was once his. For, in fact, I could see now that Pandit Gobind Das was beaming with a smile as the vast throng converged around him, throwing flowers at him and garlanding him and the other leaders seated by him, even as the procession came forward, with the cymbals crashing ahead, drums beating and men shouting hoarsely, pushing their way ahead, clumsily, heavily and yet, as though they constituted one big colossus, advancing inexorably to power and privilege.

'I could destroy them!' Victor ground the words in his mouth. 'If only Sardar Patel had not tied my hands, I could have reduced them to ashes!'

'With what? With your two bare hands and your pride! Don't give in to your weakness, Victor. You are a Rajput!'

Beyond the rath on which the Praja Mandal leaders were riding was a stately palanquin, bearing Srijut Popatlal J. Shah and Mr Bool Chand.

The very sight of the latter made Victor go mad. Frothing slightly in the mouth in an agony of helplessness, stupid and hollow, and with wild, puzzled eyes, he shouted: 'The snakes! The vipers! I shall see to it that that worm Bool Chand is destroyed! Son of a swine!'

And he peered hard through the holes of the tracery. I knew he was trying to make sure that Gangi was not there to complete his humiliation.

The shouts and slogans rose with a deafening rhythm now, as the procession nearly came parallel to the palace gates. And to increase the confusion in Victor's soul, the concourse slowed down until it came to a standstill, and a band, composed of clarinets, flutes, drums and saxophones, struck up an odd, noisy, syncopated rhythm.

Fortunately, Gangi was not in the procession, but the drumming of Victor's heart, which I could hear distinctly, continued. Apparently, his sense of coming disasters and insults was by now acute.

'Bolo Sham Pur Praja Mandal ki jai!' 'Bolo Sri Gobind Das ki jai!' 'Bolo Sri Ram Chander ki jai!' 'Bolo Sri Krishnaji Maharaj ki jai!...'

The slogans multiplied.

The band became noisier.

The drumbeats nearly tore the sky.

The sun shone gloriously and splendidly on the Praja Mandal crowd.

Out of the ecstatic confusion arose a long series of protracted tom-tom beats. And then a voice spoke hoarsely through a microphone: 'Pandit Gobind Das will speak!'

Victor got up from where he was crouching and made to go.

'Let us listen to him,' I said, and held him down.

The Maharaja yielded supinely and sat back.

The voice of Pandit Gobind Das came, metallic but raw, over the diminishing hubbub:

'Brothers, today is an auspicious day, because all efforts of the Praja Mandal have been crowned with success. The Maharaja Sahib of Sham Pur has acceded to the main demand of the States Congress – accession to the Indian Union. The Maharaja Sahib is a strange and somewhat wayward youth. He is intelligent, gracious and has, in his own way, always kept the interests of the people at heart.'

If the Maharaja was, as the Praja Mandal leader said, 'strange and somewhat wayward', then Pandit Gobind Das was no less 'strange and wayward'. At least his words were 'somewhat strange' and 'somewhat wayward', For the compliments which he had showered on His Highness were in sharp contrast to the abuse and denigration which he and other Praja Mandal leaders had lavishly bestowed on the Maharaja and his administration up to a week ago. I began to see that the real significance of the 'bloodless revolution', as it was called, which Sardar Patel had wrought, was to bring about collaboration between the Indian Government and the princes on a new basis. I could see that Victor, too, was somewhat relieved at the tone of Pandit Gobind Das's speech.

'Not so bad as you thought it would be,' I said. Victor nodded his head.

But I had spoken too soon. Pandit Gobind Das had now begun to reprimand the Maharaja a little:

'...but he is unstable, with no character, nothing to hold the various parts of his being together, heart, brain and body. There is only a lot of movement in the various parts and –'

The next few words were lost in a flutter of laughter which arose at this description. But Pandit Gobind Das's voice now resounded back from the towers on the top of the deohri of the palace, and the mass before him listened, rapt and still.

'Soon after the acceptance of office by the Congress, the ruler, on the advice of his British advisers, acted on the theory that Paramountcy had lapsed. Now the holy ghost of Britain has gone, and wiser counsels have prevailed. And the Maharaja Sahib has become the Messiah who has brought salvation to his subjects by signing the Instrument of Accession. All the Praja Mandal prisoners have been released. A representative, popular government will soon be installed and Srijut Popatlal J. Shah will act as an adviser of the Government of India to the popular ministry....'

This bit about the new role of Srijut Popatlal J. Shah came as a surprise to us. Apparently, Sardar Patel had not enough confidence in the Praja Mandal leadership and had retained his own nominee in Sham Pur.

'...the prince must be grateful that he has not yielded to the blandishments of the Satans, the Molochs around him, but has exhibited a triumph of his own spirit over the weaknesses of his flesh. Bolo His Highness Maharaja Sahib ki jai!...'

Some part of the crowd took up the slogan in an indifferent voice, because the change of Gobind Das's tone was too sudden for the people, whose hostility towards the Maharaja was too deep-seated and real. 'Bolo Praja Mandal ki jai!'

That shout was echoed back with greater fervour, being repeated *ad nauseam,* until the throats tore and the whole edifice of the palace deohri shook with the echo. It seemed that the hall in which we were would remember this occasion for centuries. For, if it was not actually stormed, its grandeur and majesty was demolished by the rancorous shouts of the people.

After the speech of Pandit Gobind Das, the procession began to move down the Victoria Bazaar.

Victor got up, his face sullen and black, his eyes bloodshot, his lips tight and his whole body hard, as though it was stiffening before it would become cold.

'Monsters!' he shouted. 'Monsters! Monsters!'

I did not contradict him, but merely touched his arm embarrassedly to direct him towards the stairs.

They have taken everything from me,' he said, going down the dark stairs. 'But they might have left me my woman – I shall teach that snorting bania, Bool Chand, the lesson of his life!'

During the next few days the actual pattern of the new set-up in Sham Pur emerged fairly clearly. A Praja Mandal Ministry was installed, with Pandit Gobind Das as Premier, and he gave the various portfolios to his chief lieutenants: one Ministry, that of Justice, being given to Raja Parduman Singh, the old cousin of His Highness. Brigadier-General Chaudhri Raghbir Singh, the Commander-in-Chief of the State Forces, was, contrary to current rumours, retained in his post. And, most important of all, the Ministry showed unusually tender solicitude for the Maharaja Sahib – the Ministers, as well as the 'Adviser', Srijut Popatlal J. Shah, having issued statements in the Press that, since His Highness had graciously and voluntarily acquiesced with the proposals of the Government of India in signing the Instrument of Accession, all old feuds should now be forgotten and due consideration and respect be paid to the benign and enlightened young constitutional ruler.

All this conduced to the acceptance by His Highness of the new order, especially because the States Ministry at Delhi gave him a privy purse of twenty-five lakhs a year and, in principle, allowed him rights over his personal lands and properties, though the exact details were left to be settled later.

Nevertheless, Victor could not really accept the changed circumstances in his heart, particularly because the 'bloodless revolution' coincided with his domestic disaster. And it offended his susceptibilities terribly to learn that Bool Chand, his ex-lackey, who had run away with Gangi, had been appointed secretary to the new Prime Minister.

The nervous tension from which Victor had suffered in the previous months now became a kind of collapse, and his habitual lying down flat on his bed spinelessly became a permanent condition of his being. There was nothing physically wrong with him; that is to say, his blood pressure was normal, his inside clear and his body intact, but he complained that he could not sleep and that his heart beat like a drum. It seemed to me that a deep malaise was eating him away slowly, and he looked thinner, shrinking visibly, and his pale face, screwed up into a knot of misery, darkened with shadows around the eyes and became set in a mould that was grim and inscrutable. Something in him was dying, the intrinsic, intimate life that he had had with Gangi, and he would not come alive again, never quite in the way in which he had throbbed and vibrated before. But the torment of this death was terrible to behold, because it was a long process in which his lucid insight into the character and temperament of Gangi, and the inevitability of the break with her, were vitiated by the return of nostalgic regrets, mainly brought about by the hold which the habits of years of living together with her had on him. And he blubbered repeatedly, bitterly, and in a strange, mad anguish, about what had been between him and her and how wantonly and stupidly she had destroyed it.

The tragedy of the onlooker in witnessing the break-up of another man's life is that the outsider cannot easily enter into the fierce, storm-tossed passions of the victim's heart. And yet the misery of the broken heart spreads like a weight on the environment, settling upon everything and bearing down the companions of the lover, steadily, into the bottomless pit of his suffering. The only thing that saved me from the boredom of the constant iterations were the memories of the anguish I had myself suffered in England when, after the hectic blaze of a three-month passionate affair I had had with a woman medical student, the question of race and colour had intervened and the college authorities had dictated that we break it off. I knew that, though my own experience was rather different, it is not possible to love, and lose that love, without being torn to shreds when the break comes. For, apart from the habits that living together engenders, there arises, in the course of the physical passion, a catharsis of emotion which grows either into a bright creative aura, if the relationship is maintained, or matures into a cancer of regrets if it breaks up. And this cancer goes on growing and paining even after the death of love, almost like some people's hearts, which are said to become harder and not to burn when the body is cremated.

Victor's will strained, with all its tension, to get Ganga Dasi back. He sent messengers all round Sham Pur to look for her. But, not being able to locate her, he wrote to her care of Bool Chand, shrieking out to her, asking why she had left him and telling her that he was desolate and lonely, and begging her to return. And when he did not hear from her, he humbled himself and wrote to Bool Chand, asking him to give her back to him. There was no answer, however, and he seemed to go through the movements of a drowning man in a rough sea, struggling to keep afloat. And I became a kind of slippery raft which he had got hold of and to which he tried to hang on for survival.

'If only she will come back to me, there will be no recriminations,' he kept saying. 'If you see her please tell her this.'

And he talked in his sleep, and even when he talked to me he seemed to be talking aloud to himself, complaining that he had been caught completely innocent and defenceless.

And all the time Ganga Dasi was silent somewhere, cold and hard and brittle, so it seemed to him, beyond his reach and unbending, relentless, in spite of the abject pleas of his letters.

I had heard of poets dying for love and read the sagas and legends where heroic princes gave up whole kingdoms for women. But I had never actually seen the spectacle with my own eyes, of the disintegration of a man through the pangs of thwarted love.

As he was free with his confessions to his staff, each person tried to soothe him with advice and help, according to the bent of his own temperament.

'There are three kinds of natures according to our ancient Hindu lore: Sattvas, Rajas, Tamas,' said Munshi Mithan Lal. 'The first is pure and truthful, the second is noble and the third is the mixed lower, carnal nature. Ganga Dasi belongs to the third group. So, Maharaj, try and forget her....'

Victor stared at him inanely from the deep sockets of his eyes, angry at the old man's insensitiveness.

'That is easier said than done,' I put in on Victor's behalf.

'There are so many women in the world,' Munshi Mithan Lal continued, 'and Victor could not marry all of them; so he should think that Ganga Dasi was one of those many women who is not his!'

I felt amused by this naïve logic, and even Victor's mouth puckered with a smile.

'You may laugh at me,' said Munshi Mithan Lal. 'But what are our little loves and vanities in the face of the sublime truth of God! We all have to die one day. Just imagine that Ganga Dasi is dead.'

Victor found this argument a little more plausible. But the stricken heart cannot admit of transcendental rationalizations. By their very nature, human beings are bound to the flesh, and detachment, or non-attachment, is outside the orbit of the worldly life unless the ascetic withdrawal becomes an ideal and is pursued with the relentless fury of the sadhu. The familiar theosophical gag, that one should practise non-attachment while being attached, is a kind of self-deception which prigs sermonize about, but which has hardly ever been practised even by avowed puritans like Tolstoy and Gandhi. Both were honest enough to admit the pull of fleshly desire up to the last; and the Count, being a supreme artist, has left a posthumous story, *The Devil*, purporting to relate the nature of the physical passion he felt for a handsome peasant girl in the last years of his life and of his fear in the face of this urge.

'It is the hangover of sex that is troubling you,' said Munshi Mithan Lal.

That statement seemed to find confirmation in Victor's soul. He nodded shyly.

'Then you must forget her,' Munshi Mithan Lal repeated, 'and face your loneliness. Once you face the fact that each man is ultimately alone, you will be able to conquer your lower nature and be free.'

'But you don't understand!' said Victor, appreciative of the kindliness of the old man, but impatient with his spirituality. 'You can't see how my life was bound with her. She is coiled up in my entrails....'

'The entrails are the seat of the carnal, animal, lower self, the kama-loka!' Munshi Mithan Lal philosophized. 'This carnal ego grows like a cancer at the very roots of life and eats away the soul, destroying the exalted harmony of life, and it causes violent conflicts in the self, which drown all calm and peace with their shrieking and noise.'

The pomposity of Munshiji's utterance did not obviate a certain profundity which was in his analysis; but he was going outside the terms of reference of the lonely heart. He had so wrapped himself in the cocoon of idealistic complacency that the anguished flutterings of the bird on to the left of Victor's physiology did not touch him at all. I felt that, apart from his loyalty to the Maharaja and his general concern for the sick man, there had come with his voice the patronizing superciliousness of the God-intoxicated Vedantist, who regards everything as Maya, illusion.

'If only – if only she would come back,' Victor said, 'I would take her to some enchanted land, to Kashmir, to Southern France, and I would lead her to the sea, or to some rock, where no one could see us, and where everything would be enchanted as in a fairyland, and there I would have her under a blue sky. In the magic of that air she would sleep in my arms, clinging to me as she always slept during our seven years together, a little child wanting protection and love and care! Oh, why was I so thoughtless? Why didn't I give her all that she wanted – houses and land and money and jewellery?...'

And he rent himself with agony.

'I know she is a harlot,' he would say in lucid moments, 'and I really ought to take Mian Mithu's advice and cast her out.'

And, for moments, he seemed to be making desperate efforts to oust her, torturing himself to get away from her.

'She is like a leopard. She is a bitch, really, a whore!'

But, in spite of his fulminations against her, he could not eject her from his sick soul.

And yet there was no news from her, and he felt the silence of the great wastes of Sham Pur beat him back. And when Captain Partap Singh, and the other emissaries whom he had sent to trace her, came back without any news of her, he felt he must accept defeat and leave her; for, if she had wanted to come back to him, she would have written or actually come.

'Your Highness, may I say something?' asked Captain Partap Singh. 'Something you may not like.'

Victor looked up at him hard. Then, thinking that the ADC was going to give some information to him which he had so far withheld, he melted.

'Sire,' said Partap Singh, 'you must have some pride. You must beckon the pride of your Rajput ancestors. And – how shall I put it, Huzoor, but you must give her up for the sake of your manhood.'

Victor kept silent but nodded assent. Then, after a moment, he said: 'To be sure, for my soul's sake, I must give up the thought of her.'

But again, with tears in his eyes, he swung back to self-pity and beggary and sobbing.

'There are other women in the world,' said Partap Singh with hearty optimism. 'Women are two a piece!'

Victor surveyed Partap Singh's tall frame with obvious affection. In the secret recesses of his mind he must have been playing with the idea of a substitute. There were other women, of course, any number of them. And he could perhaps take one. But he said: 'Partap Singh, you don't know, you don't know....It was perhaps the smell of her which mixes with mine....'

And he was sure that he was bound and imprisoned, and brooded like a superstitious fool over the reasons for Gangi's hold on him, murmuring to himself: 'Why is she all in all to me?'

'To be sure, the hill women are known to do magic,' said Munshi Mithan Lal.

'They can make a man into a goat,' said Partap Singh.

'Only in death shall I be able to get rid of her!' Victor said as he sighed.

'The bondage is of the mind,' said Munshi Mithan Lal abstractedly. 'If your soul is not free of her, then you will never be free. The mind is everything.'

'The strange thing is that I know only death will release me,' said Victor. 'And yet I do not desire death.'

'You must not be so weak, Highness,' Partap Singh pleaded shyly. 'I would rather she died, or her lover, Bool Chand, died than that any harm came to you.'

'I am weak,' Victor confessed. And then he looked at Partap Singh almost as though he wanted to see how far he would go in loyalty to him. And I had an uncanny feeling that there was a strange, mad glint in his eyes. 'I am weak,' he repeated, staring hard at Partap Singh.

'If you go on feeling like a worm....' said Munshi Mithan Lal harshly.

Victor accepted the rebuke and did not answer.

'Leave the sermons of Mian Mithu alone, Huzoor,' said Partap Singh. 'We will go to the Hawa Palace and have some fun.'

'Who will you fetch for me?' Victor said, and a gentle, lascivious smile covered his face. He seemed to be pondering over Partap Singh's formula for an easy escape, feeling perhaps that a woman, any woman, might fill the gap.

'I will bring you a peach, Huzoor,' said Partap Singh.

'You must be free of desire,' said Mian Mithu. 'Otherwise you will suffer more.'

'I can't be free of everything,' Victor said, rolling on to his side. 'I can't be free of her. Why...perhaps Doctor Shankar understands why?'

'Yes,' I said, 'I feel I understand, though it is difficult from the outside. I can sense the frenzy of desire as well as the agony of the frustration to an extent!'

'But what shall I do?' Victor asked.

'I feel you should suffer the misery,' I said. 'Like Siva you must drink the poison and become Nilakanta. And like Siva you must let Parvati trample upon your body, until she has destroyed you and left you pulped. Then, having suffered, you will begin to heal and may get some calm, though this calm may not be peace.'

'Of all the advice I have been given,' said Victor, 'yours is the most real, Hari. I will have to go through this. The nights are the worst. I rock from side to side. I feel myself slipping, slipping, and my heart thumps at the thought that Bool Chand may be having her. If only she had chosen a worthier lover!...Oh, it is a mad, black torture to think of this faithless woman whom I love! Why couldn't I love Indira? Why did I have to fall in love with a whore?'

There was an awkward silence after he said this.

No sooner had the new set-up in the state been ordained than it began to reveal contradictions among the various forces in Sham Pur life. The course of democracy, when it is merely a convenient disguise for maintaining the powers and privileges of a group, like the course of true love, when it is based only on physical possession, does not run smoothly. It was true that the bulk of power was allotted by Sardar Patel to the Praja Mandal party, which had shown democratic predilections; and the feudal chieftains had only one portfolio given to them; while the Socialists were kept out; and the Communists were beyond the pale. But the potential for the balance of power and, therefore, for mischief, remained in the hands of Srijut Popatlal J. Shah. Not only did Srijut Shah display blatant dictatorial tendencies all round, and announce an anti-Left campaign to keep the Socialists at bay, and to crush the Communists, but he manoeuvred and intrigued with the different groups to split them in order to implement his own stranglehold on Sham Pur. To give legal sanction to all this he got Sardar Patel to name him Political Administrator of the new territory which had acceded to the Indian Union.

Believing in the theory of first things first, he got the Premier to order intensified military action against the Communist guerillas in the Udham Pur and Panna districts. In order to achieve this end, he took into special favour Brigadier-General Chaudhri Raghbir Singh by offering him the bait of a higher rank if his campaign was successful. Raghbir Singh fell in with this plan, partly because it was his duty as

Commander-in-Chief of the State Forces, and partly because of the pecuniary advantages that might accrue from the consideration shown to him by the Administrator. But, having been in close collaboration with the Maharaja, he felt a trifle self-conscious, not knowing whether Srijut Popatlal J. Shah really trusted him. And the frequent presence of Mr Bool Chand in the camp of the Administrator made him feel instinctively uneasy, because of his contempt for the treacherous bania who had not only betrayed the Maharaja's salt but had run off with Ganga Dasi, fit enough, in the General's opinion, to be the mistress of His Highness or the Commander-in-Chief only, but not of a snorting ass like Bool Chand. Besides, he sensed that Srijut Popatlal J. Shah was in close touch with Raja Parduman Singh, who had no reason to love an erstwhile favourite of the Maharaja. Rent by doubts and misgivings and divided loyalties, Brigadier-General Chaudhri Raghbir Singh supplied the first important contradiction in the body politic of Sham Pur.

The second significant contradiction was between the Administrator and Pandit Gobind Das. Dyarchy is a bad form of government at the best of times. But, in times which were so out of joint as this, the dual orders emanating from the Administrator's office and from the Premier's Secretariat set going a fatal discord in which the manoeuvring powers of two highly skilled intriguers were involved.

Another contradiction was supplied by the quarrel of the minor ministers, among whom Srijut Om Prakash Shastri, who had been given the portfolio of Public Works, was demanding the key ministry of Home and Police, which the Premier had kept to himself along with the ministry of Education.

Still another contradiction was the bid that the Socialist leaders, Mr Prakash Chander Verma and Swami Shyam

Sunder, were making, as part of the campaign of the Socialists all over India, to oust the Congress Ministries.

And all these contradictions were capped by the armed struggle between the State Forces and Communist guerillas, who abounded in the jungles and the villages.

And the whole atmosphere was full of the fire of controversies, in which the voices of vainglory, gossip and contempt licked the ceiling of the sky, while the smoke of insidious intrigues, corruption, nepotism and black market spread in intricate coils around the houses and offices of Sham Pur, until, in the darkness that was daylight, one could not recognize oneself or anything else.

And yet in this very long-ago-land the sky was torn with the thunder of guns, which the Communist guerillas had seized from the State Forces and were shooting off into the smoke and darkness; burning fires that cast an unearthly glow with which to read the calligraphy of time.

The simplicity and directness of the peasants often cut through all the confusion of the learned. And since in India the old values were reversed, and nothing very new was evolved, and the Inspector of Police came to be more honoured than an Inspector of Schools, and the rich black marketeer justified, with what he could buy with his ill-gotten gains, the validity of money values, a new kind of barbarism emerged and held sway.

The disease of the thinking man in such a set-up as that of Sham Pur is, of course, much deeper. And since I was of my time, and was sick in my soul from breathing the foul air arising from the dying society, I often reflected on the nature of the more dramatic illness of Victor, because his soul was even more sick than mine and because I could see how, like a marionette, his life had been thrust out of the old grooves

and pulled by social and human forces, and pushed, not
only into minor clashes with the various layers of the feudal
and modern life, but confronted with a final challenge by
his peoples.

In essence, I suppose, the name of the malady, which affects
individuals like Victor in the transition that we see before us
today, is rootlessness.

Once upon a time, Victor's grandfather, the last known
ancestor of the dynasty, sat securely upon his throne, a
Maharaja surrounded by the love and fear of his praja, nearly
a god. In the scroll of fate revealed to him by the Brahmins,
he was styled: Maharajadhiraj Shri 108 Nara Narayan Shriman,
Mahapundit Mahasurma, Shri Shri Vikram Singhji. The
Maharajadhiraj presided over all the state functions, stood
at the head of the State Forces, on the occasion of the holy
festivals of Dusserah, Shivaratri, Dipavali, and on every Puran
Mashi, when the full moon matures. And, on all these
occasions, the temple bells rang, the drums were beaten
and bands played, and people shouted even as the
Maharajadhiraj was taken in a procession through the main
streets of the capital. And, in return for all this worship and
adoration, the head of the state threw handfuls of corns to
the poor, and free food was distributed to the beggars as
charity from the palace and in the temples. He was above
the law of the land and supposed to live within the bounds
of ancient customs, old practices, century-old precedents
and, above an, in accordance with the edicts and injunctions
laid down in the Hindu shastras for a king.

Even in the reign of Victor's father, the old order remained
secure. George VI sent an expression of his sincere pleasure
at the confirmation, by 'treaty, of the traditional friendly
relations between us', together with his earnest hope that

these relations may long continue and may contribute to the prosperity and peace of my Empire and Sham Pur'. And Maharajadhiraj Shri Vikram Singhji sat so securely on his gaddi that he offered his sincerest thanks to His Britannic Majesty for 'his gracious message' and took 'the opportunity to respectfully reciprocate the sentiments contained therein' and to 'fervently hope that the ties of friendship thus strengthened may become with God's blessings as everlasting as the mighty Himalayas'.

And everything in the garden was lovely for a few people, and as it was these few who did the thinking for the many, no one seemed to feel that the world was sitting on a volcano. When the First World War started, some people refused to fight, saying it was a war between rival empires, but, by and large, people took part in the struggle between the 'evil Kaiser' and the 'righteous British', and they preferred to live on the never-never system, a kind of deferred living, turning in upon themselves and seeking various escapes either in revived religion, or sex, or some other blind alley. And there was confusion all round, except in Russia, where Lenin and the Bolsheviks upturned the Czarist Empire and, wiping out much feudal decay, began an experiment in a new kind of community living in which men were to be united. But those people in Europe and Asia, who had cut themselves off from the traditional life of their forefathers, while retaining the forms and conventions of the old order, felt a certain rootlessness in the void in which they lived. The trouble with liberal democracy is that it takes a long time to mature, and only the most resilient men can evolve an adequate way of life out of the warp and woof of the democratic idea. So that the 'free' individual wanders about, suffering from the *mal de siècle*, unable to discriminate between one thing and another or one value and another, and so he is unable to use his 'freedom' and remains guilty, unhappy, tormented, sad, agonized ever.

Apart, then, from the other reasons which were responsible for the disquiet of Victor's spirit, there was this rootlessness, which made him the ghost of himself, a mere apparition of the feudal monarch dressed up on state occasions in all the dynamic habiliments, having all his needs met by the community – that is to say, claiming his rights as a maharaja but refusing to fulfil his responsibilities in the old structure and refusing to adopt the values of the new life.

Under the influence of Munshi Mithan Lal, he sometimes argued that his isolation was essentially like that of other human beings, who are strangers from each other and separated like islands in the sea of unknowing ever since Brahman split up his Oneness into duality, when desire arose in him; and that, like other people, he, too, was struggling to find unity in God. But when he felt the pangs of separation, these were not so much of separation from God as from Ganga Dasi, and he inclined, with a certain superficial nostalgia, towards the sets of Rajput paintings in his palace, which celebrated the loves of Radha and Krishna, in which the longing of the divine couple for each other, and the ecstasy of their union, plays such an important part.

Only in a new community can man probably find the roots which he has lost.

But from the invidious position Victor enjoyed as the remnant of an absolutist monarchy, in an age which had more or less dethroned the idea of kingship, Victor suffered from all the ills of the decaying order to which he belonged, losing his grip on the old conception of toil and prayer, and slipping down the slope, heading for a fall. Coming to the gaddi just before the Second World War, and in the period of disruption when, under the influence of the various European revolutions, the concepts of political and economic democracy began to percolate even into the most moribund fastnesses of the Himalayas, Victor began to feel the fatal contradictions of his role as a hereditary king with the urges of his people for an increasing share of power in the government of the state. And, as he could not, from the very nature of his affiliations, regain contact with the oppressed people of his kingdom, through any amount of fake worship at the temples, during the various festivals and durbars, nor extend the orbit of his consciousness to draw into himself the urges of the life-force, which still uprushed and coursed through their unquenchable blood stream, he was like a fish out of water. And his profligate education at the Chief's College, Lahore, his whole promiscuous upbringing, and his ill-assorted, unnatural life had prepared his inevitable doom, only postponed by the other manifold contradictions that kept him in a state of suspended animation.

The aetiology of Victor's malady revealed itself to me far more clearly through the news and rumours that came in the next few days from the several parts of Sham Pur, and from his own meanderings which filled the palace day and night.

We heard one fine morning that the Communist guerillas had not only divided the land among the peasantry, on the parallel of Red China and Telengana in Hyderabad, but had defeated the State Forces and were marching on the capital, being only thirty miles away from the Sham Pur old fort. And in the wake of this news came Pandit Gobind Das, the Premier, for an emergency consultation with His Highness.

Victor's temperature had not gone down for seven days below a hundred. And he lay in bed after Dorothy, the young Christian nurse, had just given him a sponge bath. He was a little rested and calmer than usual when Gobind Das was announced. I was all for telling the Prime Minister that His Highness was in no condition to see him, but Victor's curiosity about the purpose of his erstwhile enemy's visit made him insistent that the visitor be shown in.

Pandit Gobind Das came in, rather uneasy on his chappals, and anxiously assembling the folds of his homespun dhoti and tunic in his left hand, lest he should trip up on something, his small Gandhi cap sitting precariously on his round head. His face was wreathed in smiles, which accentuated the whiteness of his walrus moustache and narrowed his myopic eyes. His forehead was covered in beads of sweat. Obviously, he was excited by all kinds of fears, hopes and desires.

Victor pointed him to a chair casually.

Pandit Gobind Das did not know whether to bow before His Highness or to join hands in the usual Hindu Congressite manner. For, the European-style bedroom of the Maharaja demanded a Western courtesy, whereas the homespun ideology dictated the conventional Indian approach. And in the soul of the Prime Minister there was the confusion of the various pulls which the maelstrom in the state had created in him, dominant among which was an essential fear of His Highness, arising from the fact that he, who had ousted the Maharaja from power, had ushered the state into utter chaos since. Torn between the two forms of greetings to His Highness, he compromised and executed both, nearly tripping up as he thought he might, even as he negotiated his bulky posterior into the armchair.

'How is your exalted temperament?' he asked, without pausing to breathe calmly the breathless breaths that he was inhaling and exhaling.

'My temperament is not well,' said Victor with his usual disarmingly naïve honesty. 'I have lost my gaddi and I have lost my woman....'

'I am sorry,' said Pandit Gobind Das.

'Don't be a hypocrite!' cried His Highness. 'You have been responsible for both the disasters, and you –'

'Your Highness, I may have led the campaign of the Praja Mandal for democratic rights, but I never made any reference to your personal life.' Pandit Gobind Das's head shook involuntarily, as it did when he was a trifle excited.

'But you have employed that traitor Bool Chand, who ran away with my wife, as your secretary!' said Victor, half raising his head from the pillow.

'I am afraid I shall have to ask Pandit Gobind Das to leave if he is going to excite you like that,' I said solemnly.

'But, your Highness, I did not know that Shrimati Ganga Dasi had left you,' said Pandit Gobind Das, his innocent, puritanical and conventional mind aghast at this news. 'And I had no idea that Bool Chand had taken her away. Mr Bool Chand was imposed on me by Srijut Popatlal Shah, the Administrator.'

'Not Administrator so much as pimp,' shouted Victor. 'He himself had an affair with Gangi and then, being respectably married, he passed her on to Bool Chand!'

The prim and proper mind of Pandit Gobind Das, traditional enemy of woman, was shocked. His face went red with anger and his neck was covered with sweat. He remained silent while his head swayed, as though in a series of prolonged negations. The Prime Minister was not devoid of conscience, though he was amenable to the many influences which shape the mind of a provincial politician: ambition, inborn cunning, or rather an innate capacity for intrigue in order to achieve his ends, narrow-mindedness, tinctured by the desire not so much of power as prestige – though both these are, I suppose, the two sides of the same coin.

'I will see to it that Mr Bool Chand restores the woman of your house to you,' said Pandit Gobind Das, deliberately emphasizing each word. 'I can't oust him from his job, because the Administrator Sahib sent him to me. And that is what I came to see you about – the Administrator is acting in a very high-handed manner, sire. Although I represent the States People's Congress, I am not allowed to do anything not sanctioned by Srijut Shah. And...how shall I tell you?...But the...the Communists have defeated the State Forces and are near Sham Pur....'

Victor stared at Pandit Gobind Das with a suppressed, violent rage. If he had been in full enjoyment of his powers, monarchical or physical, he would have got up and torn him limb from limb. As it was, he ground his teeth, flushed red, lifted his head to say something, but fell back exhausted.

'Please don't excite yourself,' I said, going over to sit by his pillow and stroking his head.

'Why does he come here to give me this news?' Victor shouted. 'What can I do now that you have taken everything away from me!'

'Your Highness,' said Pandit Gobind Das anxiously, 'please do not be angry or afraid. Sardar Patel has said the Congress is not an enemy of the princely order. As a matter of fact, your Highness's name has been proposed for Raj Pramukhship of the border states union which the Sardar envisages. I have been insisting in all my speeches that your exalted person, as well as your property, be respected by all citizens of the state. Only, in this crisis, which has arisen through the Communist revolt, we have to get together. As Benjamin Franklin said, "We have to hang together, otherwise we will hang separately".' After quoting Benjamin Franklin, the Premier looked pompously towards me for approval.

I realized, almost with a sense of horror, that here we were face to face with a provincial politician, who had perhaps his own conception of duty but who was singularly unaware of anything but the crudest lumps of experience. To him the personal life of the Maharaja had no significance, because persons as such did not matter to him except as units in the scheme of government, for he was a Brahmin and thus part of a ruling oligarchy rather than a democrat, for all his pretensions to liberal ideas. Dead to his own and other people's intrinsic life, he was also unaware of the need for a wider perspective. Of course, most of us are preoccupied by the fears, hates, prejudices and sentiments of the ordinary daily life, but, increasingly, our accumulating sense of the cross currents in the shrinking world enlarges our awareness. And, especially if we are thinking people, we remind ourselves now and then of outside events, beyond the competitive jealousies and affections of our humdrum existence. We strive to keep the good of the greatest number in mind, without leaving out of account the intimate life of the individual, and thus we try to be human. But Pandit Gobind Das seemed so involved in party politics that a man or woman did not matter to him personally, and his vision did not extend beyond the horizons of Sham Pur, except to certain phrases of the great which he had picked up from the 'thought for the day' column of the daily newspaper.

'Do you realize that I have not even enough power to make a search in my own state for my own wife?' said Victor as he despairingly spread his arms on his bed.

'Perhaps she is at the house of Seth Sadanand,' Pandit Gobind Das ventured the guess, having heard that the Maharaja's mistress was friendly with the wife of Sadanand, the moneylender and capitalist.

'I am not a child!' raved Victor. He knew that Seth Sadanand would not give asylum to his mistress. And he sensed, with a shrewd enough instinct, that Gangi had not left because of her lack of security, which she might seek from the richest man in the state, but because she wanted new physical sensations.

'I only thought Seth Sadanand was friendly towards your Highness,' the Premier said, mixing his innocence about domestic matters with a clever innuendo against Victor for having supported a local capitalist who had stood outside the Praja Mandal.

'I suppose you people even resent the few friends I have left,' said Victor, quick to sense the significance of Pandit Gobind Das's subtle hint. 'I suppose you want to invite Birla and Dalmia in.... Well, do so, then! Who am I to object? You have reduced me to dust! And I am broken. I shall accept the new disasters that are coming....I can see them sometimes. I can see them coming like monsoon clouds, rolling overhead, suffocating my life-breath! I want to live. I want to fight. But you have reduced my life to dust. I feel like a ghost swirling along like a whirlwind made up of specks of dust.'

I felt that in his own mad way Victor had grasped the significance of the 'bloodless revolution' in his state. The

Congress and the Praja Mandal crowd did, indeed, want to open up the backward areas to investments by the big monopolists.

'Your Highness,' said Pandit Gobind Das, agitated by Victor's hysteria and struggling to be sincere, 'I have told you that Sardar Patel has promised not to interfere in the domestic life of the princes after the states' accession.'

'To be sure!' said Victor, bitter and recalcitrant. 'That is why the Sardar saw my cousin Raja Praduman Singh! And that is why you have given him a portfolio in the Cabinet!...Well, if the Communists have risen, it is because Raja Sahib, and the other jagirdars, forcibly occupied the lands and the houses of the tenants on my own personal estates. I hate the Communists. But I abominate my cousins more. For they have been my undoing! And you sit side by side with Raja Parduman Singh!...And yet you come to me in your time of trouble!'

It was uncanny to me to hear Victor shrewdly catch hold of the basic alliance which had ousted him from power. I realized that he had, in spite of his egoism, a clumsy but rule-of-thumb method of reckoning up his assets and liabilities as a statesman.

'This trouble in Panna and Udham Pur is also due to the fact that the army under Chaudhri Raghbir Singh was not disciplined and began to commit dacoities in the village,' said the Premier.

'Again, you are attacking my friends in the state!' roared Victor. 'I will not have charges made against General Raghbir Singh which cannot be substantiated.'

'Sire, please do not be impatient,' said the Premier. 'Chaudhri Raghbir Singh is a trusted servant of the new Government. And I am not accusing him. Only, during the quick changeover, all kinds of lawless elements have begun to take advantage of our weakness.'

'I thought it was my prerogative to be a weak ruler!' taunted Victor. 'The Praja Mandal was to usher in a Utopia!'

'Maharaj, your anger is needless,' appealed Pandit Gobind Das. 'Please have shanti and I shall explain to you our real attitude towards your Highness. We had a family quarrel in the state. Now, that has been settled by your signing the Instrument of Accession. We want to forget the past and start on a new basis. Your private property and privy purse is guaranteed. And if there are plans of building industries here, as there will be, you can have big shares in the companies which are formed. I told the same to Seth Sadanand, who was afraid of friends from Calcutta and Bombay coming in with big capital and squeezing him out. And our state will have a hand in framing the constitution. Also, the centre has given other safeguards about taxation and property. So do not harbour any fears!'

'I have not much desire left for possessions,' Victor said tiredly. 'All I want is that you order Bool Chand to restore my wife to me.'

For a moment, Pandit Gobind Das sat with his mouth half open. Perhaps he could not understand that neither worldly possessions nor the ideals of the highest good of the community, which he pretended to espouse, had any particular appeal for the Maharaja. And he seemed amazed at Victor's obsession with a mere woman.

'Of course, your Highness!' said Pandit Gobind Das. But he still couldn't get over what seemed to him to be a mere whim of the Maharaja.

'I have not slept for nights!' Victor screamed. 'I cannot sleep more than an hour or two. And I have been waking up in hot sweats and talking to myself in my sleep. I cannot bear the empty space against me where she used to lie. I cannot, I cannot! I cannot bear to be without her! She is a whore, but I want her. I need to put my arms round her to feel safe. I shall go mad if she does not come back!...' And, lifting his hands, he wrung them and then let them fall by his side, and continued to burble under his breath, 'Oh, I am broken, broken, broken!...'

I too felt a shiver of shame and pity go through my spine. For the first time I realized that, in spite of his terrific self-will, Victor could crack up if he let go of himself. I knew that he would have to become far worse before the danger point could be reached. But if the insomnia continued and the hysteria rose to a crescendo unabated under the pressure of his longing for Gangi, as well as the mounting adverse conditions around him, Victor was done for. The only hope was that his hurt might become a slow, dull pain which he could bear more easily and that the untoward outside situation would not become any worse than it was. For if there was time I could perhaps help him to endure the frustrations by explaining things to him, though he had already sunk so far down into the depths of despair that it would be impossible to help him for a long time to come.

'Your Highness must get well,' appealed Pandit Gobind Das. 'We have to stop the menace of Communism at all costs.'

'I feel there are more disasters coming my way,' said Victor, still talking to himself. 'I am afraid! I dread the future! I fear myself – my own thoughts! I feel a terrible sense of foreboding! It is all darkness, darkness, darkness around me!...'

'Highness, I can't allow Panditji to excite you any more,' I protested at this juncture. 'Your fever will never go down at this rate.'

'All I want is that Maharaja Sahib should get well,' said Pandit Gobind Das, his head shaking as though in a trance. 'I will go. Only, I would like His Highness to exert some influence on the Administrator, to help rather than hinder. After all, we of Sham Pur know the state better than he does. And he should realize that the Communists are only thirty miles away.'

'Panditji, it is an irony that you ask for help from the person you denounced as an oppressor!' Victor said. 'Well, let me tell you that the new oppressors will put us all in our places properly. It suits the purpose of Mr Shah that the Communists are advancing. He will assume full powers in the state....'

'I will defend our democratic rights, then!' shouted Pandit Gobind Das. 'And we shall not remain non-violent in that contingency!'

'Acha, I will see what I can do,' Victor assured him. 'But I expect you to dismiss Bool Chand and extort some information about my wife's whereabouts.'

'To be sure, I shall do that, Maharaj,' said Pandit Gobind Das, looking away furtively. Then he heaved himself up from the chair, his head still shaking involuntarily, and he retreated two yards, even as he bowed and moved out.

That afternoon, as I came in to tea with Victor, he waved a couple of pale blue sheets of paper before me and said excitedly: 'She has written after all.'

'What does she say? Where is she?' I asked shyly.

'She is staying in the Bara Dari palace on the banks of the Sutlej, at Madho Pur, which I gave her. She says she is staying there alone, though I am quite sure she has Bool Chand with her.'

'But what does she say? Why did she go away?'

'It is terrible,' said Victor, with tears in his eyes. 'She is accusing me of petty crimes against her. How could she be so mean? I thought she was so generous in giving, and often she helped me with advice in the affairs of the state. How could she after our seven years together! The letter is typed out in English and must have been written for her by that swine Bool Chand.'

'But what does she say?' I repeated, impatient with curiosity.

'She says that I went on favouring Maharani Indira all these years and did nothing to have my son by her recognized heir to the gaddi!' He said all this in a mouthful. 'That I did not settle the property on her which she wanted. That I was always scolding her about her past lovers. That I would not do anything to marry her and allowed her to be insulted by all and sundry, who called her my mistress! That I refused to give her enough money!...'

'She is mad,' I said. 'But with a low woman like that you can't —'

'Hari!' Victor exclaimed, affronted.

'Your relations were not equal,' I said emphatically. 'However kind and generous you were, she was in the position of a kept woman. And much as you try to think of her as an inspiring partner, the kind of courtesan of ancient days who helped kings to rule their states, she was far below that level and used the relationship for quite different ends, such as security and comfort and money and jewellery and houses....I think you are inclined to mistake her charm, and her ability to dress in modern styles, for intelligence and personality. She certainly had not developed, and she is unlikely, with her present accomplishments, to become anything. Personally, I would like to see you freed of her.'

'I chose her freely.'

'In free choice the woman has to stand on the same footing. And then if she reciprocates the love, the relationship may grow. In fact, when this happens the bonds are more real, because the ideal of such a relationship becomes the attainment of the deepest and most loyal friendship. And any break-up, or separation, becomes the greatest calamity. And men and women may then risk the highest stakes to preserve the relationship.'

'You call Gangi a kept woman, because she was not married to me?'

At that juncture, the nurse came in to clear the tea things, and behind her came Captain Partap Singh.

'Then do you think nothing can be done?' Victor asked me despairingly, unmindful of the lack of privacy.

'Everything can be done!' asserted Partap Singh vehemently, his handsome face shining with positive faith and his tall, athletic frame clad in a smart silk suit making him seem full of purposeful intent. And he continued tritely, 'Napoleon said, "the word 'impossible' can only be found in the dictionary of fools".'

I did not open my mouth until the nurse had borne the tea tray away. And then, as I was going to answer Victor's question, Captain Partap Singh said: 'I have prepared a substitute.'

And, looking in the direction of the departing nurse, he cocked his left eye, significantly.

'At the moment Gangi may be too self-willed,' I said to change the conversation, 'to want to return. And your very desire to have her back will make her more stubborn. Besides, she must be in the first flush of her new romance....'

'I will murder the bania!' Partap Singh shouted. 'The thief! The snorting ass!'

'You must remember,' said Victor defeatedly, 'that he is...well, he is part of the new Government....By the way, Partap Singh, did you give my message to the Administrator? Is he coming to see me?'

'That is what I came to tell, Highness,' Partap Singh said. 'Strange things are happening in the state. The Administrator has sacked Pandit Gobind Das and his ministers. And he has taken full charge of Sham Pur. And the Indian Army has marched in to help the State Forces to throw the Communists back. The Administrator himself wanted to see you. But he is busy and said he will be here tomorrow morning.'

Victor shuddered visibly in a violent anger. His face twisted with the will to power, born out of his disgust at his failures. And, as though in an effort to scatter the dogs who bayed at him, he barked back: 'Get out, all of you! Get out! Leave me alone!'

And then he collapsed into a sobbing fit, his fragile frame shaking with an almost deliberate effort to draw out the pain which racked him.

In such a situation, I had by now learnt, from experience, to leave him alone.

About half past one that night, when I was fast asleep, I was awakened by a gentle pressure on my shoulder, and I found the nurse, Dorothy Thomas, standing by my side.

'Who's that?' I said, startled.

'It is me,' she said. And from the break in her voice, she seemed to me to be weeping.

I sat up and switched on the light by my bedside. I could see tears streaming down her eyes. And in a flash I guessed what had happened. The casual words of Captain Partap Singh about finding a substitute had gone deep into Victor's subconscious, and the way the ADC had pointed to Dorothy with his eyes had acted as a suggestion.

'What's happened?' I said almost automatically. 'Sit down.'

'Doctor, I was asleep in the veranda after putting him to bed. I had been tired out by the day duty. Then I suddenly felt someone sitting on the arm of my chair, and stroking my cheeks. I thought I was dreaming. But the weight of his face was on me. He was kissing me! I knew it was His Highness. And I shook with fear of him. I thought I would shriek against my will. But I was afraid of a scene. "Who?" I said. "Go away." And I didn't open my eyes, though I knew that it was the Maharaja's hand, because I felt that if I opened my eyes and recognized him he might be embarrassed. He was breathing hard and leaning upon me. And he was becoming more and more familiar as I lay, my heart beating. I tried to get away. But he had his arms round me and he was pressing me. "Don't, please don't!" I protested, and said: "Leave me alone to sleep." And I watched him out of the corners of my eyes. I was terrified, like a rabbit. His face was burning. And his breathing became heavier and heavier. He bore down on me with his whole body. Then tried to lift me. I was so frightened that someone might come. I almost went mad with fear. I knew he could do anything to me he liked, and I wouldn't be able to shout for fear of a scandal. He seemed to be blind – and tried to undress me. And then...well, I took courage in both hands and pushed him away....He didn't come back to the attack. I must say this for him. Instead, he went on stroking my hair and saying, "Sleep Dorothy, sleep, my child, sleep." Then he went away. And I was so relieved and even felt guilty at having had to thrust him away like that. You know, I understand his state of mind. I quite like him and feel sorry for him, as I hear his wife has left him. But, Doctor, what could I do? I had to ask him to go. I am a nurse and our profession has been given such a bad name! Besides, in my religion – I am a Catholic – it is a sin!...Don't you see, Doctor? And now what shall I do? I thought he would never go. And I have had such a fright!'

'Acha, don't cry. And I will get you a bed made at the further end of the veranda.'

'I am so sorry to trouble you at this time of the night. I had to come to you as there is no one who would understand. I am glad I didn't shriek. Otherwise the whole household would have awakened.'

'Victor is in a bad state of mind. It was good of you to be so nice about it. I think he developed a fantasy about you and therefore came to you. Under other circumstances he would have attempted rape. I am glad he was not so violent! He is going through a very bad time.'

'I don't think the bed can be removed without him knowing. I will go back there.'

'Acha, help me to remove my small divan to the veranda outside my door and I shall sleep there and be within call,' I suggested.

Dorothy was a well-built, efficient nurse, and not only helped me to take the divan out but insisted on making my bed on it. Her tears had dried and she had become impassive, though the fear was still in her.

'Thank you ever so, Doctor,' she said matter-of-factly, and walked gingerly away, overshadowed by the horror and yet seemingly blithe in her assurance of safety now that I would be sleeping in the veranda within reach of her.

I lay down on the small divan outside. My head throbbed with the tension that Dorothy's confession had set up in me. I was relieved that she had not shouted or shrieked, and that

Victor had been saved from a scandal. And then I felt that at all costs I should try and see that there was no recurrence of this fantasy life yet for a while. Because, already ruined, desolate and unhappy, he might do something which would further prejudice his position in the state. Though it seemed to me that if Captain Partap Singh's report was true, the situation had become impossible in any case. And I didn't know what to do. The only thing was perhaps to escape, to go away from Sham Pur. But if it had only been the public crisis on the issue of accession, it would have been easy enough for Victor to quit for a little or for a long while. Unfortunately, Ganga Dasi's defection at the same time made it very uncertain that he would leave Sham Pur, knowing she was near at hand to rescue. An unknown battle raged in my mind. And there was no solution between the contending thoughts: that Victor's situation had become untenable and that he would have to 'change his bedding', as the Lamas are said to do on reincarnation, since they are not supposed to die. Sleep was difficult for me for a long time, for the weight of the unknown destiny lay on my head, but, about an hour before the dawn, I succumbed to sheer exhaustion and slept a light sleep, interrupted by dreams.

Srijut Popatlal J. Shah duly arrived at the palace the next morning at nine. And he was ushered into His Highness's presence without delay.

Victor had been tense with anxiety before he came. For though he vaguely guessed the implications of the Administrator taking over control of the state, he did not exactly know what was envisaged. Besides this, there was the guilt about the tender solicitude he had shown to Dorothy, because he asked me if I had noticed anything strange about the nurse that morning. The colours changed on his face from the unhealthy flush of the fever of 99.6 degrees to an insipid pallor. And he lay exhausted, as though he was suspended between life and death.

A tormented look came into Victor's eyes as the Administrator entered, heavy like Yama, the God of Death, and sat down in a high chair, a little way away from the bed.

Srijut Shah joined hands in hypocritical obeisance while he kept a demure silence.

Victor seemed to be sinking into the bottomless pit of fear and doubt, and 'Srijut' Shah's silence seemed to hasten the process. So he fought back with the pride of the death-defying Rajput that he was by birth. He glanced sharp and quick at the Administrator and said: 'I suppose you have come to announce my doom....May I tell you that I am not responsible for the breakdown of the administration in the state since the accession. The responsibility is yours.'

'Your Highness cannot evade responsibility,' said Srijut Shah. 'The present lawlessness is the result of the inefficiency of the past. Tyranny! Forced labour! Ruinous hunts! Illegal taxes! – these were there before the accession. And there was that great ally of the Communists, acute hunger....No, your Highness cannot evade responsibility!'

'But you and the Praja Mandal – what have you done since you came in?' shouted Victor, sitting up. 'The exploitation is being intensified! Your Gujarati and Marwari banias are coming in to spread their tentacles around the life of Sham Pur!'

'At the moment, only the army is coming in,' said Srijut Shah. 'My duty is to plug the gaps outside the capital. And this morning at 4 a.m. the Indian Union Army has joined the Sham Pur State Forces and police to stop the Communist guerillas from storming the capital. I am in earnest, your Highness. I have to stop the rot.'

'Your Praja Mandal is dishonest!' said Victor. 'Your administration is...well, I know there are all kinds of squabbles among job-seekers going on!'

'That is why I have taken over the whole administration,' said Srijut Shah. 'I have dismissed the ministry of Pandit Gobind Das.'

Victor looked at the Administrator with a soul full of frustration.

'When I told Sardar Patel that these Praja Mandal fellows were no good, he wouldn't believe me! Now he sends in the Union Army! And I, who was born to rule, am not told anything about it or trusted....The banias are in power!'

Srijut Shah looked at Victor with a cold and deliberate hostility which masked his humiliation at the insulting words that the Maharaja was using. Then he said: 'Your Highness, I have to tell you that, while we are providing for your rights and privileges, I have been asked by the States Department to restrain you from any interference in the administration.'

There was a dread flame of power in his restraint. And he sat there with his padded, dark, handsome face, exerting his will to cow down this rebellious, dissolute prince and reduce him to his proper place as an instrument in the hands of India's 'Wishmarck'.

Victor's face became darker. His humiliation was now complete, and he seemed desolate. He must have felt that everything was gone, everything, the last vestiges of everything, and that only by reconciling himself to the new rulers, by becoming an instrument of their will, could he flourish now. For he knew that the titles of Raj Pramukh or

Upa Raj Pramukh were only reserved for the more docile and amenable of the princes.

And then I noticed an aspect of Victor's weakness which had not become obvious to me before. I could sense the way he was fighting the hard, cruel streak of power in Popatlal Shah. I could see he was lacerated by the impact of the new dictum. And I could guess his torment. But equally I became aware of the complete collapse of his spirit and the emergence of the will to compromise.

'Give the Diwan Sahib some coffee,' he said.

'No, your Highness. I must go,' said the Administrator firmly. 'I have things to do.'

'You might have spared me my wife!' he said sullenly. 'You have shattered and ruined my life.'

Srijut Shah paused and looked away a little sheepishly and then said in a mild voice: 'Your Highness is mistaken. We have not taken your wife away!'

For a long moment there was an unconscious battle raging between them, a fierce battle of wills. And their faces were consumed by a strange glow.

'Your protégé Bool Chand has seduced her – hasn't he?'

The Administrator had no answer to this somewhat crude but real charge. So he abandoned the defensive position and, in order obviously to apologize to Victor without saying the words, he said: 'Your Highness, as a genuine well-wisher of yours, I would suggest that – you take a holiday in Europe and get well. A change of air will do you good.'

Victor was angrier still at this evasion. A cruel self-consciousness came over him, the shame of having been reduced to pulp. For he understood immediately that the Administrator was really ordering him out of the state and giving him no satisfaction about Gangi. He sighed as though he was in torment and lay flat, looking at the ceiling. And then with a mad rage he turned and lashed out:

'I was assured again and again that I would be well treated, that my home and property would not be touched. Now it seems that all treaties and instruments are mere scraps of paper. And nothing seems sacred, not even one's wife!'

'You should have kept her in control, then!' Srijut Shah retorted angrily.

They both relapsed into silence again.

I sank deeper and deeper into despair about this final quarrel. I knew that it would end in the rout of the Maharaja. But their protracted bickerings were odious and vulgar. And the vibrations that their fighting wills created in the atmosphere were exhausting me. In the horrible emptiness of my heart I felt dried of all content.

'I feel, Mr Shah, that His Highness will not get better here,' I said. 'Perhaps he could take your advice to go to Europe for a while. Will you make the necessary arrangements?'

'Yes, Doctor Shankar. By all means. You know that we have the greatest respect for His Highness's person. He must trust us. But you must appreciate that Sham Pur is a seething cauldron of discontent. A little strength in the Communist drive and the whole structure would have come toppling down like a house of cards. Now we have to defeat the Reds and restore order. Besides, the Government of India is pledged to democracy. We must stem the tides of the guerilla struggles and save the state at all costs. Otherwise, there will be nothing left of Sham Pur either for us or for the Maharaja Sahib. Sardar Patel has insisted that he is no enemy of the princely order....'

Victor lay apparently oblivious of us. There was sweat on his forehead, and his eyes were bloodshot. By the tremor on his lips I knew that he was holding back his tears.

I wanted to put my hand on his forehead and feel his temperature. But I did not move for fear that he would break down. I waited.

The tension continued.

Then Victor burst out loudly like a madman:

'I will destroy you all! I will! I will! I will destroy her also! And that dirty swine Bool Chand!...You can do what you like for the while! But my people love me! I know they love me! And they will not forget me! You are evil and filthy, the lot of you! – with your profiteering and bribery and corruption!'

'Please, Victor, please!' I said, touching his shoulder gently.

He thrust my hand away and, with one sharp catch of a sob, began to weep, his whole frame rocking. The sobs convulsed his body and he covered his face with his hands. Unable to withhold his tears, he turned over and hid his face in the pillow, still sobbing uncontrollably.

I stood by him unable to comfort him. I could not bear the desolateness of his hysteria. And the bitterness of the jerky sobs went into my soul. I winced before I could summon the courage to ask Srijut Shah to go. At last my mouth seemed to open.

'Please leave him alone,' I said. 'His fever will be worse.'

Srijut Shah got up quietly enough and tiptoed out.

PART 3

Sleeping and waking – or rather through the vigil of nights and days, because he could not sleep for more than an hour or two every night – Victor was obsessed by thoughts of Ganga Dasi, even after we had put seven thousand miles between him and her.

Of course, I had expected this, because it was with the greatest difficulty that he saw the facts of the situation and realized that he was not wanted in Sham Pur any more by the Administrator, and that Gangi would not return to him. I had to spend hours in persuading him to accept the logic of the events of the last few months. Even so, it was finally a written confirmation by Srijut Shah of his talk with Victor, clearly asking him to take a holiday abroad, which convinced him that the Administrator's polite and firm hint was an order. And then he allowed us to pack up. And up to the end he went on having private conferences with Captain Partap Singh with a view, he said, to tracing the whereabouts of Gangi and fetching her, so that he could take her to Europe, if necessary by force. But not all the secret agents, whom the ADC employed, succeeded in finding out her hiding-place, and, ultimately, we left for Bombay to catch the Air India International plane, 'Malabar Princess'.

Though Victor's fever abated as soon as we boarded the train to Delhi, we had not been able to continue the journey from Delhi to Bombay by rail and had to fly instead, because the Maharaja suffered from complete nervous prostration and could hardly walk ten yards through sheer weakness and exhaustion. The journey by the 'Malabar Princess' from Santa Cruz to London airport had seemed to us all, who were taking such an air trip for the first time, miraculous; though Captain Partap Singh felt that the seats were too small and cramped for his tall frame and rough bottom. The vista of the lovely Italian and Swiss Alps, after the stretch of the blue Mediterranean, seemed to exhilarate Victor, and the bottles of red wine which we drank at the Geneva airport expanded the Maharaja's spirit a little. But post-war London seemed a dull place for the congealed soul of our love-sick bird, even though the suite we had booked in Mayfair left nothing to be desired.

He was like an idiot in the Greek sense of that word, going round and round the same thought, and his hollow eyes and sunken cheeks and withering body portended disaster. He just would not believe that Ganga Dasi could leave him: that fact he could not accept or acknowledge. For he seemed to have some uncanny illusory assurance inside him that since he had been completely fulfilled in her, she too had been completely fulfilled in him, not accepting that she was a nymphomaniac. At times, when I talked to him and reminded him of the all-embracing possessiveness with which she had enveloped his life for the year or two during which I had known them together, he seemed to understand what a demon she was and how she had sucked his life-blood. But Victor had also known her in the moods when she had given and given, with a servility bordering upon abjectness, and he could not see the subtle sense in which a person of such apparent charm could also be a kind of human vampire. My inability to use strong words in defining her character, and my temperamental disability to indulge in moral condemnation when I could see 'immorality' mostly as social derangement and mental disease, made for a vagueness in which Victor could emphasize some aspect of her niceness to him. And, ignoring his own ultimate sense of the irresponsible, untrustworthy, small-minded, greedy, libidinous jungli in her, he had exalted her as a goddess in his feverish imagination and fixed this image of her in his mind to worship and long for. I had never known such an obsession. Now, it began to appear to me that I was adopting a sentimental approach in accepting the sickness of these two lovers and was unconsciously accepting the unconscious to be a kind of reservoir of all the perversities of human nature, from the most primitive trauma of birth to the most complex wishes and fantasies. In this sense, I seemed to be adopting a pessimistic view of human nature, the idealistic conception that the patient's wish to do nothing but wish is the strongest urge, because the neurotic can revert back to an easier and more primitive psychological condition, and that thus there is really no strong wish for a cure at all. And so I had begun to concede that Ganga Dasi was a harlot according to her psychological type, and Victor a libidinous hound, who found himself fixated upon a woman with a kind of primary fixation, like a spoilt child who wanted his mother and was inconsolable without her, and I was despairing of the tangle and leaving it at that. Once a harlot, always a harlot, once a decadent libertine, always a decadent libertine – that seemed the logical outcome of my acceptance of tangles in their personal relationships which could not be disentangled.

But it dawned upon me suddenly one day, while I was walking down Piccadilly and saw a well-dressed young middle-class woman talking to herself, even as she stared idiotically at the dresses in a window by Burlington Arcade, that neuroses seemed so widespread a phenomenon in our age that it must have a great deal more to do with the corrupt social system in which we were living than the healers accepted.

And from that moment onwards I felt that whether I could help Victor or not the fact was that if he was sick, it was because this sickness was inevitable to him, not merely through the wide range of his potentialities at birth but rather through his upbringing in the social set-up to which he had belonged. It was not extraordinary that his personal debacle with Ganga Dasi had coincided with his dethronement from the Sham Pur gaddi, and his virtual externment from the state. So that what had happened was not a calamity overtaking an unfortunate individual, but the concentration of all the social 'fates' in a Greek tragedy, which were bearing down on him relentlessly and might crush him, but which, given an enlightened will, he could have fought or could even now fight.

I knew that in general the social aspect of the problem which Victor presented had been in my mind, but I had been thinking too much in terms of his and Ganga Dasi's mental and emotional disorder as springing from their first failures and misunderstandings in adjusting themselves to their family relationships. For I had not emphasized that their family relationships, whatever else they may be as well, were themselves social creations, based on certain political and economic dispositions which I had seen change in Sham Pur before my eyes and which might be transformed more completely in the next few years.

I pondered deeply over this. I realized that the commonsensical materialist view would certainly help me to get rid of my obsession with Victor's obsession and see things much more objectively than I had done all this time in Sham Pur. It also occurred to me that now that Victor was free of all responsibility to the state and could do more or less what he liked, he might have a chance of recovery, unless his disease had become a complex within a complex.

I would then have to proceed on the hypothesis that he belonged to his order and was involved in the closed mental system of neurosis, bound up in the vicious circles of associations, fears and wishes which could not find direct expression because they arose from some infantile emotional situation which had not been developed and exorcized in his adult life. The symptom of his difficulty, of course, was his preoccupation with Gangi. And it had not been possible to remove it, because we had pampered him and made it seem a nice kind of feeling to indulge in under the guise of love, and he had even won sympathy from us in his invalid's privileged position.

I would, therefore, try and track his illness into a fully developed fantasy and childishness of which it was formed and try to show him that his whole obsession was founded on fantasy and was no use to him.

I found in the next few days that my optimism was ill-founded. The healing of Victor's schism was difficult, because he was still part of the diseased world of Sham Pur, involved in a closed mental atmosphere. I realized, from the kana-phusi, 'I whisper in your ear and you whisper in mine', kind of consultation that he had with Captain Partap Singh every day, that there was some secret between them, to have Gangi brought out here. And, apart from the fact that he was carrying on the intrigues of the Sham Pur palace from the suite in Mayfair, both of us were pampering him and making him feel that it was extraordinarily romantic for him to indulge in this passion for his mistress. Thus, disconsolate, he lay outstretched, staring at the ceiling as usual, or at his own image in the lovely tall mirrors of the Curzon Street bedroom.

I took him to the various restful places which had been the haunts of my student days in London, in order to distract his attention. We visited Hampton Court, Kew Gardens, the Regent's Park Zoo, the British Museum in Great Russell Street and the Victoria and Albert Museum in South Kensington. But as he had become physically very feeble, we could not enjoy these places, which required athletic English feet, and we would get back into the hired Daimler and return through crowded streets to the suite and to his bedroom.

And again, there were the same wearisome questions: 'What shall I do? Why hasn't she written? How can she do it to me? What did I not give her?...I will show that swine Bool Chand a thing or two one day – do you think she is really with him?', etc.

I answered by saying that those were not the questions he should ask, but rather: 'How can one become oneself? And what does one really want to make of life? What is to be done?'

Inured, like most Indians, to a philosophical bent of mind, he would interrogate me very pertinently by subverting the logic of my propositions: 'How can one talk of becoming oneself when one doesn't know what one is? Or when one is merely an unstable something, a half-stated truth, trying to be the complete truth and nothing but the truth? Isn't one very undefined? What is one?'

I told him that he knew that his love for Gangi was real, but that, though undefined, and perhaps impossible to state, it put him, as a human being, in a unique relationship with her.

And vaguely feeling the truth of what I said, he would then integrate enough in the background of his disintegration to become aware of himself, that he was not a separate entity in all the confusion that surrounded him, that he must do something, become himself in relation to other people. And yet he was in a torment because of that in him which had become separated from him, the usual privileges of Maharajahood. And he was so split that he began increasingly to talk to himself in his sleep, and also, when we left him alone, awake. And he turned to certain visions and far-off spoken words, till he seemed at times, in spite of his general lucidity, to border upon madness.

I dexterously arranged that we should all go out at least to one meal a day. And, saying that I thought it would be a good thing to taste the cooking of the various countries, I booked tables variously at the Spanish Restaurant in Swallow Street, at the Turkish Restaurant in Dean Street, at the Chinese Restaurant in Denmark Street, at the Hungaria, at Giro's, etc. But, apart from the endless jokes we had at the expense of the diabetic Munshi Mithan Lal, whom he remembered at mealtimes especially for the large belchings he indulged in after good food, we returned from these fashionable eating-places as morbid as we were before our visits. Except when Victor asked me to invite some old English friend of his. And then he would freely unburden himself before the guest about the unfair way in which he had been deprived of his throne and at the same time of his wife. The guests usually listened from the outside and remained politely non-interventionist in the familiar English liberal tradition, an occasional friend recommending calm acceptance.

A visit to the Old Vic was as fruitless, though Victor liked the *Swan Lake* ballet as performed by the Sadler's Wells Company, because he recognized the red-haired Moira Shearer, whom he had seen in the film *Red Shoes* in India.

We did an occasional picture, but my taste was a little too highbrow, and I preferred to go to the Curzon, the Academy, or Studio One, and this bored the others.

I soon realized that Victor was not really interested in all these things, that he was too unhappy and enfeebled to enjoy himself, and that perhaps it was best not to strain his nerves, and to let him recover slowly in his own way.

So I encouraged him to have a siesta after lunch every day and then took him for a short stroll in Hyde Park after tea. The weakening October sun fell nimbly on the copper-coloured autumn leaves of the streets by the Park Lane entrance, where we left the car, and there was a slight nip in the air, and we would take two chairs and sit down to look at the discreet glory of the homely landscape.

The air of London was so crowded with talk of financial crisis, the Third World War and the menace of Communism, that Victor joined the chorus of newspaper-talk saying that the Reds in Sham Pur had been his undoing. He wondered whether the Administrator, Popatlal Shah, had been able to arrest the advance of the guerillas outside the capital after all.

I startled him by casually dropping the bombshell that it was an ever-present possibility that, chivvied from the positions they had conquered, to one jungle hide-out after another, the Reds might carve out a free territory in the areas bordering on the USSR. And I regaled him with a brief analysis of how even some of the Lamas in the fastnesses of the Himalayas had gone Red since the victory of the Chinese Communists against Chiang-kai-Shek.

Whereupon he surprised me by saying what a fool he had been in not following up the programme, implicit in the odd remark he had made on the way back from Panna hunting lodge that he should have joined the Communists when it came to a showdown between him and Sardar Patel, or, later, when Popatlal Shah asked him to quit the state. 'For, after all,' he said, 'I could have maintained the independence of Sham Pur from the Bania Raj!'

And then, after prolonged silence, he talked nostalgically of the free, expansive life of Sham Pur, of polo and shooting and the bliss of having Gangi with him.

And at this he would repeat like a child: 'I want her. I want her.'

And as though, through the repetition of this mantra, all his passion and yearning returned to him, he would say: 'You know Majnu loved Laila as I love Gangi. When people say "What do you find in her that is so wonderful?" I always want to repeat the words of Majnu when someone asked him, "How can you love Laila, she is so ugly and black —"'

'What did Majnu say?' I asked, to keep the conversation going, though I knew the legend.

'Majnu said, "You must look at Laila with Majnu's eyes".' After a pause he continued: 'I want to be a lover like Majnu, because through such a love one can become one with God. The devotee, Chandi Das, attained sainthood by loving his washerwoman. How is Gangi inferior to that washerwoman? My heart calls to her wherever I go: my body aches for her; my soul reaches out to her wherever she is....'

'You can't revive the age of romance and chivalry, Victor,' I said. 'I think you are sick.'

'Yes,' he agreed blandly, 'I am sick. My soul is sick.' We got up and began to walk towards the Serpentine. And I asked myself for the thousandth time how it was possible to cure him short of restoring Gangi to him, or rooting out the image of her in his desire, where she really had her being, for I knew that, even if she came back to him, she would only play him up again and destroy him.

One day early in October, Victor suddenly asked me, after we had had breakfast in bed, what I thought of an idea which had struck him that he should renounce life and retire to Benaras as a yogi.

'According to the fourfold scheme of life enjoined in our Hindu math,' he said, 'one has to retire one day and spend one's time in meditation and prayer, to attain union with Brahman, the Supreme. I had graduated from the Brahmacharya student stage already into Grahast, the family life. Since I have been deprived of the chance of living in Grahast, and of even doing good works in ruling my state, I will skip this stage and become a sanyasi.'

'This is very sudden!' I said good humouredly. But as he seemed hurt at the sceptical look in my eyes, I asked: 'Do you really, seriously mean it? And what about the Queen Bee?'

'You yourself said one must discover oneself. Well, I will set my heart in the direction of God.'

'I was talking of one's need to find a direction in the obscurity, uncertainty and pathlessness of this world. But if you find the torment of the responsibility of living the ordinary life too much and know your goal in God, do certainly retire....Though I am not sure that you have rid yourself of your desires.'

'The Buddha has said,' he began quietly:

"Desire engenders sorrow, desire engenders fear,
Desire one who is freed from desire,
For there is no sorrow where there is no fear."

'Of course. The Buddha was right. Certainly, the athlete of the spirit can aspire to this ideal.'

'You don't seem sure of my capacity to do anything,' he said, raising his head from the pillow.

'No, no, Victor,' I assured him, lest he should think that I really had no confidence in him. 'I only feel that it is difficult in life to know what to do, where to go and how to become oneself in relation to other people.'

'My great-grandfather, Maharaja Hanumant Singh, renounced his wealth and position and became an ascetic,' Victor said, sitting up. 'His wife was a very devoted woman and she took him to Benaras. Perhaps I could appeal to Ganga Dasi to renounce the pleasures of the body and come with me and live in Benaras and we could together become dedicated to the worship of God. I still have a house on the banks of the Ganges by Assighat.'

I saw the meaning of his urge for renunciation. He would have Ganga Dasi with him at any price, even at the cost of giving up the marital life, so long as he could have her by him – or was this really a ruse to bring her back by offering the bait of holiness with a view to reviving the conjugal felicities? I did not know what had led to his great-grandfather's renunciation. I could only beckon in my mind a background of some sinister palace intrigue in which Maharaja Hanumant Singh had got involved and from which there seemed no way out, as, indeed, was the case with Victor.

'My great-grandfather had always been a pious man from his youth,' Victor said, with half-closed eyes and a meek manner. 'And his wife was a strong-willed woman. When she found that he could not rule the state with a firm hand, but was always busy with his puja-path worship, she decided to take him to Benaras. And she continued to rule the state as well as to...'

He was stuck for words. So I added: 'As well as to rule him!'

'You may laugh at this with your European learning,' Victor said, rather hurt, 'but in our country this can happen. Gautama Buddha also left his kingdom.'

I am afraid my imagination was straying from the subtlety of the miraculous conversion of Maharaja Hanumant Singh to the picture of him which I had seen executed by a Kangra painter: he had appeared, even in that abstract, conventionalized portrait, done by a court artist, to be a feeble, undersized man, with a grisly beard and a wicked look in his eyes, swathed in a magnificent robe of rich coloured silk, bedecked with jewels, and a nattily tied turban on his head, which told his story. And behind the Rajput painter's portrayal was, at the back of my mind, the vague figure of a Cleopatra-like queen or a harlot like Gangi, who had wanted the husband out of the way, so that she could take other lovers. And perhaps there were other more powerful forces behind the Maharani – the swarms of miracle-making, money-grabbing, unscrupulous Brahmin priests, wrapping all the violence and infamy of the court in the habiliments of words and chants from the holy books. And behind these again there were nobles, feudal lords, governors and palace servants, all intriguing within the sanctums, enclosed by the high walls and the towers and the dungeons, in a manner which seemed fantastic and incredible in the comparative light of this bedroom.

'So you don't think I can do it?' asked Victor when he got no verbal support from me.

'I must think this over,' I lied, because I just could not credit Victor with such a conversion, though I could just about believe it possible in the life of Maharaja Hanumant Singh. For, 200 years ago, when violence and tyranny was the only history in Sham Pur, and sanctity the only way to hide the nefarious intrigues, I could conceive of a situation in which a prince might suddenly tire of it all and exile himself out of his own volition. Not far from the powerful shadows of the palaces, the torchlit processions of bejewelled elephants and extravagant luxury, there stretched the ocean of squalor, emaciation and disease, in which lived people floundering in the depths of human misery. The weak little man with the wizened face, that was Maharaja Hanumant Singh, lord of the vast countryside, where men and women and children laboured with the patience of despair, straining their anaemic bodies throughout the hot day to earn a meal of crushed grain and a loincloth, may have suddenly glimpsed the wretchedness of the poverty-stricken land and decided to expiate his sins. His soul, filled with the superstitious awe of the gods, that held everyone at bay, may have suddenly been overawed. Or, what was also likely, the last of his wives, but first lady of the land by dint of her unscrupulousness, despairing of his capacity to produce an heir, might have thought of marrying him off to some stone goddess in Benaras and herself considered the possibility of securing a son of the gods in her own womb from one of the concourse of priests or ascetics who bathed and prayed and performed sundry other services to the deity on the banks of the sacred

Ganges....But in Victor's case the resolve to renounce life was certainly another of a series of romantic gestures. Because he lived, as I tried to remind him, not in the age of chivalry, where such gestures could be made, but in the period of the end of pre-history, where one's real sympathies went not to a Maharaja, however ill he might be, but to the exploited peasants, loaded with all the burdens of debt and disease, harvesting little grain but reaping a prolific crop of troubles all the year round and all through the years.

The poignant yearning for the holy life made Victor's face look a trifle bilious, especially as he seemed to be disappointed at not getting from me the unfailing response that I always gave to his more mundane demands.

'The trouble is that you don't believe in God,' Victor said in a despairing whisper, and lay back. 'I must write and ask Munshi Mithan Lal's advice.'

'Yes,' I said, unable to suppress a smile. 'You must ask Mian Mithu about this.'

'If you deny God, what do you believe in, then? What are we? How did we come to be?' Victor said frantically.

'I think that in spite of man's bewilderment and confusion about such questions as to what he is, how he ought to act and where he is going, he is the final fact of the universe. There is nothing higher and more dignified than human existence –' I felt embarrassed with my abstract words and stopped short.

'But how can one do good if there is no standard of behaviour ordained by Brahman?' Victor asked, a little querulous.

'If he gets to know himself a little better, he will know how to live and act. Because he has in him an instinctive awareness of decency, which is more or less derived from his idea of his own and other people's welfare: he is both norm-giver and subject to such norms. This kind of conscience I am speaking of is the voice of our love for ourselves and others; it is the expression of man's self-interest and –' Again my big words troubled me, and I didn't finish my sentence.

'Aren't you afraid of the unseen powers?' said Victor indignantly.

'No,' I said, warming to the debate because of the heat which Victor brought to his words. 'I don't believe that there is any power transcending man, who can decide things for him. Man is responsible for gaining or losing his life.'

'But surely, surely, there is some test by which every man has to judge his own acts,' said Victor, cutting me short, but half inclining to what I had said. 'Isn't there a higher self in man – higher than the lower self?'

'I suppose at his best man is creative and alive. And that is the only test by which he can judge his conduct. When he is most creative and uses his powers for enriching life, he is good.'

'This goes counter to the whole teaching of our Vedanta.'

'There are many philosophies in the Vedanta. Not only the idealistic, transcendentalist idea of Brahman, the Supreme God! At any rate, nowadays one's religion must become more universal and applicable to all....' My face fell with the suspicion that my words would have no effect on him whatever.

Victor seemed puzzled. Vaguely he knew that there was much more in what I said than in the ritualistic religion of his inheritance. And he was irritated that he should have felt evasive enough to want to go and become a yogi. For the glow of life remained in him, in the fast extinguishing coals that burnt in the smouldering ashes of his being, silently and unknown even to himself.

'Perhaps you are right,' Victor said in a vague, indistinct voice, even as he lay quite flat. 'But then, according to you, there is no good and evil!'

'There is no such thing as good and evil in the ordinary moral sense of those words. There is only knowledge and ignorance. All our lives are lived on the quicksands of uncertainty and doubt and inconstancy. And we have a large heritage of darkness in the subterranean caves of our natures. So to work up moral indignation, in the face of what is called evil, is only to disguise envy and hate in the cloak of virtue....' There was a vibration in my lecture which seemed to affect him, to transport him into the atmosphere where I wished to lead him.

I was aware of my influence on him now. So I went on driving the point home.

'The crucial sin is impotence and lack of the will to do something, lack of some creative purpose in one's life.'

'But my life is useless,' he confessed. 'What can I do now that I have been forced to abdicate?' And his lips trembled with a misery which was self-contained in him. And he couldn't go on, for the tears welled into his eyes.

'You despise me, don't you, for my self-pity?' he continued, his face quivering.

'No,' I said to console him, 'even self-pity and self-love are an attempt on your part to get well.'

'But I shall never be strong and firm and have character.'

'There is some chance for a person, who accepts dissolution of the personality, to become whole, because integration can only arise from a complete breakdown — provided the fire burns in one.'

He seemed absorbed for a while, as though at the significant moment he had relapsed into the darkness of his soul. But his eyes glittered as he looked at me and I felt that he was making the effort, that perhaps in his inner life there were real stirrings. And I knew that he had a considerable personal drive. Whether he would come through, in spite of the currents which buffeted him about, or held him in whirlpools, was not certain.

'The fire burns,' he said, 'but it is mixed up with the ashes of bitterness and remorse. I feel so unhappy, so lonely. I wish I could die!'

I was surprised and relieved to have confirmation from him of a feeling I had a little earlier in the conversation: that there was still a little glow left in the embers of his being.

'Don't talk like that,' I said. 'Life asserts itself.'

Life did begin to assert itself, but in the way rather more as Captain Partap Singh wanted it to assert itself than as I felt it might assert itself.

Victor came shopping at Barrots with Captain Partap Singh and myself, on the afternoon following our prolonged philosophical dialogue. We all wanted to buy a few toilet requisites in anticipation of a projected visit to Paris about which His Highness had spoken casually. We alighted from the car and were ushered into the store, through the swing doors. And we became part of the good-humoured promiscuity that resolves itself towards the lifts going up and down, all a little out of breath in the crush before closing-time. Victor liked to mingle with the herd for a fleeting hour, because now that he had lost his former grandeur as a Maharaja and was not receiving the attention which Captain Partap Singh's caparisoned presence always brought to him, he was trying perversely to cultivate the democratic manner. Thus, strictly incognito, we were part of the stream of humanity that flows into the less crowded corners of the mammoth stores, and we bought the few things we had to purchase. Due to the general depression which had settled on Victor, he was not in the spend-thrift mood which had characterized him in the old days, and we did our shopping quickly. Then I suggested that we should go to the restaurant downstairs and have tea, but Victor recalled that he wanted to buy a timepiece, as he could not wear a wristwatch, because the current of his blood always made any watch he wore go much faster.

I had noticed that throughout the shopping tour on the various floors of the store, the heart-squanderer in Captain Partap Singh had been drawn towards the schoolgirl complexion of the younger among the female shoppers and the shop assistants. And he told me that he was fascinated by their shapely legs. And, in the secret code that he had established with Victor in a language of gesture that was almost akin to Kathakali dance technique, they had shared the furtive excitements of certain sensations which shimmered and swirled in their eyes before the somewhat sublimated respectability of my presence.

After they had eyed the fine points of every passable female in the store and performed their lascivious diagnosis, their libidinous hungers were aroused enough for the inevitable to happen as soon as we got to the department where watches were sold. The young lady behind the counter was by no means Venus de Milo or Ganga Dasi, but she was a pretty, slim blonde, with her hair deliberately brushed to one side in a manner that permitted her to fling it aside with the self-conscious grace of a jerky blandishment of the head.

'What can I do for you, sir?' she said pertly, with a little glow of warmth on her pale cheeks at the sight of Partap Singh's turban and beard.

'Everything,' Partap Singh said with his usual vulgarity.

The shop assistant smiled, blushed and, averting her eyes from Partap Singh, looked towards the more subdued Victor.

Victor looked back at her and for a moment their four eyes met. Then he said almost shyly: 'We want to look at some timepieces – one of those in a case which folds up for travelling.'

The girl stood transfixed for a moment, her face suffused with an ivory pallor that showed up the specks of brown powder on her nose and on her delicate neck, above the cheap brooch by the collar of her satin blouse. She turned like a young doe in a panic towards this side and that as though she needed help.

The manager of the department, a dapper little bald-headed man with the suave grace of the experienced shop assistant, now exalted to rule over the other shop assistants, and for whom 'the customer is always right', sensed the difficulty and came flat-footedly towards the counter.

Behind him came a tall, shrivelled-up old hen in a black dress, cluck-clucking at the shop assistant: 'What do the gentlemen want, Miss Withers?'

Victor got panicky at all this fuss and, with half-closed eyes and a feeble voice, said: 'Nothing, nothing.'

'His Highness the Maharaja Sahib would like a timepiece,' said Captain Partap Singh, knowing that the announcement of Victor's title would restore the situation to its proper proportions, for the right of a Maharaja and his ADC to exact the tribute of a little confusion on the face of a shop girl was conceded by everyone, even by a prim and proper superintendent.

'Show His Royal Highness a timepiece, June,' said the manager, rubbing his hands and bowing to Victor. 'It's all right, Miss Atkinson. I'll look after the Maraja sab....'

'All right, Mr Drake,' said Miss Atkinson. And she withdrew towards the group of girls on the counter for leather goods who were whispering their comments on the scene in which June was involved.

I don't know if it was fear, terror or love that came over June, or whether standing by the counter all day with a watercress sandwich and a cup of coffee for lunch had exhausted her, but she reeled, swayed and fell forward on the counter in a faint.

'Smelling-salts!' whispered Mr Drake. And he rushed behind the counter and, lifting her in his arms, sat her down on a chair, while Miss Atkinson came with a bottle of smelling-salts produced by a girl behind the leather goods counter.

'I am so sorry,' said Victor apologetically to Mr Drake, as he came forward to help.

'What happened to her suddenly?' asked Partap Singh gallantly. And he advanced a step or two even beyond Victor and began to fan June. 'Doctor Shankar Sahib, come and look at her.'

Miss Withers opened her eyes after the smelling-salts had been applied to her nose, but closed them again, crying a half cry, while her lips trembled. 'What's the matter, Junie?' said a young man, rushing up from the leather goods department. And he looked daggers at the three of us. 'All right, Mr Cummings, all right,' Mr Drake said to the young man. 'Please give her some air,' I said. 'She will be all right in a minute.' But already she had opened her eyes and come to, wincing between the eyebrows and smiling sheepishly, even as she gasped for breath and said: 'I just felt giddy.'

'All right, my dear, you are all right,' said Mr Drake reassuringly.

She sat for a moment with a flushed face, closed her eyes, obviously with a swirling in her head, and then got up.

'I should see her home, Mr Cummings, if I were you,' said Mr Drake.

'Permit me to offer the young lady my car,' said Victor in his most deliberately gracious manner. 'My ADC will see the young man and the young lady home.'

He said this with such authoritative kindliness that the words were both regal command and supplication. And there could be no refusal, especially because he backed it all up with the swift foraging manner of the gallant who is only concerned to help a damsel in distress and is not interested in anything else.

There was a dubious frown on the eyebrows of Mr Drake, but equally the servile 'customer is always right' man smiled and bowed and scraped and shuffled on his feet as he helped June Withers to get up with soft, hypocritical words of comfort like: 'Now then, my dear, there you are....Now then...'

'Captain Partap Singh,' ordered His Highness, working up the histrionic talent of the old days when he had to act every inch a king, 'see the young lady and her friend home and come back to the suite afterwards. We will get there on our own.'

'Yes, Your Highness,' said Captain Partap Singh, coming to attention and saluting.

There were obvious tremors of excitement on June Withers's face. And she raised her head like a young colt snuffling with delight.

Mr Cummings, who was, from his proprietary airs, her young man, seemed tense and nervous and angry by turns. To him it was strange that June could accept the offer of this 'Maraja' so radiantly.

And there was a gleam in Victor's eyes as he turned with self-conscious grace and said to Mr Drake: 'I will come in to look at the timepieces another day.'

I surmised that his heart had been kindled by the romance of the situation.

He did not look back at her and carried the bluff of an unconcerned manner right to the end of the corridor where the lifts went up and down.

'Poor girl!' he said, turning to me after we had passed the knots of whispering shop assistants in the department. 'She has quite a pretty face, though she is flat-chested like all the English girls.…'

I knew that he had already decided to begin with her. I guessed that there was a revival of all the old stirrings for the unadmitted life of desire in him: in which all women were different, and each one a new prey for the eternal hunter, Man. I recoiled against the adventure, but equally felt a little relieved that he would be less obsessed with Gangi if he got involved in a minor flirtation.

It turned out to be not so minor a flirtation.

From the first day after the incident at Barrots, Victor made a dead set at Miss June Withers. He seemed a past master of the art of seduction. He had had the uncanny instinct to send Captain Partap Singh with June and her boyfriend with the dual purpose of showing gallantry as well as to find out her address. And, the next day, choosing the time when June was away at work, he sent a bunch of red roses by the ADC to her home, with a note on the back of the card asking if she would give him the honour of her company at supper that evening and informing her that Captain Partap Singh would call for her anyhow. The card, of course, bore his address and the full regalia of all his titles and honours, which he knew would impress her:

'Maj. Gen. His Highness Farzand-i-Khas-i-Daulata-i-Inglishia Mansur-i-Zaman. Amir-ul-umra, Maharajadhiraj Sri 108, Sir Victor Edward George, Ashok Kumar Bahadur, K.C.S.I., K.C.I.E., D.L. (Benaras), Maharaja of Sham Pur.'

Victor had acted dexterously. For I guessed that Miss June Withers, who had tasted the outer edge of a romantic meeting with a Maharaja in her capacity as a shop girl when she had fainted and been driven home in a Rolls-Royce by a tall and handsome man, would be suffused with the glow of a feeling that there might be a little more in the odd behaviour of the prince than he could make obvious at the shop counter. And having spent the day in a suppressed state of excitement, torn between the stares and glares of her colleagues, who had seen a definite ruse in her giddiness and the definite signs of a beginning in the Maharaja's eyes, she was not surprised when she got home and found the flowers waiting for her, red roses, the boldest confirmation of his inclination towards her, as well as an invitation to supper. And, naturally after the hesitations, occasioned by her regard for Bob Cummings, the lack of an appropriate coat to wear over the only long evening dress, the fear of consequences of such an adventure (what would Mum and Dad say?), the inner barren feeling of the shop girl about a life with mechanical repetitions, had urged her to take the plunge.

June came that evening chaperoned by Captain Partap Singh.

I was in the hall, handing over some letters to the porter to post, when I saw them arrive.

Her small face, framed by the lovely blonde hair, and her slim presence made her look like an imitation Garbo, as the great film actress must have looked in the early days in Sweden when she too was a shop girl. But June had not Garbo's self-confidence. For her little hand was trembling as I greeted her, the colour from her cheeks had evaporated and her eyes were like two miniature birds, fluttering in a panic in the strange exalted atmosphere of the Mayfair service flat.

Self-consciously, she went into the lift, awed by the uniform of the lift man and rather afraid, I guessed, because she felt people might say that she was visiting the Maharaja for only one purpose and one purpose only.

As we emerged from the lift the carpeted corridor was empty and she glided between us into our rooms.

Victor, who had dressed with greater care today than for weeks together, looked very elegant in his small closed collar, black coat and white corduroy breeches.

He took June's limp hand and kissed it in the gallant Polish manner, so that the colour rose to June's cheeks. And, in order to cover the gap of strangeness, and to put her at ease, he began to talk in his best play-acting manner.

'I am so glad you have come, Miss Withers, I thought you might be frightened – you see I know that Maharajas are supposed to be rather dangerous animals, professional seducers and all that! Come and sit down. Let me take your coat. Captain Partap Singh, please help Miss Withers. My ADC is a Sikh, Miss Withers, and his tribe is not supposed to be inured to the courtesies and graces of European life. Did you notice his rough accent? He is a peasant by birth. But Doctor Shankar was here in England and knows

English manners and customs. Now, what will you have to drink?'

'Oh, anything,' June said, breathless with the impact of his words and flushed with embarrassment.

There was a hush as Victor stopped his monologue and went towards the miniature bar we had made in the sitting room.

'May I mix you a cocktail or will you have some sherry?' Victor broke the lull.

'Sherry, please.' She was obviously unused to the world of cocktails and even sherries, a glass of beer or an occasional 'gin-and-it' being much more her line of approach through hereditary and environment, and the shop girl's modest emoluments.

'Please relax,' Victor said, noticing with an uncanny instinct that she was overawed.

June smiled demurely and dipped her eyes, then lifted them to watch the stage set for her seduction.

'Of course, Partap Singh will have whisky,' said Victor. 'What about you, Harry?'

'I'll have a little whisky too, please.' And I went over to him to help him dispense the drinks, Partap Singh following suit.

I noticed that June was transfixed, almost as though she had been numbed by the shock of finding herself, the silly goat, in a lion's den. She drummed the arm of the chair in which she sat with the forefinger of her right hand and her half-open mouth lifted towards the tall stems of the gladioli in a vase on the sideboard, with a blind appeal for help.

'Don't be so shy, Miss Withers,' said Victor, coming up towards her with the glass of sherry in his hand. 'Here's the drink. What's your first name? Mine is Vicky – Vicky is short for Victor! I was christened Victor Edward George – after Queen Victoria, King Edward VII and George V. What does your mother call you?'

'June,' came the whisper as she took the sherry. And, with the utterance, June seemed to brighten up a little, her fresh complexion colouring a vivid pink and her hazel eyes under the tiny blue-black eyelids lifting shyly up to her would-be paramour.

'I suppose you are called June because you were born in June,' said Victor casually.

'How do you know I was born in June?' the girl asked, almost as though she thought he was clairvoyant.

Victor sat down on the arm of her chair and explored her eyes.

I saw from the corner of my eye that she was looking up to him, her body still, very still. And I knew that they understood what they wanted of each other, though the colour on her cheeks showed that the virgin in her would not admit his desire without a fight.

'Let me look at your hand,' Victor asked, affecting the amateur palmist's manner.

'Can you really tell fortunes?' she said, with a childishly credulous tone in her voice.

I realized that she was a particularly dumb blonde, the usual average young English flapper, with hazy romantic notions about India and Indians, considerably frightened by the tales of hearsay about snakes and panthers and dark natives. She had heard and read many strange things in the penny bloods during her childhood, and she was fascinated by the prospects of an adventure with a Maharaja in her young coltish body.

'Ah, you have a good heart line,' Victor said, ignoring her naive question. And he smiled at her, with a mischievous glint in his eyes. 'Show me – you will have, let us see – nine children!'

June burst out laughing at this, her head swaying. And she withdrew her slim arm away from him.

'Give me your hand,' Victor said, pressing a double meaning into the phrase, but adding quickly, 'I haven't yet told you about your line of destiny.'

June let him take her hand.

'It is a lovely little hand,' Victor said, stroking her gently, and then he lifted the palm. 'Come and help me out, Harry,' he added, looking towards me.

'Were you also given the name Harry by your English friends? – and what is the pet name of the other gentleman?' asked June, obviously trying to put me and Partap Singh at ease while she yielded to the flirtatious Victor.

'All Sikhs have long hair under the turban, you know,' Victor began an explanation at the expense of the ADC. 'And as it is very hot in India, and long hair makes it difficult for Sikhs to think after noontime, I often call Captain Partap Singh "Twelve o'clock Singh".'

He made this up for the occasion to amuse June, as he had never called Partap Singh by a nickname like that. But June did not understand the joke, though Partap Singh servilely entered the fun and laughed a slight artificial laugh, adding his own quota of humour by saying: 'The best nickname given by His Highness to anyone is to his ex-tutor and Private Secretary: his real name was Munshi Mithan Lal: Maharaja Sahib named him Mian Mithu, which means parrot in Hindustani.'

No one was amused by this naive revelation and June simply did not understand all the words which were coming out of the beard, far less the joke implicit in the few words that she did hear.

There was a protracted awkward silence after this, during which Victor strained to bridge the gulf that divided him from this lovely stranger. His face darkened with the struggle to work up the necessary enthusiasm in his sick soul. He watched her furtively for a moment, then he turned aside, unable to look at her as though it hurt his eyes.

The dumb blonde also seemed to become shyer and smiled a delicately evasive smile, even as she bent her eyes to the satin sheen of the frock where it crumpled a little on her knees and while she again drummed nervously with the forefinger of her right hand on the arm of the chair in which she sat, overshadowed by Victor.

At last Victor broke the silence with a vague gesture of his right hand and asked, 'Another drink?'

'I will beg your leave, Highness,' I said, feeling that the whole thing would be easier if Victor and June were left alone.

'No, no,' Victor said. 'We shall all have another drink. Meanwhile, please ring for the waiter and we can order the food.' And he got up to pour the drinks.

'Please sit down, Your Highness, I will fetch the drinks,' offered Partap Singh, because even he seemed to be groping for a point of contact with the woman so that the sombre happiness of this meeting could be made lighter.

'Acha, you fetch the drinks,' Victor said, responding to the ADC's gesture with an exaggerated bonhomie. And then he leaned over June a little more intimately and whispered: 'I am a very unhappy man. Please don't be frightened of me....You see, I —'

I could not hear the last sentence because I was on my way to press the bell for the waiter. But I noticed that June's face relaxed immediately and lit up with a mellow smile.

'What is the matter?' I heard her breathe gently. And her eyes glowed with tenderness as she looked up to him.

As he sat silent with his head bent, so unutterably silent that his heart seemed to be weighed down by a millstone, she was filled with still more tenderness for him and pulled at his sleeve, saying importunately: 'What's the matter?'

Captain Partap Singh gave June some more sherry, and a large peg of whisky to Victor and me.

Victor's sensuality seemed to be released at the touch of her pity and he stroked her hand even as his eyes became tear-dimmed, and he searched for words for his trembling lips to utter the agony in his heart.

'I have lost my throne,' he said. 'But that wouldn't have mattered. Only, only, the woman whom I loved also left me.'

June's compassion hovered in the air before her in this critical moment. From the blossoming of her face she seemed to be drawn to him. His sorrow had apparently revealed that he could also love and was not merely a seducer. And yet her lips were pursed as though she doubted if he could ever love her, since he was suffering the pangs of having been left by another woman. Her senses seemed to have suddenly pricked up and she was transported beyond herself by the attraction of his personality.

'Why did she leave?' June asked.

Victor swept me and Partap Singh with an embarrassed glance. I wished he had let us go away when I had suggested this earlier.

'I can't understand why she did it,' Victor said, really talking aloud to himself, though he was revealing himself to the English girl. 'I gave her everything at the risk of losing everyone's respect and even my throne. But she...well...I don't know. No one will ever know how much I loved her.

You see, she was – well, always selfish – selfish and wayward! Doctor Shankar here says she is ill with schizophrenia –'

'What's that?' June asked innocently.

'A kind of split mind,' I explained. 'When one part of a person's mind does not know the other and acts independently – or rather when a person's mind is in pieces.'

'Doctor Jekyll and Mr Hyde!' said June brightly. 'Oh, I know....'

'She probably had no heart at all,' Victor continued, 'because I have done everything since then to get her back.' He quivered, and his eyes became hard. 'I have almost lost faith in women, when I used to adore women, simply worship them....'

'Oh, you mustn't feel like that,' June said, stroking his arm.

A haunted look came into his eyes, as if he wished, now that this lovely stranger had melted, to tell her everything, to throw himself at her feet. He looked towards me. But I had already got up. And, going towards Partap Singh, I took the ADC by the arm and announced:

'We will go and order the food.'

The would-be lovers accepted this suggestion without a demur.

As soon as we woke up next morning, Victor began to talk of Ganga Dasi again. I guessed that he did so now because he wanted to justify his flirtation with June Withers, while at the same time trying to convince me that the escapade of the evening was not a violation of the love he felt for Gangi. And behind the explanation was a certain masochism, a kind of heightened satisfaction at the licking of old wounds, through the re-enactment of the rage and misery and bereavement at the betrayal as well as the attempt to rise

337

above the bitterness. Perhaps, also, there was the urge to clear the previous tenant from his heart in order to admit a new one; for one cannot easily launch on a love affair when one is not free; and the murder of the previous image, or its burial alive, or safe embalmment, is necessary before the new idol can be worshipped.

'Is there no mail, this morning?' he asked significantly.

'No,' said I, as I perused the pages of the *Times*.

Victor hesitated for a moment to demolish the distance between us before launching on the inexhaustible exploration of his conflicts. His face was harrowed and tense before the passionate floodburst with its tremendous rush. My sombre preoccupation with the paper was obviously irritating him, and he rolled from side to side. But he did not allow his displeasure at my remoteness to harden into impatience, because he knew that I was the only confidant who did not show boredom in the face of his constant outpourings. In order to show consideration for me, he affected a deliberate ennui, yawned and stretched his legs. Then he lay flat. And, from the depths of his nature, from the chaotic world of ruin inside him, he said: 'You know, it is strange, but there is not a word from her, nothing at all!'

'First of all she is illiterate and can't write. But if she did write, it would upset you because she looked for quite different things in her relationship with you than you did....I don't know which is more upsetting, her writing to you or not writing.'

'If only she would be honest and tell me about herself, I would accept it.'

'I think she did seem to leave the back door open for the return in the letter she wrote to you. I have a peculiar hunch that she will ultimately come back, but then you may have June or someone else and may not want her after all that she has done. Meanwhile, the only thing to do is "to grin and bear it", as the English say.'

'But I can't grin and bear it, I want to love and be loved. I want her. I want to look after her, protect her. If you say she is ill, she must be cured. I feel responsible for her. I don't know what is happening to her. If only I knew she was happy, really happy, I would not worry so much.'

'I can see that it is no use for me to give you counsel of perfection. One can endure, but one suffers even when one endures. And yet one has to endure.'

Victor seemed exasperated even by this admission, because of the last qualifying phrase.

'I am a stoic,' he said.

'And yet you fell for June last night!' I commented cynically.

Victor shifted sharply and said impatiently: 'I don't love June, but I can even include her in the pervasive love I feel for everyone. You don't know that I felt very tenderly towards the praja in Sham Pur. My heart bled for them in their difficulties. I could not do much for them, but I often felt that I could sit down by the worst leper and tend his wounds....And I could live with Gangi even if she never gave herself to me.'

After saying this he lay motionless, still and intent, with a curiously bright tension in his face.

I did not know whether to prick the bubble of what seemed to me his newly acquired saintliness or to remain silent and let him harbour the illusions in which he was wrapping himself. I could well believe that he felt a kind of pervasive feeling for all women, but it was a strange self-deception on the part of the man who had been dramatically called the 'tyrant of Sham Pur', the levier of illegal taxes and the egotistical head of a lawlessly lawful government, whose sanctions lay in his whims and fancies, now to pose as a kind of St Francis.

'I am not too sure that you feel the same concern for other people that you feel for Ganga Dasi,' I said in a rather hesitant voice, lest I should annoy him. 'Perhaps you felt like mai-bap to the people of Sham Pur, because you were brought up to think that you should feel like a father-mother to your praja, but the people were not convinced of these feelings and rose against you. And as for living with Gangi, even if she never gave herself to you, it is mere wish-fulfilment on your part. You know you want sex. The way you looked at June last night, the way you hungered for her and ached for her – I am afraid you are deceiving yourself!'

'Perhaps you are right,' he confessed. 'But I did not look at another woman while I had Gangi.'

'I agree she fulfilled you in a way in which no other woman did,' I said. 'But she would not stay. And you were angry with her. Now you are trying to make this fixation into an exalted philosophy of pervasive love. It means that if Gangi is ill, because she had a whore for a mother and a bully for a father, your soul is also sick with a thousand neuroses. Otherwise, you would not be obsessed with the thought of her, absorbed by her so completely.'

'I know I am sick,' Victor said weakly and humbly.

'I don't know if you were loved enough in your childhood,' I ventured a guess about the reasons for his inordinate concentration on women.

'Not much,' he said, looking as though he felt rather diminished, belittled and degraded. And then he fell into a silence as though he did not want to have things dragged out of the depths.

I took up the paper again, feeling that I could not go on with my brutal fault-finding.

'What then shall I do?' he asked me after a protracted wordlessness between us, during which I felt that he felt my disapproval of his confused state of mind like a powerful presence.

'You must accept the fact, hard as it is to bear, that it is finished, it is finished, it is all finished between you and Gangi! Your only hope is June's friendship.'

Victor looked away from me.

During the next few days Victor saw a great deal of June Withers. Fortunately for them, the two days after she first came to our flat coincided with the weekend, and they went out for long drives in the country.

June was at once shy, even frightened, and wild: on the ordinary plane she seemed to be inhibited by ingrained petit-bourgeois respectability, because most Maharajas were supposed to be philanderers, and she knew that her own people, as well as others, would talk; but on the other secret plane, this liaison had released in her certain insidious romantic impulses from under the layers of convention, the 'pagan' part, as Michael Arlen might have called it, of her 'Chislehurst mind'.

After the touch of his hand, as he sat on the arm of the chair on the evening when she first came to Mayfair, her body seemed to tingle with a furtive warmth in his presence, like a bird which overcomes the original resentment of being caged and brings forth its song to its captor. And their kissing and cuddling seemed rather uncanny. In the beginning I would come into the room and find them in an embrace, with Victor quite unselfconscious and June absolutely still, her eyes closed as though she was not giving but receiving. Then, perhaps because Victor came to her with a mad, untrammelled passion, delirious with all the pent-up fury of months of frustration, which had suddenly been dissolved in his kisses, she would lie on the divan bed looking at him with open eyes, as though the rosebud was just opening at the touch of the sun. And yet there was a certain dimness in her body, and I could sense that Victor was often deliberately gentle in his approach to her, lest he should shock her with the excessive vitality of his Indian nature and send her away. As their friendship grew quickly, and they began to share the only thing common between them on the 'intellectual' plane, the swing music that came from the radiogram, their loving attained a higher intensity, which was mutual though differentiated by her essential frigidity and his ardent, flaming temperament.

I knew, however, that he was not satisfied in his confused soul. 'Give me an Indian girl for loving-time,' he let drop the phrase in one of those confidences which he often felt impelled to give me. And I realized that the spell of Gangi's high-powered sexuality was still on him, as a kind of contrast to the tentative beginnings with June Withers. Perhaps his body was in many ways finally pledged to Gangi and would never in that way belong to another, even if June had been of a hotter nature. Also, even when he wanted to give June all of himself, it was only the passion and the energy but not the flow of the real current of his life. For, in himself he seemed to have got stuck in a huge whirlpool which foamed in a circle on the top while reaching out to remote troubled centres of experience within, where mighty pulls tugged at him, breaking him, destroying him, reducing him to a soft slimy earth, which was corroded and slippery like a mass of disintegrating jelly. Therefore, in spite of his mad burst of loving in which he smothered June with kisses, caresses and soft words, his soul was bitter and ugly, demanding drink and more drink to drown itself, for what he really wanted was, like an illusion, beyond the reach of his arms, a fulfilment that was as impossible now as a bygone dream.

The hangers-on, that is to say Partap Singh and myself, were rather embarrassed when the kisses and embraces started in our presence, as outside witnesses of other people's loving are always in an invidious position because of the envy it excites in the spectators. Partap Singh went out to the lounge of a hotel in Piccadilly in search of his own prey, while I fixed one moment of shame firmly with the gaze of my mind and, accepting Victor and June as part of the furniture of the suite, began also to accept certain permutations and combinations of this furniture which seemed quite amusing. And I waited, in the unquestioning manner of the doctor, for this part of the cure to show results in Victor's person.

I found that his face looked increasingly less harrowed and the hot, insane fits of indignation, remorse, love, regret and desire were less frequent.

'How do you feel?' I asked him deliberately one afternoon when he got up from a prolonged siesta.

'As I have been making up for my lost sleep of months by having a nap every day after lunch, I feel I know the difference between life and death,' he told me.

I knew he was evading my question.

'Are you happier?' I asked him more directly, feeling very stupid after I had put the question to him.

'I don't know that I am happier, but I am wiser,' he said. And he paused as though to consider his inner feelings, and then said half embarrassedly, half jocularly, 'Someone has said that if you have a broken heart, the best cure is to try and get it broken again.'

I smiled understandingly. But I think he noticed a certain remoteness in my manner, and his face became strained with the attempt to touch me, to melt the cynicism he found latent in my expression.

'Actually,' he said, 'I did not realize how right that yokel Partap Singh was when he said that I must have a substitute for Gangi.'

As I did not want to give him the impression that I approved of the particular substitute he had chosen, I did not say anything about June, but waxed deliberately philosophical: 'It is silly for me to talk of happiness. I suppose if there is any happiness, it lies mainly in the removal of anxiety.'

'I agree,' he said. 'I still have a gnawing feeling inside me, almost like a toothache in my soul, that I have missed something in life − I feel that with Gangi's going something in me is dead for ever. Perhaps I shall never love again in the same way. I feel I will take my pleasure wherever it comes from and whenever I feel like it −'

'I wish you had waited,' I said rather priggishly. 'You might have found a nice woman.'

'I despair of ever finding anyone to suit me as Gangi suited me.' And he made a wry face.

'There are plenty of good women in the world,' I said airily, almost enthusiastically.

He waved his head negatively. And then, tilting it to one side, he looked away from me and whispered: 'I think you know that I have come to one conclusion about women: that they prefer bad men. When I was a wild young man, I could have had any woman for the asking....I feel that they are fascinated by evil.'

I laughed a wooden laugh, and tried to change the subject.

Victor seemed bored. So I sought to make the discussion interesting.

'You see, in the old days they negated woman in Europe also. She was not asked. She was just taken. And I suppose this will only alter when woman stands on the same footing as man, and love becomes a reciprocal business, embracing the whole of the man-and-woman relationship, and not being merely mistaken for sex, which is only one part of the relationship. Then men and women might live together more intensely, and their relationships might become more enduring, and non-possessive, and separation might begin to seem to both partners in a marriage a great misfortune. And through this new values would arise, in which it would not be necessary to ask whether a couple lives within or without the marriage tie, but whether the relationship is a creative one, based on shared work and mutual love and respect. At the moment people only pretend to accept this basis in our bourgeois society, but really ignore it, while in a new kind of society —'

'I don't like words like "bourgeois",' Victor interrupted.

He rose from his chair and taking a cigarette from the tea table lit it. He seemed to want to retort back to me because he found all I said to be the negation of the things he had done in his life. I knew that in his docile moods he accepted most of what I said. But when he was racked by doubts, any attempt on my part to make him question himself produced an evil will in him and he fought back. It was as though he reacted to my priggishness as Gangi was reacting to his self-righteousness. His eyes glittered as though with a malignant desire to deny me. He stood motionless for a moment, withholding his anger against me.

I sat bent-headed and rather hopeless about being able to help him or to be honest with myself.

Suddenly he seemed to see the hurt expression on my face. And he turned towards me in an obvious anguish of kindliness.

'Don't despise me too much. Please don't chastize me!'

And then he tried to hold himself hard, so that the tears should congeal in his eyes and not be seen.

I surmised that Victor was not to be purged of his remorse for the past, the guilt about the present, and anxiety about the future except through the brief moments of forgetfulness he enjoyed in the company of June Withers.

To an extent the moments with June were not really moments of forgetfulness. For one thing June's parents had begun to object to her late nights, and her young man at Barrots was making things difficult for her by prowling around Curzon Street. So that though June allowed the chill virginity of her inner life to relax in the enjoyment of the good food Victor gave her in the Spanish, the Hungarian, the French, the Greek and the Indian restaurants, the nice clothes he bought her from the fashionable shops in Bond Street and Berkeley Square, and the amusement with which he provided her in the form of the cheap musicals she liked, she felt inhibited by a certain sense of shame in the sensual voluptuousness which crowned all the entertainment.

And in the slight rigidity of her manner, and in the tension of her nerves, even in the beauty of the violently active intimate life, Victor began to sense a discord and a feeling of the temporary nature of this flirtation.

And yet warming to the excitement of a new romance with June, Victor's outward life went on, aided by all the courtesies and graces which, through gifts and tokens, bind a poor, frustrated girl to a rich suitor. But, deep inside him, he seemed to be terror-stricken at the phenomenon of his affair with the English girl. I suspected that, apart from the hangover of the heavy beauty of the licentious delight he had had in Gangi, and the comparison which these marigolds and gulmohurs of his sensibility made in view of the delicate pink roses of June's flushed cheeks, he felt a certain boredom with her vulgarity and dullness, a quite different kind of vulgarity and dullness from that which Gangi exuded. For, in the case of the harlot there were always the violent, quarrelsome words and the impatiences of the moody, dominating, sinister vampire beneath the surface of the routine life; while here, with the English girl, there was the politeness of the first days of the affair as well as reticences. The thought of the hidden resources in June relieved the situation somewhat, and he told me that he hoped he would be able to show her whole vistas of India and fill her life with riches and take her around the world. But she was slightly anaemic, listless and pale and could neither bring the energy which might cope with his ardent nature, nor open up the inner worlds behind the glistening look in her eyes, if, indeed, there were any inner worlds there worth speaking about.

Again and again, in between the moments of stepping out from the car into the suite or into a restaurant or cinema, or while holding hands in the car itself, or at supper late at night, I could sense Victor coming back to the attack. But June was not there, almost as though she was utterly frightened of the world whose powerful, glaring eyes were looking at her, exploring her whole person, like searchlights, for the guilts and the shames of giving herself to a Maharaja.

Then Victor tried a subtler approach. He stopped trying to communicate with her with words in the direct way in which he had probed her views on life; he only multiplied the endearments; and he assailed the dark confusion of her mind by an exaggerated, highly dramatized sentimentality.

The curious thing was that she yielded to this kind of lovemaking and glowed like a fire. The cold passion in her melted and she seemed to relax and open up, ready to be filled up. And although she was too dumb and baffled to understand what was happening to her, she became naked and allowed herself to be overwhelmed. And now, a slow yearning for him began to possess her, so that she would wait upon his words in an anguish of waiting, as though she was willing to receive everything, the whole universe, if he gave it to her. And, impulsively, she would turn to him and pull his cheek or hold his chin in her hands and let her blind soul radiate towards him. And they were bound up in the world of their desire.

And yet, just when they were both coming nearer to each other, Victor seemed to be thrown back into sudden moods of despair and to withdraw from the contest, as it were. And it was obvious that she was only a small part of him, a kind of stopgap before the bigger reality of Ganga Dasi, whose memories were bearing him down, compelling him, encompassing him, murdering him, annihilating him.

June noticed that he was sad, and said so now and then, even caressing him with sensitiveness; but the cold imperturbability of her nature was not really disturbed by his sorrow, and she could never realize how near death he had been. Patiently, she sat there and waited for him to return to her and take the initiative. Meanwhile, she was even glad of the freedom to be herself, detached and withdrawn, for she could devote more time to do pure gold-digging and have her hair done, and nails varnished, and feel less guilty because she was not actually committing sin.

I thought at first that Victor's moods were mostly due to the contrasts between the souvenirs of his intense pleasures in Gangi and the furtive, hole-and-corner affair with June. Also, I felt that the chill in the autumn air and the increasing absence of the sun was affecting him. But the moods became frequent and I began to see him holding prolonged secret conversations with Partap Singh, with whom I knew he had not much in common and whom he had not trusted overmuch with confidences hitherto. I thought that Victor had perhaps got bored with June and was arranging with Partap Singh to find someone else to whom he could shift his affections. But, soon, I began to suspect that their talks related to some private arrangement about a spy system, to keep surveillance on Gangi in Sham Pur, of which the ADC had been put in charge, apparently before we left the state, and about which I had not been told anything.

I felt rather hurt at not having been taken into confidence by Victor, because I realized, for the first time, that there was an inscrutable element in his nature which had not been revealed to me. And I began to speculate about the possible nature of the conspiracy in which Victor and Partap Singh were involved.

They were pretty discreet about the whole thing, however, and I just gave up nosing, only getting worried when the black fits made Victor burst into raging tempers, especially at the cost of Partap Singh, and when he became, for hours, a kind of demon, hard, overbearingly masterful and stentorian in his utterances.

'I shall revenge myself on all of you,' he suddenly burst out one day. 'I don't trust any of you! You have destroyed me! You have taken away my state. All of you, all of you, are intriguing against me. What does my life amount to now? You have all trampled upon me. All of you, all of you, all – all of you who professed to be devoted to me, "Highnessing" me!...None of you really like me! Strange, isn't it, that I have so many friends, but not one real friend – when it came to it I found that I hadn't even one friend who would stand by me!'

I protested, feeling slightly hypocritical as I did so. But, anyhow, neither my protests, nor Partap Singh's abject confessions of devotion could allay the bitterness which had begun slowly to possess Victor. And he trampled on himself with more words: 'The fool! The fool! I did not guard myself against you all. Why didn't I foresee that this would happen to me? What a fool I have been! Oh, if only, if only....'

And he again began to suffer agonies during the nights, waking up in hot sweats and in the grip of nightmares....

After the apathy and listlessness of Victor's nervous collapse had come the excitement of the affair with June, accompanied by a delirium, which was the outer index of several unresolved conflicts. And then, suddenly, one grey morning, something happened which, though really as inevitable as everything else that had happened to our Maharaja, seemed like the sudden and untoward impact of a cruel and blind fate.

A CID man, who announced himself as Inspector Ward, called on us and asked Captain Partap Singh to come with him to Scotland Yard for a consultation. He also asked to see 'His Highness the Maraja Ashok Kumar'.

Victor happened to be in the bathroom at the time. So he waited.

Nervous and distraught as I was, not only with the fear of the policeman, which is instinctive with me, but also with the dread that something terrible had happened in Sham Pur, I ventured to ask the officer the reasons for his call.

A huge, burly man with a padded face, Inspector Ward was, like Humpty Dumpty, impenetrability itself.

And this stirred the deeper levels of anxiety in me, the layers of guilt feelings aroused by my complacency in full view of the furtive talk between Victor and the ADC in spite of the sinister forebodings that had arisen in me at the very first awareness of this kana-phusi.

The atmosphere of waiting for the doom to reveal itself was fraught with the most awful, muffled anguish. The remorse about the weakness and cowardice I had shown in not resolving the contradictions in my own position, and the abject surrender of my ideas and feelings in time-serving compromises, disguised by rationalizations of affection and pity and personal loyalty for a person who was, from the logic of his position, quite unregenerate – all this shrilled out in my confusion.

At last I heard Victor come into the bedroom, and I went in to tell him that an Inspector Ward from Scotland Yard was waiting in the dressing room.

As soon as he saw my pale face with its grim expression, he said: 'Why, Hari, is there some bad news from Sham Pur?'

It seemed to me that he had a premonition of disaster.

'What has Partap Singh done?' I asked him, breathless.

'I suppose Bool Chand has been murdered,' Victor said aloud to himself. And, trembling, he sat down on the bed.

The whole thing revealed itself to me in a flash. All the furtive whisperings seemed to become eloquently clear. Apparently they had been discussing a plot which they had laid out before they left Sham Pur to have Bool Chand murdered. The fact that Victor did not want Munshi Mithan Lal to come with us, and had left him behind, seemed to me to suggest that they had also involved him in their design, and the letters Munshiji wrote to Partap Singh, which were not shown to me, had presumably reported developments back at home. So this was the end, the brutal end. And I felt sad, not because I felt sorry for Bool Chand, who was a crook anyhow, but because I felt involved in a putrescent mess, ashamed at my own weakness in not acknowledging the logic of the world of which I had become a part.

I sat down on the arm of a chair, feeling emptied of all content. I could not utter another word either of sympathy or contempt. I just felt numbed with my realization of what had happened. Something in me seemed to snap, not with a dramatic force, but merely through a sudden hardening of my nerves and an equally sudden relaxation, so that I felt I did not care any more.

Victor also seemed to have been numbed by the shock. For a moment, he looked up and saw the chaos of the bedroom, a reflection of the amorphous confusion in him. But then he hung his head down.

'The Inspector is waiting,' I said after a while.

'Oh, how I hate her, the whore!' he said in a hoarse whisper that seemed to spring from the depths. 'Look what she has made me do. She murdered me and I have murdered back! The cruel bitch left me out of sheer perversity! Just because she likes all the dogs and is not content with one!...That cur Bool Chand was also a traitor. And I had to do something for the sake of my manhood. The dog – the snivelling, snorting scoundrel did not deserve a better fate!'

'I hope you won't say all that to the CID, for your own sake,' I said.

His face became grisly pale. And he snapped:

'I won't see him. I won't see him!'

'Acha, Victor, I will tell him.'

'Has he a warrant for my arrest?'

'No, I don't think so.'

'Then tell him to communicate what he has to say to me in writing. And if there is no warrant for the arrest of Partap Singh, ask him not to worry.'

I stalked out of the bedroom and told Inspector Ward that His Highness had just finished his toilet and was not feeling particularly well and wanted to know on what business the Inspector wished to see him. I made up all this to see if the CID man had, indeed, a warrant for Victor's arrest.

'Oh, I shall call again,' Inspector Ward said, his fat red face flushing a more vivid red. 'But this gentleman had better come with me.'

'Have you a warrant for his arrest?' I asked.

'Yes,' the Inspector said confidently, looking me straight in the eye. 'Something like a warrant.'

I felt the dread of the policeman again. For Ward oozed the very stink of the policeman's soul, the tang of death. Would I also be involved in this unholy business? I seemed to be sinking into the welter, descending into the fathomless pit.

'Good morning!' the Inspector said with an artificial cheeriness. And, beckoning Partap Singh to go ahead of him, he cleared out.

I went in to see Victor. He was still sitting on the edge of the bed. And he was talking to himself even as tears rolled down his eyes.

'Why did she have to drag me through the mire like this? Why did she have to choose to go to bed with Bool Chand? I...I only wanted – what is there wrong in loving a woman? And she loved me. So she said....Oh, why did she have to make me so desperate?'

'What exactly did you do, Victor?'

'Shall I do away with myself, Hari? If one's life is empty and one fills it with hatred only, then don't you think one is justified in taking one's own life?'

'Of course one is justified in taking one's own life, but not other people's.'

'I can't stand alone. And now with this thing happening, she will be so stubborn she will never come back.'

'Oh, forget the bloody woman now!' I said impatiently, shouting in spite of myself. 'You seem to go on and on....But the situation has gone far beyond her. A man has been murdered. And now, in spite of yourself, the vicious circle is broken. Things will never be the same.'

'I am done for,' said Victor. 'Will this get into the papers?'

I didn't answer him. I only said: 'I will ring up India House and go and see the High Commissioner.'

He looked at me with a stony stare, like a madman. And his frame was rigid as though with a cold frenzy of fear, his face set into a mould paralyzed by the very excess of the fears and guilts that played behind it.

I was trying to get through to India House on the telephone to see if they knew the exact reasons why Captain Partap Singh had been taken to Scotland Yard for questioning, when the hall porter's assistant brought His Highness's mail up. And just when I had secured an appointment to see one of the secretaries, Victor handed me a letter from India House, which briefly purported to inform him that, owing to the murder, under very suspicious circumstances, of Sjt Bool Chand, Secretary to the Administrator of Sham Pur, a public inquiry had been ordered in which it was necessary for His Highness and his staff to give evidence. Therefore, the States Department of the Government of India had asked that His Highness be advised to return to India immediately. And, accordingly, arrangements had been completed to enable His Highness and his staff to travel by the Air India International plane 'Moghul Princess' the next day.

Victor had received the polite, curt note in silence. But, in a little while, he got up from the bed where he had been seated, still in his pyjamas and dressing gown, and, wringing his hands, began to hammer at his forehead, shouting the while: 'O my fate! Why have you chosen me for a victim? Why is there only humiliation after humiliation for me! Oh, God, how it hurts! This dishonour of being ordered to return home, almost under arrest! What Providence contrived to make me do such foolish things? Why, oh, why did I have to do this? May the fires of hell devour them all. May she…'

And, like the blundering buzzing cohorts of doom, the words broke forth from his mouth, echoes of his ravening soul, hating itself, loathing itself and the universe for what it had done. And as he flung himself from place to place, and struck his head with his fists and cried bitter tears, the rocking introspection made him a colossus of weariness, anger, shame and passion, trampling upon himself and the soft carpet under his feet like Caliban in the last throes of his revolt against his persecutors.

'Oh, why did I have to get bound up with this murder?' he wailed. And then, turning to me, he said: 'My father once told me: "My son, you will have many affairs. But take my advice. Never fall in love with an ignorant woman. For to do so will not only be a reflection on your taste and intelligence, but you will not be able to control her when her greed is provoked. She will want power and will destroy you in the pursuit of her ambitions. A temporary affair, yes. But not a permanent alliance. Let your emotions, if you like, dominate your physical being; do not let them cloud your brain or bewilder your reason. Many affairs are better than a few. Distribute your affections regally while you are young, then you will not be plagued by regrets when you are old." And I forgot this advice.…'

I found myself staring at him, as though unable to believe that he was uttering so lucidly perverse a statement, because his earlier hysteria had seemed to me to have annulled his being, to have crushed his ego under the immensity of the doom which had mounted from all sides around him, on to him, reducing him to the ultimate fate of non-existence. His forehead was heavy with the weight of the anguished burden as it were, and he seemed, for a moment, to be fighting back from the last ditch of his pride. Hence his attempt, I presumed, to beckon the words of his father to chastise himself with. For, more plebeian words would be an affront to the spirit of royalty, which still possessed him. I was correct in my prognostications, because he soon began to try to rehabilitate his royal ego on the throne of Sham Pur.

'Oh, come, come, my fate, and take me back to my Sham Pur! Oh, back, back, let us go to my state, to my kingdom! Oh, come, come, come and let us go where we belong, among my people. Let us go away from this wilderness of London, where my head is filled with waves till it aches — cold, monstrous, unfriendly London. Hai! I feel an utter stranger here. How all my body is chilled by the icy wind and seems to be breaking up, stripped. I feel naked, naked, naked like a murderer! But I did not murder Bool Chand. I did not do so with my own hands. My hands are clean! I tell you, Hari, they are clean!...Only, I don't know why I feel oppressed. I had dreams last night, and my head aches. Give me some medicine, will you? And tell me what I should do now....Will it all get into the papers? Is there no avail against going back like this? Can't we go to Paris for a few days? And Partap Singh?...'

The anguish of his soul seemed to become physical. His eyes glittered with a curious hard light, pushing me into a terrorized silence, stifling me with the pressure of their peering emptiness into an abject helplessness. I felt an uncanny fear that he was disintegrating and might soon lose control. And, even before I had formulated my feelings, I found him trying to stand on his head. As he could not keep his balance in two attempts to do so, he fell athwart the bed and began to say:

'That will ease the pain, Hari, don't you think? I shall perform yoga. How do you do it? Ooof!...I feel I am coming into myself, into my own self, into the single point. No pain now....Hai! But my head still aches. Oh, come, come to Sham Pur....Come, then, come, let us go.'

Giddily, his eyes closed and he lay still for a moment, his mouth slobbering.

I was very afraid for him, and thinking that he might sleep if I lifted him and stretched him out on the bed, I took hold of him by the waist.

Immediately, he stiffened and began to wriggle out of my grasp, shouting:

'No, no, I don't want to go to Sham Pur. No, no, no, thieves, traitors, I do not want to hear the echoes of my own voice. I tell you I am the Maharaja of Sham Pur. Are you not frightened of me?...Who are you? An Englishman? The Political Resident? No, Sahib, I do not want to hear your voice....Go! May your face become cursed!...Do not push me!...Go, go your way!...'

I realized that he had lost consciousness, that he did not know the meanings of the words which formed themselves in his mouth any longer, that he had gone mad.

I struggled with him and lifted him up, while he kicked and beat me with his hands. I was about to fling him on to the bed, when he hardened like a stone and dragged me down on the floor. His eyes were bright with a cold, unmoving hatred, and I felt furious with him for getting out of my control. So I tried to be rough with him and, exerting my full strength, picked him up and flung him on the bed.

This seemed to sober him a little, for his lips moved contritely from the void into which he was slipping.

'I shall give you a sleeping draught. Try to sleep.'

'I shall give you a sleeping draught,' he repeated. 'Try to sleep.'

I couldn't help smiling with grim amusement at the mockery of the mad man parroting my words.

'I can fly,' he babbled suddenly. 'I can fly. I can fly away on my own....' And he got up and, stretching his arms out, began to flap them like a bird taking off. And he fell so that his head dangled on to the side of the bed.

I tried to pull him back to a more restful position. But again he began to push me away from him, breaking the hold of my fingers with his sharp nails, with some unprecedented strength in his bones that had come into him, I did not know from where. And, thrusting me away with the ruthless frenzy of madness, he raved at the top of his voice, from somewhere in the chaos of his perjured self, the lilt of a folk song:

'Oh, where have you gone, my stranger...'

The raucous accents of the shouted Punjabi song deafened my ears, and was likely to bring the whole house to Victor's bedroom. I therefore hit him hard, even as I grappled with him by the waist, and laid him low. Pinned under my arms, held fast, he stared into the empty space with the horror of horrors and talked snatches of words in which his first and last memories seemed to touch each other in a jungle of images. His mouth was frothing with the phobia, and he made an effort to bite my ear off, till I slapped him into comparative docility and silence. And then he began to weep and sing, even as he made renewed efforts to get up. I dragged a sheet from under him with some difficulty and slowly tied him down to the mattress.

There he lay and, by turns, tittered and laughed and shouted and sang, from the impulse of the several straying herds of memories all overshadowed by the dim mist of time, where everything seemed indistinct and lost, and from which it reappeared only in the form of remnants of an existence which was half extinguished and half transformed into the emptiness of the maniacal becoming, where everything was like a naked, primeval horror.

EPILOGUE

Although we flew by the Air India international plane 'Moghul Princess', which covers the span between London and Bombay in about twenty-four hours, it was a long journey we had of it. For Victor's condition had worsened. From standing on his head and ranting in the Mayfair suite, throughout the flight he kept up a continuous monologue, interrupted by songs sung in a raucous voice, and by sporadic violence, until he became a complete nuisance to the other passengers and had to be strapped up and bound to his chair. Fortunately for me, Captain Partap Singh had been allowed to travel with us, though he was asked to surrender himself to the Bombay police on arrival at the airport; and he kept the Maharaja in hand at Heathrow, while we were going through the passport formalities, also holding him down during the early part of the journey before he was bound hand and foot and across the waist. Still Victor's outbreaks, both verbal and physical, were extremely boisterous and disturbed the voyagers greatly, particularly during the night, when he would not go to sleep. It was strange and uncanny; what a power had come into his bones through the madness. For it took me and Partap Singh all our strength to control him and keep him seated; and his eyes glowed like coals in an imitation gas fire as he stared at us between bouts of profane and less profane utterances, while he frothed at the mouth and wriggled to get free.

He had begun to be very excited at the sight of an Englishman with a full moustache at Heathrow aerodrome – the most intense and prolonged fit of violent hysteria which I had noticed. He had poked his tongue out at the gentleman and spat in his direction and abused him roundly in Hindustani as 'betrayer of his salt' and worse. It had taken me and Partap Singh all our strength to move him away from the waiting room, where this happened, towards the gangway of the plane. And, later, on the plane, it was again and again the confrontation to his gaze of one white face or the other that seemed to rouse his ire. Except that the poor Anglo-Indian air hostess, so gentle and kind, also became the object of his contempt.

For the rest, the ravings and the burblings were directed against mankind at large. And the only relieving grace was the tender and mournful atmosphere of a Punjabi verse from the epic poem *Heer-Ranja*, by Waris Shah, which he kept on reciting and singing:

> Your love, oh my Hiré, has dragged
> Me through the dust of this world.

I encouraged him to sing, because the oppression of his madness was bearing me down, destroying me with the shame of his misbehaviour and the fear that he might become much worse and do harm to the other people in the plane. The dark seething waves of power that welled up from the hidden sources of his being made him demoniac, and I felt that the potential destructiveness of his nature would demolish me completely if he did not get some release.

I found that my suggestion worked. He recited sentences of ribald old Punjabi folk songs. At first he hammered the verses which describe the two Lachis, the demi-mondaines of the village:

Akha, in one village there were two Lachian,
And it was the little Lachi who made all
The trouble...

As the original accent in which he couched his sing-song was so loud that it seemed to clamp the hold of his will obscenely on the inmates of the plane, I began to sing in unison with him in a gentler voice. This modulated the extroversion of his tormented, leonine spirit somewhat, and he softened a little. But, immediately, there was a resurgence of the ghoulish tiger from the dark jungle in which he lay and he began to growl at me with a fiendish hardness in his voice: 'How do you do, Doctor Shankar. I am Maharaja Ashok Kumar of Sham Pur. Don't you understand, you swine! – I am a prince! Why, why do you hold me like that? Let me go, let me go, rape-mother!...Let me go!...I shall allow no one to come near me, not even the Viceroy. Why did that dhobi touch me? I am a king. Do you not understand? I am the Maharaja Ashok Kumar, spoiler of my salt!'

'Come, come, Victor, you are not a little boy any more,' I rebuked him in a firm voice. 'Don't be a fool.'

This seemed to sober him. And, with a cunning candour imprinted on his face, he said: 'Why am I ill?'

'You must calm down,' I said.

But by this time the lucidity had gone and he was shouting at the top of his voice: 'Khabardar! Khabardar! The thieves are coming! Look out, folk, the robbers! the bandits!'

'Try and sing,' I suggested again, smacking my lips sympathetically.

'Try and sing,' he repeated my words, and mimicked me by smacking his lips sympathetically.

I held his left hand and pressed it warmly.

'Sing,' I said.

And he burst out with the raucous lilt of a First World War Sikh soldier's song:

Han ni, may I buy you, may I buy you
Black slippers, with high heels,
What is the use of Indian style shoes,
Ni, Harnam Kauré!...

This amused the passengers a little. And Captain Partap Singh was stirred enough by old memories, in spite of his present depression, to encourage Victor with a 'Wah Wah'.

But, instead of continuing his song, Victor began to talk gibberish, with a far-away look in his hard glassy eyes: 'My sweetheart is wearing black tights! O my little white elephant! Dance, dance, dance, ah! ah! ah! Arré wah, wah, kiya kehne hain tere, meri piari jan!...Darling, darling, darleeng...'

And then the last words became a sing-song in his mouth, ending up in a queer falsetto which was an imitation of the last accents of a baritone opera star.

Again there was a continuous flow of words; dead reverberations of his tortured sensibility, sunk in the abyss of memories and aspirations and dreams, and emerging as an assortment of isolated words in complete disorder, spilling over the boundaries of sense into a jungle of nonsense. It was as though from the primeval darkness of his soul a certain shapeless form became speech and the primal sound turned into song at the merest impact of the warm throat, hushing us into terror with the trace of fury that was in each syllable. And all the utterances became timeless, beyond understanding, but with a coherence of their own, a kind of omniform of the demented personality.

Apart from a few amused smiles, no one dared to laugh in the face of this primordial fact of the unhinged mind, even as there is no defiance possible against a bad dream, but only acceptance.

And involved in the thick undergrowth of the forest of his soul, caught in the ramifications of his dreams and fantasies, almost as though he believed that each yearning was a happening, he became a transparent mirror for each impulse, fixated perhaps in one primary fact but now scattered and homeless, without roots, much more of an orphan now than he had been in the three years during which I had known him.

I sat there whipped, whipped to exhaustion by the strain and sleeplessness, wishing that I could pity him, but unable to control a certain hardness into which I was stiffening. For his frenzy and madness, and even his suffering, had driven me into myself until I felt that my mind was insidiously devising plans to give him the go by, dump him on the scrap-heap somewhere and free myself from him.

It was then that I thought of taking him to the Poona asylum, almost as a murderer takes a victim to the place where he is going to do away with the innocent one.

And yet as soon as the thought came to me, I felt tremors of hot blood go through me and my body was sodden with sweat.

A little while later, the plane alighted at Cairo aerodrome. And as everyone had to get down while the plane was being refuelled and cleaned, I had to undergo the most terrific ordeal of all at the hands of Victor. The Egyptian policemen, each looking more like King Farouk than King Farouk himself, refused us permission to keep the mad Maharaja on board. With an insensitiveness characteristic of a defeated people, unsure of themselves, they harassed us inordinately as they scrutinized our passports. Under such circumstances, Victor let go all the brakes of his being and became a monster. He struggled to get loose and kicked and stamped and bit me and Partap Singh like a mad dog. Speaking from a mouth that was no mouth, straining from a throat that was all husk, he said words which were no words:

'Don't hold me, swines! Don't hold me! I want to fly.... Ohe, let me be a needle! Thunderbolt! Mountain goat! Horse! Woman is the beginner! The valley is green. And there grows the root. Strike up the band for a rhumba! Darling, darling, darleeng.... Go or go.... Ohe, ohe, where are we?'

And the hard light of utter lunacy came into his eyes as people in the aerodrome crowded round us. Surrounded on every side, he began to spit imaginary spittles from his dry mouth.

I shook him violently and admonished him to behave, while I dragged him towards the waiting room with the help of Partap Singh and two Egyptian Farouks.

Now he was pathetic and docile, with a poignant look in his eyes, as though he was asking me in a brief lucid moment to be gentle with him. As I turned to him, however, I could see that he merely looked sheepishly but could not understand any tenderness given to him. This confirmed me in my decision to lead him straight to Poona when the plane should reach Bombay. Perhaps they could give him shock treatment there. Meanwhile, I took the opportunity, which the break of the journey supplied in Cairo, to give an injection to Victor so that he might sleep. He was a little less violent when he got back into the plane and slept for eight-and-a-half hours at a stretch through the next lap of the journey. As we neared the end of the journey, however, he began to act a strange drama: he would call out the abject cries of a man who is being murdered, supplicating the murderer to spare him, to forgive him; and then he would shout in the voice of a murderer, hard, cruel words, pronouncing the doom of his victim.

The passengers were fascinated by this histrionic act, performed with such vigour and instinctive fidelity to the two different roles that they were completely absorbed until they had to make preparations to alight from the plane.

At the end, when the time came to deplane, he would not shift, and stiffened himself like a sulking, spoilt child. And he began to cry and lent himself to all the confusion again, abusing every one of us in the most filthy Punjabi abuse, brutally callous to all appeals from me or Partap Singh, only yearning towards his own misery in bursts of self-pity, pandering to himself with the sentimentality of the lunatic.

One of the passengers, a rich young English writer, Mr Ashley Gibson by name, who was engaged in some archaeological research in India and happened to be travelling back to Bombay after a holiday in the UK, interested himself in our plight and offered me the use of his car, which his chauffeur had brought to the aerodrome, so that I could take the Maharaja to Poona straight away. What was more, when he came to know that Captain Partap Singh had been arrested by the police at the airport, he insisted on accompanying me on the journey. I was moved by the kindliness of this stranger and accepted the offer, especially because Victor was proving to be the greatest nuisance on the face of the earth and I dreaded the journey to the mental home alone with him. I had been nearly broken by the nightmare of the air flight, during which I had had to wrestle with the madman.

The sun rose on us at Kirkee and early after the dawn our car slid into Poona, where the cantonment atmosphere still prevails, reminiscent of the polo-playing, hard-drinking Blimps who once lived in the large squat bungalows with their sequestered shade, in spite of the fact that the Rashtriya Sevak Sangh, the reactionary, revivalist, fascist Hindu volunteer Blumps dominate the town. The Buick ran smoothly across the well-metalled roads on towards Yervada, interrupted by brief pull-ups when we asked the way to the asylum. And soon we had crossed the river and glided beyond Yervada jail, famous for the generations of political prisoners who have been confined there, to the lunatic asylum. We were far too early, as the Superintendent does not arrive till ten; so we asked the warder at the gate his address and went straight on to his bungalow.

Captain Bhagwat, the Superintendent, was a demure and sympathetic man of about fifty. He was unconventional enough to ask us to breakfast. And, strangely enough, Victor calmed down in his presence and, apart from the furtive glances he cast all round, he continued to behave.

Mr Gibson and I were both fascinated by the effect that the Superintendent of the asylum had on the mad Maharaja. The spasmodic bouts of hysteria in which he had indulged, even from the midst of the injection-induced slumber he had enjoyed in the car, seemed to evaporate. The young Englishman relaxed for a few moments in the cool veranda, surrounded by the beds of flowers in the garden. Victor followed him with his gaze. And I could see that there was an antagonism of distrust lurking in his eyes, the distrust of a man who knew that he was cut off from all contact with men and had become a public enemy to humanity, which somehow keeps the uneasy balance between madness and sanity. I knew that the fits of fear and hatred were more inevitable in him than the ordinary indifferences. Therefore, I remained uneasy throughout the meal.

Captain Bhagwat cut short our ordeal by leading us quickly back to the asylum.

As we alighted from the car, however, Victor burst out into wild hysterics, stiffening and twisting like a serpent that fights back before it will enter the bag. And he shouted and yelled even as he hit out, and I felt as though he had sensed the danger he was in.

Looking past the lovely flowers on both sides of the road, beyond the gates of the asylum, I could see the barrack-like wards stretching in the huge high-walled compound. And, in a flash, the whole horror of being confined there for any length of time impressed itself upon me. How could a human being, even if he was not mad, avoid going crazy here, especially with the other lunatics raving and shouting all the time? And, although it was necessary that the fantastic egos of the madmen had to be controlled in the social fabric of this institution, I knew that Victor, with the intense egotism of the descendant of the Sun, the Rajput warrior prince, would not submit his mind as a unit in this universe of restraints and prohibitions.

'Is it possible to give His Highness a private room outside the hospital?' I ventured to ask Captain Bhagwat.

'I think so,' he said understandingly. And he pointed to a place a hundred yards away on the left-hand side of the road.

'We will walk there,' I suggested. And turning to Victor, I said, 'Come then, we shall take you to a nice annexe of this hotel.'

Mr Gibson smiled at my fairy-tale manner and, taking Victor by the arm with the gentle firmness that he had exhibited throughout the drive to Poona, he led the Maharaja onward.

Victor yielded and walked along docilely enough.

The one-room wards of the small bungalow seemed insignificant enough, but there was no avail against the poverty of accommodation provided by the mental hospital, which Captain Bhagwat said was very overcrowded.

I felt a strange sense of the cruelty and ugliness of Indian life, which was driving so many people insane. I had felt this feeling before, ever since I returned from my post-graduate course in London, that our country was going through dark days, in which the poverty, the prejudices, inhibitions and traditional restraints were ever coming into conflict with the instinctive sense of undiscovered possibilities of human life. And through the fear of the new which threw people back into the shell of the past, there were, set up in consequence, violent resentments in each soul against the brutishness of the awkward feudal self, which resulted in bitterness and chagrin and frustration, until the whole world was rejected, personal escapes made or eccentric habits developed, which led to neuroses or madness. In a way the whole of India was a kind of lunatic asylum, part of the bigger lunatic asylum of the world, in which only those who struggled against the status quo and gave battle to authority seemed to find some sense of balance through the elaboration of a new sense of values. Only, how many were there who asked themselves where they were going and what was the meaning of human existence, and how one could become aware of anything real in the midst of this great, unformed, uncreated, undiscovered muddle and wretchedness of the atomic age?

With quiet efficiency, and radiating a calm that seemed to be proof against all the tempers of madmen, Captain Bhagwat negotiated Victor into a clean bare room, furnished simply with an iron bed, a table and a chair.

Victor stood for a moment surveying the small courtyard outside the room which was bathed in the shade of a tamarind tree. Then the terror in his eyes seemed to melt, and, heavy-lidded, he sat down on the bed. His head was lowered with fatigue, and the obstinacy of the other self which had jutted out for days from the agonized, shadowy, corrosive world of his split soul, seemed to melt. He submitted to the warder who began to take his shoes off and undress him. And, as Captain Bhagwat stroked his head with casual, kindly gestures, Victor began gradually to doze off into sleep. For a moment or two he opened his eyes again, lifting the whites from the dark rings as though in supplication to us all. And he looked round again as though he was asking himself where he was, what he was, and how he had got here. Then he lay back with a thud, overcome by powerful tremors of sleep.

'I would like you also to go and rest,' said Captain Bhagwat. 'There are nice rooms in the Napier Hotel. Then please come back at 4.30 in the afternoon for tea and give me the case history.'

I felt a little relieved that I would not have to keep watch on Victor, for I was tired out by the vigil of so many nights. As I walked away with the reticent Mr Gibson I seemed to myself to be stretching out from the shrunken small person into whom I had abated through the assaults of the mad

Maharaja, and I could smell the tang of freshness in the wholesome Poona air. At last, perhaps, I was *free*.

We went back to Captain Bhagwat for tea at his bungalow at 4.30. And, in the informal atmosphere he created, I gave the Superintendent of the asylum a brief account of the private life of Maharaja Ashok Kumar of the last three years, with sidelights on the few significant things I knew about his childhood. I did not philosophize or theorize, but told Captain Bhagwat the actual facts. I found that this was a good approach, because Captain Bhagwat seemed, from the few questions he asked me himself, a practical kind of man, who regarded the ordinary social life, with its relative madness, as a norm to which he wanted most of the cases in the asylum to approximate. I realized the difficulties of having to reproduce the texture of a person's life and the care one has to take, the integrity one has to bring to judging people when one's standards are more psychological than moral. I confessed my difficulties to both my hearers and Mr Gibson said in a soft aside: 'You should write down the private life of our prince, you know. It may be useful for Captain Bhagwat and it may interest other people – it seems a fascinating story.'

Captain Bhagwat also politely encouraged me, though I could see that, having to deal with so many mental cases, and knowing so much more about them than most people, he only added perfunctorily, 'Yes, yes, it may be useful to do that.'

Perhaps it was this casual aside in our conversation which became the core for passion behind this book; for, apart from the vague desire everyone has to write at least one book in his life, I felt that I could not really see anything straight until I put down the crucial experience of the last few months on paper and got things into some kind of perspective. It seemed to me that one main thing had been lacking in my life, through the awkward crisis in Victor's life in which I was involved, and that was: poise or harmony in my own heart. And though I knew that I could not resolve my own conflicts merely by putting down someone else's conflicts on paper, I felt that I might get it off my chest and feel easier.

'What do you feel about His Highness?' I ventured to ask Captain Bhagwat. 'Do you think he will get cured?'

I knew that it was a foolish question as soon as I had asked it. But Captain Bhagwat was indulgent and did not answer in a yes or no, merely saying: 'I shall keep him under observation for the next few days and shall tell you.'

Mr Gibson was as curious as I was, and bolder for once, the writer in him forging ahead of the Englishman.

'Would it be possible some time to see the actual examination you undertake, Captain Bhagwat?' he asked.

'You could see it,' Captain Bhagwat answered, 'but you would only be bored and not understand much from it. First of all, these patients are rather uncontrollable. Secondly, there is not much possibility of a psychiatric examination until shock treatment has been given and the patient is able to say something coherent. And, thirdly, when a patient is able to talk he may say hundreds of things before anything significant is revealed.'

'Do you find it difficult to relax after examining these cases?' Mr Gibson said, surveying the lovely garden which surrounded the luxurious bungalow.

'The flight of ideas,' said Captain Bhagwat with a smile, 'is very difficult to cope with. The maniacs run from one thing to the other, and do not finish one train of thought because they want to disguise it. But they are at last in touch with reality or may be brought back to it. The schizophrenic cannot be brought back to the actual problem easily. There was a young man here who claimed that he was a genius. He had to say it because he had failed in his matric exam and would have committed suicide if he had not boasted that he was a genius. But I could always bring him back to reality in our talks and then he admitted that he was not a genius yet, but hoped to be one in the future.'

'He seems to have had a sense of humour,' said I.

'That was what saved him, perhaps,' said Mr Gibson slyly.

'Yes,' confirmed Captain Bhagwat. 'When the sense of humour is absent, as it is in most simple people who are hard-pressed by realities, then the cure is difficult.'

'Well, then, there is some hope for Victor,' said I, 'because he has a sense of farce if he has not exactly a sense of humour.'

I had turned this phrase deliberately in order to terminate the tea party. And we left Captain Bhagwat with the understanding that I should be allowed to visit Victor as often as I liked.

Mr Gibson wanted to leave the next day and expressed the wish to see Victor before his departure. I thought it was best not to visit His Highness on our way back from Captain Bhagwat, but on the morning after. Then Mr Gibson could motor back to Bombay.

So we went along about ten o'clock the next morning to the annexe where I had secured the private room for Victor.

He became very noisy as soon as we entered and began to stand on his head, while he spat and uttered filth from a frothing mouth. And the attendants had to tie him down to the bed with sheets over the shins and the abdomen. Even so he strained to sit up, and sang the ribald Punjabi song

373

about the two Lachis, the younger one of whom had made all the trouble.

It was strange, this image about the little Lachi. From what interior world of experience had he resurrected the memory of a bad little woman? And exactly how deep was the connection between Lachi and Ganga Dasi? Did he feel that the demons of his dissociated consciousness would be overcome by the frequent recitation of a symbolic name? Or was it just an irrelevant image from an odd dream memory? The concentration of his eyes on the vacant air, even as he listened to his own snatches of song, the will to move, the occasional whining despair, the comparative remoteness, followed again by animosity and the sudden compulsion of tenderness – all the alternating moods and grimaces seemed like different incarnations, multiple personalities, the split-off facets of the ego, which had been disrupted through its own weakness. And I felt that the demons in him were perhaps seeking to free themselves from the guilts, the red-glowing excesses, the terrifying deeds committed by the serpents of his unbridled passions and emotions. The unity of his life having gone with the shock of the murder of Bool Chand, which he had ordered, he had left only the yearnings towards sanity, while he was no longer capable of self-mastery. A pathetic spectacle he presented, with his deeply shadowed, sunken eyes, his drawn, haggard face and his dry lips broken for lack of moisture, his swollen gums and dishevelled hair, unable to lie down, to sleep and rest, but reaching out to be a man, to stand erect, and failing ignominiously because of the bandages which held him a prisoner. He was also frightening, with the desperate broken spasms and urges with which he lashed out at everything

374

within his reach, the surging of the demons like the hosts of Mara in the assault on what was once his essential ego.

Somehow, it was only the reserved, tall, slim Mr Gibson who could go near him and subdue him with his gentle, firm look. And I was surprised at this, because he had reacted so violently to another Englishman at Heathrow aerodrome. But I fancied that there was a difference between a full-moustached and a clean-shaven Englishman for Victor's divided mind, the subtler dialectic of the differentiation being buried in the intergrown abysses of his bowels, the seat of his experience.

He lay silent as though listening to some far-off voice when Mr Gibson stroked him gently and said, 'Now, you go to sleep for a while.'

At that suddenly, however, the all-encompassing army of demons seemed to return with all their violences, and even Mr Gibson could not soothe him. We felt that it was futile to stay any longer in the unchangeable Saturnalian realm over which the mad Maharaja established his new dread kingdom. So we came out of the room quietly, leaving Victor involved in the infinite fight of his fragile and decadent body for attainment of his personality. And we were dumb with amazement, or rather with an amazed curiosity, the avid desire of our minds to know, to grasp the meaning of the multifarious images of his distorted speech.

As we drove away, the horror of Victor's madness was still on us and we brooded, self-constrained for whiles, and contemplated the expanse of the Yervada countryside from which the earthy breath flew into our nostrils, fresh and clear.

'*Nullus amor medicabilis est herbis!*' said Mr Gibson with a rather pompously learned accent.

'My Latin is poor,' said I.

'No love can be cured by herbs,' he translated. And then Mr Gibson looked vacantly ahead of him as though he was embarrassed at the way in which he had seemed to be embarrassed when I had told Captain Bhagwat Victor's case history the previous day.

I fancied I caught a look in his face which showed that he was very taut. I put it down at first to the inhibitions which are characteristic of most middle-class Englishmen. But then the thought occurred to me that he himself might be slightly neurotic and had, apart from his generosity, interested himself in Victor with a view to learning something about the split mind. I recalled the question he had asked Captain Bhagwat the previous day about whether one could be present at an examination. And yet I felt that I was being very ungrateful in thinking of him as a case when, ostensibly, he had looked and behaved with such magnanimity.

'Don't you believe in Fate?' Mr Gibson asked me suddenly.

I guessed that Mr Gibson was fascinated and drawn towards the typical Indian fatalist attitude of mind. I answered: 'If you mean by Fate the accidental circumstances which seem to make important differences to one's life just because they coincide with a possible temperamental change, then you can use the word Fate; otherwise, it is meaningless.'

'So you consider the arrival of the news of Mr Bool Chand's murder as only a coincidental event and not the cause of the Maharaja Sahib's madness?'

'Of course, the Maharaja had a split mind and was going crazy anyhow. Lunacy is a kind of refuge for him. He was preparing for it for a long time and any accident might have brought it on.'

I thought that Mr Gibson looked disappointed and slightly peeved at what I had said.

We remained silent for a while. The car was crossing the bridge across the Sangam river which connects Yervada with Poona proper; and the lovely scene compelled one's senses to burst open and go beyond the boundaries of debate into a fleeting sense of the obvious universe. The sheer physical immediacy of the low hills and the broad valley of the dry river soothed me, and I began to feel that it would not be a bad idea to luxuriate and bask in the nimble sunshine of Poona.

Something seemed to be happening to Mr Gibson, however, for his colour changed from transparent pink to an unhealthy pallor, even as, in the silence that spread between us, he seemed to be listening to what he saw outside the car and seeing what he heard. His breath came and went a little faster and his lips were twisted into an inscrutably shy smile, the harbinger of the struggle to say something which he could not easily say.

'You Indian modernists,' he said after all, in a slightly challenging tone, 'put too much faith in science. India had such a rich anthropocentric culture....'

'A way of life approved for centuries and millenniums may not be acceptable today,' I said. 'One can take the vitality of impulse from the past; one can't take the dead routine of an old culture. The guardians of tradition often kill the new by repeating the old, old mantras.'

Again Mr Gibson became tensely silent, and his face became pink as though he was now almost hostile. I surmised that he was one of those rootless cosmopolitan young English intellectuals who had been reacting like Maugham, Huxley and Heard and the Quakers to the impact of science and believed, like our own God-intoxicated professors, in the 'spiritualism of the East' against the 'materialism of the West'. They did not believe with Darwin that man had developed from the monkey stage to a semblance of humanity, but put their faith in yoga, astrology, mumbo-jumbo and everything uncanny, except that the common-sense of their inheritance asserted itself often enough in worldly life and money matters. I have not yet come across any European yogi who hasn't got a good bank balance. And they could not see that they were merely escaping out of despair from the narrow, neurotic, hidebound cash-nexus world of Western civilization, where the struggle for existence pitted brother against brother, father against son, and mother against daughter, to a fancied Utopia of the 'spirit' called the East, with the pagan quick. Whereas in Asia the young, rising on the curves of their hopes for a better life for vast sections of wretched humanity, were prone to turn their backs on superstition, black magic, spiritualism and divining and embrace such libertarian ideas as had been promoted by the great European thinkers from Voltaire and Diderot and Bentham and Mill and Spencer and Comte to Marx.

'The bifurcation of soul and body is a vulgar heresy of conversational speech,' I continued, to ease the strain between the Englishman and myself. 'The emphasis on the first leads to idealistic views of life and to passive acceptance, isolation, agony and death; while the emphasis on the other leads to its own excesses. The truth is that man is both body and soul and a great many other things besides. And the whole man cannot admit of the stupid dualism between "spirit" and "matter".'

'Perhaps it is the comprehensive approach of the ancient Hindus I like,' said Mr Gibson tentatively. 'A kind of Hindu humanism: "The purpose of the sea is to provide fish for men to eat; the purpose of the rain is to give man water to drink; the purpose of the stars is to lighten the darkness".'

'I am afraid Hinduism was seldom humanist in the modern sense,' I said. 'It mostly regarded man as a speck in the dust, a servile creature living in the warp and woof of maya, whose illusory reality was only a remote reflection of God, the Supreme Brahman.'

'Hinduism may not have been humanitarian, but it was humanist all right!' Mr Gibson asserted dogmatically, apparently wanting to settle the argument in his own favour.

I did not answer, but looked out of the car to see how far we were from the Napier Hotel. As though to symbolize our mood of the moment the driver seemed to have lost his way in the maze of Poona Road and turned up near the railway station. I asked a policeman near the compound for the way. And our driver, a Maratha, supplemented the information which the constable, also a Maratha, gave me with more precise details in Marathi.

The parting from the liberal diehard Mr Gibson was affected by our argument. The Englishman seemed to dry up and become more reserved than ever, fancying perhaps that what I had said to him about his El Dorado made his deep sense of frustration more frustrated and confirmed him in the belief that he was doomed to extinction.

'I think, Doctor Shankar,' he said, brightening up with an artificial smile as I descended from the car, 'you must set up as a psychoanalyst in Bombay and I shall become one of your patients.'

I could not help laughing at the half-serious, half-jocular suggestion he had made.

'I will think it over,' I said. 'But we must meet, anyhow, when I come to Bombay.'

'Yes,' he said. 'I am staying at the Taj. Come and have lunch one day.'

'Thank you, I will,' I said. 'And, really, thank you very much for all the trouble you have taken.'

Mr Gibson seemed to be embarrassed by the excessive warmth of my gratitude. He waved his hand in a gesture of farewell, blushed, and turned his face away to avoid seeing me, even as he directed the driver with the staccato utterance: 'Bombay.'

I ordered some coffee as I entered the hotel and sat in the empty lounge to recapitulate the morning's experiences. Unfortunately, when one sits down deliberately to do a little thinking, one can never think consecutively. In the diaphanous world of one's silence, one goes on inhaling and exhaling, resting, waiting and watching, drifting from one thought to another with prolonged lapses, in the shadows from which one's senses awake, for brief moments, to the nearest excitation without being aware of very much in the floating stream of changing awareness. Then some intense reality forces itself upon one's notice out of the humus of existence. I recall that I only felt generally relaxed and easy in my mind after I saw Mr Gibson's car move out of the compound, a sense of release from the trammels, as it were. And time and space seemed to stretch themselves now before me endlessly.

The waiter brought the coffee, and the obsequiousness of his approach irritated me, for it reminded me of the complete joined-hands and bent-forehead servility of the servants in the Sham Pur State. On my previous return from Europe I had always felt that the relationship of master and servant in India was most humiliating to both parties, almost like that of the master and slave relationship in Roman times. I assuaged my guilt by looking away into the garden of the

Napier Hotel and concentrating on the pellucid sunshine as it embraced the lovely red bougainvillaeas.

But no one can quite escape. Everyone is captured. And I felt a kind of bell ringing in my soul, at first softly, then loudly, shattering in its oppressive dithyramb, engulfing me with its tone and almost drowning the perception in me that was seeking to become knowledge, that I had been part of a life which was rotten, where all the energy I had put into small decencies was entirely wasted, for all the elements of that society were crashing and falling and dying. Darkly, clumsily, stupidly, wantonly they were falling into the pit of madness or despair, into the grave of all despotisms. I tried to get hold of my instinctive recoil against the petty, obscene, lawless world of the Sham Pur court, with its disgusting vices and its manoeuvrings, its hellish, hysterical, tempting, lewd and irresistibly luxurious orbits. I sought to fix my inner gaze on my own hypocrisy and on my prolonged acceptance of the life of riches, of the clamorous uproar of confused voices, of a narrow circle of power-mad and privilege-loving obscurantists.

For a moment, I sought to be kind to myself with that natural kindness for oneself that always makes one accept one's own bad smells more easily than those of others. I told myself for the thousandth time that I had no reason to feel guilty because I had owed money to the Maharaja and had had to work off my debt by service. But then I realized that I could have walked off from the court at one stage or another when I felt intense revulsions against continuing, without any moral scruples about the debt which had ultimately come from money derived from the dumb peasants, and that I could have gone and served the state as a doctor more usefully in some village dispensary and thus appeased my conscience about what I owed to Victor. And I decided that if I did not feel guilty, I ought to feel guilty. I wanted to rebel, to rage and to fight against the whole system which had enveloped me in its poisonous, fungus growth and kept me rooted in the shadowy, bestial world of tyranny, cowardice, ennui and sloth.

I glanced at the morning paper and lighted on the news that His Exalted Highness the Nizam of Hyderabad was to be honoured soon with his appointment as Raj Pramukh of his state.

Strange, indeed, were the ways of the Congress democrats in our country! The man who financed the fanatical Muslim storm troopers, Razvi's Razakars, and refused to accede to the Indian Union until the Union Army marched in, was now taken up in partnership by those who had only recently protested against his ambition to be an independent king, against his infamous rule based on the exploitation of the peasantry, his personal greed and arrogance. This old fox was then still the highest in Hyderabad when his erstwhile friend Razvi was on trial! Treachery, betrayal, nepotism, complacency and corruption were the order of the day.

Another news item in the paper reported that some of the politicals in Yervada, Nasik and Sabarmati jails had gone on hunger strike, because they had been divided into A class, B class and C class prisoners and because their families were not being given any allowances and because of sundry other grievances.

Suddenly from the back of my mind arose the memory of the letter from that peasant leader détenu in Sham Pur jail, about which I had done nothing. Had he and his friends called off the hunger strike? It was inconceivable that he could have been released or his demands met. Was he then still languishing in jail?

Slowly the dying embers of my conscience smouldered within me, glowing red hot here and there but covered thickly with the ashes of my self-contempt and helplessness. The inner reactions seldom match the outer excitations uniformly. And I felt self-contained as though frightened of my own weaknesses. And yet the guilts in me about my neglects persisted.

Slowly, through self-disgust, the question arose in me: Why should a man's personal preferment matter so much? Was I afraid of starving? I knew that I could never go without a meal, considering the advantages I had been vouchsafed by my education as a doctor. Had I then cloaked my ambitions for power with the excuse that I owed money to Victor? If the truth had to be acknowledged, it was so. I was myself corrupt, wanting power and privilege and a leisurely life. I had refused to break the boundaries of a personal life and, in spite of all my kicking against the pricks, I had ignored the fact that I was only one small part of the great social fabric which was in decay. My personal comforts seemed so petty and small and subsidiary in the face of the existence to which the peasants of Sham Pur had been reduced, the so-called patient, seemingly stupid yokels, malaria ridden, sore-eyed, rickety, prey to all the diseases, trembling as though they were afraid of their own breath. Generations of maharajas and jagirdars had broken them with their taxes. The officials of the state never spoke to them except to the accompaniment of foul abuse and in the most contemptuous language. The police terrorized them with lathi blows. The army trampled over their fields and looted their granaries. Their lives were crumbling about them, even as the mud huts in which they lived were falling to pieces. And yet we lived in palaces, ignorant of what happened in the country barns. What about these 'jewels' of the earth, as they were called in the

perorations of politicians? It was no longer a question of
fine titles and names, the common man whom everyone
was supposed to love. We may invoke them in our talk to
show our sentimental love for them, but in fact we disdained
contact with them and thought of them as crude, rough
people who stank no better than their own oxen, and
sometimes worse than that. Jungli animals! And now if we
thought of them at all, it was because they were compelling
our attention. They may still join hands in obeisance to the
sahibs and the officials, and even touch their feet. But from
the spontaneous way in which Buta had defied Victor and
from the way the peasants had pelted stones at the convoy of
the hunting party, they did not love or respect their masters
very much – they who had been full of fear of the rich were
now beginning to hate them and fight them.

I began vaguely to feel that I must do something to help
these people which might make me a little more useful than
I had been to them while I was in the pay of the Maharaja.
Only in healing the poor could I live an intrinsic life, which
had been dead in me while I had been living only for the
gratification of my five senses. Something for myself but also
something for other people, as they said. I would go and
start a dispensary in a small village in Sham Pur State. I had
a little money saved up and I would start just like that, simply.

As I felt this awareness creeping into me, I also felt a certain
sense of oppression settle over me. I sat still and looked
ahead of me at the ugly heavy furniture of the hotel drawing
room, with its Victorian carved dressers, chairs and settees.
Was it the furniture which was weighing me down? Perhaps.
Because all these heavy habiliments of a tawdry existence
were associated with my past, with the errors of my past, in
which I seemed to be inescapably held.

For a few moments I stared vacantly out of the window. Then a wave of kindness for myself convinced me that only through errors did a man come to be a seeker. And that maybe I needed to go through all this to realize the futility of the selfish life. I must, therefore, accept the dread, the dread of error, accept the few things that came clear from the incertitude, and go on. In this way I could perhaps drain all my doubts to the dregs. I would have to avoid self-torment. But even if the process of accepting the new way of life brought difficulties and torments, I should accept these and not turn away. It was possible that if I submitted to the impending adventure, the hopelessness would go.

And to expunge the dread, perhaps it would be a good idea to recapitulate and write down my experiences of Victor, for in that way I could attempt a conscious appreciation of my erroneous life. I could find confirmation of my new belief from my memories, the conviction of the preciousness of integrity that I had let slip through the compromises of the last few years. And thus I may come through the portals of dread to real love for my people. And to hope for them and myself. There was still tenderness in me and faith in the search for an ideal, in spite of all the clogging shortcomings. And, being a seeking human, I would return again and again to the sources of strength in this tenderness.

My duty was, therefore, clear. I would go back to the jungle of Sham Pur. I would try to penetrate every thicket. And I would fumble about in the darkness, maybe often in despair against the odds. But I would persist and carve out a pathway for myself and others, away from the wrong roads, where I could walk upright among the men who were straightening their backs. I would struggle. For in this struggle born of tenderness was life.

When I went to have a last look at Victor the next morning, I found further confirmation of my decision to leave Poona: he seemed to be dimly aware of who I was and suddenly became very violent, even murderous.

'I will kill you!' he shouted. And, opening his mouth wide as the jaws of hell, he sat up in bed raving foul obscenities.

I stood motionless by the door, taken aback by the onslaught, aghast, almost as one is if a dog suddenly yelps when one enters a house.

I tried to calm him and said soothingly: 'Victor! Victor! Please...'

He mocked at me by repeating what I said. And he spurted more abuse, twisting his mouth, contorting it into all kinds of shapes and spitting in all directions, foaming and inundating the room with shrieks and howls, his face red and his eyes glittering. Fortunately, he was held down over the thighs and the shins by the sheets. Otherwise the roaring cataract of his body would have swept me off my feet.

I searched in my disturbed and shocked mind for the reason of this outburst against me, and I could only think that he was making me the symbol of all those who had betrayed him. Apparently, he still had some idea of reference and his vague sense of persecution had fixed upon me as the enemy now when really he was hostile to Sardar Patel, Diwan Popatlal J. Shah, Pandit Gobind Das, Bool Chand, Gangi, etc.

'How to change his mind?' I asked myself. But as I was speculating, he suddenly began to sob in the most hopeless tone of voice, like a mad dog who gets tired of raving. How should one free him from his madness? How could one help him?

The sobs had become a maudlin sing-song of weeping. And now he did not even seem to be conscious of my presence. Had he recognized me at all? Or was he now only the king of the border kingdom of nightmares whose logic was buried in him? Immediately came a partial answer. He stopped crying and said, 'Oh, Hari, take me away from here!' And then as quickly as the perception became acute enough to pass for recognition he was shouting foul abuse against me and the attendants and was enveloped in his dream world, encircled by the shadows, merged into the extinction which means the loss of any sense of reality.

I felt that I could not help him, that helping by desiring to help was mere sentimentalism and that, in fact, I was hindering his cure by my constant presence.

So I came out of the room and decided to go and say goodbye to Captain Bhagwat.

The lovely Poona sun was shining on the asylum as though it had deliberately set itself to repurify the fury-infested world inside. But fifty yards away from the main gate on the inner road, a mad man was having an altercation with the sun, looking steadily at it with wide-open eyes, and uttering certain loud, joylessly jubilant sounds, interrupted by self-suffocating, furtive whispers, half clamouring, half praying, as he raised his joined hands to Surya.

As I entered Captain Bhagwat's office, the clerk handed me three letters. The Superintendent was busy, so I sat down by his clerk and began to open the envelopes with eager fingers. I opened the brown envelope which obviously contained a communication from Sham Pur State. It was a summons from the magistrate to appear on the 10th January in the case of the murder of Srijut Bool Chand. That was that, I thought. The decision to go back to Sham Pur State was made for me.

One of the other two letters bore my address in the handwriting of Munshi Mithan Lal, but the script on the other was strange. I opened the letter from Mian Mithu next. This was a long epistle, full of gushing affection and a sentimental plea to come and help him in the 'hour of trial', as he put it. Apparently he had also been arrested and charged with abetting the murder of Bool Chand and was in jail and was not even being allowed bail. The third letter was from Maharani Indira, saying briefly that she was arriving in Poona to look after her husband and would I make arrangements for her stay.

I had hardly glanced at this note when Captain Bhagwat came out of his office, ready to go on his round of the asylum. He did not see me waiting for him. So I got up abruptly and, noticing the preoccupied, busy look on his face, simply said:

'Captain Bhagwat, I have come to ask your leave; I will be going to Sham Pur before noon.'

The Superintendent shook hands with me and said:

'Oh, I have had a wire from some maharani, saying she is coming to look after her husband. I suppose you know about her?'

'Han, she has written to me too,' I said. 'She is Maharani Indira, the wife of Maharaja Ashok Kumar – the real Maharani.'

'Well, you must tell her that she will only be able to see her husband once a week,' Captain Bhagwat said.

'I will do that,' I said. 'I will wire her and also write to her. Meanwhile, I know you will look after him.'

'Yes, of course,' said Captain Bhagwat. But his eyes were looking ahead of him and he made as if to go.

'Acha,' I said. 'I am grateful for your courtesy.' And I offered him my hand.

He shook it with a certain hurried cordiality and walked away.

I wended my way towards the asylum gates to the waiting taxi, reflecting on the irony and tenderness of a woman's love that would pursue a man even to hell to rescue him when the love was selfless and real.

About the author

About the book

Insights
Interviews
& More...

Thoughts on His Own Fiction—Mulk Raj Anand

*1) You have written more novels than your two undisputed rivals, R.K. Narayan and Raja Rao together. Which one do you consider to be your best work?**

I have no right to say which is my best work. Some books come off, not because they are really good, but because they confirm the familiar feelings of the group of critics who are swayed by partisan emotions. Actually, every book is a process, with much good and bad in it. The novel is a form too amorphous to be controlled precisely. The relative merits of a book, from the author's point of view, may lie in his feeling of how much he was able to express of the soul drama, and at how many levels. Perhaps, from this standpoint, I would consider

*This interview is reconstructed from the letters of Mulk Raj Anand to Saros Cowasjee. Every effort has been made to retain Anand's own words and phrases.

Untouchable to be a more intense work than the others.

2) There is still a lot of confusion about when you first wrote Untouchable *and when you showed it to Gandhi.*

I first met Gandhi in Sabarmati Ashram in 1927 when I showed him the immature draft in Joycean English. I did not write the book in 1930, but began it in 1925, as part of the Confession. I went to see Irene in Dublin in summer/autumn of 1926, and met A.E. [George William Russell] and Yeats. I can't vouch for the day and month in each case, but what I have put down there [in *The Bubble*] three or four times are factual references.

3) As a writer of the thirties, what did the period teach you?

I learnt that the word and act must integrate if one is to be a writer of any significance. Never mind if Gorky had already done it for Russia, Zola in France and Dickens in England. In India it had not been done. If the seamy side of life had to be written about, then there it was and it must be exposed. And this is what I did in *Untouchable* and *Coolie*. Also, I wanted to create in *Coolie* a boy in all his humaneness, as against the fantastic Kim.

LIFE
at a Glance
(1905–2004)

BORN
· · · · · · · · ·
12 December 1905 in Peshawar, now Pakistan.

FAMILY
· · · · · · · · ·
The third of four surviving sons. Father, Lal Chand, a clerk in the British-Indian army; Mother, Ishwar Kaur, a woman from a traditional peasant household.

EDUCATION
· · · · · · · · ·
In cantonment schools and at Khalsa College (Amritsar) from which he graduates with Honours in 1924. Leaves for the U.K. in Sept. 1925; earns his Ph.D. in Philosophy from University College, London, in 1929. Resides in England till 1945, with occasional visits to India and Europe.

*4) In your desire to expose the raw side of life,
were you not being documentary?*

Only when an author fails as an artist does
the question arise whether the work is
documentary or propaganda. The novel
form is fortunately loose enough to
include both scandal like *Anna Karenina*
and the echoes of the Napoleonic period
as in *War and Peace*, provided the novelist
talks in terms of human beings and not
in terms of puppets.

*5) Are treatment and form, which constitute
art, more important in a novel than content?*

It is all mixed up, this question of the novel.
Is it for burning and melting? For the
realization of the character, to see the flow?
Or is it for preaching sermons on the
Vedanta, Communism or anti-Commun-
ism? I thought, always, that the novel is a
new kind of poem, the 20th century ballad,
the folk epic of the new classes, rather
formless, but immediate in recognition
(when it is good) of the quick of life, in
little chicks, abandoned women, old
soldiers and ardent young people.

*6) You have written so much on the writing
of fiction. Are there any books on the techniques
of the novel that you would recommend?*

Percy Lubbock's *The Craft of Fiction*. In my

opinion it is one of the finest books on the subject, better even than E.M. Forster's *Aspects of the Novel*. Both books influenced me a good deal in my writing, even though I could not approximate to the points of view of either as defined in their respective approaches.

7) Even your admirers admit that you occasionally overwrite! Do you?

The first draft of each novel came in a flood. Rewriting it, one felt the instinctive truth of the spontaneous utterance. I let everything go through. Of course, in trying to integrate one's say, in human terms, with one's ideals, there is always the risk of saying too much. I admit that good craftsmanship is important. I have told myself often, 'cut, cut, cut!'

8) Have you ever thought of revising some of your 'outpourings' — if I may use that word?

I don't know if the first instinctive writing can be drastically revised. My novels come in a flood and, though I try to control the avalanche, I find that, apart from cutting down chunks, it is not possible to demolish the rhythmic flow of the ballad, rough though it be.

Is persuaded by George
Orwell in late 1941 to
work for the BBC
Eastern Service in
fighting Nazi Fascism.
Gives numerous
broadcasts till his final
departure for India.

(In India, 1946–2004)

Makes Bombay his home
and centre of activity.
Plunges into the literary
and cultural life of the
country.
Meets Anil de Silva who
introduces him to the
local bohemians. On her
advice, he founds the art
magazine *Marg* in 1946,
and remains its editor for
the next forty years.
Becomes a director of
Kutub Publishers to help
promote the publishing
industry in India.
Appointed Tagore Professor
of Art and Literature at
University of Punjab,
Chandigarh, 1963–66.
Visiting Professor at
the Institute of Advanced
Studies, Simla, 1967–68
and Chairman of Lalit
Kala Akademi (National
Academy of Arts),
1965–70.
He participates in
scores of national and
international conferences
such as the Indian Council

9) Would you say this is true of you life's most ambitious undertaking, your autobiographies — The Seven Ages of Man?

I am not writing autobiographies but autobiographical novels. It is necessary to make this distinction. I believe in the confessional novel. In the first person singular, one can be nearly honest, peal the onion layer by layer and get to one's conscience.

10) How far are you from completing it?

Just now, the deaths of my dear friends Sajjad Zaheer and Pablo Neruda, within a week of each other, have depressed me. Always, when I hear such news, I feel, apart from my sorrow, the fear for myself. I would like to live long enough to finish my seven-volume novel, slowly, maturely, and with what dynamic I may still have.

11) Are you satisfied with the progress of your writing?

I cannot answer that. It keeps growing! I write a few pages every day. I still remember most things vividly, including the facts. I am trying to trace the widening of awareness, through glimpses into the realities of life, which come every now and then but in a haphazard manner and without any linear growth.

12) What would be your advice to a young writer who is also a beginner?

Be honest. Do not be afraid. Go your own way and don't seek advice from old men like me. 'Everything old keeps a hungry grip on life,' John Cornford said. The young must break themselves free.

Writing *Private Life* *of an Indian Prince*— Mulk Raj Anand*

1) What made you choose the title Private Life of an Indian Prince? *Taken in its historical context, wouldn't* The Last of the Maharajas *have been more appropriate?*

The original title I gave to the novel was *The Maharaja and the Butterfly*, but Hutchinson altered it from the sales point of view. I never liked their title, it misrepresents my intention and what I wanted to say, but it is the sort of concession publishers often ask for.

2) Did any fiction on Indian princes influence you? Or for that matter — any authors?

There is no other work of fiction on the princes that I know of, though there are plenty of oddities described by Britishers in their memoirs. As for authors, you may detect the influence of André Gide

*This interview is reconstructed from the letters of Mulk Raj Anand to Saros Cowasjee. Every effort has been made to retain Anand's own words and phrases.

to some extent in this book, but it was much more Fyodor Dostoevsky. Incidentally, André Malraux's *Man's Fate* was very much in my mind for ten years before I wrote *Private Life of an Indian Prince*.

3) When did you first think of writing this novel?

The novel was first conceived in London before the Second World War when I heard that the prince whom I had taught in Simla in the early twenties had ended up in the Pune asylum. In 1948 I had a breakdown, and that triggered the writing. The neutral narrator, Dr Shankar, was invented to become Shiva's third eye and to burn out the dross, confusion and the chaos of emotions in order to achieve a certain balance. As you know, the sources of creativeness are far too intricate to be put down in a few words.

4) Can you throw more light on the characters? Are they taken from real life?

All the characters are taken from my intimate experience and transformed creatively from within in an almost Dostoevskian mood of pity, absolute pity for those who love absolutely – in this case the Prince. The obsession of the

Prince owes itself to the [unswerving] romanticism of Hafiz, Jami and Ali Sher Nawai, whose Persian poetry I read as a young poetaster. The narrator is modelled on one of my professors, a liberal gentleman who was private secretary to a Maharaja. I knew at least three Gangis. The last one was a Singhalese hill-woman whom I myself nearly married. I had a nervous breakdown for six months and recovered my equipoise only when the novel rushed out of me in one month. The portrait of Maharani Indira owes itself largely to the steadfastness of my ex-wife, Kathleen Van Gelder.

5) Amazing! Are you there in the novel yourself? With whom do you align yourself?

If there is any alliance between myself and a character, it is with the narrator. But, as always in my novels, the characters take charge. The novelist should try to become the great god Brahma, who created mankind but is not responsible for it, that is to say, does not determine their destiny. Distance is very important in art because art, though like life, and reflecting it, is not life. Literature and life are parallel developments.

6) Isn't your novel highly critical of the

methods employed by the Congress Government to amalgamate the princely states into the Indian union?

Political comment of the kind I have implied in my satire of Vallabhbhai Patel is perhaps permissible, though sometimes I myself become unconsciously a trifle malicious. I think Patel and Nehru did right in the integration of these princely states. They ended feudalism. The novel as private history must suggest the inner process of the shift of classes.

7) One last question: the novel would make a tremendous movie. Have you ever thought of approaching a film producer?

I turned down an offer from a producer to film *Private Life of an Indian Prince* because I knew he would ruin it. And I have, after seeing the American version of *The Guide*, been very allergic to a film of this book unless it is made by an Indian director like Satyajit Ray or Mrinal Sen. This has meant that I could not consider the bait of money. My adoption of the principle of 'poverty and active leisure' was based on a genuine wish not to regard my books, bad or good as they are, as money-making propositions.

Top Ten
Favourite Books

1. **Notes from Underground &
   the Idiot**
   Fyodor Dostoevsky

2. **Creatures that Once Were Men**
   Maxim Gorky

3. **Secrets of the Self**
   Muhammad Iqbal

4. **Sons and Lovers**
   D.H. Lawrence

5. **A Portrait of the Artist As
   a Young Man**
   James Joyce

6. **Man's Fate**
   André Malraux

7. **Tropic of Cancer**
   Henry Miller

8. **Heer Ranjha**
   Waris Shah

9. **Childhood, Boyhood and Youth**
   Leo Tolstoy

10. **The Grapes of Wrath**
    John Steinbeck